Destiny's TEAM

Destiny's TEAM

A Story About Love, Choices and Eternity

THOMAS A. GLESSNER

Anomalos Publishing House
Crane

Anomalos Publishing House, Crane 65633
©2007 by Thomas A. Glessner
All rights reserved. Published 2007
Printed in the United States of America.
07   1

ISBN: 097884534X (paper)
EAN: 9780978845346 (paper)

Cover illustration and design by Steve Warner

To my fanatical sports-loving kids, Joshua, SaraLynn, Brannan, and Jefferson.

CONTENTS

FOREWORD

Several years ago, I was traveling in Germany on business, and while there, the subject of football came up. American football, that is. I asked the individual I was speaking with to describe the German's understanding of the sport.

His answer was quite succinct and impressively accurate, stating, "The object of the game is to score points by one team advancing the football without the carrier's progress being impeded by a member of the opposition until he crosses the scoring line." And then he added, with a quick smile, "Still holding the football, of course."

In a nutshell, that is it. You see, football is actually a simple game on the surface. Yet, underneath, it consists of many intricate details, strategies, and complexities. And the guys who play the game? They are just that, simply guys. But underneath, they are guys whose lives are filled with all the struggles, decisions, and challenges that life presents. And even though most of their "conflicts" are played out in a larger-than-life arena, like every other male, they have to learn how to be men.

Destiny's Team takes us not only behind the scenes of an NFL team on the brink of the ultimate prize but also into the lives of those who play the game and the people who surround them, from family and friends to fans and the media. But Destiny's Team is more than just another football novel. Much more. It explores deep spiritual truths within the context of professional football.

Also, important aspects of culture are detailed in *Destiny's Team*, including the temptations that these talented athletes have had thrown at them from the moment someone noticed they could run faster, jump higher, or a throw a ball farther than any other kid on the block.

One of Tom Glessner's characters in the book accurately describes how we have easily become a self-centered culture. "Somehow when we are young we believe that we are invulnerable. For some reason, we feel that we can live our lives recklessly—even violently— and not have to account for our actions. We think that life will go on indefinitely, as we satisfy our inner lusts and desires and ignore the needs of others."

While *Destiny's Team* is a story about competition, friendship, and the struggle all of us face internally as well as with others, at the core of this journey is a mirror that bounces back the disturbing images of what our society has accepted as the norm. Glessner bravely confronts and demonstrates, in an intriguing story, how our society has lost respect for the value of life and how we, as a people, are on the verge of also losing the soul of our nation.

Central to the narrative are the themes of reconciliation and second chances. This book provides insights and reflections about the lasting impact that certain choices have upon relationships and how even one choice can change our lives forever.

Glessner has written a compelling story with believable characters in realistic situations, all the while keeping in mind that we need to listen to that still, small voice inside us.

Jonathan Flora, Writer/Director, *A Distant Thunder*

ACKNOWLEDGMENTS

Acknowledgements and many thanks are due to:

- Laura, my wife, with whom I have shared many wonderful hours over the years as a parent under the "Friday night lights" of high school football;
- Michelle Warner, my editor, who has diligently and professionally helped to navigate this story to completion; and
- All of the great men who have spent hundreds of hours with my sons over the years as their coaches and mentors in the great American game of football.

CHAPTER 1

Seattle had been waiting for this Sunday for years, and though the weather did not matter to the massive crowd of fanatical football fans gathered at Qwest Stadium, Mother Nature nevertheless joined in on this momentous occasion with a picturesque background of a deep blue sky with just a few small clouds, brisk air, and, as could be seen from the downtown high rise apartments, a boat-filled Puget Sound and beyond that a skyline of snow-capped mountains.

On this day, Seattle's beloved Seahawks were playing the St. Louis Rams in the final game of the National Football Conference play-offs, with the winner going on to play in the Super Bowl. After years of suffering, the fans of this sports crazy town were ready to celebrate a championship season with high hopes of winning biggest prize of all.

Seattle has had its share of mediocre sports teams. The city had even housed a few highly respectable ones, but as far as winning the big prize in any sport, Seattle has been woefully lacking. In the 1970s, the Seattle Supersonics pulled off an NBA championship that intoxicated fans. In baseball, the Seattle Mariners had some good years but always seemed to come up short of winning it all. And the local University of Washington Huskies had been competitive, even winning a national championship in football in the 1990s. Yet, all in all, the elusion of top-bragging rights in every sport has frustrated the city immensely. However, Seattle's greatest disappointment occurred when the Seahawks made it to the Super Bowl quite a few years earlier only to be beaten by the hated Pittsburgh Steelers. To add insult to injury, most Seattle fans believed that this game had been stolen from them by several controversial calls that kept the Seahawks from scoring. Some fans even suggested a conspiracy had taken place to ensure that the Steelers—known as "America's team"—would be victorious.

Several years and head-coaching changes followed that infamous defeat, but such changes did not bring the Seahawks back to the big game. And over the years, Seattle fans continued to abide in the wilderness—looking for the Promised Land.

On this day though, the Seahawks were led by their new sports hero quarterback Jason O'Connor. O'Connor was the picture of athletic and physical perfection, standing six feet five inches tall with a perfectly cut, muscular body that seemed could only belong to a mythical Greek god. Yet, O'Connor was anything but mythical in his talents on the football field, and in this season he had electrified the city as the Seahawks showed under his leadership that they were the dominant team in the NFL.

O'Connor had come into his own after suffering a disappointing career for seven years in the NFL that had seen him play insignificant roles as a backup quarterback. In the previous year, his second season with the Seahawks, he broke into the starting lineup in dramatic fashion by running up sensational passing statistics and turning what had appeared to be a mediocre Seahawks team into a legitimate championship contender.

Before his promotion to the role as starting quarterback the season before, it had appeared that it was going to be another dismal year, as the Seahawks were floundering in characteristic style. Led then by quarterback Zach Morrison, a popular NFL veteran, the team was lackluster in its performance on the field and sat on an unimpressive .500 winning percentage. Yet, despite mediocrity from the team, Morrison dazzled the football crowds with some pretty spectacular passing numbers. While he for some reason couldn't translate his individual success to the team, Morrison, nevertheless, was popular with the fans.

Morrison had played in Seattle for ten years and during this tenure had become a major figure in the Seattle community as a result of both his stardom on the field and his involvement in charitable causes off of the field. As a veteran in the NFL, he had seen his share of individual successes but had never been able to lead the Seahawks into the play-offs. Most sports pundits publicly stated that the Seahawks' inability to get into postseason play was not the fault of Morrison but rather popular opinion held that the failure to get to the play-offs was the culpability of a poor supporting cast—particularly a defense that usually found itself every season at the bottom of the league in such key statistics as yardage given up and points scored upon.

However, winning was everything to Seattle Head Coach Paul Wagner. He was obsessed with creating a championship contender, and despite the popular conception, Wagner had his doubts about the ability of Morrison to bring this about. While he could not criticize Zach's statistics on the football field, he knew that, at thirty-eight, age was catching up to him and that soon he would be a washed-up veteran ready for pasture. Wagner wanted to bring in new blood that would provide a foundation for the team to build upon in the coming years.

When Wagner came to Seattle three years earlier, he promised the Seattle fans that a championship would soon follow. He came as a successful head coach of the New York Giants and was hired as both head coach and general manager of the Seahawks. He arrived in Seattle with a reputation as a tough, no-nonsense coach who expected results from his players. He usually got those results. Past performances and reputations meant nothing to Wagner. If a player didn't produce, he would be benched and eventually traded despite the player's past record of performance.

One of the first items of business that Wagner undertook after signing with Seattle was to trade for O'Connor. Wagner had watched Jason closely when he was playing in college and believed that he had all the tools, both physical and mental, to be a great NFL quarterback. Nobody was more surprised than Wagner that Jason had bounced around the league for seven seasons serving time as a backup quarterback to several veterans on three different teams. Wagner believed that with the right supporting team, Jason O'Connor could show the athletic talent in the NFL that he had shown when playing for Washington State University.

Indeed, Jason's failure to be a star in the NFL had been a mystery to most sports pundits. When he did play, he showed signs of promise, but because of his lack of consistency and failure to make the big play at the right time, he was never trusted by his NFL coaches to become a starter.

The scuttlebutt among the football experts—both coaches and sports pundits—was that Jason O'Connor had as much natural physical and athletic talent as any quarterback in the league. Yet, he had never proven himself in a big game.

In college Jason was an all-American for two years at Washington State University and his senior season was the runner up for the Heisman Trophy, the highest award acknowledging the best college football player in the land. However, despite his individual heroics and statistics, he twice failed to lead his team—the Cougars—to a victory in postseason play. His junior year the Cougars were destroyed in the Rose Bowl by Michigan, 38-7, and in his senior year, they lost the Rose Bowl to Iowa by three touchdowns. The Cougars were expected to win both times, but, instead, their lopsided losses tagged Jason as the leader who could not win the big game.

Despite the questions regarding O'Connor's leadership in the big game, Wagner believed that if given a chance and pushed hard enough, Jason O'Connor would be a star quarterback for the Seahawks. Wagner had had an innate ability to spot talent throughout his career as a coach. He had developed and trained many NFL stars whom others had written off, and Wagner dared to believe that Jason O'Connor would be another football talent that he could develop to full potential. Thus, Wagner traded for and signed O'Connor with the clear intention of putting him in the lineup at the first opportunity.

O'Connor's first year on the team was uneventful, as Morrison enjoyed the best season of his career. Even though he did not lead the Seahawks into the play-offs, he was named a starter in the Pro-Bowl in recognition of his superior passing statistics. With a performance like this it was virtually impossible for Wagner to get O'Connor into the lineup his first season with the team.

While it appeared that Morrison was riding high and at the peak of his career, Wagner had no sentimental feelings for him. In fact, Wagner secretly loathed the image of Morrison as a great community leader who gave back to the city with his much-publicized efforts to support charities. To Wagner what a football player did on his own time away from the team was his own business, but he personally preferred that players stayed away from what he referred to as "sentimental do-gooder" causes. Wagner had a distain for social activism in general and felt that when football players attempted to be so involved, it distracted them from concentrating on achieving their best on the football field.

Morrison's popularity with the Seattle community was based, in part, on his involvement in the community with underprivileged teens and other such charities that worked with the poor. In being so involved he was constantly featured in the Seattle media—both television and radio—promoting causes he supported. Telethons and fund-raising events for numerous charities were common on Morrison's speaking circuit in the off-season.

Morrison was, in Wagner's mind, simply a grandstander who sought the limelight outside of the football arena. While Wagner personally distained this kind of activism, he could tolerate it in a player as long as he produced results on the football field. This was Wagner's bottom-line, and he hated seeing a flashy quarterback, such as Morrison, preside over mediocre team performances. Wagner was convinced that O'Connor would make a difference if he replaced Morrison in the lineup.

When the decision to start O'Connor was announced, however, there was a howl of protest from the Seattle sports media and the fans. Wagner's tough personality made it easy to buck this tidal wave of anger and criticism because he was convinced that this personnel change was the correct move for the franchise. He had never been more right in his life.

O'Connor started the ninth game of the previous season with the Seahawks sitting on a 4-4 win-loss record. His performance on the field immediately ignited the team. His first game against the San Francisco 49ers was spectacular. He threw five touchdown passes, passed for 433 yards, and ran for another 65 yards as the Seahawks crushed their opponent 49-3. The next week with similar statistics O'Connor performed with brilliance, leading his team to a 38-14 victory over the New York Giants. Jason's sensational play was unexpected but resulted in such obvious successes that the fans realized his replacement of Morrison was, indeed, the correct decision for the good of the team.

By his third starting game, the city was abuzz with excitement over its newest sports star. O'Connor and the Seahawks did not disappoint, winning seven of their last eight games and landing in the play-offs. Seattle fans actually dreamt of reclaiming the lost Super Bowl title that had slipped through their fingers years before. By the time the opening play-off game rolled around, the town was in ecstasy, and many national sports pundits predicted that the team would go all the way and win the Super Bowl. But such glory was not to be, as the Seahawks lost the final conference play-off game to the St. Louis Rams on a last-second field goal. St. Louis went on to win the Super Bowl.

While the Seattle fans again experienced heartbreak and frustration, there was also hope in the air for the next season. This time the worn-out exclamation of "Wait till next year!" did not seem to be a futile, delusional cry from never-say-die Seattle sports fans. Jason O'Connor had proven himself, and Seahawks fans believed that with some astute trades in the off-season, their team would triumph the next season.

Immediately after the season ended, word came down from Seahawks ownership that money was no object in obtaining the right players to put the team over the top. Jason O'Connor himself was awarded with a lucrative thirty-five million dollar contract over five years and was even allowed to project himself into the off-season deals by insisting that his old college buddy and roommate, Bobby Childs, a wide receiver and Olympic caliber high hurdler in college, be signed. The Seattle front office obliged, and in addition to Childs, signed four critical players to shore up the defensive line and linebacking corps.

The new season started with anticipation as O'Connor and company picked up where they had left off. A local radio station began using the old rock and roll hit "Hold on Tight to Your Dream" as the season's theme song for the Seahawks. Indeed, by mid season all of the radio stations were playing this song on a regular basis to promote the team, and the Seahawks organization began to play the song through the loudspeaker system at halftime at all home games.

Jason O'Connor performed nearly flawlessly in game after game. The acquisition of his friend Childs turned out to be the best trade of the season, as Childs and O'Connor teamed up for sixteen touchdown passes. O'Connor broke the NFL record for most touchdown passes in a season, held for years by Hall of Famer Peyton Manning, by throwing for fifty-seven touchdown passes—more than three each game. All season long the two former college buddies lit up the scoreboards in stadiums across the country and were the highlight of ESPN sportscasts.

The Seahawks rolled to a 15 –1 regular season record with their only loss resulting from another last-second field goal by the St. Louis Rams. But the team entered the postseason with the highest degree of confidence. The best quarterback the league had seen in decades led them, and he was backed by a team of individuals who had performed to the potential that Coach Wagner believed they had in them. The only serious threat to the title came from the St. Louis Rams, who had ruined the Seahawks' previous season and spoiled a perfect season this time around—both times with their last-second (some would say lucky) wins.

However, on this crisp, winter day, the Seahawks had their opportunity for revenge and redemption. The despised Rams were in town to play for the conference championship and the right to move on, but the Seahawks were ready to settle old scores and advance to the next level—the Super Bowl.

The home crowd had no doubts as to the outcome of this game as the opening kickoff took place. They expected the Seattle surge to continue and to take them to a revenge match with the Steelers. Yet, despite being heavy underdogs, the Rams came to play football and show that their previous wins over the Seahawks were not accidents. They intended to remind people that they were the reigning Super Bowl champions and did not intend to give up their title without an all out war.

Indeed, the St. Louis offensive took immediate control of the game in the first quarter as they received the opening kickoff and marched eighty-five yards down the field to take a 7-0 lead. With an offense that mixed up passes with runs and one unorthodox reverse, the Rams made the Seahawks defense look like a middle school team. The crowd sat in stunned silence while St. Louis drew first blood.

Jason O'Connor was not to be denied. He immediately showed why he led the league quarterbacks in passing yardage and completion percentage as he took his team down the field. Six straight completions (three caught by his buddy Bobby Childs) put the Seahawks on its opponent's eight-yard line with the end zone in sight. However, O'Connor was then sacked for a five-yard loss, and on third down his pass in the end zone was picked off by the St. Louis secondary to end the drive.

St. Louis again took advantage of the situation and drove down the field with precision. Five yards here. Then ten more. Another first down. And then a completed pass for twenty-five yards to the Seattle ten-yard line. The crowd began to get restless and booed the Seahawks for the first time all season. Whether or not such fan displeasure was justified, it seemed to motivate the Seahawks defense as they rose to the occasion and kept the Rams offense out of the end zone. St. Louis had to settle for a field goal, but the deficit now grew to 10-0.

Once again, O'Connor began to move the Seahawks down the field, and as the first quarter came to an end, they were sitting on a first down at the fifty-yard line. A quick completed pass to Childs for ten yards and then a bootleg run by O'Connor for twenty-five more placed the Seahawks on the Rams fifteen-yard line. The Seattle crowd came alive as they anticipated breaking out of what seemed to be a bad enchanted spell. But once again fate killed their hopes when O'Connor threw his second interception in the end zone as Childs ran the wrong receiving route. For the first time all season Jason O'Connor had thrown two interceptions in one game. The fickle Seahawks crowd again began to boo loudly and show its dismay at the play of O'Connor and his teammates.

Coach Paul Wagner was among those bewildered at the performance of his star quarterback and called him over as the Seattle defense took the field. "OK, O'Connor, what is going on out there? What happened to Childs on that last play?"

"He blew his assignment, Coach. He ran the wrong route, and I simply threw to where he was supposed to be. That's it."

Wagner cursed in Jason's face and responded condescendingly, "Well listen here, pretty boy. The buck stops with you. Do you hear me? No more excuses. The next time we get the ball we will score. Failure is not an option. Do you understand that? I know Morrison understands that very well!"

Jason was shocked at the reference to the benched veteran Morrison. The inference was clear, and he resented it deeply. He had worked hard to bring victory to this Seattle team and believed that he should have earned the respect of his coach.

The Rams continued to stick it to the surprisingly weak Seattle defense. Taking the ball from their own twenty-yard line, they marched up the field mixing runs with short passes while taking time off of the clock. With five minutes left in the first half, they scored again on a three-yard plunge by their fullback. With the score now reading 17-0, the incensed crowds shouted obscenities at the team and the decibel level of the boo birds began to rise.

The teams traded possession of the football on the next two series, and the Seahawks got the ball back on their own twenty-yard line with one minute and thirty seconds left in the half. O'Connor was determined this time to punch in a score before halftime and called for a pass out of the team's shotgun formation. More disaster happened on the first play of the series. As O'Connor called the signals from the Seattle ten-yard line, the Seahawks center snapped the ball on the wrong count catching Jason by surprise. His worst nightmare became reality as the ball slipped through his hands and quickly bounced toward the goal line. As the ball rolled into the end zone he plunged on it just before the speedy Rams defense piled on him to score a two-point safety. The score, now 19-0, remained unchanged until the end of the first half.

Coach Wagner was briefly interviewed by a television reporter on his way to the locker room. "Coach, what adjustments are you going to make in the second half to get back into this game?

"Well, we didn't get the breaks in the first half, and this game should really be a lot closer than the score indicates. We are going to have to hold their offense and then find some ways to score," Wagner replied while holding in check his seething anger at the play of his team.

"Will you be replacing O'Connor with Zach Morrison in the second half?"

Wagner artfully dodged the question by stating, "We will make the proper adjustments after talking this over with the team in the next few minutes."

The Seattle crowd was stunned and restless. Grumblings about O'Connor's performance and questions about his inability to win the big game freely traveled throughout the stadium. The fan sentiment was probably best expressed by the popular radio announcers Jake McGee and Robin Everson.

"Well, Robin, I guess we have to catch our breath here and try to figure out what happened in this first half. That simply wasn't the Seahawks team we have seen all year."

"Listen, Jake, I need to express something that everybody is thinking right now. Jason O'Connor was simply awful in the first half. I think I am being kind to put it that way. But we have to be honest about some things here. O'Connor's performance raises the question that has been dormant for most of the season. Since the Seahawks have been wining all year, nobody has cared to raise the issue about his ability to rise to the occasion and win the big game. I think today is going to finally answer that question once and for all. So far, he is failing the test."

McGee responded, "Well, let's look at his track record. In college he put up spectacular statistics. Many thought he should have been the winner of the Heisman trophy his senior year. Yet, he failed to win any bowl game for his team. And in the pros we are now seeing a similar pattern."

"Right you are, Jake. He had not been a starter prior to coming to Seattle so it was hard to predict what he would do when Wagner traded for him. But look at the record so far. Last year he excited the city in an unbelievable way but couldn't lead the team past the Rams, and this year the Rams again have stood in his way of success. Why can't this guy come through in the big games? And now, in the biggest game of his and his teammates' careers, he comes up with the poorest first half performance imaginable."

"I guess, Robin, we should give him the benefit of the doubt with all he has accomplished this year, but this game is just too big. I think many

Seahawks fans are wondering if Zach Morrison will replace him in the second half."

"Not only am I wondering that, I am earnestly praying for it to happen. Listen, Morrison had a terrific season two years ago, and he was playing almost as well when Wagner pulled him in the middle of the last season. You know that I was one of the sports media that was highly critical of that move. I still think it was the wrong decision."

"And a lot of other Seattle fans think the same," responded Jake McGee. "I guess I need to go on record now as saying I don't believe Seattle can pull this one out in the second half unless there is a change at the quarterback spot."

"I am with you on that, Jake. Zach Morrison is a seasoned veteran and knows how to respond to this kind of challenge. I think Wagner needs to make this move at the start of the second half and let Zach take the reigns. There is simply no tomorrow. All is on the line now."

As the crowd murmured and complained, McGee and Everson continued to pour on the criticisms of Jason O'Connor. In the meantime the Seahawks team sat in stunned silence in the locker room awaiting the entry of Coach Paul Wagner. Wagner was not known for his motivational speeches in the locker room. He was no Knute Rockne as far as inspiring a football team.

Immediately after entering the locker room, Wagner loudly cursed and kicked over a trashcan. He proceeded to pick up a football and throw it as hard as he could against the wall. He then looked down the row of pro football players until he saw Jason O'Connor sitting quietly at the end of a bench with his helmet still on. He screamed loudly, "O'Connor! Get up, and answer for yourself. Come over here now!"

As Jason stood up and began to walk toward his Coach Wagner met him halfway. He immediately grabbed the facemask of O'Connor's helmet and pulled it right up to his own face.

"OK, hot stuff, since when do two interceptions and a fumbled snap from center in one half ever occur on this team? Can't you take the heat, boy? This is the big leagues, not some sand lot football game!"

Jason O'Connor stood quietly and accepted this humiliation in front of his teammates with grace. Jason was a proud man and not accustomed to being talked to in this manner. But Wagner was the boss. Not only was he the head coach who demanded results, he was also the general manager who had the power to destroy a career through a trade or simple release of a contract.

Wagner continued his tirade. "We are paying you a lot of money to perform, and we expect results! Do you understand that?" Wagner then began to curse in a high-pitched tone that shocked even the most profane of this group of pro athletes. Wagner continued to scream, "I will not accept this subpar performance from you or anybody else on this team. Am I understood, Mr. O'Connor?"

As soon as Jason responded with a "yes, sir" Wagner released his grip on the helmet and began to scream and curse at the rest of the team.

"This isn't just O'Connor's doing," he shouted. His ranting turned into loud cursing. "Where is the defense? They drove all over you as if you were a bunch of schoolboys playing flag football. I am walking out of here in a few minutes and will turn you bunch of little girls over to the assistant coaches to seriously discuss adjustments in the second half. But let me make one thing very clear. There is more than just a game on the line here. Anybody who doesn't take seriously his role out there today can count on either being traded or having his contract terminated. I don't think free agency will sit well with many of you. Remember the contracts we enter into do not give you job security. You have to earn your place on this team. Anybody who doesn't contribute will be gone!"

Wagner was for the first time resorting to a threat that always hung over this team but had never been outwardly mentioned in a team setting. Yet, it was constantly in the back of each player's mind. The contracts entered into between the Seahawks front office and each player had a huge escape clause for the Seahawks. Simply put, each contract entered into with every player stated that if in the opinion of the head coach a player is underachieving, the coach can either have him traded in the off-season or have the contract terminated for breach by the player. Wagner had insisted on this kind of authority when he agreed to be the general manager, and now he was using it as leverage to get the kind of production he desired from the team.

Wagner began to walk out and turn the meeting over to the Seahawks assistant coaches.

Just before he got to the locker room door, he pivoted and shouted at Jason, "And by the way, O'Connor, you have exactly one possession to show you can turn this game around." He then looked at Zach Morrison. "Morrison, I want you warming up that arm on the sidelines immediately. Don't stop throwing until I say so." With that command he walked out of the locker room, slamming the door behind him.

The Seahawks assistant coaches, both offensive and defensive, began the work of building up the team that had just been broken down by the ranting of what some might believe to be a lunatic. They went over every defensive set and assignment to break down what had happened in the first half and where the adjustments needed to be made. The offensive coaches likewise meticulously talked about where the offense had broken down and what needed to be done to fix the problem. However, halftime in a locker room is not long, and there simply wasn't enough time to adequately deal with all the holes the team had shown in the first half.

When the team was notified that it had five minutes before it had to take the field, Jason O'Connor rose to address his teammates. Jason had never been a fiery speechmaker in the locker room. He usually led by quiet example and stellar performance on the field. However, on this day, he believed he needed to say something to calm his teammates down and give them confidence in his ability to lead them.

"I suppose that most of the fans out there are doubting we can do this thing. Some are questioning our will and desire to win this game. Some believe that we are not serious about our mission here today.

"I don't know about you guys, but I intend to prove these people wrong! We have worked too hard this year to get to where we are and then throw it all away. Sure, we stunk up the field the first half and have no excuses, but we can't change what has happened. It is gone and over with. It is only the here and now that we can deal with.

"We can control our destiny. None of us in this room today believes that the Rams are the better team. None of us believes that they should return to the Super Bowl because we know something deep in our gut that the Rams do not know. I think we all have a feeling of destiny that has culminated since our first win. Our play together this year has been something special, and despite the score right now, I still have this feeling of destiny inside me. I believe that all of you do as well."

"So guys, let me make a deal with you. I don't care about tomorrow, the next day, or even a week from now. I care only about today, and I know that victory is ours if we just trust each other do the job that we know we can do on the football field. Each of us has a mission to accomplish. So my promise to you is that I will accomplish my mission. Can I count on each of you to do the same?"

The locker room was silent as the players let O'Connor's words sink in. "Well," shouted Jason, "What are we waiting for? A conference championship awaits our arrival, so let's go get them!"

And with that the Seahawks locker room erupted with war cries of men ready to go to battle and accomplish the improbable. No team in a conference championship game had ever come back from this kind of deficit at half time. Yet, the air in the locker room was filled with determination. If any team could possibly pull off this kind of miracle, each one of the Seahawks believed that it would be this team.

Jason O'Connor and his teammates returned to the field with an intense determination to be victorious. The song "Hold on Tight to Your Dream" blasted through the loudspeakers as the Seahawks made their way onto the field from the locker room. The crowd was on their feet now swaying and dancing to the music and screaming with all of their might for their hometown heroes to comeback and win the game.

Jason determined that he was not going to be benched. He was not leaving the playing field. He intended to show his coach and the world that he was the right man at the right time to lead this franchise to win the conference championship and go on to the Super Bowl. His face showed determination as he trotted onto the field to lead the offense after the kickoff return.

On the first play from scrimmage, O'Connor kept the ball and ran a bootleg around the left end for twenty yards. He then completed three consecutive passes, two to Childs, to put the Seahawks on the twenty-yard line and within striking distance of the goal line.

Three short running plays left the Seahawks with a fourth down and inches to go for a first down just outside the Rams ten-yard line. Wagner signaled O'Connor to sneak the ball for a first down. However, as he approached the line of scrimmage, Jason nodded to Childs to break for the goal line. Instead of safely sneaking for a first down, Jason risked everything as he stood back and fired the ball at the streaking Childs, hitting him right on the numbers as his college roommate scored the first touchdown for the Seahawks. With the extra point successful, the score was now 19-7, and the Seattle crowd came to life.

The Seattle defense, however, was still struggling. St. Louis again marched down the field after the ensuing kickoff. Mixing up their offense with short runs, quick passes, and play action passes, the Rams threatened to score again with a first down at the Seattle eight-yard line. The Seahawks called timeout to regroup, and the defense headed to the sideline to talk things over with the coach.

Yet, Jason O'Connor was so emotionally charged up that he intervened and wouldn't let Coach Wagner have a say. He screamed at his teammates in order to be heard over the noise of the crowd.

"Listen, you chumps. This whole team is relying on you. The whole city is relying on you. I am relying on you! Do not let them in the end zone! You can do this. They are not stronger than you. Dig deep. Don't let them in. We need a gigantic effort from each of you. Don't let us down!"

O'Connor's words seemed to take hold, and the defense fought hard. Three straight running plays netted the Rams just two yards as they faced a fourth down on the Seattle five-yard line. The Rams opted for a field goal, increasing their lead to 22-7.

The game then settled into a defensive struggle with each team unable to move their offense in any significant way. Some brief excitement occurred when O'Connor teamed up with Childs for a dramatic fifty-yard pass play to put the ball inside the Rams twenty-yard line, but the play was called back because the Seahawks had been called for holding.

On the very next play, Jason ripped off a beautiful twenty-yard run on a quarterback draw, only to have it nullified by another penalty. Coach Paul Wagner seethed with anger on the sidelines as the smell of defeat began to set in.

Time was now becoming a factor as the game moved into the fourth quarter, and the clock ticked away precious minutes. The Seattle fans were getting restless, and the real possibility of defeat was sinking in when the Seahawks received possession of the ball on their own thirty-five-yard line with three and a half minutes left to play. In the huddle O'Connor decided to gamble in hopes of catching the Rams off guard.

O'Connor looked at Childs and asked, "Hey, Bobby, you can outrun both of those defensive backs one on one can't you?"

"Of course, give me a head of steam, and I will leave them at the train station."

"I thought so," replied Jason. "Here is what we are going to do. We are going to thread the needle with a post pattern over the middle. You run ten yards down, and then break right between those two defenders. As soon as you get a little ahead of them, look back because the ball is coming to you."

Childs and the whole team knew what had to happen for this play to be successful. First, Childs had to utilize his Olympic quality speed to beat both men down the field and get behind them. Second, O'Connor had to throw an absolutely perfect pass. The ball had to be thrown with precision in order to hit Childs on the numbers just as he is accelerating down the field. If the pass were off even a few inches to the right or to the left, it would undoubtedly be intercepted and the game would be over. O'Connor had to literally thread a needle with the football to make this work.

If Jason O'Connor had any flaws in his passing abilities, they couldn't be detected on this play. After receiving the snap O'Connor dropped straight back and looked down the middle of the field. Childs accelerated to near superhuman speed as he broke down the middle between the two Rams defensive backs. As soon as he was a step behind them, O'Connor rocketed the football toward him with a perfect pass, hitting him right on his numbers at the very moment his speed was in top form. Childs caught the ball on the run and pulled away from the defenders, scoring easily on a perfectly executed sixty-five-yard touchdown pass.

The Seattle crowd went berserk. They were on their feet wildly shouting and hugging each other, as it now seemed possible that their beloved Seahawks could pull a win one out. The successful extra point conversion made the score 22-17 with a little over three minutes left in the game. Strategy now became a critical factor for Seattle, as the Rams were to receive the kickoff and merely needed to run out the clock to preserve the victory.

Jake McGee raised the question to his sidekick Robin Everson in the radio booth. "OK, so now what does Seattle do? Should they try an on-side kick in hopes of getting the ball back to score? Or should they kick it deep and hope the defense can hold and get the ball back?"

Everson replied, "This is a real tough call for Coach Wagner. There are only three minutes left in the game. All St. Louis has to do is get three first downs, and the game is virtually over. On one hand, the Seattle defense has been determined this fourth quarter, so if we kick it deep, there is the hope that the defense will hold, and we can get the ball back with time to score. On the other hand, if we recover an on-side kick, we would be in good position to score with plenty of time on the clock. What would you do, Jake?"

"I gotta tell you that I think I would take a chance on the defense. An on-side kick rarely works. And if it fails then St. Louis has the ball around the forty-yard line. Even if the defense holds, they would punt us deep into our territory with little time left to do anything."

Paul Wagner himself was conflicted. In the end he decided for the on-side kick, believing that St. Louis would be expecting a deep kick and would be caught off guard. It failed miserably. St. Louis easily recovered the ball and now had possession on its forty-five yard line with less than three minutes to go.

But the Seattle defense was not to be denied. It held its ground like a concrete wall. Three straight runs up the middle produced only three yards, and St. Louis was forced to punt as the two-minute warning was announced. The St. Louis punter showed why he was the best in the NFL, as he nailed a fifty-yard punt that went out of bounds on the Seattle two-yard line. Less than two minutes to play and exactly ninety-eight yards to score was all that stood between Jason O'Connor's Seahawks and a trip to the Super Bowl.

In the world of sports every athlete has a defining moment. It is a moment when he is faced with adversity and impossible odds that only a superstar can conquer. If the athlete overcomes and triumphs, then immortality, fortune, and fame may follow. Perhaps his likeness might even appear on a Wheaties box. If, on the other hand, he falls short nobody will remember his career and name within a few years. Most athletes fall short in these moments, for superstardom in any sport is achieved by only a select elite.

This was Jason O'Connor's defining moment. To lead his team to a touchdown and victory would undoubtedly place him in the direction of the NFL Hall of Fame. Jason was aware of what was at stake and determined within himself that he would succeed.

In the huddle before the first play he asserted his leadership. "All right, men. This is it. Everything we have worked for our whole lives is coming down to the next two minutes. Follow my lead. We are going to win. Give it everything you have. Let's go!"

The first play called was a forty-five play action bootleg left. This play gave O'Connor the option of keeping the ball and running around the left end if no receivers were open. Jason did not consider the possibility of passing this time and determined to run the ball from the outset. He was the best passer in the NFL statistically, but he also was the best running quarterback. His big frame and unusual height teamed up with better than average speed to make him a very difficult player to tackle once he turned the corner and headed up the field with the ball under his arm. On this play he showed why he was so tough to bring down.

O'Connor took the snap, faked a hand-off to his running back, and then briefly looked down field as if to pass. However, he then took off running toward the left side of the line. After turning the corner he was hit hard by a Rams linebacker but broke the tackle, sidestepped another defender, and eventually was brought down on the twenty-seven-yard line—a run of twenty-five yards.

On the very next play Jason hit his tight end with another pass down the middle of the field and the receiver rambled for eighteen yards to the forty-five-yard line. The Seattle crowd was hysterical—everyone on their feet, screaming loudly for the home team to continue the drive.

Seattle called its last time out with a little less than one minute to play. Jason O'Connor went to the sideline to talk to Coach Wagner.

"O'Connor, you have got to work the sidelines now. We have no time outs left. If we are caught in the middle of the field get the team to the line and immediately spike the ball to stop the clock, and then we will work out a series of plays."

Jason was breathing deeply from the physical exertion he had undertaken this afternoon. As he caught his breath he said to Wagner.

"Childs has been beating their corners all day. I think we will work them on both sides down the sidelines. If Childs is not open, I will throw it out of bounds."

"Good call. Just get the job done, and I will forget that it was that cursed safety at the end of the first half that is preventing us from tying the game with a field goal. Now go do your job."

Three straight completed sideline passes to Childs and the Seahawks were on the Rams twenty-yard line with twenty seconds left on the clock. The noise now from the crowd was deafening as the hometown fans feverishly rooted their team on. Word came from Wagner into the huddle that there was time for three plays, so O'Connor was instructed to throw to the corner of the end zone each time in hopes of scoring and securing the victory.

The first attempt went nowhere, as all receivers were covered, and O'Connor was forced to throw the ball out of bounds. The second attempt didn't fare much better as Jason tried to hit his only open receiver on the five-yard line in hopes that he would catch the ball and step out of bounds. The throw was high, and sailed over the head of his intended target.

One more play was all time would allow. Twenty yards stood between the Seahawks and victory. The St. Louis Rams knew that the only option their opponent had was to throw into the end zone in hopes a receiver could make the catch. So the Rams resorted to a prevent defense with seven pass defenders placed between the ten-yard line and the goal line.

Jake McGee had been a popular sports announcer for many years in Seattle. When he became excited everyone listening got caught up in the emotion of the moment. He had the vocal ability to create excitement out of a slug race. His voice was stressed to the limit as he called the final play of the game.

"The ball is snapped to O'Connor as he fades back looking into the end zone for Childs...no receiver is open, and O'Connor rolls to his left. He now reverses his field and moves right...There is hot pursuit, and he is hit hard at the twenty but breaks the tackle...HE IS GOING TO RUN IT! HE HAS ROOM! HE IS AT THE TEN...THE FIVE...HE IS HIT HARD AND DIVES TOWARD THE GOAL LINE...DID HE GET IN? DID HE GET IN? THERE IS A BIG PILE OF PLAYERS NEAR THE GOAL LINE WITH NO SIGNAL FROM THE REFEREE YET...DID HE SCORE?"

It seemed like an eternity to Seahawks fans as they waited for the referees to dig into the pile of bodies at the goal line. The radio and television audiences awaited the final call in deep suspense. The fans in the stadium were paralyzed and couldn't move. Finally, the referees got to the bottom of the pile where O'Connor was lying facedown with the football, and the signal was made.

Jake McGee's screaming said it all. "TOUCHDOWN! MY GOODNESS, O'CONNOR DID IT! TOUCHDOWN! THE SEAHAWKS HAVE WON! THE SEAHAWKS HAVE WON! UNBELIEVABLE! O'CONNOR IS A MIRACLE WORKER! THE SEAHAWKS HAVE WON! SUPER BOWL HERE WE COME! THE SEAHAWKS ARE THE NATIONAL FOOTBALL CONFERENCE CHAMPIONS! "

Jake McGee's excitement was only a microcosm of the joy and delight experienced by the Seahawks fans at the game and around the city. Upon the touchdown signal, the stadium exploded into cheers of ecstasy. Men and women alike screamed and cried at the same time. Fans hugged each other and hugged people they didn't even know. Tears flowed freely down the faces of many who had waited so long for this moment. The streets of Seattle crowded with celebrating fans. People danced in the streets, and in the sports bars football addicts danced with each other, simultaneously laughing and crying.

It was a moment of pure joy for a city that had waited so long for a champion. "Hold on Tight to Your Dream" now blasted through the stadium as the loud celebration continued. However, in the excitement of the moment one thing went unnoticed—Jason O'Connor lay flat on his face at the goal line, his body totally lifeless. On his touchdown run O'Connor had evaded several tackles but was hit with a bone-crunching tackle at the five-yard line. His momentum had carried him forward as he staggered toward the goal line and then dove for the end zone. At that same time he was hit in the head by a ferocious 250-pound all-pro linebacker in a superhuman effort to stop him from scoring. His last conscious moment came as he stretched his arm with the ball just over the goal line before going down.

Jake McKee seemed to be the first to notice O'Connor and announced to the radio audience, "Hold on, Seahawks fans. O'Connor appears to be seriously hurt. He is not getting up and is lying flat on his face. The Seahawks trainer is out there now and kneeling over him. Let's hope he just had the wind knocked out of him."

Jason certainly had the wind knocked out of him, but it was much more serious than that. The team doctor would shortly announce after examining him that he suffered a serious concussion. At this moment of uncertainty, however, the crowd began to quiet down as they looked on the field in hopes that the injury was minor.

O'Connor gained consciousness after a few minutes of the trainer using smelling salts to revive him. He was then placed on a stretcher and taken immediately into the locker room to be checked out thoroughly by the team physician.

Silence descended over the stadium at the sight of O'Connor being carried away on a stretcher. McKee attempted to put the most positive light on the situation, "It is unfortunate that this glorious day in Seattle sports history has to end like this. We will keep you posted on updated news. We trust that Seattle's star quarterback and hero of today's game will be OK and cleared to play in two weeks in the Super Bowl. That's all I can say right now."

CHAPTER 2

Jason O'Connor clearly did not know where he was as the Seahawks team physician examined him. He had no memory of his thrilling touchdown run and could barely recall why he was at the stadium on this day. But slowly as he talked to the doctor his memory returned.

"You took quite a shot to the head, O'Connor. Do you remember what you were doing?" the doctor inquired.

Jason struggled for a moment but then replied, "Well, Doc, I think we won didn't we? And didn't I run it in for the final score?"

"That a boy, Jason. Keep working at it, and the details will come back. You suffered a mighty big blow and concussion to the old brain son. Does your head hurt?"

Jason remained quiet for a few moments and then spoke, "OK, sure, Doc I have a splitting headache right now. It hurts like nothing else I have ever felt. My head just keeps throbbing; man it feels like it is going to explode!" He then noticed Coach Wagner approaching him.

Wagner interrupted the conversation. "OK, Doc, the press is waiting for some news. What can I tell them. I need to make an immediate statement."

"Well, Coach, it is clear that Jason has suffered a pretty serious concussion. I will order a CAT scan to be done this evening at Providence Hospital. We need this to help us assess the extent of the injuries. I am going to give some painkillers to get him through the night, but Jason needs to be ready to go to the hospital as soon as everything gets cleared out."

"Oh shove it, Doc," Wagner replied. "I have to go out there in a moment and deal with the press. I need to have something positive to say. They are going to want to know if he will be ready for the Super Bowl in two weeks."

Jason interrupted, "Coach, my head is throbbing and feels like it is going to split open. But let me go with you. Just fill me in on what happened on that last play. I can fake it pretty good."

Wagner's impatience grew. "Doc, I need something to say. Will he be ready? Can he practice this week? What do I tell them?"

The team physician replied, "Coach, I will not know the extent of these injuries until we do the CAT scan, so tell them for now that Jason will be kept out of contact at practice this week because of a concussion but should be ready to go for the big game. Do not tell them we are doing a CAT scan tonight. That will lead to all kinds of speculations."

"That sounds fine for now. O'Connor, let's go. I will fill you in on what happened on the last play by describing it to the press from my perspective. Remember, you are definitely going to play in two weeks. That's all you need to say."

Coach Wagner and Jason O'Connor walked together to the pressroom. Cameras began flashing as Wagner and O'Connor approached the podium and microphone. All the bright flashes merely increased Jason's excruciating headache.

Wagner immediately began talking when he got to the microphone.

"This was the most inspiring victory I have ever coached. Jason O'Connor is a true hero. It took plain guts for him to decide to run that ball from the twenty and score. And it took incredible athletic ability to fight off the tackles and dive for the score."

Jason listened intently as he now was hearing what actually happened.

Wagner continued, "There is no greater quarterback in the NFL right now. O'Connor will be our man in the Super Bowl. I understand we will be playing the Steelers. Well, bring 'em on. With Jason O'Connor at the helm, we are going to be a tough team to beat."

The questions from the press began to fly. "Coach, after the dismal first half performance, did you consider replacing O'Connor with Morrison? We all noticed Morrison warming up at the sidelines at the beginning of the third quarter."

"No. I believed in Jason O'Connor when I first brought him into the franchise. I knew that from his playing days in college he had the ability to be a winner in the right NFL setting. He has proven me right, and I believe in him now. At no time today did I consider taking him out of the lineup. Even at halftime, I had a feeling that Jason would pull this one out, so I stayed with my instincts, and they turned out to be correct."

"But Coach, why then was Morrison warming up on the sidelines at the beginning of the third quarter?"

"Morrison was throwing the ball on his own, without my instruction. I believe in this man," he said pointing to Jason sitting at the table on the side of the podium.

Jason's memory was beginning to resurface as he recalled the locker room scene and the direct threats to replace him in the second half. He sat stone faced in front of the press, however, even though he was furious at hearing such dishonesty from his coach.

"So, Coach, what does the doctor say? Will O'Connor be ready for the big event in two weeks?"

"Absolutely! Jason will be held out of contact this week at practice but will be ready to go for the Super Bowl. He suffered a bump on the head and a minor concussion, but that is not going to stop him from the task at hand."

"Jason, what were you thinking on that last play? You ran the ball from the twenty-yard line instead of throwing it. Did you not see any open receivers? Tell us your thoughts."

Jason O'Connor rose to address the question from the microphone, wincing in pain. The lights in the pressroom and the flashing cameras further contributed to his agony. He hoped that nobody noticed his obvious discomfort as he spoke.

"Well, let me first just say something about the entire game. At the beginning of this season, I had resolved within myself that no team was going to stop us from going all the way. At halftime I knew that there was no way the Rams were going to beat us today because we have been committed all season to winning it all. They are a great team and they deserved the Super Bowl last year. But this is our year. At no time today, even at halftime, did I ever doubt the end result."

Jason continued, "Now, about that last play. I think the replay will speak for itself. I obviously could not find anybody open. I was looking for Childs but, of course, he was triple-teamed and covered. I had no other choice but to run the ball."

Another reporter jumped in, "There was a huge pile at the goal line, and we had to wait for the referee's signal. When did you realize you had scored?"

Jason, not remembering a thing about the run, did a masterful job of faking it.

"Well, recall I took a nasty blow to the head and was out for a moment, but I knew I had scored when I heard the thunderous cheers from the crowd after the referee's signal."

"You mean to say that even while trailing 19-0 at halftime you were confident that the team would comeback and win?"

"Let's just say that at no time did I expect to lose this game today."

"Will you be 100 percent ready for the Super Bowl?"

"No question about that. The doctor wants me out of contact this week, but I will be ready to go after that. Nothing is going to stop me from playing in this game except an act of God."

With that response Coach Wagner grabbed Jason's arm and led him off the stage toward the exit door. Wagner shouted as they left, "It's been a tiring day for this young man, fellas. Let him enjoy the moment with his teammates, and we will talk again tomorrow."

The Seahawks locker room was a madhouse as Wagner and O'Connor walked in. Reporters, who had special permission to be in the locker room, fired questions related to O'Connor's injury and whether or not he will be ready to play in two weeks. Jason O'Connor's teammates greeted him with cheers and hugs as he made his way through the sea of bodies. Before he got to his locker a television camera and reporter interrupted him.

"Jason O'Connor, that was one of the most exciting comebacks in the history of NFL play-offs. Give us your comments."

Jason struggled to speak. The pain in his head intensified as his weary and beat-up body absorbed the emotional energy of the locker room.

"We are a team of destiny," he responded. "Nothing was going to stop us from winning today. Nothing!"

"How do you size up your chances against the Steelers in two weeks?"

"Let us enjoy this victory right now. We will be ready for the Steelers on every front."

"And will you be leading the charge?"

"Absolutely. As I said before, only an act of God will keep me from playing. Only an act of God." Jason then abruptly walked away to his locker where he hoped he could find a little bit of solace and privacy.

On his way Zach Morrison suddenly hugged him. "Listen, O'Connor, I am sorry about the way Wagner messed with you at halftime. I never want to be caught in the middle of that kind of exchange, but what can you say except that he is the boss. You were superb man. Awesome. I couldn't have done what you did. I am glad you are our leader. Anything I can do to support you I will do."

"That means a lot coming from you, Zach," replied Jason. "Thanks a lot. I am glad you are there to cover for my bonehead mistakes."

Morrison looked at his younger teammate with respect and said, "Well, give me a call soon. Let's make sure we bury the hatchet if one exists. I want this next game more than anything. And you are the guy to take us there."

"OK, Zach. We will talk soon."

Jason sat on the bench in front of his locker for what seemed to be an eternity. His exhausted body ached from the beating he took in the game. All he wanted at this point was to breathe slowly and ignore his throbbing headache that just would not subside

As he sat thinking about the game and its turn of events, Bobby Childs came alongside and sat down. Childs had been a close friend since their college days at Washington State University. They had been fraternity brothers, best friends, and a dynamic duo on the football field. Their relationship as friends bonded them from the beginning. This along with their unique and special athletic talents made their achievements on the football field lethal to opposing teams. Both had been first team all-Americans their senior years, and both were selected in the first round of the NFL draft. While their pro careers had separated them for a few years, they were teammates once again and now in the unfolding Seahawks drama.

Childs sat for a few minutes beside his friend. Both were silent and reflective on the events of the day. Then he spoke.

"Hey, buddy, we have come a long way from our days at old Wazzu, haven't we? I just can't tell you how inspiring you were to all of us today. Your run was amazing. One for the record books. It will be on NFL highlight films forever. You are incredible, man. Thanks for leading the way."

Bobby then hesitated a bit before continuing. He looked seriously at his friend and asked, "Are you sure you are going to be able to play in two weeks? Frankly, you don't look so good."

Jason smiled. Compliments from his old friend were far and few between but, when given, were genuine. Because of their longtime friendship, Jason was safe in confiding with Childs.

"Bobby, you were the inspiration out there. That touchdown pass in the third quarter was what kicked us into high gear. You know we couldn't have done it without you. But I need to be honest. My head is giving me an incredible amount of pain right now. I am worried that I won't be ready."

"Wow, what did the doc say?"

"He prescribed me a major pain killer, and I am going in for a CAT scan tonight. Please keep quiet about that for now. The official word is that I suffered a mild concussion and will be out of contact this week but ready for the Super Bowl."

Childs sat silent for a while, mulling over the scenario if his friend were not able to play in the Super Bowl.

"OK, buddy. Listen I understand that mum's the word on the CAT scan. I won't say anything, but frankly, I know you would never let them take you out of the biggest game of our lives. Missing such a game is not in your blood. I am confident that you will be with us leading the way."

"Let's hope so, man," responded Jason. "Let's hope so. I want to hit you with a couple more touchdown passes before this season ends. So let's make it happen. A deal?"

"It's a deal, " said Childs as he and his buddy threw up their hands in a high five. "Now I have something I need to mention to you before we get out of here."

"What is it? Don't tell me you are finally settling down and getting married," he said with a grin. Childs had quite a reputation as a lady's man both in college and as an NFL star.

"Not quite. At least not yet." Bobby paused briefly, took a deep breath, and then continued. "Do you remember Mandy Brooks? Of course you do, what a silly question."

Mandy Brooks was a name out of the past for both O'Connor and Childs. It was a name that brought up painful memories for Jason. These were memories he did not want popping up at this time in his life. He responded, "Of course I remember her, but I would rather forget. Why do you ask?"

"Well, she and I have been in touch. She lives in Seattle and wants to get together again and talk. She mentioned you briefly but figured that you would not want to see her. However, I am planning to have dinner with her tomorrow night."

Jason sat back and stared at his friend before responding. "How did she pop up all of the sudden? You can't be serious man. She is bad news. She chewed you up and spit you out like tobacco. And I certainly can't believe she would want to talk to me again. What's she up to anyway?"

Childs replied, "Well, I don't know a lot of details. She said she has a son who idolizes me and follows the Seahawks closely. She said she was afraid to try to connect after all these years but decided it was worth the try."

Jason was livid. "Hey listen, brother. This is pretty clear isn't it? You are now a big star in the NFL with lots of bucks. She is a gold digger pure and simple. Don't let her mess with you now. At least wait until after the season is over."

"No, I don't believe that is the case. She seems very sincere and sorry about the past. She said she just wanted to clear the air and make things right between us. So I invited her to dinner tomorrow night. That's all it is—dinner and conversation with an old college friend. I asked, and she said it was OK if you came along as well."

Agitated at this turn in the conversation, Jason replied, "Listen, Bobby! I don't want anything to do with her. You apparently haven't learned anything. She still has you tied up in knots. Man, don't you remember what she said and did? Personally, I want to forget it. Go ahead, but leave me out of it."

Jason then shouted at his friend, "Just leave me alone! Get out of here! I need some peace and quiet."

Childs slowly got up and walked toward his locker.

Suddenly, he turned to Jason but paused before speaking. Bobby had gone through many months of soul searching regarding his own life. He had come to realize that football was not everything there was to living. And he knew that both he and Jason had demons in their past that they must confront. Mandy Brooks was one of those demons. Bobby was prepared to face this ghost from his past. Jason was not.

Bobby spoke quietly but with strong resolve to Jason. "You will not bury the past until you come to terms with it my friend. Remember that."

Despite his exhaustion Jason couldn't let that remark go. He stood up from the bench and responded, "The past? Don't you ever lecture me about the past you hypocrite! Don't you dare come to me so high and mighty and preach about the past! You have no right to do so. Leave me alone!"

Bobby Childs gave his friend a very cold stare and started to respond. However, he quickly held his tongue and turned away, leaving Jason O'Connor alone for the first time that day.

Jason showered, soaked himself in the whirlpool, and relaxed his mind. The two tablets of painkiller seemed to be finally having some affect in reducing his headache. He closed his eyes and stretched out in the pool, allowing the jet streams of warm water bathe his aching muscles. He was feeling totally relaxed and momentarily absent from the tensions of his life when he was interrupted again. This time it was the boss—Coach Paul Wagner himself.

"Don't get too comfortable in there, O'Connor." Wagner gruffly stated. "You have five minutes more and then need to get out. We will be driving you to Providence Hospital for your CAT scan. And remember, this has to be kept quiet. We don't want any undue speculation from the press as to your condition right now. So let's be real quiet and nonchalant when we leave here."

"OK, Coach. I'll be out in five." Jason closed his eyes one more time, seeking the nirvana of the comfortable Jacuzzi bath in which he was sitting.

"And by the way, Jason. I know I was a little rough on you in the locker room at halftime. But it worked. Nice job in the second half. You did all you were asked to do."

"Thanks, Coach. It was all in a hard day's work." Jason smiled to himself upon hearing this non-apology. He wondered if Wagner would have been so magnanimous if his effort had fallen a foot short of the goal line on the last play of the game.

Jason finally pulled himself out of the whirlpool and slowly got dressed. The locker room had cleared out, and he was alone with himself for just a brief moment. His altercation with his friend Bobby Childs was on his mind. Childs was his closest friend and the closest person to a brother that he had. They had some wild and crazy times in college, but those days were long gone. He thought to himself that Bobby was right—it was finally time to grow up and bury the past. He was sorry he had been so harsh with Childs and promised himself that he would call and apologize when he got home. But the name Mandy Brooks still haunted him, and he realized that his short conversation with Childs was not going to leave his mind easily.

After a brief time, Coach Wagner came in again and sat down next to O'Connor. "Jason, I can't underestimate the impact a victory next week will have on everybody. Sure the players and coaches all want this and have been playing for it for years. But it is bigger than that. This city is counting on a Super Bowl win big time. Those fans that come out Sunday after Sunday to support you and the team are living their fantasy dreams now. They have been loyal and you know that the tickets they buy are not cheap. They are not as financially privileged as we are."

"Coach, I am aware of this. So what are you telling me that I don't already know?"

Wagner stood up and looked straight at O'Connor. "Many people are counting on you now. You simply have to play in the game and give it your all. I frankly don't care what this CAT scan shows. You have to be ready to play. Do you understand me?"

Jason was somewhat taken back by the assertiveness of his coach. The Super Bowl was his dream as well, and he thought he had made it clear that he intended to play. "Coach, I am going to be there leading the team forward to victory. You have my word. I am not going to be intimidated by anything the doctor says."

"That's all I need to hear, O'Connor. Now lets get to the hospital and get this thing over with. Remember, regardless of what is said by the physicians, the official team position is that you will be held out of contact this week but will be ready to go full strength in two weeks at the big game."

Jason inquired, "What if that is not what the doctors tell us, and the press talks to them?"

"The front office will handle all of this. Believe me, we have the doctors under control. What they might say privately will not go public. Now, let's get out of here and get this thing over with."

O'Connor and Wagner made their way out of the dressing room and toward the stadium exit. It was the end of a very draining day—both emotionally and physically. Both men wanted to get the CAT scan over as soon as possible and then crash at home. Neither wanted more stress or excitement. And neither was prepared for what was about to happen.

They approached an unfinished parking garage across from the stadium. The Seahawks front office had for years pressured the city to build more parking facilities for the public. However, this new parking garage was somewhat controversial, as it was the result of the city of Seattle, through the eminent domain process, taking over and tearing down buildings of businesses that had existed for years and had become a part of the Seattle downtown culture.

One such business was a popular art gallery that had helped young, starving artists show and sell their artwork to the public. When the city announced that this gallery was going to be condemned and torn down, there was a public outcry led by none other than Zach Morrison. This was the kind of cause in which Morrison loved to get involved. At the time, Morrison was unaware that the Seahawks front office was behind the city's condemnation efforts. He even appeared in several television interviews to plead the case for the art gallery. However, Wagner, upon learning that his veteran quarterback was causing public relations problems for the Seahawks, immediately put the brakes on Morrison making any further statements to the press. Morrison vanished from the controversy, and the art gallery was left to fend for itself. This guaranteed certain doom for the gallery as far as staying in the building it had occupied for years.

Even though the crowd had pretty much cleared out of the stadium area, it was now virtually impossible for Jason O'Connor to go anywhere without being noticed. Wagner and O'Connor walked swiftly toward the garage, but a small number of people began to follow seeking an autograph or possibly just a closer look at the new football superstar of Seattle. As they approached the first level of the garage where Wagner's car was parked, a few fans seeking autographs and a couple of sports reporters with microphones came into view. Coach Wagner looked at Jason and said, "Stand back a little, and let me handle this."

One reporter immediately put a microphone in front of Wagner and asked, "Coach, do you have a specific game plan ready to stop the Steelers in the Super Bowl?"

Trying to be polite, Wagner replied, "We are aware of their strengths and weaknesses and will be ready to play in two weeks."

The reporter continued in an annoying fashion. He pointed to O'Connor, and said, "And of course this big fella over here will be ready to play, right?" O'Connor, standing about ten feet away, looked amused by the irritation he knew his coach must be feeling.

As Wagner began to respond he heard a loud scream among the small group gathered around him. His head jerked toward the noise, and he saw a large, burly man dive toward Jason, tackling him and knocking him down. At nearly the same time a concrete beam crashed down from the unfinished, second level, landing only a couple of feet from where O'Connor was now lying. Had this man not acted, the beam clearly would have hit Jason—seriously injuring if not killing him.

Jason was caught off guard and was not prepared for the body blow he received. The tackle was as bone crunching as anything he had experienced in a game. It knocked him down, causing his already injured head to slam hard onto the concrete pavement. Nobody else was injured in the commotion, and for a few seconds the small crowd stood paralyzed, stunned from the unforeseen event.

The immediate concern was for Jason, who now apparently suffered an additional injury to his head. Emergency aid was summoned and arrived on the scene without delay to deal with the injured O'Connor. Wagner began to give orders.

"OK, everybody step aside; give us some room.," he shouted as the emergency aid vehicle moved in, and the medics jumped out to assist Jason.

Jason was not totally unconscious from the blow, but he was feeling groggy. His eyesight was blurred and, of course, the pain to his head was piercing. Finally, he was able to speak as his stretcher was lifted into the emergency vehicle.

"Coach, what happened? Man do I ever see stars. And who was that guy who tackled me?" Then with some humor he added, "You know we could use a good linebacker like that."

Wagner responded tersely, "Apparently the construction crew for the parking garage left a concrete beam hanging over the edge of the second floor. It came crashing down toward you. As for the guy who tackled you? Well, let's just say he saved your life. We will find out more about him later."

Wagner and O'Connor engaged in some small talk as the vehicle immediately sped them to the hospital. However, neither mentioned the greatest fear that was on their minds. Would this new injury compound the head injury received in the game in such a way that Jason O'Connor would not be able to play in the Super Bowl?

As the ambulance moved quickly through the streets of Seattle Paul

Wagner, dialed front office personnel from his cell phone to explain what had happened. After explaining the unfortunate turn of events, Wagner strongly gave orders to the Seahawks management team. "Listen, carefully to this now. This is very important," he said. "There was a reporter on the scene. He saw everything, and I am sure he is going to immediately get this on the wires. But try to find out who he is, and contact him. I really don't want this out in the press. See what you can do, and then report to me."

However, Wagner's attempt at keeping the incident away from the press was doomed.. The reporter who had witnessed the accident did not keep it to himself but rather immediately phoned local television and radio news sources with the story. Once the story was out, reporters from the media were sent to the hospital where Jason was being taken.

Wagner and O'Connor were taken to the emergency room entrance at Providence Hospital, arriving about ten minutes ahead of the press. Immediately, they were ushered into a room where the CAT scan was to be run. Not long after a physician entered and addressed them both.

"Good evening. I am Dr. Jim Nevin, the head of the Radiology Department here at the hospital. I understand that you have had some serious head trauma today," he said looking at Jason. "I watched the game and have seen the hit to your head quite a few times—the news keeps playing it over and over for the public. But I understand you have had an additional blow to your head as well? Tell me about it."

Paul Wagner took the lead and explained what had happened while Dr. Nevin examined Jason's eyes and head. Nevin wanted as much detail as possible about the last blow Jason received when his head hit the concrete walk by the parking garage.

After completing his initial evaluation Dr. Nevin spoke, "We will go ahead with the CAT scan now, but I need to tell you that from what I have heard and now see, Mr. O'Connor has suffered some serious injuries to his head. The first concussion was bad enough, but this last hit has made the injuries far more severe. The CAT scan will tell us what we need to know, but I am afraid that Mr. O'Connor is seriously injured."

"So what are you saying, doc?" Jason asked.

"I am saying that I do not believe two weeks will be a long enough time for you to recover from these injuries. Let me put it bluntly. If you suffer another blow to the head, even a mild blow, there could be serious permanent injuries to your brain. We do not want to risk that now do we?"

"Well, doc, I expected you to give us good news. This organization is depending on the health of this man," Wagner exclaimed in an emotional voice.

"We will know more after we get the results of the scan and can spend some time studying it. That will be sometime tomorrow. In the meantime, Mr. O'Connor is to stay out of all physical contact. I will make sure he is given a strong pain killer so he can sleep tonight."

Paul Wagner, never being one to not get what he wants, replied, "Jason will be ready for the Super Bowl, period. And I expect you and your cohorts to do whatever is necessary to make that happen." With that response, Wagner abruptly left the room to allow the CAT scan to be taken.

After the scan was completed, Dr. Nevin met briefly with both men. "We will have the results and recommendations sometime tomorrow by early afternoon." He then looked at Wagner. "Coach I understand your concerns. I am a very big Seahawks fan myself. And I know I can't make you follow my recommendations. I just want to prepare you for what I think will not be good news as far as Mr. O'Connor playing in two weeks. I am professionally obligated to give you my advice. Whether you two gentlemen follow it or not is up to you."

"And will you talk to the press about this?" Jason inquired.

"Only with your permission, Mr. O'Connor. These are your medical records, and they are private unless you personally release them. If you refuse to do so, I can say nothing about them to anybody outside the Seahawks front office."

"All right, doc, we will deal with the information when it comes. For now the official word from our organization is that Jason O'Connor will be out of contact for one week only but will be ready to go full strength after that. And he will definitely be the starter in the Super Bowl. I will expect your call as soon as possible tomorrow."

Wagner and O'Connor slowly made their way toward the lobby of the hospital to exit. They were not aware that the press had gathered at the hospital, waiting to talk to them and get a report. When Wagner saw the reporters in the lobby he said to Jason, "Make sure we keep to the party line, O'Connor. It will be important for you to speak and alleviate the fears people undoubtedly have right now. So think about what you are going to say."

"Right, Coach. I'll do fine," replied Jason.

As they walked into the hospital lobby, they were greeted by a swarm of reporters and television camera lights. Jason flinched in pain at the lights but smiled into the cameras and waived to the reporters, who immediately started the inquisition.

"Jason, first tell us what happened outside the stadium," inquired the first reporter.

Jason smiled and chuckled a little before responding. "I guess I have a harder head than most people give me credit for. Apparently, a loose concrete beam fell off of the second floor of the new parking garage and was headed straight for my head. Someone—I don't even know his name yet—tackled me and knocked me over to avoid the falling beam. I landed smack dab on the back of my head."

Another reporter chimed in. "The guy's name is Mr. Josiah Johnson, or Joe as he likes to be called. Apparently, his wife and son are very big Seahawks fans and come to every game. Have you ever met him?"

"No, I never have, but I understand he saved my life. I plan on trying to see him this week to thank him."

"When will that be?" a third reporter asked.

"Oh come on, fellas. I will work it out this week, but this has been a brutal day. I need to go home and get some sleep."

"What did the doctor say? Will you be ready for the Steelers in two weeks?

Paul Wagner was waiting for that question and immediately jumped into the fray. "Nothing has changed. We will hold O'Connor out of contact this week; although, he will definitely practice. Then he will be ready to go full steam the next week as we prepare down in Miami for the Super

Bowl. So guys, listen, I agree with Jason. It has been a long day. We will talk more tomorrow after our practice session. Let us get out of here and get some sleep."

Jason and his coach abruptly walked out of the emergency room ignoring follow-up questions from the reporters. But as they exited, the voice of what sounded to be like that of a child shouted at them from a car parked on the side of the road. As Jason looked over he saw a young boy no more that seven or eight shout, "Mr. Jason, Mr. Jason, you were awesome today! You were awesome!" Jason smiled and waived to the youngster as he headed toward the limousine sent by the Seahawks organization to pick Wagner and him up.

As they got into the limousine neither spoke. They were both contemplating the question that neither wanted to verbalize to the other.

What if Jason O'Connor cannot play in two weeks?

CHAPTER 3

Jason couldn't have been happier to walk inside his condominium over-looking the serene and majestic Puget Sound. The time was getting late—9:30 pm—, and with a team meeting and practice scheduled for 10:00 AM the next day, he wanted to just hop in bed and sleep. However, the very moment he stepped inside his place of solitude, the telephone began to ring. He hesitated briefly, but then picked up the phone and answered.

"Hello, Jason, buddy. This is Zach Morrison. I am calling to make sure you are OK."

"Sure, Zach. Why wouldn't I be?"

"Cut the bull, O'Connor. It is all over the news. You took another hit on the old noggin again. That can't be good. What did the doctor say?"

"Listen, Zach. Everything will be fine. Keep me out of contact this week, and I will be ready to go. I promise."

"All right, Jason, but I just want to say that it is important to me and the rest of the team that you will be ready to play. That's all. You gotta be ready, man."

Jason thought that this was odd for Zach Morrison to say. He was a veteran quarterback who lost his starting job two seasons ago. One might think that he would relish the thought of finishing a distinguished career by starting in the Super Bowl as the quarterback. He responded with that in mind.

"Hey, Zach, if I don't start you will. And everybody knows you can do it. That would be a great thing for you after all these years. Some people think you should be starting anyway. So I think we are in good hands either way it turns out."

"You have become our leader, Jason. You have accomplished what

I couldn't in all of my years in the league. Winning the Super Bowl means everything to me, and you are the one who can get that done for us—not me."

There was a long silence on the other end of the phone before Morrison continued, and what he had to say next stunned Jason.

"OK, my friend. I am going to play it straight with you. What I am about to say is known only by two people on the team—Wagner and me."

Jason gulped hard in tense anticipation of what he might be hearing next.

"The truth is I can't play anymore. I have had a degenerative disk in my back for over two years, and it is getting worse. Yeah, when Wagner replaced me with you last year I was doing pretty well statistically, but my back was getting worse. I knew I couldn't continue and asked to be benched and have you replace me."

Jason gasped before responding, "Are you telling me that you were in favor of being benched all along? You even encouraged it?"

"Absolutely. Listen, this thing has been coming for a while. When you first took over it wasn't too bad, and only Wagner knew about it. My private doctor did the diagnosis and told Wagner and me that I needed to have surgery in the off-season. But Wagner kept it hushed because he believed that you would perform better if you thought I might be replacing you if you messed up. He seems to only want to motivate through fear and intimidation. That is his style."

"And so all this crap in the locker room today about you replacing me was . . ."

"Crap! That's all it was—crap," interrupted Zach. "Wagner had no plans to put me in. He knew I couldn't do the job. In fact, I was in agony throwing the ball on the sidelines. I can barely throw the ball over thirty yards now. That is hardly acceptable for an NFL quarterback."

"So why didn't you get surgery in the off-season?" inquired Jason.

"Well, I did. Nobody knew about it. Wagner insisted that it remain a secret, and he worked it out with Providence Hospital to do it without fanfare. When I reported to camp last August, I was actually feeling fine.

But my back began to deteriorate as the season progressed. I guess the surgery simply couldn't restore me to whole. And as long as you were doing great, there was no concern. You did notice that I have thrown the ball very little in practice?"

Things were now beginning to make more sense to Jason. No wonder Wagner was so concerned that he be ready to play in two weeks. He is all the Seahawks have at quarterback.

Jason replied, "Well, now that I think about it, I did notice you have had very little action during practice as the season progressed. I guess my ego wanted me to believe that I was so great they just didn't need to be concerned about ever having to bring you in."

Morrison laughed. "We all have that ego problem, Jason."

Jason replied, "Yeah I guess so. But I am curious about one thing: why didn't Wagner put you on the injured reserved list and trade for another quarterback sometime in the fall."

"Because both Wagner and I believed I would improve as time went on and be fully capable of playing by mid-season. At least that is what the doctors told us to expect. But the truth is I haven't gotten better. In fact, I am worse. And when that became apparent, it was too late in the season for Wagner to make a trade. So now we are stuck with the current situation."

There was a few seconds of silence and Morrison spoke again. "Listen, I want to let you in on a secret that even Wagner doesn't know."

"OK," said Jason, "Give it to me straight."

"I am retiring after the Super Bowl regardless of whether we win or lose. I am just happy to be there, and I owe that all to you. I never would have taken this team this far even if healthy. We are there because of you my friend. So don't let us down. You gotta play and give it all you have because, unfortunately, I will be on the sidelines. I simply can't play at the level necessary to win this game."

Jason was touched by this expression of confidence. All he could say in response was, "I will be there Zach. I will not let this team down."

"Glad to hear it, buddy. I need to sign off now, but you better check out the sports news before you go to bed tonight. You are the main topic, and it isn't just because of your heroics on the field. It seems that all they want to talk about is the condition of your skull. And they have some interesting information on that dude who apparently saved your life."

"Will do. I guess I should take a look at the television tonight before hitting it. You take care, Zach. I will see you tomorrow."

Jason was totally fatigued and wanted to go to sleep but flipped on the television to the sports cable channel to see what was being reported. He still was not clear on what had happened at the parking garage after the game and wanted to see if the sports media could shed light on the subject. He particularly wanted to find out more about the fan who saved his life.

"Good evening, this is Bart Craiger, your host for this evening's edition of *NFL Today*. And do we have an interesting and exciting broadcast for you tonight. First, let's report the news out of Seattle. In a thrilling comeback the Seahawks, led by their all-pro quarterback Jason O'Connor, came back from nineteen points down at halftime to win on the last play of the game."

Craiger went on to describe O'Connor's second half heroics highlighted by his touchdown run on the last play of the game. The game video showing the violent tackle, which knocked Jason out as he crossed the goal line, replayed several times. After thoroughly discussing the head injury Jason received in the game, the report switched to the second injury he received at the parking garage after the game.

We have a live reporter at the hospital now, Mark Wiggins. Mark, what can you tell us about this bizarre turn of events?"

"Well good evening, Bart. Jason O'Connor was here earlier this evening along with Coach Paul Wagner. Apparently, a CAT scan was done and the results will be made known to the Seahawks and the public tomorrow."

Craiger inquired further. "Mark, were any statements made by Wagner and O'Connor as they left the hospital? What is the prognosis of O'Connor playing in two weeks?"

"Bart, both Wagner and O'Connor appeared adamant that Jason will play. The plan for now is to keep him out of contact for a week but that he will be ready to go for the Super Bowl."

"Well, one more question for you, Mark. Do you have any more detail on the accident and on the person who pushed Jason O'Connor out of the way of the falling beam?"

Mark Wiggins responded, "We only have sketchy information right now but will undoubtedly have a lot more on this in the next twenty-four hours. The person who knocked O'Connor out of the way and probably saved his life is Rev. Josiah Johnson. Rev. Johnson is a minister of an inner city church who in his day—about thirty years ago—played some pretty mean football for a small college in the Midwest. Apparently, Rev Johnson, his wife, and a small son are very big Seahawks fans and come to every home game. However, they cannot afford tickets to the games so they park near the stadium and listen to the game in their car radio. I guess that gives them the feeling of being actually at the game inside Qwest."

"Interesting," Craiger responded. "It sounds like we might have a great human interest story here. I hope the Seahawks reward Rev. Johnson with at least some season tickets for next year."

The news on Rev. Johnson fascinated Jason. He was grateful to this man who had saved his life and wanted to know more. However, his throbbing headache and aching body reminded him that he needed to lie down and try to go to sleep. He would make it a point to find out more about Johnson the next morning. He turned off the television, took his pain medication, and headed toward his bedroom when the phone rang again. This time it was his buddy, Bobby Childs.

"Hey, man, how are you doing? The news is just incredible. How in the world did that accident happen?"

"Well, to tell you the truth, Bobby, I have no idea." Jason replied. "It all happened so fast. I know that Wagner and the front office will be looking into it in the next couple of days. Man, my head just hurts. All I want to do is sleep."

"I understand. I'll let you go but listen man. I am sorry about that altercation we had in the locker room. I should have known better than to bring up the name of Mandy Brooks with you. I am sorry."

"Well, Bobby, I am sorry too for flying off the handle, but I am concerned. We are on the verge of accomplishing the dream of our professional lives. You just can't let that woman back into your life and mess with your head again."

"Jason, I promise you; it won't be like that. I am having dinner with her to clear the air tomorrow night and that will be the end of it. I won't even bother you with the details. So I'll let you get some sleep now and won't mention this again. We need to keep our thoughts on the big game and beating the Steelers."

"Right, buddy. Good night, and I'll see you tomorrow at the stadium."

Upon ending the phone call Jason immediately turned off the ringer on his phone. He was now ready for a very deep slumber, but the mention of Mandy Brooks made him uneasy. This was a woman from his past—a friend to him and a lover to Bobby Childs. He wanted to forget that this woman ever existed, and he was worried that the meeting with Childs would interfere with his friend's concentration on what needed to be accomplished to beat the Steelers.

As Jason settled into bed, his mind now began to reflect on his past and where he had come from. He marveled to himself how he could have progressed so far in the world of professional football. His was clearly an all-American story. A story of a kid from humble circumstances who overcame the odds and ended up on top. As he closed his eyes he reminisced about his life and what he had accomplished.

Jason O'Connor grew up in Mansfield, a small farming community in the eastern part of the state of Washington. This small town never had a population of more than 350 people. Its school from elementary to high school had no more than seventy-five students at any one time.

Jason's father was a wheat farmer who died from a farming accident when Jason was only two years old. His mother turned the farm over to Jason's uncle who failed at the endeavor and bankrupted the family. Eventually, a corporation purchased the farm from the bankruptcy court and operated it for several years before closing it down because of its unproductivity.

Jason's mother succumbed to a very rare blood disease and died when he was seven. His paternal grandmother, a teacher at the town school, raised Jason, but in actuality, the entire town raised him. Mansfield was populated with hard-working, decent people who took the loss of Jason's parents very hard. Jason grew up with more self-appointed aunts, uncles, and cousins than probably any kid in history. He was in fact the darling of the town and became their symbol of pride later on as he proved himself on the football field.

During the summers Jason did strenuous farm work. Such work undoubtedly contributed to the maturation of his young body and the development of unusual strength for a boy his age. Baling hay, building and repairing fences, and driving farm equipment were all part of his summer days in the hot sun of eastern Washington.

As Jason grew older his unique physical stature began to unfold. He got his growth early and by the time he entered high school he stood at almost 6' 4" in height and weighed 210 pounds. (His physique when he entered professional football was not much different. As a rookie he was 6' 5" and 225 pounds.) However, as a growing teenager it became very obvious early on that he was not only blessed with physical stature but also had a very unique, God-given athletic prowess.

Football was Jason's first and only athletic love. His strength in throwing a football was evidenced by the fact that by the time he was a senior in high school, he could routinely kneel on the fifty-yard line of his school's football field and throw the football into the back of the end zone.

The high school at Mansfield usually had no more than thirty students at any time and the boys numbered no more than fifteen. The school did, however, have a tradition of fielding a very competitive eight-man football team. The state of Washington allowed very small high schools, like Mansfield, to compete in football in an eight-man division. In order to do so, Mansfield had to have virtually every boy in the school play on the football team. When Jason played they had twelve of the fifteen male students on the team. The other three played in the pep band.

Eight-man football is quite unique. It utilizes one running back behind the quarterback and six linemen. The tackle in the line opposite of where the end or split receiver is lined up is eligible to receive passes.

The quarterback in this kind of offense is the critical person, even more so than in regular eleven-man football. This is the position Jason owned from his freshman year until his senior year, and his devotion to winning football games gave the citizens of the small town of Mansfield some wonderful Friday night memories.

Jason's own physical strength and better than average speed allowed him to dominate on the football field. He simply mowed his opponents down when he ran. More lethal, however, were his passing skills. The only problem he faced when passing was getting his receivers to hang on to the ball. He threw a football extremely hard and because of this the intended receivers dropped many of his passes.

During his teen years Friday night football from September through November was the highlight of the town. Virtually the entire town of Mansfield closed down as its citizens turned out for these games, cheering Jason and his teammates on to victory. Victory came often to this little high school under Jason's leadership. In his four years of quarterbacking an eight-man football team his team, compiled a record of 34 wins and 2 losses. Most of these wins were by lop-sided scores of 63-7, 54-0, etc. While there was no state-tournament for these small schools, there was a state poll that ranked the top teams, and the Mansfield Wildcats were ranked number one in the state in these polls all four years.

After graduation it was unclear what Jason was going to do. Most kids who graduated from the high school left for bigger things and never returned. However, Jason had given this town some pride. When drivers passed by Mansfield on the interstate they would see a billboard by the freeway proudly proclaiming, "Welcome to Mansfield. Home of Jason O'Connor and the Mansfield Wildcats—State Football Champions the Last Four Years!"

Jason had been literally raised by the town, and they were very anxious to keep him. In regard to football it was clear to most that his days were over. No player from a lowly eight-man football team, regardless of what statistics he compiled, would ever be considered for a football scholarship at a major university. The consensus of the town was that Jason should remain, perhaps attend a Community College in the area, but eventually settle down and be part of the town the rest of his life.

Jason was conflicted as to his future but did enroll at Wenatchee Community College, a short distance from Mansfield. Wenatchee CC had a football team and it was Jason's intention to play there and dazzle football fans with his passing skills. The football coach and staff at the college were delighted to have him try out but harbored serious doubts that he could play competitively at this level. Being a star in small town, eight-man football was one thing. Being a star at the college level—even the community college level—was quite another issue. But, for Jason O'Connor, this level of competition was what he needed to prove to himself and others what he was all about.

Almost immediately after fall practices started for the community college, Jason showed what was to come. He impressed the coaches with his athletic ability and the only problem he had in his passing was, as in high school, finding receivers who could hang on to the ball. Eventually the Wenatchee team found a couple of receivers who could not only run fast but also could catch the ball on the run, and Jason became the star of the state community football league. In his first season he passed for nearly three thousand yards in ten games and rushed for over four hundred yards. Statistics like this made the scouts at the top universities in the state—the University of Washington and Washington State University—take note. However, a scholarship was not offered by either of these schools because Jason's grades were not high enough. He was counseled by both schools to work hard on the grades his second year, and they would take a second look at him.

The summer after his first year at community college Jason returned home to Mansfield and seriously contemplated leaving school. He worked at the only grocery store in town and was offered a full-time position in the fall as store manager if he did not return to school. The offer was tempting because Jason simply did not like school and studies. He loved football, which was the only thing that kept him in school in the first place. However, the likelihood of him ever going further in football was small. His realistic chances to remain in the sport he loved was to play in college, get a degree, and then coach in a high school setting.

Jason struggled throughout the summer with his decision to return to school and play football. Ultimately he decided that he wanted to go for his dream. He decided that he would achieve such impressive statistics that the major schools could not ignore him. And that is exactly what he did.

His second season playing football at Wenatchee CC was all he had hoped it would be. He was simply a phenom on the field. His team ran through every opponent scoring 553 points in ten games. Jason set the passing records for the community college football league, and the scouts from major universities began to call. Both Washington and Washington State were now clamoring to obtain his services on a full ride scholarship. Jason had passing grades so it appeared that indeed he would advance to the next level of competition.

In the end, Jason chose to go to Washington State University because it is the school that has the loyalties of those in the eastern part of the state. Washington State is located in Pullman, Washington, in what is known as "Palouse country." If not for the university population, Pullman would be a small town, and it still had a small town atmosphere that made Jason feel at home.

Plus, Jason had always been a Washington State Cougar fan, so this was an easy choice. He was offered a full ride—tuition, books, and room and board—to play football at "Wazzu" and gladly accepted. To the townsfolk in Mansfield there was both disappointment that he would not be returning but also a sense of pride that one of their own was going on to bigger horizons. At the end of July, just before he left for football camp, the town gave him a going away party that was fit for royalty. There was a parade in his honor followed by a huge community picnic and the awarding to him of the key to town. The president of the city council ended the event by announcing that they had passed legislation to rename the main street in town to "O'Connor Ave."

Jason was truly moved at the showing of affection from his hometown friends and vowed to make them proud of him at "Wazzu." For him it was the next step in finding out just who he was and how far he could go in pursuit of football perfection. He had no dreams for himself other than being the best quarterback the game has ever seen. The thought of obtaining a degree and going into a profession was not really on his mind. His life was football.

Jason's introduction to big time college life was a bit of a shock for this small town farm boy. Life on a college campus is somewhat different than life in a small farming community. So Jason struggled initially to fit in.

On the football field it was a different story. In practice it became very clear that he was going to win the starting job from the outset. It had appeared that this would be a very big year for Cougar football if they could find the right quarterback, and Jason seemed to be that person. His skills complemented the Cougar offense perfectly, and they had the right kind of receivers for him. Included in this receiving corps was a cocky kid named Bobby Childs.

Jason's social life on campus required a little more time for him to adjust to his change in environment. Fraternities who were anxious to have the prestige of a football player in their ranks immediately recruited him. He ultimately joined the Sigma Nu fraternity. This was a fraternity with a variety of students from the brainiac scholars to the athletes to the party animals. Bobby Childs had been in this fraternity for two years and recommended that they recruit Jason as a member. It was here that Childs and O'Connor's friendship solidified. They were roommates in the frat house and quickly bonded on the football field as the perfect passing combo to take the Cougars to a championship season.

The first football season with the Cougars was spectacular. O'Connor to Childs became the dynamic duo of Division 1 NCAA football. O'Connor led the nation in passing yardage with over four thousand total yards, and his pal Bobby Childs caught eighty-five passes for fifteen hundred of those yards. The Cougar team itself met expectations, losing only one game all season before being crushed by Michigan in the Rose Bowl on New Year's Day. This was the first big disappointment in Jason's career. However, at this point in his career nobody questioned that he could not come back and win the big game. Both Jason and Bobby were voted onto several all-American teams after this season and expectations were very high for the Cougars the next season with O'Connor and Childs returning.

During the winter months after that first season, Jason and Bobby solidified their friendship and also discovered the joy of being campus football heroes. As such, neither had to work too hard to get a date for the weekend date dashes and fraternity formals. Bobby had become quite a partier over the years in the fraternity and was never lacking in his ability to attract the opposite sex. Eventually, both settled down with one campus sweetheart. For Bobby, it was Mandy Brooks. For Jason, it was Rachel Thomlinson.

Jason met Rachel at a party at the Sigma Nu fraternity house. She was a freshman from Seattle and a member of a campus sorority—Delta, Delta, Delta. Jason had never been comfortable around the opposite sex. In high school he never had a girlfriend and rarely dated. When he first saw Rachel, however, his interest in romance dramatically changed.

She was, in Jason's eyes, the prettiest, sweetest, and sexiest young woman he had ever seen. She stood 5' 2" with brown hair and hazel eyes and had a sparkle about her that touched Jason's heart and emotional senses. They met at the bar in his fraternity house during a social between his house and her sorority. When they first caught each other's eyes, Jason simply smiled at her and began to walk away. Rachel, however, was a little more aggressive and spoke.

"Hi, there. Aren't you Jason O'Connor? My younger brother back home is a big fan of yours." She continued, "Do you think you could maybe give me an autograph to send back home to him? He really would be thrilled."

Jason was initially caught off guard, but once the ice was broken, the conversation flowed freely. "Sure, glad to do it," he nervously stuttered, and then blurted out, "so, where are you from?" For the rest of the evening Jason and Rachel were side by side talking nonstop about school and football until the early morning hours.

Jason learned that Rachel was the daughter of a prominent Orthopedic Surgeon in Seattle. Her mother was a teacher in a local school district. She had one brother, age twelve, who was a die-hard fan of Jason O'Connor and the Washington State Cougars. He also learned that Rachel's best friend in the world was Mandy Brooks who was dating Jason's best friend, Bobby Childs.

From that moment on, Jason and Rachel were inseparable. They studied together and met everyday on campus for lunch. In the evenings when they were not studying, they were snuggling together in the fraternity television room watching a movie or one of their favorite sit-coms. Within a few weeks it was clear that both Jason and Rachel had become smitten with each other. They were an item.

O'Connor and Childs did a lot of double dating on and off campus. Bobby was wilder in his lifestyle as was his girl Mandy. The latter two always wanted to party at a local bar where alcohol flowed to all—even to minors. Jason and Rachel preferred to avoid such activities. All in all, however, the two couples had fun together and made up what looked to the outside as the ideal campus romances.

Rachel was a hopeless romantic and became deeply committed to Jason as time went on. Jason was frankly scared of what was happening to him and tried to avoid the topic of commitment. His focus was football, and he intended on winning the Heisman trophy his senior year. He was determined that nothing would side track him from achieving that goal—not even the love of a campus beauty like Rachel Thomlinson. However, the sweetness and charm of Rachel was becoming harder and harder to resist.

On one particular night, after the spring formal dance at Rachel's sorority, she gave Jason a special gift. As they sat cuddled on the couch in his fraternity house, she spoke to him sweetly and shared about the interest her father had in collecting coins. She said, "You know, Jason, my dad is a long time coin collector. He has some really beautiful coins from all over the world. Can I show you one?"

"Sure, go ahead," said Jason not understanding where the conversation was heading.

Rachel pulled out a chain that had a coin attached to it, and she put it around her neck. Grabbing the coin she said, "This is an English half-penny that they actually call a ha'penny. They don't make these in England anymore. What do you think of it? Isn't it pretty?"

Jason looked at the coin that had been polished up and saw that it was quite attractive on the gold chain around Rachel's neck. "Sure, Rachel. It is pretty. So why is this so important to you?"

She replied, "Well, I have been thinking about this. I think that each of us is like a ha'penny. We are perfectly good and spendable on our own. On our own we have value, but someday we can come together and become a whole penny. Twice as valuable and twice as spendable."

Rachel smiled and blushed a little, as she thought that maybe what she had just said was a little too corny. Jason kissed her softly on the forehead and said, "And when did you become such a profound philosopher?"

Rachel giggled a little in embarrassment, but then pulled out of her purse another gold chain with a ha'penny on it and placed the chain around Jason's neck. Jason was caught off guard, and all he could do was smile.

Rachel gently kissed him and got up to leave. She turned to Jason and said, "Well, OK, maybe that was a little silly, but keep the ha'penny as a token of my feelings for you. Maybe someday that ha'penny will become a whole penny." She then departed, leaving Jason a bit unnerved and feeling awkward at such a showing of affection from this young woman. He knew he loved Rachel but was not sure he was ready for the relationship to move so quickly into discussions of the future..

Jason avoided further such talk with Rachel as he prepared for the upcoming football season. However, changes were happening to him. He was a big campus hero and had virtually everything he wanted, including certain amenities supplied to him by alumni of the school. On more than one occasion he found in his campus post office box an envelope with one thousand dollars stuffed inside and an accompanying note saying, "Just want to show you how much we appreciate your efforts on the football field for our university." On another occasion he found keys to a new Ford Mustang for him to drive with a note saying, "It's just on loan but enjoy it until graduation."

The fraternity party life was also changing Jason's outlook on things. His pal Bobby was a big partier. Bobby on occasion would drink hard and encourage Jason to do the same. Both were athletes who cared about their bodies and did not want to abuse them. But on occasion, usually at the pleas of Bobby Childs, both men would drink to excess and enjoy the thrill of intoxication.

Then there was the issue of sex. Around the fraternity Bobby Childs made no secret about his about his sexual escapades. Every member of the fraternity all had heard by the Sunday afternoon of every week what Childs and his girlfriend Mandy Brooks had been up to over the weekend. Jason really did not like this kind of behavior from his friend, but when he complained and told Bobby to keep to himself his sexual activities, he was mocked by Childs and a few other fraternity brothers who called him a "closet virgin."

This kind of chiding bothered Jason a great deal, as he continually felt pressure to succumb to the promiscuous lifestyle of a college fraternity. Jason was the big star on campus and could easily find sexual activity with many young women. Yet, there was Rachel whom he never wanted to hurt. His solution to this temptation was to pressure his girlfriend to become involved intimately in a sexual relationship. As he became more and more arrogant and prideful, he became more and more aggressive and demanding of Rachel in their relationship. Rachel was a sweet, young woman who had strong feelings about abstinence as a lifestyle for single adults. Yet, she loved Jason dearly and finally gave in to his sexual demands.

The spring of Jason's junior year started out promising but turned into a nightmare. Spring football was proceeding as expected with Jason and Bobby looking every bit as good as the national sports pundits had predicted. Jason was the most popular guy on campus and treated Rachel as a trophy that hung on his arm around campus.

At the very end of the spring semester, Rachel gave him alarming news. They were sitting on a park bench on campus enjoying the spring weather. Rachel was planning to return home and live with her parents for the summer.

As they sat in silence it was clear to Jason that she had something on her mind. He asked her directly, "Are you mad at me? What's wrong?"

"It's not you, Jason. It is both of us," she said. "I know you don't understand that."

Jason laughed. "Right you are. Now tell me what you mean."

"OK, Jason. I am pregnant."

Jason sat stunned for a few seconds before responding. "Nice try, Rachel. But it isn't April Fools' Day, so tell me what is really on your mind."

In an uncharacteristic emotional tirade, Rachel repeated herself forcefully. "I said I am pregnant! How much clearer can that be? I took a pregnancy test earlier this week at the Student Health Center, and it showed positive. I then went to a local doctor to double check the results, and he confirmed the diagnosis. Now what part of this do you not understand?"

She paused for a few brief moments and then began to cry. "The doctor says I am due sometime at the end of October."

Jason drew a deep breath and leaned back, closing his eyes for a few minutes. The next few months were critical for his future. The expectations on him in the fall were high. He simply could not be diverted with this kind of problem. He was not ready to be a father. And though he cared about Rachel, he certainly was not ready to be married. As he thought of what to say, he let his emotions get the best of him. The ensuing conversation with Rachel was one that would haunt him through the years. It was one he later would be willing to pay millions to take back.

Jason finally spoke, "Well, you know that neither of us is ready to be a parent. We have our lives ahead of us with plenty of time for that. And these next six months are crucial to my future. You know that full well, Rachel."

Rachel looked at him incredulously and responded. "So what are you saying, Jason?"

Jason's temper came through as he responded. "Oh, knock it off, Rachel. I didn't ask for this, and you have the ability to solve this problem in a heartbeat. I for one am not going to be blackmailed into becoming a daddy ahead of schedule. So it is up to you to do the right thing here."

Rachel's cries turned into sobs. "You can't be suggesting that I…"

"Of course I am!" shouted Jason. "Get rid of the problem. It is that easy. Bobby knows a doctor in Spokane that can help and money won't be a problem. So do the right thing, Rachel!"

Rachel Thomlinson now realized something for the first time about Jason O'Connor. The sweet country boy she had fallen for had rapidly changed over his months of notoriety. He was now an arrogant and selfish guy who didn't care about her. He didn't care about anybody but himself and his future in football. She looked at him at this moment and couldn't believe the anger she saw in his face. She thought he loved her. And regardless of whether he did or not, she was carrying his baby. How could he now be so heartless and cruel? Her sobs increased as she struggled to gain her composure and speak. Finally, she responded.

"I can't believe I have heard these things from you, Jason. You are a different person than the one I met last year. What happened? Have fame and fortune truly destroyed you?"

Jason O'Connor was now enraged and began to shout at his girlfriend. "Do not ever talk to me that way again. I have a future, and I won't have it destroyed by your little sentimentalities. Get rid of the problem!"

"Sentimentalities? Is that what this is? And our baby? That is a problem to you?"

Rachel got up to leave. "Don't worry about your future. I will deal with this. And I don't need any money either. Take your stinking money, and do with it what you want. I am leaving tomorrow for the summer. Your problem will be dealt with!"

She began to walk away, but turned quickly to say to Jason, "Don't bother to call me. I will be fine." And with that remark Rachel Thomlinson walked out of his life. At the time Jason believed that things would be worked out. However, little did Jason realize that this would be the last time he would ever speak with Rachel again.

The summer months went by quickly as Jason prepared hard for the start of fall football practice. He thought of Rachel off and on but did not hear from her until the end of August. She mailed him a small handwritten note that strangely was not postmarked from Seattle where Rachel's parents lived. Instead, it was sent from Moses Lake, a town in the middle part of the state. The note tersely read.

> Dear Jason,
> Your problem is taken care of. Nothing can ever again be the same between us. We will talk when I return to school. I will not be back in the fall, as I need to take time off. I will see you spring semester.
> Rachel.

August football camp started for the Washington State Cougars and Jason O'Connor with high hopes. Jason was careful to stay focused on the goals of his team and did everything possible to avoid dwelling on Rachel and their breakup. Both O'Connor and Childs looked sharp in preseason camp, and the national sports media took note. *Sports Illustrated* magazine featured O'Connor and Childs on the cover of its *College Football* edition and picked the Cougars as the third best team in the nation. In this issue, Jason O'Connor was picked as the odds on favorite to win the Heisman trophy.

The Cougars started the season strong, erasing any fears of a "*Sports Illustrated* jinx" that some had raised after the magazine featured the team. They crushed opponent after opponent, and the O'Connor to Childs passing duo brought to life the football fans in the state of Washington and all over the nation. After ten games the Cougars were undefeated, and Jason had passed for more than four thousand yards with Childs hauling in ninety-two passes for sixteen hundred yards. It truly was an amazing season for the dynamic duo from the Palouse and for their team.

The final game of the season against archrival Washington was the crucial game for the Cougars. The rival Huskies were always a quality opponent in this traditional Apple Cup game, even when they were not having a particularly successful season. This year, however, the game promised to be a classic match with both teams totally committed to victory. For the Cougars a win meant another trip to the Rose Bowl and a possible national championship. Everything they had worked for all season was on the line.

Jason O'Connor and his buddy Bobby Childs knew clearly what the game meant and responded accordingly. The Cougars were unstoppable as the two fraternity brothers teamed up for pass completion after pass completion. The final score of 42-28 in favor of the Cougars made the game seem closer than it actually was. Victory was never really in doubt from the opening kickoff until the final gun. O'Connor passed for 476 yards and five touchdowns. Childs made fifteen receptions for 240 yards.

With an undefeated season wrapped up and another shot at the national title secured, the celebration began in earnest at the Washington State campus. O'Connor and Childs were the toast of the town. Fraternity Row at the campus was crazy that night with wild partying and celebrations like never before. At the Sigma Nu fraternity house, the beer kegs flowed, the rock music was loud, the dancing was raunchy, and O'Connor and Childs were the men of the hour.

The fraternity party went well into the morning hours. Bobby Childs, quite inebriated, was particularly loud and boastful about his accomplishments on the gridiron. Jason O'Connor was more subdued but equally boastful of what he had accomplished, and he did not mince words about what he intended to do in the Rose Bowl game.

"It is all in the bag before it happens. Bobby and I will take them down, and the national title will be ours. Count on it and take that to the bank!" Jason shouted at one time during the intoxicated celebration.

At sometime during the gala, Mandy Brooks quietly entered the house and sought to get the attention of Childs and O'Connor. Bobby was so intoxicated that he could not comprehend much, so Mandy sought out Jason first. When she finally got his attention, she pulled him aside, grabbed him by his arms, and began to cry.

"That's OK, Mandy," Jason stated. "A lot of people are crying right now. This victory even makes grown men weep for joy."

"Oh shut up, you arrogant jerk! Just shut up and listen to me!" Mandy replied as she slapped him across the face to get his attention. Jason, stunned by the response, became silent, realizing that something was drastically wrong. Before he could talk, Bobby Childs walked over to confront his girlfriend..

At the sight of her boyfriend, Mandy blurted out, "Bobby, I am glad you are here to listen to this. I have some horrible news. You two have to come down to planet earth and listen to me for just a minute."

Bobby Childs shouted in his girlfriend's face. "OK, Mandy, tell us what is so important that you would interrupt our moment of glory like this."

"It's Rachel," she said between sobs, barely talking with any coherence.

"OK, now listen. I've had enough," responded Jason. "Rachel and I are through. We are history, and I don't need to hear anything right now about her. This is my night, and I am not going to let you ruin it. Do you hear me?"

Childs chimed in. "Enough, Mandy. We don't care about Rachel now. We have worked for this moment for four years, so don't trash it. Rachel had a chance to be part of this, but she refused. It is her problem."

Mandy Brooks could take it no longer. She began to scream at the top of her lungs. She screamed so loud that she could be heard over the noisy party atmosphere at the fraternity house. People suddenly quieted down, and a crowd gathered around the threesome as Mandy spoke.

"You two arrogant jerks! Listen to me. I don't care about your stupid celebration, nor do I care who won this game today. Rachel was in a serious accident tonight. A drunk driver hit her car head on. She is in a hospital in Seattle, and they don't think she is going to make it. I just talked to her mom on the phone."

Jason was truly taken aback. The news paralyzed him as he froze in his tracks staring at Mandy with disbelieving eyes. After a moment of silence he finally spoke.

"Tell me you are joking, Mandy. This cannot be true. Tell me this is just a joke. It is a joke right? Of course it is just a joke now. Although I don't think it is very funny."

Mandy fell into Jason's arms sobbing and pounding on his chest.

"I only wish it were a joke. She loved you, and you sent her away. If it weren't for you, she would be here right now."

Bobby now was alert although still quite inebriated. He and Mandy had not been getting along for quite sometime. They had been fighting more and enjoying each other's company less lately. This moment did not seem particularly different to Bobby than the previous months he had spent with her. He began to raise his voice and shout in her face while the crowd around them grew larger.

"OK, now listen you stupid woman. Enough is enough. This is Jason O'Connor, my friend, you are talking to, and I won't let you speak to him this way. So lay off!"

Mandy Brooks looked at her boyfriend, whom she thought she cared for, but now saw someone quite different from the man she had once believed was worth giving her life to. She lowered her voice and spoke in a controlled but forceful manner.

"So that's what I am? A stupid woman? Is that what you think Bobby? Rachel is dying, and you call me stupid? Your jerk friend here treated her like garbage and sent her away. Now she is dying, and you call me stupid? Listen, buster, go ahead and be the big football hero. It won't last. Just like our relationship is now over so will your great football career be gone someday, and then what will you do with your pathetic life?"

Bobby began to respond, but Mandy cut him off and continued. "I know one thing. You abandoned your babies and me months ago. You threw them away just like you have thrown me away. So yes, stupid I was for falling for you. But now being a much smarter person than before, I am saying goodbye to you and your arrogant friend Jason O'Connor and this university forever. To hell with you, and to hell with football."

With that comment Mandy Brooks stormed out of the fraternity house never to return again. A few days later she withdrew from school and moved back home to Seattle.

Jason and Bobby stood in stunned silence in the middle of the group of students who had gathered around to observe the loud discussion that had ensued. Jason spoke first. "I need to call Rachel's parents right away and find out what is going on. I can drive tonight and be in Seattle sometime before noon tomorrow."

"And what will you accomplish by that man? You can't do anything for her now. What do you think you will achieve by going over there tonight? We have football to concentrate on now man. Don't let this divert your concentration to what we need to do in the next few weeks."

Suddenly a couple of female students, friends of Mandy Brooks, approached Bobby and interrupted. "OK, Bobby Childs explain that comment from Mandy about throwing away your babies. What was that all about? Do you care to tell us?"

Upon hearing this Bobby went into a drunken rage, swearing and shouting obscenities at the two women. "It is none of your business, so butt out." He then took the bottle of beer in his hand and threw it as hard as he could against the brick fireplace. The crashing sound of the glass silenced the entire party once and for all. With that stunt Bobby Childs bolted out of the fraternity house.

Jason left the party in a less flamboyant manner. He immediately went to his room to call Rachel's parents in Seattle and get the full story. Mandy had recited the details accurately. Rachel had been driving home alone after seeing a movie with a friend when a drunken driver going in the opposite direction crossed the middle lane and plowed into her car head on. The drunken driver was killed upon impact. Rachel suffered serious head injuries and internal bleeding. The doctors at the hospital could not stop the internal bleeding and advised Rachel's parents that it was just a matter of hours before she would expire. She apparently was slipping in and out of consciousness and could not recognize anyone in her hospital room.

When Jason got off of the phone, he packed a few of his belongings as fast as he could and started the five-and-a-half hour drive to Seattle. He told nobody where he was going and began the long drive not entirely sober, as his emotions were telling him that he needed to be at the hospital as quickly as possible to be with Rachel and her family.

Jason drove all night. He was fortunate that most of the drive was over a stretch of freeway not heavily traveled on a Saturday night because the effects of the alcohol he had consumed had not completely worn off. After a few hours he sobered up enough to safely navigate his way toward the Seattle hospital where Rachel was desperately fighting for her life. He pulled into the hospital parking lot around 8:00 AM and immediately rushed into the building toward the reception desk.

He was told that Rachel was in intensive care and could only be seen by family, but when he told the receptionist that he was Rachel's brother, he was given the room number and its location in the hospital.

When Jason arrived in the room, he saw Rachel's mother weeping in the arms of her husband. Rachel's younger brother was sitting in the corner of the room with his head in his hands and tears streaming down his cheeks. Rachel's father simply acknowledged Jason's presence with a slight nod of the head and continued to hold his wife very tight.

Jason's arrival was just in time. He walked toward Rachel's hospital bed and looked intently into her face. Her eyes were closed, and she was breathing irregularly into an oxygen mask. She was connected to a monitor at the side of her bed that measured her heartbeat.

Finally, after a few minutes Rachel's mother spoke. "Thank you for coming, Jason. This whole thing has been such a shock. We don't know if Rachel is aware of any of us in this room. She seems to go in and out of consciousness."

Jason could only nod his head acknowledging that he had heard the statement, but his emotions were overwhelming at this time. He wanted to cry, but he had never shown emotion to others in his life. Why now? He could not remember crying at his father's funeral as a child. And he certainly could not remember crying at the news of his mother's death when he was young. Why then, he asked himself, was he now ready to lose it? Why were tears welling up inside of him as he stood at the bed of Rachel Tomlinson, his girlfriend for less then two years?

Jason had grown up pretty much without experiencing the love of a father and mother. He had become a self-sufficient man. He now realized that Rachel was a person in his life who had loved him unconditionally. And as he stood at the side of the bed of this young, dying beauty, his heart broke.

Suddenly and without notice Rachel opened her eyes and looked directly into the eyes of Jason. Jason looked back into the eyes of his girl-friend whom he had deserted and wronged. The eye contact lasted only a few brief seconds, and then ended abruptly with Rachel closing her eyes slipping back into unconsciousness.

For a few more minutes Rachel lay with her eyes closed, but then the moment had arrived. She briefly gasped for air, and then opened her eyes once again. She again looked at Jason, but this time it appeared that she was looking through him. It seemed that she was seeing something he could not see. A big smile came to her face as if to say everything would be all right. She then closed her eyes and stopped breathing. Her monitor began to beep loudly indicating that her heart had stopped. The nurses in the unit rushed to the room to see if they could keep her heart beat-ing, but to everyone present it was clear what had happened—Rachel was gone.

Rachel's passing was difficult for her family, but for Jason it was dev-astating. He had thought when she left school for the summer that they would patch things up and get back together. He had no idea that his conversation with her earlier that spring on campus, when she revealed her pregnancy, would be the final goodbye. He was emotionally devas-tated by her death. It caused him to lose concentration on his studies and his football. His final grades that semester were barely passing. And he lost focus on the upcoming New Year's Day Rose Bowl game.

Likewise, the confrontation with Mandy affected Bobby Childs's concentration and play. Needless to say both had sub par performances in the Rose Bowl that January with disappointing results for the team—another loss in the Rose Bowl and a blown opportunity for a national championship.

All of these thoughts about Rachel and his past troubled him as he lay in bed with a stinging headache. The serious concussion he had suffered made it difficult for Jason to go to sleep. Jason was also keyed up due to the reentry of Mandy Brooks into the life of his friend Bobby Childs.

What in the world did that woman want to say to Bobby? Why did she reenter the scene after ten years? Jason was very worried that the emergence of Mandy Brooks would now affect his friend's concentration on the challenge that lay ahead of them in the Super Bowl. Would she impact their play like she did years before with her tirade at the fraternity house?

Deep down Jason feared that the reemergence of Mandy Brooks would revive profound emotional trauma and wounds that he had buried within himself for so many years. And as he finally dozed off to sleep, his subconscious mind began to replay the memories of Rachel and the brokenness he had experienced but, until this moment, thought had been laid to rest.

CHAPTER 4

J ason O'Connor was not the only person having trouble sleeping that night. Insomnia also plagued his friend Bobby Childs. Bobby was rattled by the sudden reconnection with his old girlfriend, Mandy Brooks. They had not spoken since their confrontation and her departure from the fraternity house that night so long ago.

Bobby was not the type who dealt well with personal conflict. When Mandy left him he simply closed that chapter in his life and obscured it forever in his mind—at least that is what he had thought. But now this conflict from his past was raising its ugly head at a time when he needed to stay focused on the upcoming Super Bowl.

Unlike his friend Jason O'Connor, who was raised in a rural farming community, Bobby Childs grew up as a child of privilege. His father was a very prominent trial lawyer in Spokane, Washington, who not only made a small personal fortune from his legal work but also established major state precedents in the area of personal injury law. His mother was a licensed social worker and an accomplished concert pianist. The family was well established in the upper levels of cultural life in Spokane and held considerable political clout with the governing authorities.

Because of his family's connections and wealth, Bobby was denied nothing while growing up. When he turned sixteen, his father purchased for him a convertible BMW. When he graduated from high school, he received a convertible Mercedes Benz. His summer vacations always included extended stays at wealthy resorts across the country and sometimes even included travel to Europe and hot vacation spots along the Riviera.

At an early age it became quite apparent that he was a gifted athlete. Whether it was playing Little League baseball or school sports, Bobby Childs was always the first among his peers. His father, recognizing the potential in his son, made sure that he attended the best sports camps in the summer and that he had the finest personal instructors available. At a prestigious, private high school, Bobby dominated in his sports of football, basketball, and track.

In track he showed incredible promise as a sprinter, being the individual state champion for four years in the 100-meter run, the 200-meter run, and the 100-meter hurdles. At home Bobby's trophy case was filed with awards received at all levels of competition. His trophies were proudly placed by his parents in the entry area of the home as monuments to the accomplishments of perhaps the most gifted athlete to come out of the Spokane area.

In the summer after his senior year, he was invited to attend the Olympic trials and attempt to make the Olympic team. After serious consideration of the offer, he finally decided to stay focused on football and stayed at home to work out and get ready for the upcoming football season in college.

As a high school football player, Bobby, like his friend Jason O'Connor, excelled above the crowd. However, while Jason played for a small rural high school in the eight-man football division, Bobby starred at the Triple-A high school level in a major metropolitan area in the state of Washington. As such, his name was constantly in the sports headlines and college scouts took notice.

During his senior year in high school, Bobby had some important decisions to make. Where would he go to school, and what sport would get his sole concentration? He was offered full scholarships to seven different major universities in both football and track. He finally decided upon Washington State University, which was the alma mater to both of his parents. The track and football programs at the school both wanted him and both offered scholarships. In the end football won out as Bobby and his parents harbored ambitions for a future NFL career. Track was just another sport that allowed him to condition his body for his real love—football, the sport that afforded him the greatest satisfaction and feeling of accomplishment as an athlete.

He was a running back in high school, but upon his arrival on campus, the coaches placed him at wide receiver. They recognized that his speed and quickness could prove to be a lethal offensive weapon if teamed up with the right quarterback. Bobby was not large in stature, as his height was slightly under six feet, and he weighed around one-hundred and eighty pounds. But his ability to catch a football complemented his natural athletic abilities to run and jump and made him a superb football receiver.

For Bobby's first two seasons at this position, he performed admirably but did not stand out above the competition in any meaningful way. It took the arrival of Jason O'Connor onto the scene as the quarterback for the Cougars to bring out the best in Bobby Childs and make him a true college football star. Jason had the needed skills at quarterbacking to complement Bobby's superior receiving skills. A quarterback with the precision passing accuracy of Jason O'Connor was what was needed to push Bobby to the maximum potential he had as a wide receiver.

As a freshman Bobby became the stereotypical fraternity jock. He worked hard at his sport and made a place for himself in the football program, but he was just an average student majoring in business and never applied himself to his studies. Academically he did what was needed to pass and graduate. But his driving ambition was to play professional football, and he devoted long hours in the gym during the off-season to improve his athletic abilities in every aspect.

Bobby was also a social animal at his Sigma Nu fraternity. He partied hard, and in the early part of his freshman year became known for his "animal house" behavior—particularly around the young ladies. That was before he met Mandy Brooks.

Mandy was from the Seattle suburb of Burien on the other side of the state. She was a cute and sassy young woman who knew how to attract the boys by flaunting her seductive physical appearance. She grew up as an only child in a single parent home. Her mother had died of cancer when she was in elementary school, and she was raised by her father who worked long hours as an engineer for the Boeing Company.

Mandy knew how to attract the boys and always attended the main events of her high school, such as the prom and homecoming dances, with the date of her own choosing. Growing up without a mother and with a father who worked long hours caused her to be independent at an early age. In school she was involved as a cheerleader and played flute in the band. As a student she was slightly better than average but did not stand out above most of her classmates.

When Mandy came to Washington State University, she had no particular ambitions other than to meet and marry someone who was, as she would say, "going places." She was indeed a social climber, and her assessment of any particular young man that she might be interested in dating was mostly influenced upon whether, in her opinion, he would amount to a financial success.

Bobby and Mandy met in the fall of her freshman year at a social gathering between his fraternity and her sorority, Delta, Delta, Delta. Bobby, then a cocky sophomore football jock, was always overly confident in his demeanor around the opposite sex. For Mandy Brooks he became a challenge and a wild stallion to tame.

They bumped into each other at a weekend dance jointly sponsored by the two organizations. Her striking blue eyes caught his attention immediately, and she was attracted to his boyish looks and athletic physique. They both knew in an instant that they belonged together, but such coming together would first have to survive a few silly dating games.

Upon seeing her Bobby looked into her eyes and said, "And shall we dance?" To which Mandy replied, "And give me one good reason why we should?"

The arrogant Bobby Childs was immediately thrown off balance. No young woman had ever turned down his charm before. He thought that she just did not realize who he was, so he responded, "Well, listen, I really know how to shake it on the dance floor because as a wide receiver on the football team I have to have some coordination."

Mandy was not falling for the line and pretended not to be impressed. "Oh, so you are one of those jocks who thinks he owns the campus? No thanks. I am more interested in the studious type," she said as she began to walk away, quietly giggling to herself.

Bobby was taken back by this response but was not going to be deterred. A young woman to whom he was attracted had apparently rejected his advances. He did not like the feeling but was up to the challenge. He decided to try a more humble approach.

Slightly laughing he said, "OK, now, I am sorry if I were being rude. Playing football is what I love to do, but you don't have to be impressed."

"Believe me when I say I am not." Mandy knew she was lying through her teeth.

At that point they looked at each other and both began to laugh. Finally, she broke the ice. "My name is Mandy Brooks. I am a lowly freshman majoring in English, and even though I don't play any sports, I still have enough coordination to dance."

"And my name is Bobby Childs. So, shall we dance then?"

"Sure, why not?"

What Bobby didn't realize was that Mandy Brooks was a very skilled dancer. She had taken ballet, jazz, and modern dance since she was four and loved to dance to all kinds of music. Throughout her growing up years, she had performed in many recitals and even won awards in several dance contests. She had considered becoming a professional dancer before she finally opted to get a secondary education. In short, Mandy was to dancing what Bobby was to football—an extremely talented young person who not only enjoyed the activity but also performed to perfection. Dancing was a joyful expression of who she was and how much she enjoyed being alive, and her gleefulness expressed on the dance floor was infectious to those who watched her.

Bobby soon learned that he had gotten himself into an embarrassing situation on the dance floor. He looked rather clumsy compared to the graceful and energetic Mandy Brooks. The music was upbeat and fast paced. Poor Bobby Childs. On the football field as a wide receiver he was first among peers, but on the dance floor with Mandy Brooks he was awkward and most uncoordinated. She smiled and laughed as he tried to keep up with her. Eventually he got some moves down, but he knew then that he had better learn some real dance steps if he wanted to keep up with this young lady.

"You didn't tell me you were such a good dancer," he said when they took a break and sat down.

"Well, you told me as a football player you were coordinated on the dance floor," she said laughing. "But I guess there are a few things I can teach you if you want."

"Sure, as long as you let me teach you about football. Do you like football?"

"Like football? What a question! I don't like football at all. I love football!"

After this meeting the two were together constantly. They later took dancing lessons on campus and began to look like a professional dance team. Many of their campus friends encouraged them to enter into some dance competitions, but their lives were just too busy to add on an additional activity like that.

Mandy knew how to tame this wild young buck rather quickly, but she also knew how to use the relationship to her benefit. Prestige was important to her, and to be known as the girlfriend of an up-and-coming athletic star gave her the prestige on campus that her insecurities craved. Growing up without the companionship of a mother and with a distant relationship with her father, Mandy came to college with the desire for acceptance, recognition, and intimacy from others. She did not necessarily yearn to make a name for herself, but she did long to feel important to others and to be loved by a man. Her relationship with Bobby Childs filled this void in her life.

The first year of their relationship was innocent enough. Together they were known as an "item" on campus—always being seen with each other, studying in the library, eating in the student cafeteria, or partying together on weekends at one of the campus social functions. Mandy's influence on Bobby was quite positive in many regards. Her project to "tame" him, as she would describe it, seemed to work quite well. Bobby's well-known partying antics quieted down as the dating relationship matured, and he seemed to take his studies more seriously than he had before meeting her.

The social culture on campus had its expectations and pressures, however, that were difficult for the couple and to deal with. Appearances at weekend functions were not only routine but were somewhat expected by the social mores of the campus. This was particularly true for a football star and his girlfriend.

Then there was the issue of sex. At first no pressure was placed upon Mandy, and Bobby seemed to be content to keep their expressions of affection to heavy kissing and touching. However, after a few months Bobby began to demand more. Mandy was resistant at first. While she enjoyed being seductive with him, she thought that such actions on her part were not to be seen as serious invitations for sex. Eventually, however, she gave in to his demands because she did not want to lose the relationship. Initially, her relationship with Bobby Childs was, in her mind, non-committal and playful. But it didn't take long for her to fall in love with him. Once that happened, she did not want to lose the security the relationship had given her.

Mandy wanted love and acceptance, and sex was simply the price to pay to obtain what her emotional needs desired. To a young aggressive athlete who had been given everything he ever wanted all of his life, however, sex was expected. Indeed, in the "jock and fraternity" setting in which he lived, Bobby was expected to be a conqueror in all things—including conquering the woman he was dating. This simply meant sex as often as possible. And Bobby did not keep his escapades secret to his fraternity brothers.

Eventually, an intense sexual relationship developed between the two. While Mandy always felt guilty about this, she compromised her feelings in order to make her boyfriend happy. Such compromise, however, enabled her to be able to exert some control over him as well. She learned quickly that one thing she could do to make Bobby perform in the manner that she desired was to withhold sex.

At the beginning of Mandy's sophomore year she met Rachel Thomlinson. Rachel was an incoming freshman who pledged the Delta, Delta, Delta sorority. The two were assigned as roommates and became fast friends. They had much in common, as they both loved music of all kinds, dancing, reading Shakespeare, and, of course, football players.

Their commonality became even more obvious when Jason O'Connor arrived on the scene.

Rachel and Mandy were not only sorority sisters but were best friends who shared every aspect of their lives together. Likewise, Jason and Bobby became true brothers with common interests, goals, and ambitions. This foursome shared an exciting period in their lives, and the good times they had together seemed destined to continue indefinitely. Marriage for either couple was never seriously discussed but was always assumed by both Rachel and Mandy. This was not the case for Jason and Bobby.

The only issue regarding marriage in the minds of the two young women was simply when it would happen. They knew that they had to await the results of the final senior football year for Jason and Bobby and then await the results of the NFL draft before they would have further specifics on their futures as football wives, but they were both content and patient to wait.

In the spring of his junior year during spring football practice Bobby began to experience difficulties in his relationship with Mandy. They were arguing more and enjoying each other less and less when they were together. The stress and pressure of the expectations on Bobby with the football program had something to do with this tension, but the sexual relationship between the two and Mandy's underlying feelings of guilt about it were also playing a major factor in the conflict.

After football practice one afternoon, Mandy confronted her boyfriend directly with some important news. She met him outside the locker room of the athletic facility and demanded some time from him.

"We have to talk now and it can't wait," she said with a tone of urgency that got Bobby's attention quickly.

"Wow! What's up with you? I just finished a bruising practice and would like a little down time. Can't this wait until at least I get something to eat?"

"OK, let's go out and eat, but it is not small talk tonight. I have a lot on my mind."

Bobby began to brace himself for another night of conflict and accusations. Mandy had lately been accusing him of caring more about football than he did for her. She was continually bringing up the topic when they were together, and when Bobby got defensive the discussion usually ended in an argument—sometimes a rather heated one. Bobby was expecting more of the same as he and Mandy secured an isolated table in the corner of a campus restaurant.

As they awaited their food Bobby broke the silence. "All right so what is so important to you tonight that we have to talk about? It sounded rather urgent outside the locker room. So go ahead and spit it out."

"All right, Bobby. I am pregnant."

The words he had just heard hit hard. The anxious and distressed look on the face of his girlfriend told him she was not joking, and the ever so confident Bobby Childs was now a very frightened young man.

"So are you sure? How did you find out? You could be mistaken you know."

Mandy began to cry. "No, Bobby. I am sure. I went to the doctor today, and he confirmed my pregnancy. After the positive pregnancy test was done he performed another exam that allowed him to actually see inside my womb. I think it is called an ultrasound. There is no question about it. I am pregnant. In fact, I am very pregnant. I am carrying twins."

Bobby sat stunned at the news. He mumbled to himself. "When bad luck comes, it comes in double doses, and I have my share now."

"Bobby, you should have seen the little hearts beating. They were so precious." She then began to sob and looked into his eyes longing for compassion and softness.

"So what am I supposed to do about this? You can't really suggest that I take time off of football, become a devoted father, and learn how to change diapers do you?"

Mandy was now crying uncontrollably. "I know…I know…I can't quit school and have a baby, and you certainly can't be burdened with this. But Bobby, can't we work it out? Can't we survive this? You should have seen their little hearts beating."

"Enough!" Bobby's voice became stronger and more intense. At his response Mandy moved over beside him, looked into his eyes, and then collapsed in his arms. They held each other for a few moments neither one speaking.

Bobby's tone suddenly became softer, more compassionate. "It's OK, baby. We will work this out. My dad knows a very competent doctor in Spokane who can take care of this for us. You won't have to quit school, and I won't have to worry. And best of all, the good times won't have to end."

Mandy looked up at her boyfriend fully understanding what he had just said. In her emotionally vulnerable state, she had no response. She had nothing further to say. She was overwhelmed with a deep sense of anguish and sadness.

She stared into the Bobby's eyes for what seemed to be an eternity. Finally, she spoke. "OK, Bobby. I understand. You are not ready for this. I can't force you into fatherhood. It is a choice these days. So how do I contact the doctor?"

"Let me call my dad tonight, and he will take care of it. Don't worry about the cost; that will be handled as well."

Bobby then paused and stared blindly out the window into the night sky. Finally, he continued. "This is all for the best. In a few days life will be back to normal, and it will be like this has never happened. Trust me on this one. This is the right thing to do."

"OK, I trust you."

"You will be in good hands. I will call my Dad tonight, and the matter will be taken care of."

With tears in her eyes Mandy just nodded her head and got up to leave. As she began to walk away she turned to Bobby and said one more time. "Bobby, the little heart beats; they were so precious."

"You are only making this harder on us, Mandy. Let it go! I will call you tomorrow with the details."

That next weekend she made the trip to Spokane by herself to see the doctor that Bobby had referenced. Afterward the relationship between Bobby and Mandy was never the same.

Nothing was ever said again about this experience. Both of them wanted to bury the matter and leave it in the past. However, their times together became increasingly tense as they argued and fought constantly over trivial matters. Mandy resented Bobby as time went on and, finally, lost all of her composure the night of Rachel's accident when she walked away.

Bobby thought Mandy had left his life forever after that fateful night at the fraternity celebration. While his pride refused to allow him to admit his loss and hurt, deep inside he grieved losing her. Deep inside he knew that he had been selfish and cruel, and deep inside he knew that he loved her and needed her. He just didn't know how to make things right. He decided that he would not let his emotions and the self-inflicted wounds from this relationship influence his future. He resolved within himself that his relationship with her would never brought up again. To him Mandy Brooks was history.

Bobby was never the same. The loss of Mandy in his life and the death of Rachel shook him emotionally in a manner that he could not address, and this affected his ability on the football field. His less than stellar performance in the Rose Bowl his senior year was only the beginning of his sub-par performances on the gridiron. His first eight years in the pro ranks were disappointing, as he was traded four times and failed to live up to the athletic promise he had as a collegian. He only started a few games with each team and rarely provided the skills needed in tight games to become the impact player most NFL scouts had thought he would be. His career had become so disappointing to him that he was ready to retire from the NFL when he was traded to the Seahawks upon the urging of his old college buddy Jason. The trade was a rebirth to Bobby. Jason O'Connor had just finished an incredible year for the Seahawks, and they were being projected to do big things the next season. The thought of teaming up with his old fraternity brother and repeating their college gridiron performances at the pro level energized Bobby and give him hopes of finally achieving success in the NFL.

On a personal level Bobby never let himself get close to a woman again. He dated and had the reputation of being a swinging bachelor, but he knew that was a front, an image to project to the public.

Ten years had passed before Mandy contacted Bobby. After dropping out of Washington State University she moved back to Seattle and lived with her father for two years. She finally married a Seattle lawyer, but the marriage was strained from the beginning. Eventually it ended in a bitter dispute with allegations of physical abuse against her husband. She had a young son who was emotionally and physically abused by Mandy's husband.

Mandy finally had begun to follow football again when Bobby was traded to Seattle. Even though ten years had passed since their confrontation at the fraternity house, she had more to say to both of Bobby and Jason. However, her spirit toward them had changed significantly over the years. Instead of the anger she expressed the night of Rachel's accident, she now felt sorrow for the wounds that she knew they both were secretly harboring. She did not want to reopen painful memories, but she had an important message that she needed to deliver. This message had troubled her for many years, and for a long time she did not know how to proceed. Finally, on the day before the conference championship against St. Louis, she made her move.

She knew that Bobby Childs would not be listed in the telephone directory, so she made her attempt at contacting him by calling the Seahawks front office. When she asked to leave a message for him, she was promptly told that she should send a letter to the office, and they would deliver it to him. She became insistent, however, that she was an old friend and wanted to talk with him. Finally, the front office agreed to take her phone number and give it to Bobby to call back if he desired.

On that day Bobby happened to be in the Seahawks locker room checking out his equipment. He was contacted by the front office on the locker room phone.

"Mr. Childs, I am so sorry to bother you, but we have received a very insistent message from a woman who claims to know you and wants you to return her call."

Bobby laughed. "Not another one. Listen you know I don't have time for this." Bobby still had an irresistible charm to the female gender and had to constantly refuse to respond to such requests. To him it was just another adoring female fan eager to land a date. "Tell her I am too busy to respond."

"OK, Mr. Childs I will do so, but she says that she is a long time friend."

"Did she leave her name?"

"Yes, sir. She said she was Mandy Brooks, a friend of yours from college."

Bobby was speechless for a few moments and struggled to get words out of his mouth. Finally, after a long pause he blurted out, "Mandy? Did you say Mandy Brooks? Did she leave a number?"

"Yes, sir. I will leave her message for you in your box here in the front office if you'd like."

"Please do and thank you for the message."

Bobby sat down to catch his breath and think. Why would this woman be contacting him now after all these years? The last time he saw her was a disaster, and it ruined his concentration on the Rose Bowl. Now, on the eve of the biggest game of his life, she was back wanting to make contact. He wondered what her motive could possibly be, but Bobby was also sincerely happy to hear from her. After obtaining her phone number from his mailbox he drove home and debated in his mind whether he should call her. Finally, after thinking through what he would say, he dialed the number.

Nervous sweat began to form on his face as the phone rang. After what seemed an eternity a female voice answered. "Hi, this is Mandy. How can I help you?"

"Mandy Brooks, how are you? Do you still shake 'em down on the dance floor?"

Mandy laughed and responded, "Nah, I gave that up a long time ago cause I lost my dance partner. But if you want to apply for the job, just send me your resume."

Jason relaxed. "So what in the world are you up to? I thought that maybe you had gone off to a convent and become a nun."

Mandy laughed again. "Bobby, you never could get serious now could you? I am fine but don't have a lot of time to talk now. I guess I just wanted to call and take the time to say hi. I have lived in Seattle since I left old Wazzu."

"Well, then you have probably been following the football escapades of your two old buddies. We haven't done too bad for ourselves after a few years of failure."

"Well, you sure have excited this city like never before. I am proud of both of you. My son worships you."

"Your son? You have a son? Wow, and he follows football?"

"Yep, a typical male. Just like his daddy. He loves football."

Mandy's voice then changed to a very serious tone. "Listen, Bobby, I know how we parted, and I know you really don't want to see me, but I need to see you at least once more. I have something very important to tell you."

Bobby was quiet for a few seconds before responding. "Really? Listen, Mandy, I do want to see you, but I am afraid of dredging up the past. It messed me up big time before, and I won't let that happen again."

"Bobby, the past is the past. I am not trying to change anything. I don't plan on upsetting you. I just have one important thing to tell you, and I can't do it over the phone. Would you just please consider meeting me for a brief dinner next week so we can talk? After that I promise that I will not bother you again."

Bobby as he wrestled with his response. He did not want his focus on beating St. Louis and getting to the Super Bowl to be broken. He did not want to hear Mandy dredge up the past with allegations against him and Jason. Yet, something seemed to be telling him that he should see Mandy. Something was telling him she could be trusted, and he knew that after all the years that had gone by he still was interested in this woman. Finally, after a very long pause, he spoke.

"OK, Mandy. I would like to have dinner with you, but I am not going to get into any heavy stuff right now. It will be just a couple of old friends getting together to reconnect. And that will be it. Agreed?"

Mandy lightened up and with a little chuckle said, "Agreed your honor. I promise I won't bore you too much with the details of my life since I lost my dance partner." She then laughed and said, "Bobby, I promise that I am not going to eat you alive. You can handle me. Trust me."

He heard those words— "trust me"—and they cut through him. He remembered when he had said those very two words to Mandy but in the end had betrayed her trust. Would she do the same now? He wondered if this was her revenge after all of the passing years.

"OK, Mandy. How about Monday night at 7:30 PM? I like a quiet little restaurant near the stadium named "The Trolley." On Monday nights it is not very busy, and I can go there without too much fanfare."

"Yes, I know where it is."

"Well, stranger, I look forward to the reunion."

"Me too. And, Bobby, there is one more thing."

"What is it Mandy Brooks?" Bobby replied, trying to sound annoyed at her persistence.

"Well, I know they have a jukebox there. You owe me one dance for old time's sake."

"Oh really now? My, my, I can see myself injuring my ankle trying to keep up with you again on the dance floor. Is that your agenda? You are a spy for the Steelers with instructions to take me out before the big game, right?" Bobby said laughingly.

Mandy responded with a giggle. "Well first you have to beat the Rams before the Steelers would be worried about you. But no, no, I am not smart enough to have thought of something like that. But come to think of it, I do believe that the Steelers would probably pay big bucks for that to happen. Do you think I should call them and get an offer?"

"Good night, Mandy. I will see you on Monday night"

"Good night, Bobby, dearest."

With the end of the conversation, Bobby felt strangely excited. He was looking forward to the meeting with her, but vowed to not let anything she would say rattle him and take his mind off of the upcoming football challenges. He hoped that he could finally make peace with her and bring closure to this unresolved chapter in his life.

All of these things raced through his mind as Bobby lay in bed attempting to go to sleep. The game had been exhausting. Normally Bobby would simply crash after such a game, but on this night, he could not sleep as his mind was fixed on the details of his upcoming meeting with Mandy.

What did Mandy really want to say? Why did she wait to reappear in his life at this time? He knew that he would be taking a risk in meeting with his former girlfriend, but something was compelling him to do so.

CHAPTER 5

While Jason slept, his subconscious mind remained active. In fact, his mind was so active that it delivered a dream that was haunting and disturbing. It was a dream that he desperately wanted to understand.

In this dream Jason found himself walking on an endless beach with his feet in the cool water. He did not know his destination, but felt a compelling need to walk in the tide and follow it along the shoreline of the beach. He noticed in the sky streaks of light that looked like lightning but in fact were shooting stars. The numbers of such stars were too many to count, and it appeared that they were all headed his way on the beach. Yet, strangely, he felt no fear. Instead he watched in awe, knowing that there was some intelligence behind this celestial light show.

The color of the ocean water was a blue-green and unlike any color he had ever seen. While it seemed to be a tropical body of water, the weather was not hot and humid as might be expected in such an area. Instead, it was pleasant. Warm but not hot and a cool breeze actually blew on his face as he walked.

As he continued along the beach, he came upon an inlet with a small river that flowed into the ocean. He turned to follow the river and began to walk upon its banks.

He now unrelentingly exerted himself toward his yet to be disclosed destination, and as he did so, he noticed a strange glow in the sky. The view seemed to be of a sunset, but it was like no other sunset he had seen before. The sky's colors were magnificent, and the setting sun was a glorious light show emitting different shades of yellow, red, and orange. As he looked, Jason saw ongoing shooting stars rapidly shooting across the twilight sky . No fireworks display ever invented by man could compare to what Jason was seeing.

Jason continued his journey along the bank of the river until he began to walk up a path that led up a mountain. The river water flowed alongside the path and up the mountainside, contrary to the law of gravity, and he saw beautiful birds of all colors flying upward along the riverbank toward the top of the mountain. He also saw animals of all kinds—both wild and tame—running up the mountain path, unable to resist the compulsion to move upward toward the top of the mountain. Tigers, elephants, cats, dogs, rabbits, reptiles, and other creatures hurried up the path and were totally unaware of each other's presence as they ran. The wild feline animals seemed like joyful and playful kittens as they scurried on toward the top. Likewise, the other animals—both large and small—all seemed to act like playful newborn cubs, stimulated by the unexplainable compulsion they had to head up the mountain path.

Jason began to climb the path. He did not tire but, in fact, became stronger and more energized as he moved on. As he continued to hike, he began to hear strange melodious sounds that initially were not recognizable. As he walked further, he began to identify the sounds as female voices singing in the distance. The closer he came to his destination, the clearer the voices were, and the more alluring they became.

Just like the Sirens in Homer's *Odyssey*, these voices drew Jason toward them and motivated him to continue his journey. He picked up his pace and began to run up the path, longing to come to the source of the angelic voices. He did not recognize what the voices were saying in their song, as they appeared to be singing in a different language, but he was unable to resist them and believed that they were calling him to come.

At the end of the path, Jason found himself looking over a clear meadow covered with plush green grass. Animals continued to come up the path and onto the meadow field, which appeared to be miles in both width and length. Somewhere in the distance the voices continued their melodic enchantment, and Jason renewed his quest toward them. He began to run as fast as he could across the soft, grassy blanket as the heavenly voices called him onward, and as he ran, he outpaced the animals so that within a short period of time he was far ahead of the fastest of them.

The voices grew louder and more vibrant as a fog began to arise out of the meadow that blurred his vision and his ability to see. He slowed his pace and began to walk more deliberately as the voices grew louder, but his ability to see was greatly hindered. After what seemed to be miles of walking, he saw something in the distance that appeared to be silhouettes of humanlike bodies, and it became clear that these beings were the sources of the unspeakably beautiful music that he had been pursuing.

Jason continued, and as he walked forward the fog began to lift. At first the silhouettes were just dark figures, like shadows, against the backdrop of a spectacular blue sky, but as the fog continued to lift, the silhouettes began to take on more shape and substance.

Eventually the fog lifted entirely, and Jason saw numerous beings in the distance who appeared to be dancing, singing, playing, and laughing. Their demeanor reminded him of small children at play in a schoolyard with no concerns at all, just enjoying their lives. He continued his walk toward these figures in the distance.

He came closer and one of the beings, apparently a young woman, began to look his way and started to walk toward him. Jason picked up his pace to meet her. As he got closer he began to see the figure of someone he knew. She was familiar to him in everyway—it was Rachel Thomlinson. Once he recognized her, he ran toward her with all of the athletic speed his body owned. He longed to take her into his arms once more.

Rachel ran toward Jason as well. The closer they came to each other the more detail Jason could see. She was stunningly beautiful in a way he had never seen before. The word "angelic" simply did not describe what she had become. She smiled at him, and her bright hazel eyes pierced his heart. As Jason saw her more clearly, he began to call her name as he ran with the pace of an Olympic sprinter.

Rachel was also running hard calling, out his name and urging him to come to her. Both of them were at top speed moving toward each other when suddenly they each made an abrupt stop. The meadow had ended and before both of them stood a deep abyss. They were only perhaps twenty yards apart, but the abyss prohibited them from coming together, and it was too wide for even an athlete of Jason's caliber to leap over.

Jason looked down the abyss that appeared to be endless with no visible bottom. He then looked up and across the divide at Rachel and their eyes met. Nothing verbally was said, but the connection in their eyes said everything. In her eyes Jason saw love, compassion, forgiveness, and peace. He longed to hold her again, and tell her how sorry he was for what he had done, but he knew that she understood his feelings of guilt and remorse. And he knew she had forgiven him.

Jason desperately wanted to come to her, so he began to run alongside the edge of the meadow looking for a bridge or at least a narrowing of the abyss so he could leap over. He kept his eyes on her as he ran. Although she did not move her body, she seemed to follow him as he moved. It was like a reflection that follows a person as one moves alongside the water. So too in this manner did Rachel's likeness and eyes follow Jason as he ran along the edge of the abyss to find a bridge and a way to come to her.

It seemed to Jason that he had run up and down the edge of the abyss for miles but found no way to cross over. He was not physically exhausted from these efforts, but he was getting frustrated at his failed quest. Finally, he stopped trying. He could see that there was no way that he could cross and be with her. It was impossible. He resigned himself to stand at the edge of the abyss and look into her eyes communicating that he could not come.

Rachel smiled lovingly at him. Her face did not express anguish that she could not be with him. It did not show sadness that there was no way they could be together. Rather, her countenance showed total peace and contentment and indicated that she wished the same for him. The enchanting voices of song in the background quickly became more noticeable to Jason, and then the fog began to rapidly rise from the ground. It first covered her feet and slowly worked its way up her body. Jason noticed that the fog was beginning to engulf him too, and he realized that soon he would lose sight of her.

He began to call out her name. "Rachel, Rachel, don't leave me. I am so sorry Rachel. Don't leave me now. Please don't go. Please forgive me my love. Please don't go!"

Jason's cries were to no avail. Eventually the fog totally covered Rachel, and her image disappeared.

Jason violently jerked awake from the sound of his voice to find himself in his bed crying out in sorrow, "I am sorry! I am so sorry! Please forgive me! Please forgive me!" Sweat drenched Jason's body, tears streamed down his face, and exhaustion overwhelmed him.

The dream had ended.

CHAPTER 6

Jason slept very little the rest of the night. He finally pulled himself out of bed at 7:30 AM to shower and get ready for the day. His head continued to throb in pain and did not feel significantly improved from the previous evening.

He immediately turned on the radio to listen to the sports news of the day. His favorite sports show was *Morning Sports Talk* hosted by Jake McGee and Robin Everson. The entire morning show was devoted to discussing the previous day's game and the hero of the game—Jason O'Connor.

Jake McGee opened up the show, "Good morning Seahawks fans. And what a day yesterday was at Qwest Stadium. In one of the most thrilling sports dramas in Seattle history, the Seahawks, led by their every-thing quarterback Jason O'Connor, pulled a victory out with a dramatic second half comeback. This is an incredible season my friends, and I don't want to be wakened from this dream. After all these years, the Seahawks are going back to the Super Bowl."

Robin Everson chimed in, "Yes, it was a day for celebration, but the day ended in a very bizarre way. Jason O'Connor was seriously in-jured on the last play of the game, which was his dramatic game-winning touchdown run. Apparently, he took a pretty heavy blow to the head and suffered a mean concussion. But things got more bizarre after the game as he took another blow to the head when a fan tackled him to push him out of the way of a falling concrete beam from the new parking garage across from the stadium."

McGee responded, "You know, Robin, we are going to get into some detail about that bizarre event later in the show, and we will be interview-ing Coach Paul Wagner to find out more about the condition of Jason

O'Connor. Right now, though, we want to go straight to the phone lines and hear from our listening audience. What is your take on the events of yesterday? And how do you size up the Seahawks' chances in the Super Bowl in two weeks against the Steelers?"

"Good Morning and welcome to *Morning Sports Talk*. What's on your mind?" McGee said as he took the first caller of the day.

"Hey, Jake and Robin, good morning. I just wanted to say that yesterday's game was the most exciting sports event of my lifetime, and I have lived here and followed Seattle sports for over three decades. I just thought it was over at halftime, and I couldn't believe that O'Connor could do anything right after that stupid safety right before half. Thank God he proved me wrong."

"Lets talk about that first half for a minute," Robin said. "You know, Jake, I for one have been very skeptical about Jason O'Connor and have been so ever since he was elevated above Zach Morrison. So, as you know, at halftime yesterday I was actively calling for him to be benched and replaced by Morrison. But boy, am I a believer now. That winning touchdown run was the prettiest thing I have ever seen over the years, and only Jason O'Connor could have made that run."

"Well, Robin, you and I have disagreed on O'Connor for the last two years. I thought it was a very good move made by Wagner when he traded for him. O'Connor has all the qualities to be a great NFL quarterback, but for some reason he just didn't jell in the league until he came to Seattle. Zach Morrison, while a great quarterback over the years, is just getting older and less effective all the time. So I think it was a good move when Wagner benched Morrison two years ago and went with O'Connor. And now yesterday's game shows us that Wagner's football instincts have been right all along."

For the next thirty minutes McGee and Everson took phone calls from the fans to let them talk about the Seahawks and express their excitement about the upcoming Super Bowl. Eventually, however, the discussion turned to the events that followed the game.

"We have to now talk about that bizarre accident after the game yesterday and what effect it will have on O'Connor's ability to play in two weeks. Robin, what can you tell us about it? What in the world happened?"

"Jake, this is the strangest thing I have ever heard of. It is just plain weird. That is the only way to describe it. Apparently, Wagner and O'Connor were walking out of the stadium to get to their cars and drive to Providence Hospital to have Jason's head checked out when reporters and fans wanting to hear more about the game surrounded them. They were standing right at the entrance to the new parking garage across from Qwest stadium when a concrete beam that was hanging over the edge of the second floor of the garage fell and was headed right for Jason O'Connor. A very alert fan saw what was happening and immediately tackled Jason to knock him out of the way of the falling beam. While he probably saved Jason's life in doing this, he did in the process knock Jason to the concrete pavement causing another serious injury to his head."

McGee responded, "We are going to have Coach Wagner on in a minute to tell us how seriously Jason has been hurt, but before that happens, do we know anything about the fan who saved Jason's life?"

"Not a lot but we should know more very soon. His name is Josiah Johnson. He is an African-American minister who has a small church in the Central Area of Seattle. We know that he and his wife attend every home game, but they can't afford to pay for the tickets so they park their car on the street by the stadium and listen to the game on the radio. Apparently, being this close to the stadium makes them feel like they are actually at the game inside the stadium."

"It appears that he is a true blue dyed in the wool Seahawks fan."

"One more thing, Jake. The Johnsons have a young boy about the age of ten who comes with them to the games every Sunday when the Seahawks play at home. Apparently he is handicapped and cannot speak or communicate well but loves the Seahawks, and we are told that Jason O'Connor is his hero."

Jason had been listening intently to all of the details on whom it was that saved his life.

"Reverend Johnson was a pretty mean football player in his day playing for a small college in Indiana. That is about all I can tell you now, Jake, but more information will be forthcoming today on this."

"Now we have a special guest on the line— the head coach and general manager of the Seahawks, Paul Wagner. Good morning sir, and congratulations on a thrilling victory."

"Thank you very much, Jake. It is always a pleasure to be on your show."

"Listen, Coach, before we talk about Jason O'Connor and his injuries, let me ask you a few questions about the game. You were behind 19-0 at halftime, and there was a lot of murmuring going on in the stadium. Did you consider switching quarterbacks in the second half and going with Zach Morrison?"

"Never. Absolutely not!" Wagner continued, "You know I was heavily criticized when I first traded for O'Connor, but I saw his talent and followed his career when he was in college. I always believed that he had the tools to be a great NFL quarterback. I knew if we could give him a supporting cast that he would come through for us. I know that my professional judgment was brutally assaulted in many parts of the media last season when I benched Zach Morrison and went with O'Connor. But Jason proved all of these critics wrong yesterday. He is our man."

"Coach, what did you say to the team at halftime to get them turned around. I have to admit that the first half was pretty depressing and left us with very little hope of a victory."

"Well, Jake, you know that these are professional football players, and they know that sometimes the breaks just don't go your way. You have to play through those times. You have to keep your head up and keep believing in yourself knowing that you can get the job done. So that is all I told the team at half. I wasn't down on them. I told them to just keep playing the way they know how to play and that the breaks would turn around for them. And I was proved right."

Jason was ready to turn off the radio when the next question from Robin Everson caught his attention.

"Coach, we are all concerned about the physical condition of Jason

O'Connor. What can you tell us about that? Can you assure the Seattle sports fans that Jason will be ready to go for the Super Bowl?"

"Absolutely, Robin. Absolutely. I was with Jason last night at Providence Hospital when he was evaluated and received the CAT scan. We are going to be talking with the doctors the first thing this morning about the results, but I was assured last night that there should be nothing to concern us about the physical ability of Jason to play at full speed in the Super Bowl. Our game plan is not going to change in preparing for the Steelers. And Jason will be an integral part of the game plan. He is going to be held out of contact this week but will practice fully in every aspect next week when we are in Miami preparing for the big game."

"Before we let you go, Coach, let me ask you about the strange incident that occurred after the game at the parking garage," said Jake McGee. "What in the world happened there?"

Coach Wagner chuckled. "Well, Jake, I have to agree with you that it was a rather strange occurrence. However, we can thank Rev. Joe Johnson for saving Jason's life. I was right there and the whole thing happened in front of my very eyes."

"And what did exactly happen?"

"You and the rest of the media have it right. An unattached concrete beam somehow became dislodged from the second floor of the garage and came hurling toward Jason. Rev. Johnson saw the danger and alertly moved Jason out of the way with a very forceful tackle. Let me tell you something—he looked like an All-Pro linebacker on that one."

"And is there concern that Jason further injured his head when it impacted the ground?"

"We are going to find out more about the full extent of Jason's injuries later this morning, but all I can tell you now is that the doctor last night did not seem overly concerned about the injury affecting Jason O'Connor's ability to play in two weeks."

"You know, Coach, that the Steelers' defensive line has been virtually impenetrable against the run all season long. The only way they are going to be beaten is through the Seahawks' passing game of O'Connor to Childs. That is why people are so worried about Jason's ability to play right now."

"I totally understand and agree. Of course, remember, that we do have the best backup in the league in Zach Morrison. If, in the unlikely event, Jason cannot play, then we will be in good hands with Zach at the helm."

Robin Everson responded, "That is comforting to all of us and particularly so to those fans, like myself, who until yesterday's miracle comeback believed that Zach Morrison should have been the Seahawks starting quarterback all along."

"Zach is a veteran of the league, Robin, and certainly has the capability to lead us to victory if need be," Wagner replied. "The Seahawks are just very fortunate to have two high quality quarterbacks on this team, so I am not worried."

The more Jason listened to his coach deceiving the listening audience, the more nauseated he began to feel. "If they only knew what I know," he muttered to himself under this breath.

"But let me assure you and the public," continued Wagner. "Jason O'Connor will be ready to play and stick it to the Steelers on Super Bowl Sunday. That is guaranteed."

"That is great news to hear, Coach. Thanks for your time, and good luck this week and next as you prepare for the Steelers."

"Thanks for having me guys. It is always a pleasure."

Jason left his radio on as he walked away seething with anger at his coach. Jason wondered what kind of treatment the coach would receive from the press if it became known that Wagner had failed to obtain an adequate backup quarterback during the season, knowing that Morrison could not physically play. One thing lingered in Jason's mind as he got ready for the day—he did not trust nor respect his coach.

As Jason prepared himself for the day the radio talk show continued with more callers expressing their opinions on the Seahawks' chances of winning the Super Bowl if Jason was not able to play. Opinions were mixed. Some believed that Zach Morrison was an adequate backup and could do the job. Other's felt that all would be lost without Jason at the helm. Still, others were adamant in their opinion that Jason was overrated and needed to be benched in favor of Morrison, regardless of whether or not he were able to play.

McGee introduced his next radio guest. "On the phone with us now is Sammy Jensen, well-known sports reporter and columnist for the *Seattle Post-Intelligencer*. Welcome to *Morning Sports Talk* Sammy."

"Thanks, Jake. It is a great morning to be a Seattle Seahawks fan isn't it?"

"Yes, indeed. What we want to ask you about your upcoming series of articles on the dynamic duo of the Seahawks—Jason O'Connor and Bobby Childs. Can you give the public a preview of what they will be reading the next few days in the paper?"

"I am very glad to do so. Since mid-season I have been working on a series of articles on Jason O'Connor and Bobby Childs that will be appearing in the *Post-Intelligencer* beginning this week. What I wanted to do is to really study these two. I wanted to look at their backgrounds, their upbringings, what makes them tick together as a unit, and, really, just do a good job of reporting on these two guys who have brought so much excitement to the Seattle area this year."

"Can you give us a few specifics of what we can expect to find in your articles?" Asked Robin.

"Well I have found this project to be one of the most fascinating studies that I have ever done. I am going to be calling this series 'The Brotherhood.' As you may recall, they both had incredible senior seasons at Washington State. Jason was the runner-up in the Heisman voting after his senior season and they both made every all-American team. However, they just didn't come through that year in the Rose Bowl against Iowa. That game was an unmitigated disaster for both of them and the Cougars. It was a very unusual and disappointing game in that both of them gave very sub par performances. O'Connor's passing in both yardage and completion percentage was far below his norm during the regular season, and I believe that Childs caught only two passes for about twenty yards."

"And this disappointment followed them in NFL. While they both went high in the first round of the draft, neither seemed to show much promise in the professional ranks, as they both settled in backup roles for years. That was until last year, of course, when Jason got another chance and came through big time. And this year the career of Bobby Childs was reborn as he came to Seattle to play with his old buddy. Its like the two just can't accomplish much apart from each other. Together they are unstoppable, but apart they just don't make the grade."

Robin Everson spoke up. "You raise an interesting point here, Sammy. Most of our broadcast has centered today on Jason O'Connor. But it was Childs yesterday who made the most incredible acrobatic catches that kept that thrilling fourth quarter touchdown drive alive. And remember it was his lightning speed and that sixty-five yard touchdown run that brought Seattle back from the brink. I wonder if Bobby Childs is not the real MVP for the Seahawks this year."

"You might be on to something. Remember the Seahawks only traded for Childs in the off-season at the insistence of O'Connor. I think maybe Jason knows that he can't do it alone, without his buddy. I believe that their performances this year indicate that they need each other to play at their highest potential."

Robin Everson continued with the interview by asking, "You know, Sammy, you are a well-respected sports reporter here in Seattle and have been for years. However, I recall that you were pretty tough on O'Connor when he first was elevated to the starting quarterback position, and he had some pretty strong words to say about you as well during those early days of his ascension to the starting job. Is there any ill will between you two, and if so, has that affected your ability to be objective in your evaluation of him in these articles?

Jensen replied, "That is a fair question, Robin, and I admit I did have some tough things to say about him in the press during those days. I think I called him an underachiever and a total disappointment when one remembers the expectations people had of him after he graduated from Washington State. Yes, Jason, was pretty upset with me then and probably still feels like I won't give him a fair shake. But listen, I am a professional and just want to report honestly and fairly about a sports figure in this town. I only call the facts as I see them, and if I am wrong, I will apologize."

"Do you apologize for calling him an underachiever?" Jake McGee asked.

"No, not really because at the time I said that it was true. Look at his record. After his dismal Rose Bowl performance his senior year, he did absolutely nothing until Wagner benched Morrison for him. So at the time it was a true statement. But now I can say he is playing to his potential. Like all of the Seahawks fans I am very happy about it."

Jake McGee chimed in, "We have little time left in our broadcast today, Sammy, but can you quickly tell us anything more about your articles?"

"I believe I am going to leave you all hanging for now," laughed Jensen. "I think the public will find these articles very interesting and entertaining. The first will appear in Thursday's paper and will focus on the different backgrounds of these two guys. Their different upbringings make them a highly unusual pair to team up and connect so well together. The later articles will add more detail and bring us up to the current situation as the Seahawks prepare for the Steelers in the main event. There will be one article everyday for five days."

"We look forward to reading your work. Thanks for filling us in, Sammy."

"And thank you too, guys, for having me on this show. I look forward to more conversations as we get closer to the Super Bowl in two weeks."

"And with that, Robin, it is time for us to sign off as well," stated McGee. "We will keep you fans posted on the breaking news regarding Jason O'Connor's head injuries. We expect to be hearing some official word from the Seahawks office later this morning. Thanks for listening sports fans."

As McGee and Everson ended the show, the radio station began to play the now all too familiar unofficial theme song for the Seahawks, "Hold on Tight to Your Dream."

Jason, now fully showered, was sitting eating breakfast. He had missed the radio interview with Sammy Jensen but would have turned off the radio sooner had he known Jensen was going to be on. He loathed this reporter. Jensen had been highly critical of Jason from the moment he became a Seahawk. There were countless columns written by Sammy attacking Jason's football ability after Jason replaced Zach Morrison. Jason felt that many of the articles were simply personal attacks. He remembers one article that called him a "country bumpkin farm kid from Eastern Washington."

As Jason got up to leave and go to the stadium the telephone rang. It was Paul Wagner.

"Hey, O'Connor, I just wanted to call and see how the old noggin is feeling right now."

"Well, Coach, I am sure that it is not comforting to you to say this, but to be honest, my head feels like it is going to explode."

"I figured as much. You took a couple of pretty hard shots. The doc from Providence will be in the office the first thing with the CAT scan results. I want you to be there about 9:30 this morning to go over those results."

"Sure, Coach, I will be there. I am as anxious as you to find out more."

"OK, but let me tell you something. These docs are far more cautious than they need to be. They have been sued one too many times and cover their backsides pretty carefully. As an old football player myself, I know that a player of your caliber will rise to the occasion on a big game like this and play through any physical pain. We are simply too close to achieving the ultimate to let it slip through our fingers now. Do you understand what I am saying?"

Jason, of course, wanted to play in the Super Bowl, but he was seriously questioning whether physically he could do so. Yet, he knew had to give Wagner the response that he wanted because Wagner held all the keys to Jason's future career in football. Jason replied, "Listen, Coach, nobody wants to beat the Steelers more than I do, nobody! I am playing no matter what the doctor says, so don't even worry about it. This should be the last time the matter is even brought up."

"That's what I like to hear, O'Connor. We are going to have a press conference after practice today, so stay positive and keep on that message. Everything will work out in the end; it always does."

"I agree, Coach."

"One more thing, Jason, before I go."

"I am listening."

"Well, that big lug that saved your life yesterday—Reverend Josiah Johnson."

"Yes, tell me about him. What do we know?"

"I am not sure of all the details yet, but we will have enough information when you get to the stadium this morning. I do know that this is a grand opportunity for some really good public relations. So tomorrow after practice I want you to go over to his house. Hug his kid. Pet his dog. Give them an autographed football, and we will throw in some season tickets to give his family for next year. We are setting this up with the media. The press will arrive, and when they do, you are to smile for the cameras and say some nice things. After that, get out of there, and don't think about it again."

"Can't Zach Morrison handle this one?" Jason said jokingly, with a half-hearted laugh. "He is much better at these human relation type stories than I am."

"Very funny, O'Connor. Cut the bull. To be honest you need to thank Reverend Johnson for saving your life. I was there, and believe me, if he hadn't done what he did, you would have been flattened—most likely dead."

"I understand Coach, and believe me, I am grateful, even though my head does not feel like thanking anybody right now. But I will do it. He sounds like a pretty decent fellow anyway. I will see you at the stadium shortly."

"See ya, O'Connor."

Just as Jason hung up, the phone rang again. It was Reporter Sammy Jensen.

"Hey, Jason, I hope all is well with you. How is the head feeling?"

"Do you think I would be straight with you about that? No matter what I say you will probably report that I am dogging it and do not have what it takes to play through pain like a champion or maybe, in your opinion, play like Zach Morrison would."

"Listen, Jason, I know you don't like me. That is OK. It is not my job to be liked. I only report what I see as objectively as I can."

"Yeah, sure, Sammy. Sure thing. So what do you want now?"

"Well, I have been calling you for several days now, and you don't seem to want to return my calls. I want to do an interview with you in the next two days for the series of articles I am writing on you and Childs for the *Post-Intelligencer*. You two guys are a fascinating duo, and I think that Seattle sports fans would enjoy knowing more about what makes you two tick."

"No dice, Sammy. Write whatever you want, but write it without my help. I know you have been snooping around about my past and calling people who have known me over the years. That is fine. Do what you want. I am sorry to disappoint you. I know my life has been pretty boring, and you don't have much to tell."

Jensen laughed. "Oh, don't be too sure, O'Connor. I have found that you and Childs together make a fascinating story. It is actually inspiring. I just want to get your perspective firsthand on this before I go to print. That's all."

"Listen, man, all I want to do now is concentrate on the Super Bowl. This is the dream I have been living all of my life, and I want to be ready for it. I won't be diverted from that by you or anybody else."

"Can I quote you?" laughed Sammy.

"Oh, give it a rest, Jensen. OK, listen, sometime on Wednesday after practice I will give you thirty minutes, and that is all. Take it or leave it."

"Well, you know the first article is appearing in Thursday morning's paper. It is simply a review of your college days with Childs so I guess we can talk Wednesday afternoon. You will have time to read the first install-ment of the series and see that I do not mean you any harm and then you can comment. Fair enough?"

"Fair enough."

"One more thing, O'Connor, before I sign off here. I understand that you are sometime today or tomorrow going to be meeting Josiah Johnson and his family. Is that right?"

"Who?"

"Reverend Joe Johnson, the guy who saved your life, man."

"Right, right. Yeah, Wagner wants me to go over there sometime tomorrow after our practice to thank him. I am anxious to meet the guy."

"Well, Wagner has invited the media to show up and take some pictures as well as interview both you and him. I just thought I would let you know that I will be there along with some others."

"Fine. I am sure this will give you guys the kind of human interest story that you want to write. Frankly, I think you should do a great fluff piece on the guy and give him some notoriety. It will take the spotlight off of me for awhile."

"I don't think so, Jason. Haven't you gotten it into your head by now that you are the Seahawks franchise. Everybody wants to know about Jason O'Connor. And your buddy Childs makes it all the more interesting."

"I gotta run now, Sammy. I guess I will see you later and remember—you have only thirty minutes on Wednesday."

Jason was glad to finally be rid of Sammy Jensen for the time being. He found Jensen to be an obnoxious reporter who somehow had it in for him. He didn't trust what he was up to but realized that probably the only way he could be rid of him for good would be to grant the interview. Hopefully, he thought, this would end the annoyance of Sammy Jensen in his life once and for all.

Jason left for the stadium and arrived at 9:15 AM—about fifteen minutes ahead of schedule. As anticipated, upon his arrival numerous reporters seeking to get a comment from him as well as fans who hoped to get a glimpse of their hero and maybe even an autograph greeted him.

One reporter shouted as he walked to the locker room. "Hey, Jason, can we get a comment or two about yesterday and what happened after the game?"

"Sorry, not now, but we will be having a press conference later on today to fill you in."

"Are you going to be playing in two weeks against the Steelers?"

"You can count on it. Only an act of God will keep me out of the game."

Jason made his way to the locker room and sat down on the bench in front of his locker with a sigh of relief. He was glad to be alone with himself for a few minutes and reflect on the events of the previous twenty-four hours. He placed his head in his hands and closed his eyes. All that came to his mind was the dream and the way in which Rachel had looked at him across the great abyss. He wanted desperately to find a bridge to reach her. He knew that this had been only a dream, but for some reason, he felt as if it were very real and that he had actually seen her.

"Hey, O'Connor, wake up, and get your butt in my office," sounded a gruff voice. Paul Wagner called from across the locker room, "We need to have a pow wow before the doctor from Providence comes in here. I want to make sure that we are on the same page."

Jason slowly made his way across the locker room. He entered Wagner's office while the coach sat back in his chair and smoked a cigar.

"Listen, O'Connor. I am annoyed about all that has to be done today regarding your situation, so let's just start out by saying it will be a lot easier on everybody if you buy the party line here and don't deviate from it at all."

"I am not sure what you mean, Coach."

"I had a discussion with the doctors at Providence earlier this morning and got a preliminary report about the CAT scan. According to them, it is not good. They didn't say this in so many words, but I think they are going to recommend that you not play in two weeks. You and I both know that is totally unacceptable."

"Can't we get a second opinion?"

"Right, sure thing. We will just go out and get another doctor to say something different? Is that what you are suggesting? Listen, these docs at Providence are the best in the business. Their opinions are as good as gold."

"So what do you suggest we do?"

"Well, as far as I am concerned, you are going to play. Of course, they are going to tell you not to play because that is the safest position for them to take. If you play and something bad happens, they can say that they warned you."

Suddenly, the intercom on Wagner's telephone buzzed and a secretary in the front office said, "Coach Wagner, Doctor Nevin from Providence hospital is here to see you. I knew that you are expecting him, so I have sent him your way."

"Thank you. We are here waiting for him." Wagner then turned to Jason and stated, "Let me do most of the talking here. I can handle this thing fine."

Before long a knock was on the door and Paul Wagner opened and invited Doctor Nevin to come in. "Hi, Doc, we have been waiting for you. Have a seat."

Jason got up and shook the doctor's hand and then returned to his seat. The doctor sat quiet for a moment before he spoke.

"Well, Mr. O'Connor, I take it that Coach Wagner has filled you in on what we found out."

"Yes, he has, and listen, doc, I appreciate your concerns, but just let me tell you right out. I am playing. My head will be fine. I am not going to miss the biggest game of my life. Nothing you can say will change my mind."

Doctor Nevin sat still for a moment and then spoke again. "Mr. O'Connor, you have received serious head injuries. Another blow to the skull could have permanent consequences. I just need to advise you of that."

Wagner interrupted, "Jason knows everything, Doc I have filled him in. We are going to make sure that he has a special helmet fitted for him for extra protection. And our line is going to make sure that he is well protected the whole game. Everything will be fine."

He then turned to Jason and said, "O'Connor, you can go now. I will finish here with the doctor. Remember the press conference after practice, and I will fill you in on the details at that time regarding Joe Johnson."

"Right, Coach. And thank you doctor for your concern. I understand your position, but please understand mine and the position of the Seahawks.

"Oh, believe me, Mr. O'Connor, I do understand. More than you could ever realize. I do understand."

After Jason left the office the doctor again sat in silence for a moment before he erupted in a rage at Paul Wagner. He raised his voice as he said firmly. "OK, Coach, what is going on here? I told you about the head injuries. There has not only been a serious concussion, but there is a small fracture to the skull of Mr. O'Connor. If he takes one more serious blow to the head, he could suffer irreversible brain damage. He could suffer paralysis or worse, death. Did you tell him all of this? What is the matter with you anyway?"

"Cut the bull, Doc Jason is a strong young guy who will play through pain. Without him we lose the game, pure and simple. Neither he nor I want to risk that."

"Does victory mean that much to you? Is that what it will cost? The permanent health or maybe even the life of a player? Is winning a game that important? Or maybe you are just trying to cover your own backside for the totally inexcusable manner in which you handled Zach Morrison's serious injuries."

Wagner replied more forcibly, "Don't push me doctor. I call the shots here. You and your hospital are subject to my decisions on this. I am not going to jeopardize our chances of winning the big one by listening to your whiny incompetence. We are going to win the Super Bowl, and you are not going to put a monkey wrench into that."

"Is that what this is all about, Coach? Winning? The life of one or your players is not more important than winning? I am not going to stand for this," shouted Nevin as he rose from his seat.

"Well shut your big fat mouth doctor before I shut if for you!" shouted Paul Wagner. "Jason has been informed and has made this decision on his own. You have nothing to say about it. And remember his medical records are confidential; you are not to release them unless Jason gives you permission. If you do you will have the biggest lawsuit levied against your sorry rear end that you can imagine. So don't push me!"

"Oh, I know this so well, Wagner. I remember the advice you were given about Zach Morrison after his back surgery. You ignored our advice and put him in contact before his back had properly healed. Now, his condition is worse, and he could eventually end up in a wheel chair. I don't think the Seattle media would take it too kindly to know about your cover-up of his condition. Because of your failure to obtain another quarterback, Seattle doesn't even have an adequate backup to O'Connor for this game. Is that why you are now risking the health and life of Jason O'Connor?"

Upon hearing this, Paul Wagner lost it. He began cursing and shouting obscenities at Nevin and, in his own patented way, threatened him. He rose from his chair, walked over to Dr. Nevin, and with his big six-foot three-inch frame directly in front of the doctor, said, "OK, you lousy medical quack! I am going to remind you once more and then this discussion is ended. Morrison made his own decision to play just like O'Connor is now making his decision to play. You are not given authority to release these medical records on any condition. And I don't have to remind you that this organization has some very close friends in the administration at Providence that will not take kindly to a doctor who acts unethically and releases medical reports without the proper legal authorization. Do you understand me fully?"

Doctor Nevin glared at Paul Wagner for a moment and then moved toward the door of the office. "Oh, I understand you full well, sir. You don't have to say anything more." He then left the office, slamming the door hard behind him.

Wagner sat stewing in his office for a few minutes before he picked up his phone. He dialed the personal cell phone number of Doctor Bill Zirinsky, head of the radiology department at Providence Hospital. He received only a recording but left a very strong message on the voice mail.

"Hey, Bill, this is Paul Wagner. I just had a rather contentious discussion about the results of the CAT scan on Jason O'Connor with one of your radiologists—John Nevin. I just want to make sure you understand something here and that you make it clear to Nevin. The medical records of both Zach Morrison and Jason O'Connor are not to be released on any condition. I don't think I have to remind you that the Seahawks give several million dollars each year to your hospital for cancer research and your cancer ward. Just remember what hand butters the bread, and we will be fine. It would be a shame to see Providence having to cut back on the resources at the cancer ward for a lack of money."

Wagner continued to sit at his desk in a very agitated mood and puffed hard on the cigar in his mouth. He then picked up the phone again and dialed the personal cell phone to Robert Mahoney, the CEO and administrator of the hospital. Mahoney answered the call.

"Bob, this is Paul Wagner."

"Coach! Hey what's up? I don't usually get any calls on this line unless it is important. By the way, sorry about the news on, O'Connor."

"Listen, Mahoney, and listen good. Jason O'Connor is going to play in the Super Bowl. He has made his own decision on this, and I for one am not going to overrule it. Your doctor Nevin apparently thinks he can, but I want a lid put on him now!"

"Well, Paul, I don't get involved in telling doctors what to say in making a diagnosis and prognosis. You know that. So what are you saying to me?"

"Let me spell it out real clear, Mahoney. You know how much the Seahawks have given to Providence and its cancer ward as our selected charity. Not only does two million a year go directly to you, but we also lend our co-sponsorship to your annual fund-raising telethon. I know that event also brings in millions. It would be a shame now if we decided to put our efforts elsewhere."

Mahoney was quiet for a few seconds then spoke. "All right, Coach. But I don't quite understand what you are suggesting."

Wagner lost his patience, which never was much of a personal attribute anyway. He began to raise his voice.

"Let me spell it out for you! I will only say this once! The medical records of Zach Morrison and Jason O'Connor are not to be released without my express authorization. Any violation of this is going to cost you and Providence Hospital big time. I don't think the board of directors of the hospital would take kindly to knowing that their big time, high paid CEO lost a major financial supporter like the Seattle Seahawks. Have I made myself clear, Mr. Mahoney?"

Ten seconds of silence ensued until Robert Mahoney responded in a very calm voice.

"I have heard you, coach. Of course we cannot legally release medical records without authorization from Morrison or O'Connor, so I assume you are speaking for them. Without hearing from you further on the matter, rest assured these records will remain private."

"Just make sure that Nevin understands that!"

"Of course. Have a good day, Coach, and good luck in the upcoming Super Bowl."

After slamming down the phone Wagner sat in his chair still fuming for a few seconds. He puffed on the remainder of his cigar and then left for the conference room to meet with the coaching staff and go over the game film from the previous day. His plan of action for the day was simply to review films and talk about game strategy for the Super Bowl, but the verbal warfare he had just been involved in clearly unsettled his mind and ability to think clearly.

Paul Wagner was an aggressive and highly competitive person. He had played ten years in the NFL himself as a lineman with the Minnesota Vikings as well as with the New England Patriots. He made the pro-bowl as a player on three occasions and had a distinguished career. After leaving the ranks as a player he served as assistant coach for several franchises until he landed head coach for the New Orleans Saints. After three years at that job, he was hired as the headman for the New York Giants.

Wagner served the Giants for five years, getting them into the play-offs every season but failed to get them to the big dance. When Seattle hired him, they offered not only the job as head coach but also the position of the general manager. He would be totally in charge of the organization from top to bottom. The opportunity was just too tempting to pass up. Wagner took the job, vowing to take the Seahawks all the way to the top.

And now he was almost there. The big game was in front of him, and in his mind nothing was going to stop him from achieving the dream of every player and coach in the NFL.

The morning went by quickly. Wagner and his coaching staff went over game films with the team and then discussed strategy for the upcoming game against the Steelers. The Steelers had a defensive line that was virtually impenetrable against the run, and running the football was not one of the Seahawks' strengths.

On the other hand, the pass defense of the Steelers was mediocre at best. Everyone knew that the Seahawks' passing attack was the key to victory, and this was why the physical condition of Jason O'Connor was so crucial. Nobody on the team, except for Jason, knew about the true physical condition of Zach Morrison so the anxiety level for the players was minimal. In their minds if Jason could not play Zach would be more than an adequate backup and could lead them to victory. However, both Wagner and O'Connor knew full well that Morrison's ability to throw the ball no further than thirty yards meant he was far from capable of providing the kind of winning performance needed from the Seahawks quarterback. The ability of Jason O'Connor to play at top performance was essential if Wagner and the Seahawks were going to be able to achieve their dream

A press conference was scheduled immediately after the practice, and in quick preparation for this, Wagner called Jason into his office for a brief talk.

"OK, Jason, you know that these guys want to first know about your condition. How are you feeling?"

"Better now, Coach. The pain killers are helping and of course not getting hit on the noggin helps some too."

"Yeah, well that's good. We are having a specially padded helmet made for you to wear to just make sure nothing happens, but I know you are going to be fine. Make sure you let the press know this and let them know your determination to play and win."

Jason chuckled. "I am surprised you feel that you need to tell me this. I am playing. This is a dream come true for me. I won't be denied."

"Glad to hear it, O'Connor. So let's go out there now and make this as brief as we can. Let me handle most of the questions."

"Sure thing, Coach."

Wagner and O'Connor then went into the pressroom and sat down at the table in the front of the crowd of about fifty media representatives. The questions immediately began to fly.

The first question was to be expected.

"Coach, please give us the status of Jason O'Connor and his ability to play against the Steelers?"

"Jason took quite a pop to the head on two occasions yesterday. But his old Irish cement head is holding. He is an example of what they say about the Irish. You know in Ireland they bury people with their heads above the ground because it is cheaper than a tombstone and lasts twice as long."

The reporters all laughed at this unusual show of humor from Paul Wagner. He continued.

"We have conferred with the top medical experts in the country at Providence Hospital and while, of course, we don't want Jason to take another pop on the head like yesterday, he will be ready to play against the Steelers. We will hold him out of contact this week, but he will be ready to go full strength next week."

"Jason, could we have your comments?"

"Sure thing. Nothing is going to keep me out of this game. I know I will be ready to play. Right now I feel fine and am anxious to just concentrate on beating the Steelers."

The next question was also expected.

"Can either of you, or both of you, comment on the strange situation that occurred after the game outside the stadium? What in the world caused this to happen, and what can you tell us about Reverend Johnson?"

Wagner again took the lead in answering. "Well, as to how this incident happened, I do not know. I do know, however, that this was a clear case of negligent behavior by someone who is responsible for that very dangerous steel beam hanging over the ledge of the parking lot. We are looking into that now, and believe me, legal action will be taken against the party responsible. As for Reverend Johnson, let's just say that the Seahawks organization is very grateful for his quick action. We plan on expressing our deep appreciation to him later this week."

"Coach, do you know any further information about Reverend Johnson than what already has been reported?"

"Well, no, not yet anyway. We have people in the front office working on this and finding out more. We have to respect Mr. Johnson's privacy, however, and understand that he probably doesn't want to be in the limelight. Because of this we are not going to dig into his background very much."

Jason O'Connor spoke up, "Let me say that I am extremely thankful and appreciative to Reverend Johnson. The thing happened so quickly that I did not know what hit me. And I can tell you, that man can hit! I understand he used to play football. Well, what do you think, Coach? Maybe we ought to offer him a try out in summer camp."

Everyone in the room laughed as Wagner responded, "As I said we are appreciative that our all-pro quarterback was spared serious injury due to some knucklehead's negligence. Because of Mr. Johnson's quick action, we have Jason available to lead us to victory over the Steelers."

"About the Steelers, Coach, how are you going to prepare? They have a defense that is simply impenetrable against the run but is vulnerable to an effective passing game. This is why everyone is so concerned about O'Connor's physical condition to play."

"We know the Steelers are tough to run against, but that doesn't mean that we won't be running. Listen, this is the Super Bowl. All stops are going to be pulled out. Of course, we are going to pass a lot—we have done so all season long. But everyone on our team is going to be giving 1,000 percent to win, and that includes our line in its blocking schemes and our running backs."

"In the event Jason can't play or is not at full strength do you have confidence in Zach Morrison's ability to lead the team?"

"Zach Morrison has had a great and productive career in the NFL. He is a veteran and knows how to prepare for the big game. We all have confidence in him. If he is called upon to help I know he is up to the challenge, but I want to again emphasize that Jason O'Connor is going to be at full strength for us."

Jason chimed in, "I respect Zach a lot. But I plan on playing every down. As I said before—only an act of God will keep me out of this game. We are destiny's team, and I intend to lead us to a win against the Steelers."

After a few more questions ensued about the Seahawks' strategy against the Steelers, Paul Wagner ended the press conference and bid the reporters farewell until the next day. On the way back to the locker room he said to Jason, "Good job, O'Connor. You stayed on message and gave the Steelers a lot to think about in preparing for us this week."

As Jason retrieved some personal belongings from his locker and was getting ready to leave, Bobby Childs approached him. "Hey there, buddy. Nice show with the reporters, but tell me, how you are really doing? Play it to me straight man."

Jason looked at his friend and knew that he could not keep anything from him. He responded, "Bobby, I hope for the best, but my head continues to hurt bad. Wagner tells me the doctor's concerns are not to be taken seriously because they are covering their backsides to avoid potential legal action in case I play and get injured further. But man, I don't know. I am having trouble seeing today. Everything is blurry."

"I thought as much. But we all have confidence that you will be ready. I don't think the docs would allow you to play if there were serious concerns."

"Yeah, you are right on that one. At any rate I am not going to be taken out. We have worked too long to be here. This is the time I have been dreaming about all my life."

Bobby then changed the subject. "You know that I am meeting Mandy Brooks for dinner tonight."

"Don't remind me man! She is up to no good, I know that full well. I am sure that she wants back in your life to get something from you. You have struck it rich, and the money probably looks good to her right now. Don't let her do it, man. I just don't understand why you are meeting her in the first place. Do you not remember what she did to us at the height of our college careers?"

"Of course I remember, Jason. How could I forget? I just think that Mandy and I need to resolve some things. I have felt so for a very long time, and now she pops up and asks to see me. I couldn't turn her down for some reason."

"Did she tell you what she wanted to talk about?"

"She just said she wanted to meet with an old college friend and wish him luck in the play-offs and Super Bowl."

"And that's it? Oh come on, she is up to no good and wants something more! I really want you to cancel, but if you don't, just be on guard. Don't let her mess with your head like she did last time."

Bobby Childs placed his hand on the shoulder of his friend and replied. "Jason, buddy. Listen to me now and believe me when I say that nothing is going to take me off my concentration and focus on beating the Steelers. Nothing is going to do this so don't worry."

"All right then, Bobby, do what you have to do. You don't even have to tell me about the meeting and what is said. But please be careful with her, and don't take any crap!"

Bobby smiled a big smile, put his right hand in a military salute, and said, "Aye, aye, sir. You have nothing to worry about, Captain."

Jason laughed and said, "OK, showboat. Enjoy your dinner and just be careful."

"I will, Jason. I promise you that I will."

CHAPTER 7

Bobby Childs arrived thirty minutes early that evening for his dinner date with Mandy. He wanted to collect his thoughts and prepare for the reunion, and he was suddenly feeling ill at ease. The moment to confront his personal demons from the past had arrived.

Why did Mandy want this meeting? What did she want to say to him? Was she still angry for the manner in which he treated her? Should he express regret and even remorse for the way he acted toward her when they split?

All of these questions haunted him as he sat quietly in the corner table of the restaurant awaiting her appearance. Of course, there was the primary question in his mind that he could not shake—were there still feelings between them? Maybe the reason he had not been able to completely free his mind from thinking about her over the years was that he still cared for her.

Bobby ordered a couple of sodas—one for him and one for Mandy—as he tensely kept an eye on the entrance to the restaurant. Finally, at exactly the right time a familiar face appeared through the front door. Bobby smiled as he looked at her and remembered that punctuality was always one of her virtues.

She looked virtually the same. Ten years had not changed her appearance. Her long, wavy, brunette locks highlighted her beautiful face and blue eyes. Her countenance drew attention to her seductive and almost perfect figure. He knew immediately upon seeing her walk through the door that the magnetic attraction that had originally brought them together still existed—at least it did for him. Whether she had the same emotions was another question to be answered sometime later. Whether she would even let him know her feelings was a completely different matter. For now, however, at this moment in time Bobby looked upon Mandy Brooks with a glow in his eyes and realized that he had been a fool to let her out of his life.

Mandy walked into the lobby of the restaurant and began to look around. Their eyes met as she spotted him in the far corner of the restaurant. She shot a big smile his way, waved, and then walked forward. Bobby got up to meet her halfway finding his legs shaking and weak. They greeted each other with a slight hug, and then Mandy kissed him on the cheek.

"Well hello there, stranger," she said. "Do you care to dance, or are you afraid I am going to show you up again?"

Bobby laughed. "You look good, Mandy. Real good. I guess life has treated you well."

"Lately it has, but there have been a few hard knocks. That is true for all of us I am sure."

They sat down and shared in small talk for a while as they ordered their dinner. Bobby knew this was going to eventually be a deep discussion about something, but he wasn't sure how that would start or end. He began to probe Mandy.

"OK, Mandy Brooks. So what have you been up to for the last ten years? Since I know you have a son I have to believe that you didn't go off to a convent and take vows of celibacy."

She laughed and then responded, "Bobby, you know that the manner in which we split was very angry and hostile. So initially it was hard. I dropped out of school and didn't get my degree, and I have to tell you that I have gone through some pretty rough waters since then."

"Did you continue your dance talents somewhere along the line? I always expected that you would eventually end up in a Broadway musical."

Mandy laughed, "Well, it did pay off a little. I taught dance to young girls for several years at a dance studio in Seattle. I even danced a little ballet in a production of the Nutcracker for a few years. I was a party parent in that performance—nothing major. And oh yes, I did get married, and yes, I have a son. He worships you by the way. He is a very big football fan and plays Pop Warner football himself."

Bobby smiled. "Well, who is the lucky guy that landed you, and what does he do?"

"We are divorced and have been for three years."

"I am sorry, Mandy."

"There's nothing to be sorry about. It's OK. The relationship was wrong from the beginning. It was a rebound romance after we broke up and should never have happened."

An uncomfortable moment of silence ensued before Bobby responded. "Mandy you don't have to tell me anything that you don't want to share. I am sorry that this went so badly for you."

"I want to tell you. He is a lawyer in Seattle. A very successful lawyer by the way, and he makes very good money. I met him at a club in Seattle a couple of years after I left the university. He was very charming and romanced me to death; although, he couldn't dance a step on the dance floor. Unlike someone I know."

Bobby gave a self-conscious laugh. "Well, at least he was there for you when you needed somebody."

"Yeah, I needed somebody, but he wasn't the one. We married shortly after meeting, but things went wrong almost from the start. He worked long hours and drank way too much. We began to argue incessantly when my son was very young, and he was physically and emotionally abusive to both of us. Eventually, I just said that I had enough and filed for divorce."

"That's sounds painful."

"Bobby, you don't know the half of it. It was a very angry divorce. I had to get restraining orders against him, and my son was very frightened of him. We moved out of the big home on Lake Union and in with my dad. We still live with my father."

"Why was he so angry anyway?"

Mandy grew very quiet and still. She finally spoke. "Do you really want to hear this?" When Bobby nodded that he did she continued to talk.

"Well, first Jim was very possessive and insanely jealous of any male in my life other than him. That included my dad. And he knew all about my relationship with you in college."

"Me? Oh my goodness. What did I have to do with this?"

"I talked about you periodically because Jim is a big football fan. At first he just listened with interest about me dating a football player. As time went on, however, he became more and more jealous of you, and he began to bring up all sorts of silly things. He mocked you for being a backup receiver, and when we fought he always would sarcastically mention your name by saying, 'Oh yes, if I was only as perfect as your ex-lover that loser Childs.'"

"Wow, Mandy. I am sorry I caused such an ongoing problem for you. I am sure that my name was really the last one you wanted to hear. I am surprised you even mentioned me to him."

Mandy now looked deeply into Bobby's eyes for a few seconds without saying a word. She then briefly touched his hand and spoke. "As hard as I tried, I could not forget you."

"Well for someone who has experienced so much stress in life, you seem to be at peace."

Mandy then clutched the small gold necklace that she was wearing. Bobby noticed that it was a pretty gold cross. She responded, "Peace isn't the absence of stress. It is the presence of God."

Bobby was speechless. His life since that infamous night long ago at the fraternity house had been virtually downhill until he came to Seattle to play. His career in the NFL was, for the most part, a big disappointment. He had never quite lived up to the expectations placed upon him, and he felt that he had let a lot of people down. His life since saying goodbye to Mandy had been far from peaceful. Bobby knew full well that below his outside surface—that seemed so self-assured to the public—was a frightened man who had not figured out who he was and where he belonged. He desperately needed to win the Super Bowl to prove to everybody that he really was a champion who could achieve the ultimate, but peace in his life was nowhere to be found, and he doubted that even a Super Bowl victory would bring him that.

After a few uncomfortable moments of silence Bobby responded. "You know, Mandy, I have put up a pretty good act over the last ten years.

The public and the media think that I am a shallow playboy who works and plays hard. The truth is that inside I am a frightened little boy."

Mandy smiled and said, "Oh, I know that full well, Bobby Childs."

"Well here is the big secret about me that hasn't gotten out yet. Are you ready to be the first to know?"

"I am honored that you would tell me."

"That playboy image is a total sham—a complete fraud. It gives me great cover to avoid getting close to anybody. The fact is that since we split, I have never been close to anybody, except for Jason, but here is the real kicker that nobody knows yet."

"And what is that?"

Bobby laughed and said, "Well when you clutched your cross I decided I could trust you with this, but you gotta promise not to blow my cover and tell people. It would ruin my hard fought for reputation."

"I promise. Scout's honor."

"OK. For the last two months I have been going to church."

"No way!" Mandy laughed. "Not you. It can't be true."

"It is. I promise you. It is."

"And what brought this on?"

"I guess at sometime in your life you have to believe that there is something bigger in this universe than just your puny little surroundings. You have to believe that life is more than just a football game. I have always had these instincts, but I never knew where they came from or what they meant. So I started going to a very large church in the University District. There are several thousand people there every Sunday, so it is safe. I can just slip in the back pew and nobody knows I am there. As soon as the last hymn is sung, I quietly slip out and am not bothered by anybody."

Mandy began to laugh uncontrollably much to Bobby's consternation. She finally stopped.

"Oh, Bobby, please don't misread me. It's just that I knew you were going to church because I have seen you there the past two Sundays."

"You what? How could you?"

"Hey, like you said it is a big church. My son and I sit up in the balcony in the corner, and I have seen you slip in and go out." She paused, gave him a playful look, and then continued, "But don't worry. Your secret is safe with me."

"So why didn't you track me down after church and say hi?"

"Well, first, Mr. Childs, I was up in the balcony—a little bit a ways from you, and you sprint out of the church as fast as you can so nobody can even try to talk to you. How in the world could I move fast enough to catch you?"

Bobby nodded his head, expressing that he understood.

"But I have to confess to you something."

"And what is that, Mandy."

"I have been frightened to death to talk to you. Even if I could have caught you right after church to say hi, I think I would have been too scared to try. I was not sure that you wanted to talk to me."

"How do you feel about that now, Mandy?"

"I feel like old friends should feel after they have had a long period of separation. I feel good being with you. I am glad you are not still angry. At least it seems that you aren't."

Their eyes again met, and they gazed at each other for a few moments before Bobby spoke. "Of course I am not angry, Mandy. I have nothing to be angry about. You are the one who should be mad. I am glad you contacted me, and I am very glad to be here with you tonight. But I have this feeling that there is something more that you want to tell me—that you have a reason to see me other than just catching up with an old friend."

Mandy immediately began to look around until she spotted the jukebox that was in the corner on the opposite side of the restaurant. She then responded, "Bobby, let's take a breather from the heavy talk for awhile and just relax. You know you owe me another dance here," she said pointing to the jukebox.

"Oh, come on, Mandy, you can't be serious. There is little room to dance, and this really isn't the place to do that anyway."

"What's the matter, Bobby Childs? Are you afraid you can't keep up? Or maybe I will leave you in the dust like I used to at old Wazzu?"

Mandy then went over to the jukebox and paid for one song. It was a rocker from the past with a nice lively beat—perfect for a couple who had enjoyed dance lessons together in college and who loved to dance old style dances like the jitterbug.

"Come on now, Bobby Childs. This is for old time's sake."

So Bobby got out of his seat, walked over to Mandy, who was moving to the music in the middle of an aisle and they began to dance together. Mandy had not lost her step and ability to move and swing to the music, but Bobby was rusty in the moves. Yet, together they danced like two young children playing with each other in an open field on a summer day. The small number of customers at the restaurant began to take notice and smiled in amusement as they saw the couple swing and move to the beat.

In the middle of the dance Bobby began to notice the words of the song:

But I want you to know after all these years;
You're still the one I want whispering in my ears;
You're still the one who makes me laugh;
Still the one that's my better half;
We're still having fun and you're still the one.

Mandy began to notice the words too as they danced, and then she looked at Bobby and began to sing along. Bobby joined in singing, "We're still having fun, and you're still the one."

When the song ended, they laughed and hugged each other as the small crowd of patrons applauded. They were ready to talk about more serious matters and went back to their table for a few moments to finish their meal. Bobby spoke next.

"OK, Mandy, I know there are some serious things on your mind; I am ready to hear now. But before you start in, I want to thank you for being with me tonight. In some ways I feel like nothing has changed. On the other hand, of course, things have changed. How could they not have? That was a pretty nasty way in which we parted."

"Bobby, I am not here to spew anger, and I have no vendetta against you at all. I wish you the best. I always have." She paused for a few moments to catch her breath before continuing. "And I know you probably won't want to see me after tonight. That's OK. I don't expect things to really ever be the way they were, but I have some very important things to tell you, so please try to be patient and listen to me for awhile."

Bobby gulped hard and drew a deep breath. "I am ready, Mandy. Tell me what you have to say. Don't hold back. I want to hear everything on your mind."

"Bobby, I need to speak to Jason. I have something very important to give him, and I need to warn him."

"Warn him? About what? Now, listen, Mandy, this isn't the time to play with his head. We have the Super Bowl coming up, and he needs his full attention on that."

Mandy paused for a moment, collected her thoughts, and then continued. "I knew you would react that way at first, but let me try to explain why this is so urgent. I have been getting calls from a reporter asking all sorts of questions about you, Jason, me, and even Rachel."

Bobby was beginning to feel angry. "Who in the world is this reporter?"

"He said his name was Sammy Jensen. I don't read the papers much, so I didn't recognize the name at first. Now I understand that he has a popular sports column and wants to do a series of articles on you and Jason before the Super Bowl."

"Sammy? What is he up to that he would want to talk to you? I have talked to him quite a bit the last few weeks. Yes, he is doing a series of articles on Jason and me as part of the Super Bowl hype, that's all. Jason hates the guy and refuses to talk with him, but I don't have a problem with him. So this shouldn't be a big deal."

"I think it is. He has been very insistent when talking to me. After my initial discussions with him I have refused to say anything more. I think he intends to do harm to both you and Jason—but particularly to Jason."

"Now why do you say that?"

"Well, first he seemed to know everything about us. He asked about our relationship, and he asked if I had ever seen Dr. Barton in Spokane for anything."

"Who in the Sam Hill is Dr. Barton, and what does that have to do with these articles?" Bobby replied sounding more than just a little annoyed.

Mandy became quiet and waited for what seemed to be an eternity. Finally, she spoke, and her voice began to quiver. "Dr. Barton is the doctor your dad set me up with to see in the spring of our junior year."

Bobby was stunned. It finally hit him what Sammy's true agenda in his articles might be. Jason had never trusted Sammy, and Bobby now understood. Sammy was more of a tabloid reporter who wanted to dig up dirt on people than a true sports reporter, and now it appeared that Sammy wanted to trash both him and Jason in a series of articles on the eve of the Super Bowl.

"Well, if you haven't talked to him about it, then he has nothing to write, so we shouldn't worry at all."

"Not quite, Bobby. I wish that were so."

"What do you mean?"

"Well, Jim, my ex, called me last week. He was surprisingly very friendly; although, it was clear he was drunker than a skunk when he called. He began to trash you and Jason and the Seahawks in general."

"I thought you said he was a Seahawks fan."

"He is a football fan but, as I said before, he was insanely jealous of you since you had been part of my past. When you arrived at Seattle to play, we had been divorced only a short time, and Jim's attitude toward the Seahawks changed. My few communications with him were short, but they always included a tirade from him about what a loser you are and how he hated the Seahawks for playing you and Jason."

"OK, so your ex is a stupid bum. What does that have to do with Sammy Jensen trashing us in the newspapers?"

Mandy realized she just had to spill it out, so with a deliberate voice, she looked into Bobby's eyes and slowly stated, "Bobby, Jim knows all about you and me. He knows about Dr. Barton. And he knows all about

Jason and Rachel. He has obviously talked to Sammy and filled him in on the details."

"What? How does he know this, and are you sure he has said anything?"

"Jim was my husband, Bobby. I tried to share everything about me with him. I thought that was what husbands and wives could do with each other. I had wounds that I needed to talk about. Discussion of my past was not off limits. My relationship with you, with Rachel, and with Jason were all talked about. He knows everything."

Mandy paused again for a moment. She then said with a great deal of emotion in her voice, "And he knows about Dr. Barton."

"So, how do you know that he has talked to Sammy Jensen about this?"

"When Jim called me he began to tell me that he was a very important person. He said that you were not such a big shot and that he had information to take you down. I just thought he was out of his head because he was so drunk, but then he told me that he had been talking to Sammy about Jason and you and that he had told him everything he knew. He then cruelly laughed and hung up the phone."

"Well, like you said, he was drunk. Surely, Jensen is too professional to take the word of such a guy. I don't think Sammy would stoop that low to write a trashy tabloid piece based upon this kind of information."

"Let me continue," responded Mandy. "A day later Sammy called me. He began to ask a lot of questions about Jason and Rachel. And he wanted to know about you and me. He wanted to know about our personal life, and yes, he had the audacity to ask about our sex life."

"That guy is slime! I should have listened to Jason about him. I trust you didn't say anything."

"Of course not! I told him to bug off and that I wouldn't talk. But before he hung up he asked me one question that sent chills down my spine. He asked me if I had ever seen Dr. Barton for any medical problem."

"And what did you say?"

"I lied and said I did not know who Dr. Barton was."

"And?"

Mandy's voice began to quiver with emotion. She fought back the tears and responded. "He laughed and said that my medical records tell a different story. Then he hung up."

"Now why would he have access to your medical records? They are confidential."

"A few years after I saw Dr. Barton, I decided that I wanted to sue him for malpractice. I was an emotional basket case and he had not informed me of the aftermath results that could happen after my kind of surgery. I never did follow through with a suit, but I sought out a lawyer to review my claim. The lawyer was in Jim's law firm, and my file in the firm has all my medical records. Jim has seen them and undoubtedly has copies. I think he has provided copies to Sammy Jensen."

Bobby sat very still taking this all in. He was speechless and angry. But he was not sure with whom he should be angry. Should he lash out at Mandy for coming back into his life and once again playing with his emotions and mind? Should he be furious at her ex-husband who seemed hell-bent on destroying him and his friend Jason—two men he had never even met? Or, should he just be angry at himself for the life he had lived, for the cover-up that had taken place, and for the way he had so brutally injured Mandy Brooks emotionally?

Bobby began to ramble. "I am taking this all in Mandy and trying to be calm. We can't stop Jensen from writing what he wants. He has been part of the Seattle sports media forever and is respected. Actually, I have a hard time believing that he wants to destroy the Seahawks right now. This is our big moment. It is Seattle's big moment. He is also a big Seahawks fan. Why would he want to hurt us now? It doesn't make sense. I think he just wants to write some kind of dramatic piece that will sell a lot of papers. I have to believe that these stories are going to portray both Jason and me as sports stars and heroes."

Mandy composed herself and drew a big breath before she spoke again. She looked at Bobby Childs and remembered those words "trust me" that he had spoken to her once long ago. She also remembered that he had betrayed that trust. She thought of the lonely nights after their breakup and her departure from the university. She thought of her financial struggle to survive until she married, and then she reminded herself of her painful marriage and of the isolation of being a single parent. All of these things in her past would have been different if, in fact, Bobby had been a person who was trustworthy.

As she sat in the restaurant thinking of what she should say next, she realized that a major choice was in front of her. She could get up from the table, thank Bobby for his time, and then walk out of his life for good. If she did her conscience would be clear, and she would be at peace knowing that she had done all she could to warn him and Jason of what was coming against both of them. On the other hand, she could one more time take a risk and trust Bobby with the additional information she needed to tell him.

Mandy cleared her throat and began to talk but abruptly stopped as she noticed two familiar people walk into the restaurant. It was her father and her young ten-year-old son. Mandy's countenance immediately changed and a big sunny smile engulfed her face. Bobby instantaneously noticed the change and looked toward the door as Mandy called out to address the two who had entered the restaurant.

"Hey, what a surprise to see you two here! Come on over and let me introduce you to an old friend." Mandy got up from her seat and went immediately to her dad and son and gave them both a big hug. They then went back to her table, and she introduced them to Bobby. Mandy's dad spoke. "It is such a pleasure to meet you Mr. Childs. You and Jason O'Connor have thrilled this city in a way never before felt." He then turned to Mandy and said, "Honey, I am sorry for interrupting." He then pointed to the young boy beside him and said with a big smile, "It is just that this young man couldn't stand the thought of not meeting his hero knowing you were with him. So he talked me into coming just for a few moments to say hi."

Bobby Childs smiled and breathed easily. He was thankful for the reprieve from a very emotional and stressful conversation. He looked down at the youngster who was staring at him intently without saying a word and holding a football close to his chest.

"Well, your mom tells me that you are a wide receiver too. Is that right?"

"Yes, sir. I caught a touchdown pass in my last game and we won."

"Good for you. Hey, give me that ball, and let me sign it for you."

As Bobby reached for a pen in his shirt pocket, the young boy handed over the football with a gleam in his eyes. Mandy and her dad looked on, smiling broadly as they witnessed a dream come true for this little guy who was so much a part of their lives.

"Well, so tell me as I write, what is your name?"

"It is Bobby, sir. My name is Bobby Harrison."

Bobby Child's hands immediately began to quiver, and he could hardly write. He briefly looked at Mandy. Their eyes connected, and the look given deeply penetrated each of them. This look told Bobby the truth as he struggled to complete the autograph.

"Well, Bobby Harrison, I hope that you are going to root us on to victory against the Steelers," he said as he handed the ball back to the youngster. "So what do ya think? Can we take them?"

Young Bobby continued to stare and finally blurted out. "Oh yes, sir. I think you will win by three touchdowns. And you and Jason O'Connor are going to be on fire."

Bobby Childs laughed and then responded. "I hope you are right buddy. Tell you what; if we do win by three touchdowns then it is dinner on me for you, your mom, and me. A deal?"

"Wow! Really? OK. It's a deal!" Young Bobby shouted and then gave Bobby Childs a high five before his mother stepped in to interrupt.

"OK, dad, thanks for coming, but it is time to get Bobby home. I know he has an early school day tomorrow and needs to get his sleep."

"Right, honey. We need to go. Have fun catching up, and I will take care of the youngster here. Mr. Childs, it has been a real pleasure. A wonderful treat for Bobby and me to meet you."

As they shook hands, Bobby responded, "The pleasure is all mine sir. Thanks for coming, and Bobby, remember, we got dinner if we come through like you predicted."

After they left, Bobby sat speechless for a few moments, looking out a window at the night traffic. Mandy sat patiently waiting for him to speak. He was frightened to ask her the major question on his mind. Finally, he spoke.

"So your son's name is Bobby. How come you didn't name him after his dad?"

Mandy grabbed Bobby's hand and looked him squarely in the eyes. "Bobby, I did name him after his father." She paused as tears came to her eyes. Her voice quivered as she continued. "I told you that he loves football—just like his daddy. He takes after him in everyway. He even plays the same position as his daddy."

Bobby was now paralyzed. He could not move. He could not talk. He could hardly breathe. He sat staring into Mandy's eyes for the longest time. He could not even smile. He simply could not respond.

"I was pregnant with him when I walked away from you that night at the fraternity house. I didn't know it for sure at the time; although, I suspected it might be true. I went home to live with my dad, and he looked after me during my pregnancy. Dad doesn't know who the father is. I didn't tell him, and he didn't bother to ask. My dad is a really good man even though he was quite distant from me after my mom died, and he was left to raise me alone."

"So, why is his last name Harrison?"

"My ex is Jim Harrison. After we got married Bobby went by that name. Bobby was only two when we married."

"And he never was adopted?"

"No, Jim didn't even like Bobby taking the last name. Jim never accepted Bobby at all. He emotionally and physically abused him. Harrison was my name at the time. I changed back to my maiden name after the divorce, but while we lived together as a family it was convenient that we all shared the last name."

Finally, Bobby gained his composure and began to speak very forcefully.

"OK, Mandy, so what is it you want from me? Ten years ago you ran off and had a child of mine without letting me know. Ten years go by, and

I don't hear a peep from you— not a word. And now on the eve of the biggest event in my sports career, you show up and simply lay unbelievable news on me. So what is it, Mandy? You want money? Sure, that's it isn't it? You know I am now a big shot pro football player with a lot of money, and now it is your time to dig up some gold? Is that it, Mandy. You better come clean with me lady. Tell me the truth!"

Tears were now streaming down Mandy's cheeks as she tried desperately to compose herself and respond. Her voice shook with emotion as she answered the angry charges leveled at her.

"First, Bobby, please believe me when I say that I did not invite my dad to come tonight and bring Bobby with him. I was very surprised they came. That is the truth."

"Yeah, right, Mandy Brooks, and I am also an all-pro defensive tackle. Now neither of these statements are true, and you know it!"

"No, you are wrong. I did not plan on telling you about your son. This was not the reason I wanted to talk with you. I am not here to ask for money. I have lived without your money for ten years, and I will continue to do so. I did not come to black mail you. I came to see an old friend and give him some information that I thought was important. You have to believe me because it is true."

"Why should I believe you, Mandy? Why didn't you contact me with this information long ago? Why are you doing this at this time? Jason warned me not to see you. He said that you were going to mess with my mind and you know something? He was right! I should have listened to him."

Despite the tears rolling down her cheeks, Mandy continued to respond to the accusations.

"Bobby, just listen to me. I know you are angry and upset. Maybe you have a right to be. Maybe I should have told you about Bobby long ago. But I was afraid to do so. My experience with Dr. Barton tore my heart apart. I hated him. I hated you, and I believed you hated me too. My life has been in a downward spiral since, and now the information about me seeing him is about to go public unless you can stop Sammy Jensen from writing about it. But please believe me when I tell you that I never planned to bring up our son to you at all. I did not intend to tell you tonight. That was not in my plans. You don't have to see me again if you don't want. I won't blame you if that is what you decide. But you have to at least hear me out. I have not said everything I need to say."

"OK, Mandy, what other surprises do you have in store for me tonight?"

"I have to see and talk with Jason. It can't wait."

Bobby's voice rose dramatically as he responded, "Why in Sam Hill do you want to talk to him? He won't talk to you. I know that for a fact. He warned me about you, and I should have listened."

"I have something to give to him. It is from Rachel. He must have it immediately."

Bobby had heard enough. He put a fifty dollar bill on the table to pay the bill, and then got up to leave. He began to make his way to the front of the restaurant without saying anything more to Mandy. He was angry that he had taken the time to see her, and he was not going to pull his friend Jason O'Connor into this at all. Whatever Mandy wanted to give to Jason would have to wait until after the Super Bowl. Bobby headed out the restaurant toward his car with Mandy following close behind pleading with him to listen to her.

"Bobby, please you must listen to me. It is important. I promise I will not bother you again if you just listen and help me see Jason. That is all I ask."

As he reached his car, Bobby turned around, looked sternly at Mandy, and replied, "OK, so what is so important that cannot wait? And how dare you try to bring Rachel Thomlinson into this. She is gone. We all were very wounded by that, but the wounds have healed and it is time to move on. I cannot imagine anything you have from Rachel that would be important enough to give to Jason now. Don't you understand how much you would be messing with his head? And don't you understand how much you have messed up my head tonight?

Mandy struggled to gain her composure as Bobby Childs stared coldly into her face. She took a deep breath and responded as deliberately as she could.

"Bobby, I have a letter that Rachel wrote to Jason shortly before she died. The envelope has been sealed. I do not know exactly what the letter says, but I know the basic contents of it. It is extremely important that Jason have this information now."

"And how do you know what is in the letter if you have not read it?"

"About a week before the accident, I was home visiting from school and saw her. Rachel told me she had written this letter to Jason but was not sure whether to send it or not. She showed me the sealed envelope and asked me to keep it until she decided what to do. She felt that if I kept the letter she would have time to think about sending it and would be prevented from mailing it out of emotion. She really wanted to do the right thing and was conflicted as to whether this should be given to him. A week later she died, and I kept the envelope not knowing what to do. Jim urged me to destroy it, but I never felt that I should. Deep inside I thought that someday Jason would want to know about it."

"So you kept it all this time? You never opened the envelope? Are you sure you know what the letter is about even though you have never read it?"

"I am very sure, Bobby. Rachel and I had a long conversation about it when she gave it to me."

"Again, why is this so important now? Can't we just bury the past and move on?"

"Bobby, I think that Jensen is going to write about some things that are in this letter. Jim knew about the letter and its contents. I am sure that he has told Sammy Jensen all about it. Jason must be warned. He has to know!"

"So why don't you tell me what the letter says? I will be the judge of that. I am not going to sabotage my friend with this until I am sure he needs to hear the information."

"Bobby, you will know what the letter says sooner or later, but I will not tell you until after I give this to Jason in person. That will allow me to explain some things to him. And I will not open this letter and read it to you or anybody. It must be read by Jason alone because that is what Rachel wanted."

Bobby Childs stared coldly at Mandy for a few moments. As he gazed at her he began to look into her eyes and his stern look began to soften. He looked at her beautiful face and sparkling eyes and began to remind himself of how he had abandoned her. He thought of their son who had lived ten years without knowing his father, and he began to understand how terribly lonely Mandy must have been all of those years trapped in a loveless marriage having to raise her son without the help and guidance of a caring companion.

A moment of decision had now arrived. Bobby could get in his car and drive away and, in doing so, walk away forever from a woman whom he knew he still loved and with whom he had sired a child, or he could finally face his responsibilities to her and to their son. He could finally be a man and offer comfort and protection. He could finally become a knight in shining armor that rescues his damsel in distress, and he could protect his friend Jason O'Connor from being sabotaged by a vicious reporter who wanted nothing more than to write about scandal and destroy reputations.

Bobby's eyes softened considerably as he looked at Mandy. She stood in front of him teary-eyed and pleading with him to grant her request. After a few moments of quiet soul-searching, he spoke.

"OK, Mandy, I will talk to Jason tomorrow and try to convince him to see you. I know he has an interview with Jensen on Wednesday after practice, and I am not sure that we can see him before then. I can only ask."

"Will you tell him how important it is? Will you tell him that he doesn't have to talk to me ever again? Just let him know that I need to give him this letter and explain. After that, I will be out of both of your lives forever."

"I will tell him, Mandy." Bobby paused for a moment and then continued. "And what ever gave you the impression that I wanted you out of my life forever?" He then softly stroked Mandy's long flowing brunette hair and said, "Don't you think that we have a lot of catching up to do?"

Mandy looked into his eyes. With her voice quivering and tears filling her eyes she said, "Oh Bobby, you should have seen their little hearts beating. They were so precious. They were so very precious." She then fell into his arms, buried her face into his chest, and sobbed uncontrollably.

With tears in his eyes Bobby responded, "I'm sure they were, Mandy. I am sure they were."

CHAPTER 8

Sammy Jensen had been a sports reporter with the *Seattle Post-Intelligencer* for more than twenty-five years. Growing up in Seattle, he had attended the University of Washington and graduated with a degree in journalism. As a student, his ambition was to be a muckraking reporter who uncovered scandal and, in so doing, helped rid the nation and the world of both corporate and political corruption.

Sammy went to journalism school during the Watergate era and admired Robert Woodward and Carl Bernstein, the two reporters from the *Washington Post* who uncovered political scandal and brought down a president. Nearly every journalism student during that time period fantasized about uncovering some widespread outrage and, by bringing it to the light of public scrutiny, achieving a more just society. Jensen was no exception.

After graduation from college, Sammy was frustrated in his pursuit of a glorified muckraking journalistic career. He had been only an average student at the university, with mediocre grades, and offers of employment were non-existent. He briefly interned with a large metropolitan newspaper in the mid-west but was offered no permanent position. He returned to Seattle in hopes of landing a job as a political commentator with one of the city's major newspapers, only to be rebuffed in his efforts. He finally took a temporary job as a sports reporter for a small weekly paper in a Seattle suburb, covering the high school sporting events of the community.

It was a less than fulfilling job for him. Sammy dreamed of writing big journalistic scoops and uncovering slimy deeds of political cronies undertaken out of the light of public scrutiny. Instead, he found himself reporting on a weekly basis the facts about high school athletes. Only the parents of these kids ever cared about what he wrote, and even then such stories would be forgotten within a day or so after going to print. The longer he stayed at this job, the more frustrated he became. He saw himself as destined to be a significant player in the shaping of public attitudes and political trends. He did not see himself as a sports reporter covering touchdowns, baskets and balls, and strikes. Yet, that is where he found himself.

He continued to seek employment as a political commentator, but opportunities did not come his way. After a few years of sports reporting at the small local paper, Sammy was offered a job with the *Seattle Post-Intelligencer*, a daily, to cover the metropolitan high school sports. With this offer of employment, he finally abandoned his dream of being a muckraking reporter fighting corruption. The new position was a far cry from what Sammy's ambitions had desired; yet, it allowed him to refine his reporting and writing abilities. Eventually, Sammy began to cover and report on the major pro sports franchises in the area and finally, he began to do a bi-weekly sports column that allowed him to express his opinions on matters.

After a year of writing and expressing his views, his column—"Sammy's Corner"— began to attract a loyal readership. Sammy's opinions could sometimes be very biting. His critical and unrelenting, negative reviews eventually eroded public confidence in two head football coaches at the University of Washington who were forced to step down. He also had a great deal of influence in the periodic decisions of Seattle area pro sports franchises to trade certain players as well as whom to draft. Seahawks Coach Paul Wagner was a big reader of Sammy's column. Knowing the influence he had over public opinion, Wagner made extra efforts to stay on his good side.

However, Sammy and Paul Wagner began to butt heads when Wagner traded for Jason O'Connor. Jensen felt that O'Connor had been a colossal failure in the NFL and was not worth the effort and money that the Seahawks were ready to invest for his development. For weeks after the trade Sammy's columns hammered away. He slammed Wagner for making the trade and for, in Sammy's opinion, "throwing down the toilet the support of the loyal Seahawks fans."

Wagner further antagonized Jensen when he benched Zach Morrison for Jason. Of that decision Sammy wrote:

Perhaps, I am just too mentally slow to understand certain things in the world of professional football. I certainly am limited in my own understanding of the strategic thinking and logic behind some sports trades. For the most part, however, I understand that a trade in professional football is always a gamble, and sometimes the experts simply know more than us common folk.

While I was critical of the trade that brought Jason O'Connor to Seattle, I have come to accept it, desiring to believe that the Seahawks front office just knows more about these things than I do. However, for the life of me, the recent benching of Zach Morrison for Jason O'Connor makes absolutely no sense.

Morrison is a veteran, perhaps even a Hall of Famer, and one of the few bright spots on a mediocre Seahawks football team. Jason O'Connor is the biggest bust of any draft choice in the history of the NFL. Morrison is having another banner year, despite the team's mediocre record. It is not his fault that the team isn't doing better. Maybe if Paul Wagner would trade for a few decent offensive linemen to protect Morrison, things would be different. Instead, Wagner decided to go for a former college hot shot that has produced absolutely nothing in the world of professional football.

Welcome to the big leagues, Jason. This isn't old Wazzu—it is the NFL. Jason O'Connor has shown no promise other than to be a sophomoric cheerleader on the sidelines during the Seahawks games. So what gives here, Wagner? Have you completely lost it, or am I just too dense to understand what seems to be obvious to you.

When Jason immediately began to lead the Seahawks to victory after victory, Jensen cooled his negative rhetoric considerably, but he never directly apologized for his harsh criticism of the decision to trade for Jason and eventually play him as the starter. Instead, Sammy's columns aimed its arrows at Jason's character and ability to win the big game. After the Seahawks' only loss to St. Louis in the current season, Sammy wrote, "Jason O'Connor is a gifted man. He is blessed with God-given physical prowess and athletic abilities. His physical stature is one only enjoyed by the mythical gods of the Greeks. Perfectly sculpted and blessed with speed and strength, this man would seem to have it all. Sadly, however, he is an underachiever of the highest magnitude. One must ask the tough questions about Jason O'Connor. When has he led his team to victory in the big game? When it is really on the line and matters, what has he accomplished? To date, absolutely nothing! Let's hope that this season will be different, but yesterday's loss to St. Louis does not give us reason to be optimistic."

Jason was outraged by the column and incensed that Sammy seemed to want to continue to pile on him. When Sammy later called him to ask for an interview about the St. Louis loss, Jason was terse in his response.

"Why would I want to talk to you? You write what you want, and I will prove you wrong." With that comment Jason hung up the phone.

As the Seahawks renewed their winning ways after the loss to St. Louis, Sammy's columns grew more complimentary, even if grudgingly so. O'Connor's league-leading statistics were just too overwhelming to ignore, and even "Sammy's Corner" had to acknowledge that Jason just might be the best quarterback in the NFL. Although recognizing in his columns O'Connor's superior ability to score points on the board and run up fabulous game statistics, Sammy continued to raise doubts about Jason's ability to win in the big game. Such misgivings became the underlying thoughts of Seahawks fans during halftime of the conference championship game with the St. Louis Rams.

During the Seahawks winning streak, Sammy began to take an interest in the relationship between O'Connor and Childs—whom he officially dubbed "the dynamic duo." He became fascinated with their friendship and wanted to know what made it tick. He decided to investigate the relationship starting from its beginnings at Washington State University. His initial desire was to simply write a series of columns reporting on the polar opposite roots of Bobby and Jason and how these two superb athletes joined forces in a brotherhood to bring thrills to Seattle sports fans. The name of the series would be simply "The Brotherhood."

As Sammy dug into their past, however, he began to piece together a picture of two wild and crazy college guys who were obsessed with football, partying, and women— in that order. This was truer of Bobby than of Jason, but, nonetheless, it seemed to be a common theme describing both of their collegiate lives. Sammy liked this slant for his series of articles and believed that it would put a face on both Jason and Bobby of which the public was unaware. So, he methodically went about calling sources to find names of people who knew both men or could provide information on them for his articles.

In his research, Sammy was able to call many old friends of O'Connor and Childs. Some were teammates on the Washington State football team and others were acquaintances from college. Some knew both men very well and lived with them in the fraternity. Others had more limited knowledge but were able to steer Sammy in the right direction. That direction led to Mandy Brooks.

Sammy first made contact with Mandy one week prior to the conference championship game against St. Louis. He was not sure what to ask her, so he simply decided to pretend that he had information regarding Bobby and Jason that he wanted her to verify. The conversation was a pure bluff on Sammy's part, but it paid off as far as obtaining leads. When Sammy obtained her name and was told that she lived in Seattle, he went to the phone directory and came across a "M. Brooks" with a local listing. He dialed the number hoping that he would have success.

"Hello, may I speak to Mandy Brooks please?"

"This is she. How can I help you?"

"Ms. Brooks, it is so nice to speak with you. My name is Sammy Jensen, and I am a sports reporter with the *Seattle Post-Intelligencer*. Perhaps you have read my column that we call 'Sammy's Corner.'"

Mandy had not followed sports since leaving Wazzu, but somehow did recognize the name. She responded, "I believe I know who you are. But why are you calling me? I don't really have much to do with sports these days."

Sammy chuckled and continued. "Well, you are in the same place as most of the public. But I was told that you might help me with some information I am seeking. I am writing a series of columns that will be published in a few weeks about Jason O'Connor and Bobby Childs. I understand that you knew them both in college at Washington State University. Did I call right Mandy Brooks?"

Mandy froze and could not talk. She was aware that both Jason and Bobby were playing in Seattle with the Seahawks, and she had seen Bobby sneak in and out of church lately, but she went out of her way to avoid knowing anything more about either of them. Her memories of the past were too painful to talk about. She immediately became suspicious of Sammy Jensen and his intentions. Mandy remained silent.

"Hello, Ms. Brooks? Are you still there?"

Mandy swallowed hard and answered. "Yes, sorry, I had something caught in my throat and was trying to clear it. I didn't want to do that over the phone and be rude."

Sammy chuckled again. "I appreciate it. But as I was asking, did you know Jason O'Connor and Bobby Childs in college?"

"Most certainly. I dated Bobby for a few years and Jason dated my best friend Rachel Thomlinson." Mandy immediately knew that she had said too much.

"Really? Well, very good, then I think you can probably help me in my research. Do you mind if I ask the nature of your relationship with Bobby Childs?"

Mandy now became defiant and a bit hostile. "It is none of your business, sir. What does that have to do with football and the Seahawks? We broke up ten years ago and haven't talked since."

"Well, sorry ma'am, I am not trying to pry. I just wanted to verify the level of your relationship so I would know how credible my sources are."

Mandy grew more hostile. "How credible your sources are? What are you trying to do? Create some scandal and write about it to sell papers? I don't think I will talk to you anymore. My past with Bobby Childs is the past, and I intend to keep it that way."

Sammy realized that he was about to lose an important source of information so he had to think fast to keep Mandy from hanging up on him. He attempted his "humble servant of the people approach"—a tactic that usually worked to obtain additional information from a source.

"Ms. Brooks, I am so very sorry if I have offended you. Please forgive me, but you have read me wrong. The whole city is thrilled about the Seahawks, and Jason O'Connor and Bobby Childs are the toast of the town. My articles are going to highlight them and their remarkable sports accomplishments. I just want to make sure that my story is accurate. The people who read my column deserve the highest level of integrity from me when I report facts, so I have to verify them with reliable sources. You certainly understand that, don't you?"

Mandy was not budging, but she remained on the line. What she briefly said next she would come to regret..

"Of course, I understand. Just like I understood when my ex-husband Jim would come home drunk from work and tell me that he had been drinking to relieve the stress from his work day. He expected me to understand that too."

Sammy again chuckled but saw an opening that he had to follow-up on before he let Mandy hang up. "Yes, that is always the case with guys who drink too much. They find some way to justify their behavior but please, Ms. Brooks, don't put me in the category of your alcoholic ex-husband, what did you say his name was, Jim Larsen?"

"Jim Harrison. He's a very prominent attorney in town, but I am not going to tell you about that relationship either. So please just leave me alone, and don't call me again."

With her response Mandy hung up the phone, but she knew she had given Sammy too much information. Upon hanging up Sammy smiled and went to the telephone directory to find the number for Jim Harrison. It was listed under "Attorneys" with the law firm of "Michelson, Radley, and Harrison." He quickly dialed.

"Michelson, Radley, and Harrison, attorneys at law. How may I direct your call?"

"Mr. Jim Harrison, please."

"And whom may I say is calling?"

"Sammy Jensen. I am a reporter from the *Seattle Post-Intelligencer*."

"Please hold, Mr. Jensen. Mr. Harrison will be right with you."

The beginning of their conversation was brief and to the point. Jim Harrison was a rude person who did not like to be side tracked, but once he understood the nature of Sammy's inquiries, he became more engaged in the call.

Sammy wanted to know information about Mandy and her relationship with Bobby Childs. He wanted to obtain additional information about Jason and his relationship with Rachel Thomlinson. Jim Harrison, still very bitter about his hostile divorce with Mandy, was more than anxious to provide Sammy with as much information as he had. And he had plenty to give.

Sammy was overwhelmed at his discovery. A source like Jim Harrison comes along rarely in a journalist's career. Harrison provided Sammy with information, which, if verified, would turn his series of articles into real prime-time reading. His only concern was whether Harrison could document the matters. Sammy had to keep in mind that although Harrison was a prominent attorney, he was also an alcoholic whose judgments and perceptions could be seriously skewed.

"OK, so you tell me that you have the medical records of Mandy Brooks at your office?" Sammy inquired.

"Yes, sir. Her file contains all her medical records and indicates that she was clearly treated by Barton. I will fax the pertinent records to you as long as I remain an undisclosed and confidential source."

"Of course you are. I won't do business with you any other way. Whatever happened to Barton anyway?"

"He eventually lost his license to practice medicine. I guess there were too many malpractice complaints against him and the state board removed his license."

"Where is he now?"

"Who knows? The last I heard he was living it up in the Bahamas. He made a lot of money in his practice."

"You can verify that he lost his license to practice medicine?"

"All you have to do is call the state medical licensing board. They will verify it for you."

"Can you get possession of the letter that Rachel Thomlinson wrote to Jason O'Connor to verify what you have told me?"

"That is much more problematic. Mandy kept that letter in our home safe, locked up. When we split Mandy took the letter with her. I never thought about the need to take the letter and copy it. But that letter deals with a case that was highly sensational and had a lot of publicity around it ten years ago. I know that your newspaper covered the story. You can go and look it up in your paper's archives."

"Well, sure but those stories won't provide the link to O'Connor and Rachel Thomlinson. Only this letter will."

"I wish I could get it for you. But I would have to commit a felony to break into her house and retrieve it. I am not willing to do that. I think if you call her back and are a little coy with what you know, she just may spill the beans and verify this."

"OK, Jim. I will work on it at my end. I assume you will be available if I have further questions."

"Count on it."

"Thanks again. You have been extremely helpful."

A day later Sammy received by fax Mandy's medical records from her visit to Dr. Barton. They confirmed everything that Jim had told him. Sammy was beginning to smell a big story, and his journalistic juices were heating up. Maybe, he thought, after all the years of being just a sports reporter, he had finally hit on a big breaking news story that transcended sports. He began to imagine how he would portray O'Connor and Childs—his two main characters in the plot. They were heroes in the Seattle community, and heroes they would remain in his articles. But all heroes have flaws. All heroes are human. All heroes have dark secrets that they are hiding. O'Connor and Childs were no different. Sammy surmised that the public had a right to know about these two. It was public support that made them millionaires and celebrities. Thus, the public had an unshakeable, fundamental right to know all the details about the celebrities that their hard-earned dollars paid for. This includes both the bad and scandalous details as well as the good information.

After reviewing Mandy's medical records Sammy picked up the phone to call her again. This time he planned to be more forceful; although, he would not tell her exactly what he knew. His goal was to pull information out of her. His demeanor was cold and calculating in assessing his strategy when the phone rang and she answered.

"Hello again, Ms. Brooks, this is Sammy Jensen from the *Seattle Post-Intelligencer.* I am hoping that we can continue the discussion we had the other day."

"I am not sure there is anything to discuss. I told you that I haven't seen Bobby for ten years and discussing my past with him is off limits to you."

"I am not trying to pry. I just want to understand and verify some information I have received from others. So please bear with me if you don't mind."

Mandy was now beginning to panic. After thinking about her previous conversation with Sammy, she was very certain that he had made an attempt to call her ex-husband. She knew that Jim Harrison would relish the thought of providing embarrassing and scandalous information to the press about her and Bobby Childs. Jim hated Bobby, and this would give him sweet revenge over her from the financial pounding he took in their vicious divorce proceedings. Her heart was pounding rapidly as she contemplated hanging up the phone without responding.

"You are quiet and not talking. I know you think I am up to no good, but I just want to assure you that I do not mean to bring harm to you, Bobby Childs, or Jason O'Connor by my articles. These articles are going to be an in-depth series discussing the lives of the two newest and biggest sports stars in our area. I just need you to tell me a bit more so I can confirm my stories."

Mandy responded, "OK, Mr. Jensen. What do you want to ask me?"

"Well, I understand that Jason had a girlfriend Rachel Thomlinson who was your best friend and that she tragically died in an auto accident Jason's senior year."

"Yes, Rachel was the best friend I have ever had in the whole world."

"How do you think her death affected Jason and Bobby?"

"What do you mean?"

"Well, the Rose Bowl that following January was probably the poorest performances that both of them gave in any football game. It appeared that their heads were not into the game at all. And frankly, until they came to Seattle, their play in the NFL was far below expectations. Do you think the trauma of her death had something to do with all of this?"

"Possibly. But I am not certain because I broke things off with Bobby the night Rachel died and have not talked with him since."

"Why did you break things off? He had nothing to do with her death."

"Bobby and I were not doing well together for several months. We had been fighting a lot anyway. He betrayed my trust. His response to Rachel's death that night set me off. I determined that I was finished with him for good after that."

"And what about Jason's response? "

"I haven't talked with Jason since then either. I assume that her death hit him pretty hard and probably had an impact on his performance in the Rose Bowl."

"Is there some secret that Rachel was keeping from Jason at the time of her death?"

Mandy was stunned at the question. She now knew that Sammy had been talking with her ex-husband because only Jim Harrison would know such information. She was not sure how to answer and became agitated that she had even started talking with Sammy in the first place.

"I am not going to talk about Rachel with you, so drop it."

"OK, but can I ask you one more thing about your relationship with Bobby Childs?"

"Ask if you want. I am not sure I will answer."

"Did you have a child with him?"

Mandy was stunned by the question. Jensen aggressively continued his questioning.

"Everyone I have talked to about this said that Bobby Childs was quite verbal and explicit about his sexual escapades with you. Do you deny that you and he were sexually involved and produced a child out of wedlock?"

Mandy now was trapped. To respond would be an admission of her deepest secret and would allow it to go public. Yet, she was now certain that Sammy had the information on her son and that she probably could not stop him from printing it. Not even her dad knew who had sired her son, and her precious boy, little Bobby, did not know the truth about who his real father was. It now appeared that all would be brought to light and that the two most important people in the world to her, her dad and her son, would be hurt.

"You are getting too personal, Mr. Jensen, and I think we are going to end this call now."

"Oh, please, I don't mean to personally attack you. That is not my intention, Ms. Brooks. You are not the person of interest here, but I do think that the public has a right to know if Bobby Childs is a deadbeat dad who has failed to support his son for ten years."

Mandy remained silent while Sammy continued his interrogation. "Did you ever seek medical treatment from a Dr. Barton in Spokane?"

"Who? I don't know a Dr. Barton."

Sammy snickered a wicked, little laugh. "Your medical records say otherwise, Ms. Brooks."

Mandy slammed the receiver down. She went into her bedroom weeping hysterically and threw herself down on her bed. Her life had been such a struggle up to this point, but she had survived. Now, however, it was beginning to unravel and possibly in an irreparable manner.

After gaining her composure, she did what she had vowed she would never do. She picked up the phone, called the Seahawks office, and asked to speak with Bobby Childs.

CHAPTER 9

Jason O'Connor awoke on Tuesday morning feeling marginally better than the day before but still experiencing a stinging headache. He had pretty much slept through the entire night thanks to the medication he was taking and did not experience any further disturbing dreams. Hence, his overall condition, both physical and mental, was somewhat improved. However, upon awaking he felt anxious, as his immediate thoughts were on Bobby and Mandy. He wondered about their dinner engagement the night before.

Jason sat up in his bed and stretched his arms over his head. He pondered whether or not to call his friend and inquire about the previous evening, but as he stood up to start his day, the phone rang. The caller ID indicated it was Bobby. He immediately answered.

"Hey, Bobby, what's up? And should I ask how last night went or is that a topic that is off limits?"

"Well, buddy, I knew you would want a report, and I feel that I owe one to you, but before we get into that, tell me how you are doing this morning. Is the old head feeling any better?"

"I guess I am feeling as well as possible considering the two horrendous shots to the skull that I took.

"Well, glad to hear it. As long as there is improvement we can be hopeful."

"Yeah, we can be hopeful. Let me just say my head does not feel worse. There is a slight improvement. But now tell me about last night. What in the heck did she have to say to you anyway?"

Bobby paused and took a deep breath. He knew that this was going to be a difficult conversation, and he was not sure whether he could get

Jason engaged enough in what he had to say to get him to agree to see Mandy. He gave it his best shot.

"Jason, buddy, she has some things she needs to talk to you about. She asked me to set up a meeting because she has something to give you. She said it couldn't wait and that she needed to see you immediately."

Jason was unimpressed and responded accordingly. "What in the world does she have to give me after all these years that I would want to even have? Come on, Bobby, what is her game now? You can't possibly be serious about this. Why didn't you just get up and leave instead of listening to her crap?"

"Jason, I am sorry, but she has some important information that I think you need to have. It is in regard to Rachel. She won't tell me exactly what it is but says you have to have it immediately."

Jason was taken aback. He was, in fact, stunned and felt like he had received another jolt to the head from an all-pro NFL linebacker. At this critical stage in his life and football career, the last thing he wanted to have was information about Rachel Thomlinson. In his mind, she was someone from his distant past. Now, however, in light of his dream the night before and in light of this new event, it appeared that his life was still not free from the effects of his relationship with Rachel ten years ago. Jason was not sure how to respond.

"Bobby, I don't know what to say. I warned you about this meeting. I am sure that Mandy is up to no good and that she wants something from you or maybe something from both of us." Jason's voice and emotions became more intense. "What in the heck could possibly be brought up now? Why does Mandy Brooks believe it is so important to give this to me now after ten years? This is the worst possible time for this to happen—right at the time we are preparing for the biggest game of our lives. Is she working for the Steelers?"

Bobby took another deep breath and paused. He was not sure how to proceed, but the longer he thought about it, the more confident he was that a meeting between Jason and Mandy was the right thing and had to occur.

"Jason! Listen to me! Hear me out man! I know this is hard, but try to first understand why I am asking you to consider meeting with her.

You have to know that I am your best friend and that I would do nothing to take away your concentration from the big game. I care as much as you do about beating the Steelers. I don't want anything to upset your preparation for the Super Bowl. It is, in fact, because of this that I think it is wise that you meet with her very soon and get this matter out of the way quickly. You need to hear her and get her information so that you can be in he best frame of mind to prepare for the Steelers. Please believe me when I say I want that for you more than anything."

Jason was quiet for a few moments, trying to understand what Bobby had just said. He realized that, of course, his friend would do nothing to disturb his preparation for the game of their lives, and he knew that his friend had only good intentions for him and would not want anything to come between him and success in the Super Bowl.

"OK, Bobby, I know your heart is in the right place, but how do I know that she has not hoodwinked you? How do I know that she has not simply conned you?"

"Jason, old Sammy Jensen is on the war path."

"Well, so what else is new? Isn't he always?"

"You know he is doing a series of articles on us in preparation for the Super Bowl?"

"Oh yes, the expectations in the media are high, and I am sure that Sammy thinks these articles are going to get him a Pulitzer Price. I don't trust the man, but I have agreed to see him Wednesday after practice."

"Well, Mandy believes that he has some information on both you and me that will be very damaging. He knows all about you and Rachel, and he knows all the details about Mandy and me—he even knows about Dr. Barton."

"Now, how does he know all of that?"

"Mandy is divorced and has been for three years. It was a very ugly and bitter fight, and apparently her ex is getting his revenge by talking to Sammy and feeding him information."

"Her ex knows all these things? She told him?"

"They were married. I assume most married couples share with each other such things about their past."

Jason was silent as Bobby continued.

"And one other thing, he knows about little Bobby."

"Who is little Bobby?"

"My son."

"Your son? Since when? How long have you been harboring this bombshell?"

Bobby went into detail about his son. He told Jason about meeting him and Mandy's father, and how he discovered that he had sired little Bobby. His voice quivered with emotion as he shared his emotional pain upon realizing that he had abandoned his child for ten years.

Jason was aghast as he heard the details, but as he listened further, he realized that his friend was in agony. After a few minutes, Jason interrupted and tried to provide comfort.

"Bobby, listen to me. All these years you did not know you had a son. You would not have abandoned him if you knew. This is not your fault. She hid this information from you. How were you to know? She is the one who walked out. And ten years have gone by with no information from her. It makes me even more suspicious that she is up to something. While you were just a backup in the NFL bouncing from team to team, she didn't bother with you. But now, now that you are a big star and a millionaire, she wants back into your life. She is nothing but a gold digger. You need to seek legal advice before she takes you to the cleaners."

"Sorry, man, but I don't buy this. I thought like that at first, but after meeting with her, I believe she is sincerely concerned about both you and me and what Sammy intends to do with the information. I just believe her—that's all. "

"You know I have reasons not to trust Sammy. I can see his slant right now on this. He will portray you as a swinging bachelor, who parties hard, gets his girlfriend pregnant, and she has a baby that he doesn't support for ten years. Great tabloid headlines that's for sure."

"Not to mention the connection to Dr. Barton."

"Yes, old Sammy really has it going for him, and I know he wants to pile it on. He never did like either of us, but for some reason, he particularly dislikes me. Now, it looks like he is going after you."

"He may be going after you big time too, and that is why you need to meet with Mandy."

Jason again was silent for a few moments. The topic of Rachel Thomlinson was just too painful for him to bring up. He did not want to face this again, and yet, it was now becoming clear that there was some unfinished business that needed attending. He wondered if his dream about Rachel the previous night was sent to him to begin this process.

"Listen, what is it that she wants to give me?"

"OK, pal, are you sitting down? I hope so."

"Give it to me straight, Bobby, and stop the crap. I can take it."

"OK, my friend, here it is. Two weeks before she died Rachel wrote you a letter. It has been in a sealed envelope since then. She gave it to Mandy to hold and keep while she decided if it should be mailed to you. Mandy has not read the letter, but says she knows its contents because she talked to Rachel about it. Mandy is absolutely insistent that you read the letter because she believes that Sammy knows about its contents and will be writing about it."

Jason sat back down on his bed and moaned in disbelief. What secrets were contained in this letter? Why was it not given to him after Rachel's death? What is in the letter that would be of interest to Sammy Jensen? And what is Mandy's motivation in bringing this up now? Jason's already seriously injured head began to throb with pain as the stress of the situation sank in.

"I feel like I am living a nightmare and can't wake up. Why do you trust Mandy so much on this one Bobby? Isn't it clear that she is setting us both up? Does she want some money to go away?"

"No. I believe she wants to protect us. You have to see her, read the letter, and then proceed from there. I think it is extremely important that you don't talk to Jensen until after you have read the letter."

"I am supposed to see Jensen after practice on Wednesday. After practice today, I am supposed to go and shake hands with Rev. Johnson and meet his family."

"That is the guy who tackled you and cracked your skull on the concrete?"

"Yeah, that's him. Wagner wants a real PR show on this one, so I am obligated to go. I guess I could see you and Mandy later tonight after that. I have to tell you though, I am very nervous about this. What can you say to assure me that she is on the up and up?"

"I just have a positive feeling about her. She was not angry and really seemed to want to make things right. She didn't ask to see me again and even said she expected that both you and I would not want to see her again after she gives you the letter. But she was absolutely insistent that you have the letter. She wants to be present when you read it to explain and answer any questions."

"I hope you are right."

"Well, don't you think she would be working with Jensen on this if she wanted to set us up? And if she were, then she wouldn't be trying to tip us off on all of this. No, she would just be giving Jensen the information and let him go to press without us knowing."

"That makes sense. OK, I will go with you on this. Let's make this as quick and painless as possible. I am not sure what is in the letter or what to do with it once I read it, but we can talk about that later. If I have to, I can put Sammy off for a few days."

"I will call Mandy this morning and tell her that you will meet us at my place tonight at around six o'clock. Is that fine with you?"

"Sure, Bobby. I will be there. But let me make one thing clear. Nothing is going to take away my focus on the Super Bowl, and this woman better not take away yours either."

"I couldn't agree more. We stand together on that buddy. I will see you later today at practice."

As Jason arrived that morning at the stadium, he was greeted with the usual crowd of reporters asking questions and fans seeking pictures and autographs. The questions being shouted out as he made his way to the locker room were predictable and dealt with his physical condition and ability to play in the Super Bowl. Jason ignored all inquires as he entered the side door of the stadium into the locker room area. Just before entering, he turned to the group of inquiring reporters and said, "We will talk about all of this after practice in the press room, fellas. See you then."

Paul Wagner had already been at the stadium for about an hour when Jason arrived and sent to word that he wanted to see him right away. Jason went to Wagner's office without delay. Immediately upon entering the office, he saw Wagner with his feet propped up on his desk, his hands behind his head, and puffing on a cigar.

"Come on in, hard head. Sit down, and tell me how you are doing today."

"Better, Coach. The head hurts but not like yesterday, and I slept well last night. I am sure that I will be ready to go when needed. Don't even worry about it."

"That's good to hear. Just make sure you keep telling this to the press. The team will be having some contact today after watching more film of the Steelers, but you are going to be on the sidelines until next week when we fly to Miami."

"I assume that we will be having a press conference after practice today?"

"Of course, like always. We will be having one everyday until the Super Bowl. And everyday you are going to be swarmed with questions about how you feel and whether or not you will be playing. Just stay on message. Don't give the reporters reason to doubt that you are not going to play. If you do, then that will be all that they will report on and the whole speculation will divert us from our focus of beating the Steelers."

"Coach, you have to play this one straight with me now. What did the doctors really tell you? Are they concerned at all? I am playing despite anything they have said, but I do need to know what their concerns are."

Wagner got up out of his seat and began to pace a little behind his desk. He was chewing on his cigar heavily and was staring out the window at his view of Seattle. He looked briefly at Jason and then turned away. Jason knew he was withholding information from him but waited patiently for the coach to respond.

"Listen, O'Connor, you have received two very serious blows to the head. Nobody denies that. If I had taken the beating you did, I probably would be in a coma in the hospital now. But I am not you. And the truth is, nobody in the world is like you. You have been blessed not only with incredible football talent but with a physical strength and stamina unlike any player I have ever seen. If it were any player other than you, he would not be playing. But it isn't any other player. It is Jason O'Connor. It is the one guy who can play above this injury and will lead us to a win."

"You didn't answer my question, Coach."

Wagner sat back down and responded without looking into Jason's eyes. "The doctors are overly concerned. Of course, we all know if you get another hit to the head it could be serious. So our job is to make sure that you don't get hit in the head again. The offensive line is going to be pumped up to protect you. They are not going to let you down. You are going to have a specially fitted helmet that will give you extra protection. Everything is going to be done to prevent another blow to the head. You can play resting assured that you are not going to be at risk."

"Bottom-line, Coach. Please, I just need to know. I am playing regardless, but you have not answered my question. What have the doctors said to you that I don't know?"

"All right, O'Connor. They are saying there is a serious risk of permanent brain injury if you get hit again in the head. But as I told you before, these doctors are just covering their backsides from legal action. They have to talk like this. I have seen this over and over again in my career. Sure, we don't want you to get hit again, and that is why you are being kept out of contact this week. But, you are not going to get hit like this again. Everybody on this team is ready to die protecting you. You are just too valuable to us to have you on the bench."

Jason decided to see if he could bring out an admission from his coach by mentioning Zach Morrison. While looking directly into the eyes of Paul Wagner Jason retorted, "Well, I am confident that Zach Morrison will be able to do the job if I can't, so make sure he is ready to go if I do get another hit to the skull."

Wagner again refused to look his quarterback in the eyes. He turned his head slightly and tersely responded, "Zach is ready, but he won't be needed. You are our man. Now let's get out there to practice. We need to go over game film first, and then we will have our team meeting to review the game plan. After that we hit the field, and you will be at my side at all times. When it is over, we go to the pressroom, and let's try to keep that at a minimum today. I want to begin talking to reporters about our plans to beat the Steelers instead of the condition of your head."

Wagner was a master of evasion. Jason marveled at his ability to respond to questions without really giving answers, but he was fully satisfied that his coach was dishonest in his answers to his questions. He certainly knew that he was not speaking truthfully about Zach Morrison. Inside Jason was seething with disrespect and anger, and he got up to leave with a quick response.

"I will see you out there shortly, Coach."

"One more thing, O'Connor. Remember that when we are done today, you need to make your way to see Rev. Joe Johnson and his family. The front office has directions to his place that you can pick up after practice."

"I haven't forgotten, Coach. I am looking forward to meeting the man."

"As I told you before, I will be arriving about thirty minutes after you get there, and there will be some reporters with me. Johnson has a handicapped kid that is a big fan of yours, so when you get there, give the kid an autographed football, and chat with his parents for awhile."

"Yeah, I know. You want me to do the Zach Morrison community outreach thing."

"Yes, and do it well. We can use the PR. Oh, and one other thing before you go."

"What is that, Coach?"

"Be careful where you park your car. Apparently, the Johnson's live in a very rough part of the city. You don't want your car stolen or broken into while you are there.."

The Seahawks had a routine practice. Zach Morrison took snaps from center at the practice but rarely threw the ball. When he did, the passes were short yardage plays or screen passes. No deep passing routes were called and Bobby Childs, the Seahawks premier receiver, had an easy practice, hardly working up a sweat.

At the end of the practice, Bobby approached Wagner and asked, "Hey, Coach, what gives? Don't you think we should have Morrison throwing a few long balls in practice, just so we can get loosened up?"

Wagner responded gruffly. "Shove it, Childs! I have it under control. Don't question my practice plans. Just do what you are told."

The press conference afterward was predictable. Question after question came at Wagner about Jason's physical condition and ability to play. While he tried to divert the questions to other topics, such as the game plan against the Steelers, inevitably the inquiries came back to Jason's availability to effectively pass the ball. Wagner began to get testy in his responses.

A reporter again asked about the topic of concern. "Coach, clearly anybody who takes the kind of shots to the head that Jason O'Connor did on Sunday is going to be weakened considerably. Even if he starts and plays, do the doctors assure you that he will be 100 percent?"

"Listen, I have said it before, and I will say it again, but I am growing weary of this conversation. Jason O'Connor is not like anybody else in this league. It doesn't matter how somebody else would have responded to these blows. This is Jason O'Connor, and he is different." Wagner then tried to add some humor by looking at Jason and saying, "I guess that old Irish hard head is working to perfection these days, huh O'Connor?" The press chuckled, but Jason did not appear amused.

Finally, after dominating the answers to the questions Wagner let Jason speak about his physical condition in general and about the Super Bowl game plan. Jason addressed the media with emotion.

"I can't emphasize enough to all of you what this games means to me personally. A lot of people have put their faith in me—my teammates, Coach Wagner and the staff, and the fabulous Seahawks fans. When I came to Seattle not long ago my career in the NFL was going nowhere. Some of you thought I was a bust. But being here has given my career new life. I will not let people down. This is the chance of a lifetime—perhaps, my only chance to win it all. And I intend to do just that. No blows to the head are going to stop us. As I have said before this is destiny's team."

Jason then noticed Sammy Jensen sitting in the group of reporters taking meticulous notes. He nodded at Sammy and then continued look-ing straight at him.

"I have had my share of problems with the press while in Seattle. Some of you questioned the wisdom of the trade that brought me here. Others have strongly disagreed with the decision to start me ahead of Zach Morrison, and despite achieving much on the field since then, some of you still continue to question my ability to lead this team to victory in the big game. That's OK. You can have your opinions and write whatever you like. All I know is that I am faithful to my teammates and myself. I will give everything to this effort. I am not going to let people down and nothing that is written in the press by some of you will stop that—nothing!"

Jason again nodded at Sammy. He and Wagner promptly exited the pressroom ending the questioning. As they walked into the locker room, Wagner motioned to Jason to join him in his office for further conver-sation. Jason followed his coach in silence and closed the door behind him.

"Nice going, O'Connor. You stayed on message, and hopefully we can get on to other topics tomorrow. I am a little concerned that you seemed to be singling out Sammy Jensen by your last comments. You know he can have a poison pen."

"I am not worried about Jensen. I just want to concentrate all my mental faculties on the Steelers. Let him write what he is going to write. What he says won't matter after we win the big one. "

"Listen, we are moving on after today, and this will not continue to be a topic for discussion. On a separate note, don't forget, you have that meeting with Rev. Johnson and his family after you leave here."

"Do the Johnsons know the press is coming?"

"I am not sure they comprehend the nature of this. They have been told that you are coming to meet them and thank them. They know I will join you later with an expression of thanks from the front office, but I think it is probably a little fuzzy in their minds that the reporters and cameras are coming."

"Don't you think it would be courteous to them to just let them know?"

Wagner responded in his patented testy manner. "Listen, let me handle this thing, and you just do as you are told. Quite frankly, this is a chance for you and the Seahawks to rise and shine, and we need good publicity on this. The Johnsons will respond more naturally if they are surprised by the visit of the press and will be less likely to have something prepared in advance to say. I want the cameras fully rolling when I give them the season passes, and I want to capture their honest reactions. I know it will be a great show. It will be good for everybody and maybe bring an end to all this speculation about your ability to play. So do your job, O'Connor, and do it well, but when it is over today don't look back. Don't get sentimental. This is just part of the job."

Jason felt further distain for his coach. He sincerely wanted to thank Joe Johnson, but he did not believe that Wagner's phony, orchestrated show of sentimentality was right. It only further implanted in his mind the realization of how much he did not want to play for Wagner after the season ended.

After he got the directions from the front office, Jason went to his car and headed out. Following the directions given he soon found himself in a part of the city where he had not been before. Wagner had told him it was a rough part of town, but in Jason's mind that was putting it very mildly. All of the few business establishments in the area had iron bars on the windows, and it was clear to him that street crime infested the area.

Jason noticed, as he drove through this part of the city, several groups of young men at street corners involved in probable drug trafficking, and he passed several young teenage streetwalkers who smiled at him and tried to flag his car down. He shook his head in both disgust and sorrow wondering how such people could continue to live in such hopelessness.

He was extremely happy to arrive at his destination. As he pulled his car in front of the address given him, he noticed that right next to the house was a small church with a sign that read, "Community Church of God, Rev. Josiah Johnson, Pastor. All are welcome to come." Jason had found the right place.

CHAPTER 10

The Rev. Josiah Johnson was a lifetime resident of Seattle. He had grown-up in the inner city—raised by his grandmother from the age of three until he left home after high school. He had never known his father, and his mother died in her teenage years hooked on heroin after a life of drugs and streetwalking.

Joe's maternal grandmother—Gramma Grace he called her—raised him. Grace saw life differently than Joe's mother. Grace was a fervent Christian woman who attended church several times a week. She prayed daily for her grandson as she attempted to raise him in the drug and crime infested atmosphere of the inner city. Her efforts to keep Joe in church, however, met a setback when in his early adolescent years he became deeply involved in the street life of the community.

As a young teenager, Joe belonged to a vicious and violent gang that centered its activities on street crimes terrorizing the local merchants. Drugs, sex, and violence were no strangers to him, as his life appeared to be headed on a collision course that would either kill him at an early age or send him to prison for life. Two things changed all of that—God and football.

When he was sixteen, he was pressured by Gramma Grace against his will, or so he thought, into going to a weeknight revival meeting to hear a guest speaker who had played professional football for the Seattle Seahawks in the early days of the franchise. The speaker had been an all-pro linebacker during his playing days but seemed to put little emphasis on his football past. Instead, he talked about the present and his future—as a child of God. The speaker, a minister in a Seattle area church, was simply known as "Preacher Ken." Joe listened intently that night to the words spoken. It seemed like the speaker was talking directly to him.

"Somehow when we are young we believe that we are invulnerable," Ken said softly. "For some reason, we feel that we can live life recklessly— even violently—and not have to account for our actions. We think that life will go on indefinitely as we satisfy our inner lusts and desires and ignore the needs of others."

Joe perked up from his pew, listening attentively. He saw nobody but himself in the words of the preacher. Ken continued on, "And for a time it even seems like things will continue going your way. You become cocky, thinking nothing can stop you from taking whatever you want from whomever you want. So you continue to live your life for yourself, ignoring and even abusing others."

Joe thought of the drug trafficking he was involved in. He thought of the young women he had sexually overpowered and abused in pursuit of his own selfish pleasures. And the realization was coming upon him that living life for himself was meaningless and a total waste. As Ken spoke Joe understood that his life was a priceless, one-time gift, never to be repeated. If he threw away this precious gift in pursuit of his own selfish desires, he alone would be the loser.

Ken's voice began to boom out over the church audience. "I tell you friends, life can be like that for the young because it was like that for me. Until one day I crashed. I overdosed on drugs and went violently berserk. It took four policemen to finally pin me down to the ground and keep me from killing somebody. And after that I spent a good time in jail and prison, thinking about the sorry mess I had made. I then realized that I was not created to live for myself, but rather God created me for himself and for his pleasure. I knew I would only have meaning if I surrendered to him and not until then."

Joe continued to take note to the words coming from the preacher's mouth. Everything was making sense to him as he listened. He did not want to continue the ways of the streets. He wanted his life to count for something, and as he let Ken's words pour into his soul, he knew that God was speaking to him.

After about thirty minutes Ken concluded his remarks with a very soft invitation. "I have spoken too long already, and I have to stop now because I don't want you to hear me anymore. I want you to hear and listen to that still, small voice inside you calling you to come to him. Do you hear it? Do you feel it? It is the voice of God calling for his kid to come back home and enjoy the blessings of the father."

Joe's eyes were misty. His body began to shake and tears came to his eyes..

"I believe that some of you in this room tonight are listening to that still, small voice and want to change. For those of you who are doing this right now, I want to simply ask you to get up out of your seat and come forward so I can pray with you."

The church choir began to sing softly the hymn "Amazing Grace." Young Joe had no control over his reactions. Later he would say he felt like something or somebody just pulled him out of his seat and pushed him forward. He was compelled to get up and respond. The grace being offered to him at this moment was irresistible. Like an unborn baby coming down the birth canal for the moment of birth, Joe was moving forward toward his moment of rebirth.

As he walked forward, his eyes were filled with tears and his heart was filled with contrition. Preacher Ken laid his hands on him and prayed. Joe prayed too. He prayed that God would give him a new heart and a new life. Joe was never the same after that moment. His heart was made new. His life had been reborn.

Joe's experience with Preacher Ken had another major impact on his life. As an ex-football player Ken immediately saw the football potential in Joe, if for no other reason than his extraordinary size. At age sixteen Joe was six feet three inches tall, 255 pounds, and wore size fifteen shoes. He was a football coach's dream lineman. Ken contacted the football coach at Joe's high school and urged him to make contact with this young man. August football practice for the school was around the corner, and this was the perfect time to get Joe involved in a sport he would come to love like none other.

The diversion of his energies to football came at just the right moment, when he needed to make his break from gang life and pursue a calling of virtue. For anyone else a conversion to Christianity would have brought on jeers, mocking, and even threats from his former gang, but because of Joe's physical stature, the gang members were smart enough to leave him alone.

Joe's size and speed made him a natural lineman on the gridiron, and he quickly showed that he belonged on the football field. For three solid years Joe was a high school football star, leading his inner city school to high rankings in the state polls and even a bit of a run up the state play-off ladder his senior season. However, because his grades were slightly mediocre, college offers did not come for him. Instead, after graduation he enlisted in the army and saw action in Southeast Asia at the tail end of the Vietnam conflict.

Joe's experience in the war would stay with him the rest of his life. He was in combat in treacherous battles and saw several close friends killed before his eyes. One of them was his best friend—a field chaplain he affectionately called Sparky. Joe gave him that nickname because he simply put a spark of life into everything around him. A war zone is a time of tremendous stress and fear for most, but Sparky was there for all of the soldiers with a message of hope and love in the midst of blood and death. Many times before and after a battle, Sparky and Joe would pray and read the Bible together. It was these times that gave Joe the strength to continue on. He believed that if not for his devout friend in the war arena, that he would have lost his faith as he witnessed death and destruction around him.

Joe was right next to his friend when the fateful stray bullet hit Sparky directly in the temple, immediately killing him. Joe held his friend tight when he died, and he wept and cried out to God, "Dear Lord, not Sparky. Not my friend Sparky. Tell me it ain't so, Lord. Don't take my friend Sparky from me now. Not Sparky, Lord. Please don't take Sparky." But Sparky died in his arms, and Joe was left on the battlefield without his spiritual mentor.

Josiah Johnson grew stronger in his faith, however, from his war experience. He had seen destruction, suffering, and the death of a close friend and had come to understand how swiftly life passes. Joe vowed that when he returned from the war, his life, no matter how long or short, was going to make a difference. Accordingly, he took advantage of the federal GI Bill to enroll in a small liberal arts Christian college in Anderson, Indiana, with the intent of studying for the ministry.

Anderson College had a football team, and upon learning this Joe immediately made himself available for the college gridiron. No small college could pass up a physical specimen like Josiah Johnson, and just like in high school, Joe became a star lineman for this small Midwestern College. Joe was a popular person on campus, starring not only for the football team but also deeply involved in the spiritual life of the campus.

During his junior year Joe met Helena. She was a Vietnamese, young woman who had fled to America with her parents several years earlier, before the end of the war. In Joe's eyes Helena was the most beautiful woman he had ever seen. She had a strong Christian faith and identified with Joe's war experience and passionate faith that came from it. She was majoring in education and history and, as a naturalized American citizen, had developed a great love for the American experiment in representative democracy. Because of her experience as a Vietnamese, she appreciated more than most the American heritage she had adopted and cherished her privilege of being an American citizen.

Together Joe and Helena made a great team. The two were married right after their graduation from college and immediately moved to Seattle—Joe's home turf—to start an inner city church and pursue their mutual calling to reach out and touch those in need.

Upon their return Joe and Helena started the Community Church of God in the inner city of Seattle. The location of the church was directly in the middle of the drug traffic of the city. Being a war veteran Joe believed that victories are never won unless the battle is fought on the enemy's turf. That is exactly how he went about the business of starting and building a church.

With some start-up money from a few charitable foundations, Joe purchased an old, dilapidated church building along with the house beside it and went about the work of renovation and recruitment. When the church building was fit for use, Helena opened a day care center to help single mothers in the area who had to work. Joe began to knock on the doors of the citizens in the area to invite them to his church. In the process he met many seedy characters, some of whose lives had been devastated by drugs and crime. As years went by many of these people cleaned up their lives and became stalwart members of the church, helping Joe and Helena in their inner city work.

What was lacking though for Joe and Helena was a child. They both desired to have a family, but physically it was impossible. Hence, the adoption route was pursued. Joe and Helena placed their names with numerous adoption agencies in the Seattle area hoping that eventually a child would be placed with them. However, adoptions are in great demand, with far more couples available to adopt than accessible children. Because of this, Joe and Helena had to wait their turn in line to receive the desired call from an adoption agency telling them that a child was available. It took years for such an event to happen.

After waiting over two years, the call finally came. One fall Saturday afternoon they received a call from Bethany Adoption Services in Seattle telling them of a very unusual adoption need. A baby had been left in a basket at the steps of the adoption agency that previous morning. No note was left with the child, and there was no clue as to the identity of the mother. The child, a boy, was no more than four or five weeks old and appeared to be very sickly. The agency without delay put him in the intensive care unit at Providence Hospital and began the process of placing him in a home for adoption.

The Seattle media picked up the story of the child being left at the agency, and for several days, articles appeared about the matter. Editorials also were written in the newspapers about the tragedy bemoaning the lack of established legal procedures for agencies to deal with such situations. After a few days, however, the ruckus died down, and Bethany was free to proceed with the adoption out of the spotlight of the media.

Joe and Helena were thrilled to be selected as the adoptive parents. However, the doctors in examining the baby were suspicious that the child might be a special needs child. After a few weeks, it was determined that the child indeed had Down's syndrome. In addition, it was clear from the beginning that the child was unusually weak and sickly despite robust efforts to strengthen him. It was later determined that the baby suffered from an extremely rare blood disease that guaranteed he would not live much past the age of twenty.

Before the adoption was finalized, Joe and Helena were advised of the child's physical condition, but such handicaps made no difference to them. They had both committed their lives to serving others and this adoption was simply another act of such service. The physical condition of the child did not matter. As Joe would later point out in regard to his adopted son, "red and yellow, black and white, we are all precious in his sight."

The fact that the child was left at the doorstep of the adoption agency in a basket reminded Joe of the biblical story of Moses, who was put in a floating basket in the Nile River by his sister to escape the death decree of Pharaoh. Moses of old was spared by that act and lived a life with a special calling and purpose. To Joe and Helena this baby also had a special calling and purpose. So he too was named Moses, as a reminder of where he came from and that there was a purpose for his life.

As Moses grew older it became clear that the degenerative blood disease weakened him greatly and prevented his normal physical development. Likewise, having Down's syndrome he was further prohibited from other activities that parents would pursue with their children during the nurturing years. Regardless, Joe made sure that Moses would understand at least one great love of his life—football. When Moses became old enough, Joe and Helena took him with them to the Friday night football games at Joe's high school alma mater, and, of course, Joe made sure that he and Moses spent Sunday afternoons after church in front of the television set watching the Seattle Seahawks.

When Moses turned nine, Joe decided that he wanted to experience the Seahawks with him in a bigger way. Joe and Helena could not afford tickets to attend the games, but they decided to do the next best thing. Every Sunday when the Seahawks were playing at home, Joe and Helena would pack up Moses after church and head down to Qwest stadium where they would park their car and listen to the game on the radio. Being so close and hearing the crowd outside their car gave them the feeling of actually being inside the stadium. Such Sunday rituals became a special time for the family. Joe especially enjoyed the time explaining to Moses what was happening and cheering along with the stadium crowd that they could hear outside their car.

The degenerative blood disease from which Moses suffered was of a constant concern. The boy periodically would need to be breathing from an oxygen tank with a tube attached underneath his nose. Although he was not crippled and could walk normally, the weakened condition caused by the disease required that he be in a wheel chair when going out for long periods of time.

As Moses grew older, there was a noticeable deterioration in his condition. He could not walk on his own for any length of time and was spending more and more time in the wheel chair. Further, he would sleep long periods of time—sometimes sixteen hours a day—slipping in and out of consciousness. Joe and Helena knew it was a matter of time before Moses would go into a comatose condition and not wake up, but they cherished every moment they had with him.

Family physicians advised Joe and Helena from the beginning that Moses would eventually need to receive a series of blood transfusions in order to survive into his adolescent years. The transfusions would only prolong his life for a few years, as nobody expected him to live past the age of twenty.

At age ten, Moses had already received two complete transfusions, but they seemed to effect little improvement in his condition. The doctors stated that the best hope for an effective transfusion would be if the donor were related genetically to Moses—a blood relative such as a father or brother. However, considering the conditions surrounding Moses's adoption, the identification of such a donor was simply impossible. Still, Joe, Helena, and their entire church family held out hope for a miracle. No church service went by without intensive prayers being offered up for Moses and for the discovery of a blood relative that could be a donor for Moses.

Moses learned to love football, and his times with his parents outside the Seahawks stadium on Sundays were very special. He knew all about the Seahawks and their star quarterback Jason O'Connor. When he watched the Seattle team play on television, he constantly would smile and cheer for "Mr. Jason" as he called him. When Jason O'Connor scored a touchdown or passed for one, Moses would break into a deliciously wonderful laugh and smile that brought sunshine into the room. Such moments were precious to Joe and Helena.

Moses and his mother were watching from the car on the infamous day when Joe saved Jason O'Connor from serious injury from the falling concrete beam. They heard Joe scream and then looked in horror as they saw him lunge toward Jason, tackle him, and pound his skull into the concrete pavement. Moses did not understand why his father did such a thing and became hysterical at the sight. Joe and Helena were not able to calm the boy down until hours after the incident had passed.

On Monday following the incident, Joe got the call from the Seahawks front office advising him that Jason O'Connor would be visiting the next day to express his thanks. He was also told that Coach Wagner would be dropping by to present him and his family with a gift of appreciation. Joe was not told that the media would be coming along with Wagner.

When Joe told Moses that "Mr. Jason" would be coming, he was ecstatic. His excitement was so great that even with his weakened deteriorating physical condition, he had trouble sleeping the night before. On the day of the visit—about two hours before Jason's arrival—Helena was finally able to get Moses to nap. Moses was sleeping soundly when Jason O'Connor knocked on the door and Joe answered.

Jason was not sure what to expect. He did not know what Joe Johnson looked like; although, from the blow he took he knew he had to be built like a Hall of Fame linebacker. He was not surprised at Joe's appearance when the door opened, and he was greeted. "Hello, Mr. O'Connor. Thank you for coming to see us. We are honored. Please come in." Joe said holding out his hand for a vigorous handshake, Jason noticed that the man's handshake was firm and strong, as it nearly crushed his own hand. His slight grimace of pain went unnoticed as he responded.

"It is so nice to meet you, sir." Looking behind Joe he spotted Helena and approached her as well. "You must be Mrs. Johnson. Thank you for taking some time to spend with me."

"Now before we get any further here please call me Joe, and this is Helena. We are on a first name basis only with our friends."

Making his way to the living room couch, Jason responded, "Of course. And please call me Jason."

Initially, Jason was at a loss for words and began to wonder why he had agreed to come to the Johnson home. Likewise, Joe was not sure why he was being thanked. He was glad that he wasn't being blamed for further head injury to Jason, but he was puzzled as to why such a commotion was being made over his actions. Finally, he spoke and broke the silence.

"Well, Jason, I feel a little awkward about all of this. I hit you pretty hard and your skull took quite a shot when we went down. I hope all is well and you are going to be able to play in the Super Bowl."

Jason laughed. "You know, Joe, after I came through the shock of all of this, I recommended that the Seahawks give you a shot in training camp next summer. We could use a linebacker that can hit like that. I am serious when I say that I have not be hit harder by anybody in my life."

"It would be wonderful to do that, but, of course, I am an old man—over fifty now—and would get killed out there. My knees would be the first to give way. I did my thing in college. No way am I going to punish my body like that again."

Jason again responded with laughter, as he was becoming more comfortable in the conversation. "I tell myself the same thing all the time, but punishment on the old body is part of the game. When you can't take it any longer, it is time to hang the spikes up and do something else."

"So are you going to be ready for the big game?" Helena interjected.

"The docs tell me that I will be fine. I am staying out of contact this week and will have light contact the week of the game. But I promise you one thing—I am going to be ready. I have never been more ready for anything in my whole life."

"Well, we are big fans and that is what we want to hear," Joe replied. "Helena, could you see if Moses is awake. I know he wants to meet our guest."

Helena went to check on their son and returned to say he was beginning to come out of his slumber, but it would be a few more minutes before he would be able to come out and visit. Joe explained the situation to Jason.

"Our son is very sick. He has an incurable blood disease that apparently afflicts only one person in one hundred thousand. There is no cure, and it makes him very weak. Sometimes when he sleeps it is hard to wake him."

Jason felt an unusual surge of compassion upon hearing this information. "I am sorry to hear this Joe. Could you tell me a little more about him?"

Joe took the next ten minutes to explain the circumstances surrounding Moses and his adoption. He told Jason of the manner in which the baby was found and about the Down's syndrome and the blood disease. Jason listened intently.

"So there is no cure to this? And you tell me that apparently the blood transfusions are not having an impact."

"They don't appear to be. Our only hope is to find a blood relative, so we can have an genetic match, but that would appear to be impossible."

"Yes, it would appear to be."

Helena now spoke, "Jason, I want to show you something very special before Moses joins us. Would you come into the dining room area with me for a moment?"

Jason got up from the couch and followed Helena into the next room. As he walked through the door, she pointed to the far wall. He looked and saw a framed oil painting of him fully dressed in his football garb and raising his arm with a football as if ready to throw a pass. Helena smiled as she watched Jason's facial expression show amazement and surprise.

"Wow, where did you get that?" Jason exclaimed.

Helena responded, "Well, by now you know that Joe, Moses, and I have made regular trips to the stadium on Sundays to listen to the game on our car radio and be part of the home crowd. At halftime last year we began to take a break by getting out of the car and going into an art gallery that used to be where the new parking garage now sits."

"Oh yes. That infamous art gallery that Zach Morrison tried to save before the Seahawks front office told him to cool his jets."

"Maybe if Zach Morrison had been successful, then we wouldn't be talking here today, and your head would in shape to play ball." Joe chimed in.

"Yes, that's the one." Helena continued. "The nice lady who owned the gallery took a special liking to Moses. She would give us hot chocolate on the cold days. One time Moses noticed this painting, which was done by a local artist. He was so excited when he first saw it he gave his infectious laugh and started pointing at it and shouting 'Mr. Jason, Mr. Jason.'"

Joe continued the story, "When the city moved the gallery out, we went down to say goodbye to the owner. She took the painting off the wall and gave it to Moses. She didn't charge anything. She just said that seeing our child smile was payment enough."

"That was very nice of her," Jason responded.

"Yes, it was," replied Helena. "You should know that Moses worships the ground you walk on."

Jason was visibly moved. "I am not sure that I am worthy of that kind of adulation. But I am very touched."

Joe responded, "Well, Jason, you may feel that way, but you have been put in a position of great influence in this city. Many kids in our church look up to you. There is a lot of crime around here, and the temptations these kids face are enormous. But football provides an escape for many—I know that it did for me. And the Seahawks provide all of us with a wonderful diversion from the very hard realities of the inner city. You and Bobby Childs seem to be the talk of many of these kids these days."

Jason was speechless. He had never seen himself as a role model. He was just an ordinary guy who happened to be athletically gifted and could play football very well. He certainly knew all of his own personal flaws. He did not think that he was a person who should be admired. Football was simply his love. It was his career. He wanted to be the best he could be and accomplish the maximum as a player, but he had never seen himself as accomplishing some greater good in society and changing lives in the process. Yet, Joe Johnson was telling him that he meant something to the kids in the inner city and to Moses, his own handicapped son. Jason was deeply moved.

Helena finally walked into the room holding the hand of a youngster who appeared to be in a stupor from not having awakened completely from his deep slumber. It was Moses.

Helena walked with him until he was face to face with Jason and introduced the two. "Moses," she said, "I want you to say hi to Jason O'Connor."

Jason had never before personally seen an individual with Down's syndrome; although, he had seen pictures of the condition. To Jason this youngster looked quite normal, but it was apparent that he suffered from some degree of mental retardation. Jason put out his hand and responded. "Hey there, buddy. Give me five, would ya?"

What happened next was totally unexpected. Moses stared at Jason for a few brief seconds, as if paralyzed. Then suddenly, without warning, Moses jumped into Jason's arms, hugging him as tight as he possibly could, and repeated over and over, "Mr. Jason, oh, Mr. Jason." Tears came to their eyes as Joe and Helena watched in amazement at the show of affection.

Jason was also overcome. He did not know what to do next, but after taking a deep breath he pulled Moses away, looked him in the eyes and said, "Hey there, buddy; I have something for you." He then took a pen out of his pocket and signed the football he had brought with him. It read, "To my pal, Moses. Jason O'Connor."

When he received the ball, Moses began to laugh with exhilaration and tucked the ball under his arm as if he were playing football. He began to run in the living room like an all-pro running back headed for the end zone.

The three adults watching the display of joy all laughed and smiled. Helena then turned to Jason and said, "You don't have any idea how much this means to all of us but especially to Moses. I don't think we can ever repay you for this."

"Helena, don't mention it. I am the one in debt to all of you. If Joe hadn't been alert, I may not even be here right now, let alone preparing for the Super Bowl."

The three adults continued their silence and watched Moses at play with his new treasure. Finally, Jason spoke, "Coach Wagner will be here shortly to give you a token of appreciation from the Seahawks front office. Some members of the media are coming as well. I understand that you were aware of this."

Joe and Helena looked at other with bewilderment. Joe then responded, "Actually, Jason, we were not aware that the press was coming. I don't mind it, but it does make me a little nervous. What am I supposed to say? I hope that this doesn't intimidate Moses too much. Are they expecting to talk to him as well?"

Helena piped up, "I wish I had known. I am kind of embarrassed about the way the house looks. I hope they don't take pictures."

Inside Jason was furious. Jason knew what it was like to deal with nosy reporters, and he truly could see the stress in the eyes of his new friends about dealing with the press. He felt like these very decent people had been set up, and he was very sorry.

Jason responded calmly, "I am so sorry that you were not told. I guess there was a mix-up in the front office on this one, but trust me. This is no big deal. All they want to do is ask a few questions about the incident and take a couple of pictures. Believe me when I tell you that Joe is a hero to most sports fans in Seattle."

"It's OK," said Joe while looking at Helena trying to calm her with his eyes. "I think we can handle a few questions."

At that moment Wagner and his press entourage arrived in several vehicles that pulled up directly in front of the Johnson home. Along with the coach were two cameramen, a photographer, and three reporters— one of which was Sammy Jensen. Jason burned with anger as he looked out the window and saw Sammy. He believed that this person could never be up to anything but mischief.

Joe Johnson opened the door and after briefly introducing himself let Wagner and the media party into the house. Immediately upon entry the cameras began to roll and Wagner began to speak.

"Mr. and Mrs. Johnson, on behalf of the Seahawks organization and Seahawks fans everywhere, I am here to thank you, and especially thank Joe, for his alert reactions that have preserved the ability of our all-pro quarterback Jason O'Connor to lead us to victory in the Super Bowl."

The cameras immediately went to the Johnsons to get their reactions. Helena stood looking very uncomfortable as Joe finally responded, "Coach Wagner, the thanks is really all mine. The Seahawks have given us wonderful pleasure this year. It has been an opportunity to share something special with my family. I can't imagine this team without Jason O'Connor. So I did what anybody would have done. I don't consider my actions special at all."

Wagner hammed it up for the cameras. "Well, spoken like the true humble person that you are, Mr. Johnson, but let me assure you that we think your actions were extraordinarily courageous. You could have been seriously hurt yourself."

Joe smiled sheepishly as Wagner continued. "As a token of our appreciation the Seahawks would like you to have this." He then handed to Joe and Helena an envelope that they immediately opened. Inside was a Seahawks guarantee of season tickets for the next year on the fifty-yard line at Qwest Stadium. They were overjoyed at the gift and hugged each other. Moses who was standing in front of his mom holding on to her tightly did not quite understand the significance of the gift. Helena spoke to him gently as the press looked on.

"Moses, this is all wonderful news. Next year we are going to be able to watch Mr. Jason and the Seahawks play football right in the stadium every Sunday they are at home. Isn't that great!"

Upon hearing the news, Moses immediately ran again into the arms of Jason O'Connor saying, "Mr. Jason, oh, Mr. Jason." It was great press. The sight of the Moses jumping in the arms of Jason, and the joy on the Johnson's faces at the news of the gift was not only great theater but was everything that Wagner had hoped it would be. With the cameras rolling the reporters, led by Sammy Jensen, began to ask questions to Joe and Helena.

"Mr. Johnson, Sammy Jensen here from the *Seattle P-I*. Would you please share with us what drew your attention to the falling concrete beam that resulted in your swift life-saving actions on Sunday?"

"I am not really sure, Mr. Jensen. I guess I was just looking at the right place at the right time. My eyes were for some reason on the upper level of the garage when I saw the beam start to fall squarely in the direction of Jason. I just reacted as fast as I could."

Sammy continued his questions. "Mr. and Mrs. Johnson, can you tell us a little bit about your life with your son and how big of a role football plays in your family?"

"Well, Mr. Jensen, our times following the Seahawks with our son have been precious. Moses has a very rare blood disease and will not be with us forever. But the times we have cheered on the team from our car radio have been really something. I wouldn't trade those times for anything in the world—not even Seahawks tickets."

"I understand that the circumstances surrounding the adoption of Moses were quite unique and even got some media coverage a few years ago. Do you mind giving us a little more detail about that?"

Joe and Helena Johnson immediately froze up. Moses did not know about the details of his adoption, and they had definitely avoided over the years giving him much information. They certainly did not want him to know how his mother had abandoned him on the doorsteps of the adoption agency.

Jason sensed their unease and jumped into the fray. Moses was still holding on to him as he spoke. "Hey, Sammy, that is totally irrelevant now don't you think? What matters is that these wonderful people have done something for which I am extremely grateful, and because of that they are going to be Seahawks season ticket holders. As for Moses, I think all in this room can see that he is very happy today."

The cameras then began to click catching the sight of Jason O'Connor hugging the handicapped, adopted child of Joe and Helena Johnson. Wagner loved every moment of this and anticipated a big national story the next day.

Finally, after assessing the situation for a few more moments Paul Wagner determined that all had been accomplished and ended the event with a few words. "Well, guys," he said to the press, "I think we have intruded enough into the private lives of these good people. Let's leave them in peace." He then turned to Joe, Helena, and Moses and addressed them directly.

"Again, thank you so much for who you folks are. We look forward to having you at the Seahawks games next year."

As the camera crew and the reporters began to depart, Wagner mumbled under his breath as he walked past Jason. "Nice going, O'Connor. It was a great show."

Jason stayed behind as Wagner and the media left the Johnson home. After all had finally left, he spoke.

"Listen, Joe, and Helena, I am really sorry. I honestly thought you knew that the press was coming over to ask questions."

"It's really OK, Jason," responded Joe. "It took us off guard for a little bit, but we are fine. I know that Helena and Moses share my joy in knowing we can actually go to the games next year and watch you play."

Jason smiled at Joe's comment before responding. At this point he was not so sure he wanted to play for Paul Wagner again. He knew he would be demanding a trade after the season ended, but he was also feeling strangely very connected to the Johnson family, even though they had just met, and did not want to disappoint them in any way.

"I am glad you are not offended, Joe." He then looked at his watch and realized that he had an appointment to meet with Bobby and Mandy in less than an hour. "If you will please excuse me now, I have to be somewhere and will be fighting that awful Seattle traffic to get there on time."

Joe got up from his chair, walked over to Jason and gave him a big bear hug as he spoke, "Jason, my friend. You are in our prayers. I trust the Lord to make sure you are going to be in the big game leading the way. We need you."

Helena and Moses also walked toward Jason as he moved toward the door to exit. Moses was standing in front of his mother facing Jason while she had her arms around his neck and chest and said. "Jason, you just don't know how much your visit means to us."

He looked down at Moses to say goodbye but could only smile. Moses had won his heart. Moses smiled and looked deeply into Jason's eyes. Jason knew that a profound emotional connection had occurred between him and this young handicapped boy. After a few brief moments of looking into Moses' eyes, Jason said his final goodbye.

"Joe, Helena, and Moses, all I can say is that the pleasure has been all mine. I am going to be thinking about you all as we prepare for the Super Bowl."

He then looked down at Moses and said, "Listen, little buddy, after we win I am going to bring the game ball directly back here and give to you. That's a promise." Moses smiled broadly at Jason, and Helena fought back tears.

Jason left the home hurriedly, as he was running late for his appointment with Bobby and Mandy. His stomach was in knots as he realized that he was going to finally find out what deep dark secret was in the letter from Rachel Thomlinson. He did not relish the thought of this meeting and wished that he could avoid it, but he knew that he had to pursue the course set before him—wherever it may lead.

Jason drove away from the Johnson home with his mind focused upon Rachel Thomlinson and his dream two nights before. He wondered if the dream had some strange connection to this upcoming meeting. His body began to tremble at the thought that this encounter might answer his questions concerning the dream.

As Jason drove away his mind returned to the past once again and began to battle the demons that had haunted him for over ten years. He hoped that such demons would, once and for all, be laid to rest.

CHAPTER 11

Bobby Childs paced up and down the living room of his expensive and swanky town home in suburbia Seattle. It had been agreed that Mandy would come to his place an hour before Jason arrived, to talk further about issues and prepare for the presentation to Jason.

Bobby had slept little the previous night. He knew that he and she still had some unfinished business to discuss, but he also knew that they were miraculously starting their relationship anew. For this he was excited and grateful.

He looked out the window of his home as Mandy drove up. He watched her get out of her car and look up at him. She waved immediately upon recognizing his face, and he smiled back. Such a brief moment confirmed to him that this woman was indeed meant for him. He felt like a young adolescent on a first date with his first and only love.

Bobby eagerly and immediately went and opened the door before Mandy walked up the steps. "Hey there, lady. Glad you could make it. I was getting worried that you might be a no-show."

Mandy laughed and responded. "Hardly, Mr. Childs. But I have to confess that at times my nerves were making me think of chickening out. I am glad I am here, Bobby."

Mandy came into the house as Bobby poured her a soda on ice. She sat down on the couch and took a deep breath as he sat beside her and handed her the drink. Both felt a bit uneasy and said nothing for a few moments until Mandy piped up.

"So, did you sleep well last night? I know that I laid a lot on you and wasn't sure that you really wanted to see me again. I wouldn't blame you if that is how you feel."

Bobby laughed nervously, and then got up from the couch and began to pace. "Jason was very reluctant to meet us tonight, but I talked him into coming. He will be here in about an hour."

Bobby continued to pace back and forth in the living room as he struggled with what to say next. He was frightened to say what was on his mind. He looked at Mandy as if to talk and then turned his head and gazed out the living room window. "Cat got your tongue? When is Bobby Childs ever speechless?" laughed Mandy.

Bobby sat down beside her on the couch. He cleared his throat and looked into her eyes. They were the deepest blue eyes he had ever seen. The thoughts that he wanted to express were numerous, but he didn't know where to start, and he felt a deep sense of regret for his past actions toward Mandy. Finally, he realized that he had to speak because time was moving fast, and Jason would be arriving soon. He knew if he were going to express his innermost thoughts, he would have to do so immediately, or the opportunity would be lost.

"Mandy, my parents came of age back in the seventies, and I remember my mom telling me about a pretty dumb slogan that was going around then. I think it said, 'Love means never having to say you are sorry.' Have you heard of that?"

Mandy again laughed. "I think so. That sure is a hokey line. About as dumb as it can get."

"Yes, indeed," laughed Bobby. "I remember my mom telling me about it, but then also saying true love means being able to say 'I am sorry.'"

"That makes sense to me," responded Mandy.

Bobby then took her hand and looked deeply into her eyes. He cleared his throat, and licked his dry lips. He then said in a soft and tender voice, "Mandy, I am sorry. I am so very sorry."

Tears came to Mandy, and she could not speak. All she could do was look at Bobby as he stared into her eyes. She knew if she said anything now, she would lose her composure and become an emotional basket case. With Jason arriving soon, she definitely wanted to be in control of her emotions.

Bobby got up from the couch, as she remained silent and went over to a desk. He pulled out two envelopes and brought them over to her. "I have something to give you. Please open this one first."

Mandy took the envelope and opened it. She saw its contents and squealed with delight. In the envelope were three tickets to the upcoming Super Bowl and three round trip plane tickets to Miami for the game. She threw her arms around him and hugged him tight.

"Oh, Mr. Childs, you really do know how to make up now don't you. I am assuming that the other two tickets are for my dad and son as well."

"Absolutely! And the seats are on the fifty-yard line—the best seats in the house. I stopped by a travel agency after practice and got the plane tickets. I hope that Bobby can get off of school because I am sending all of you to Miami for most of next week as part of the Super Bowl gala activities."

"I am sure we can work it out. He will be the envy of every kid in his school. Of course, dad took early retirement, so he won't have a problem tagging along."

Bobby then took the second envelope from her hands for just a moment before giving it back. "I am afraid when you open this one you might leave. I won't blame you if you do, but I hope you don't go. I didn't have time to buy the real thing, but take this as an offer for a future purchase."

Mandy looked at him suspiciously saying, "I thought I was the one who was bringing the surprise in an envelope, but I guess you outdid me." She then opened the envelope and looked at its contents with bewilderment. She then looked at Bobby, wanting an explanation.

The envelope contained a picture cutout from a magazine. It was a picture of a diamond ring surrounded by tiny rubies. Bobby got up from the couch, looked at Mandy, and then got on one knee.

"Mandy, seeing you last night did something to me. It tore at my soul. When I met little Bobby and realized who he was, I was overcome. I was overcome with guilt and remorse. I realized that the wounds I had given you were deep and that I hurt for this little guy of ours that had to endure important years of his life without a real father. And most of all

I hurt for myself and realized what an incredible fool I was to let you go out of my life. Worse, it was inexcusable that I did not try to contact you again over the years. Believe me I have thought a lot about you."

Bobby remained on one knee looking into Mandy's tear-filled eyes. He continued, "I have made a lot of mistakes regarding you and me. But I know I am being given another chance, and I am not going to blow this one. So, Mandy Brooks, you would make me the happiest man on earth if you consented to marry me and bring our son into my life as well. I know I will let you down at times because I am not perfect. But I will never intentionally do so, and I will immediately ask for your forgiveness when I do. I also know that I will never again abandon you, and I will love you, Mandy Brooks, until the day I die."

Mandy remained speechless for a few moments. Her tear-filled eyes remained fixed, looking deeply into his eyes. She then leapt into his arms, almost knocking him on this back. Bobby laughed and said, "Hold on, lady. You might injure me and keep me out of the Super Bowl."

They both stood, and then tightly embraced as Mandy finally spoke. "You have always been my love. I never dreamed that one day we would be together. But, Bobby Childs, you will make me the happiest woman on earth if you become my husband. Of course I will marry you."

They looked at each other intensely as they stood together in the embrace. Finally, after ten long years, their lips touched and came together. This was not a sensual kiss like the one they had engaged in so many times in college. It was not a kiss that was just a preliminary activity to a sexual experience that their young bodies had once craved and required on a regular basis. Rather, this kiss was a cleansing act that brought two broken hearts and lives back together. It was an act of contrition on the part of both a man and a woman who had grieved each other and suffered the consequences of unrepentant actions. Now, as they united in this kiss their hearts were flowing with forgiveness for each other and with pure and innocent love. Tears streamed down both of their faces as they continued the embrace.

After what seemed an eternity of simply being in each other's arms, they broke free and both took a deep breath. They then sat back on the couch in silence, as Mandy rested her head on Bobby's chest. He stroked her long, beautiful hair, and they remained still for several minutes, trying to comprehend what had just happened. Finally, Mandy broke the silence.

"Can I tell you about Timmy and Tina?" She asked. "I have wanted to do so for so long."

"Of course, but who are they?"

Mandy cleared her throat. "They are our twins. The ones I saw in the ultrasound when I found out that I was pregnant."

"Oh….are sure you want to talk about this?" Bobby fearfully asked.

"Very sure, my love. We need to deal with this if we are going to move on. Should I continue?"

"Yes. You must. But you named them. How do you know it was a boy and a girl?"

"Believe me, Bobby. A mother knows these things. I named them a couple of years ago as I tried to come to grips with what had occurred. I even wrote them a letter asking for their forgiveness."

"Do you think they got the message?"

"Oh yes, they got the message. I am sure of it."

"How can you be so sure?"

Mandy gripped the gold cross around her neck and replied. "I have first had to deal with forgiveness for my part in this. When I found the forgiveness I needed, I then had to forgive myself. My God is in the business of forgiveness. He didn't let me down, and I know that he relayed my message to our two precious little twins." She then continued.

"I then had to forgive you, Bobby. That was the hardest part. I felt so let down and abandoned. I wanted you there in the midst of the crisis, but you weren't. I hurt badly for years. I hated you for so long."

Bobby remained speechless. He was dealing now with the ghosts that had haunted him since Mandy's departure from his life that night at the fraternity house. He knew that his moment for cleansing had finally come, but he was not sure how to proceed or what to say. He remained silent as Mandy continued to talk.

"I followed your career with mixed emotions. When you were doing poorly, I rejoiced on the outside but deep inside I hurt for you and for me. I knew you were better than that. I knew you were meant to be an NFL superstar. But I also knew that you were hurting too. My pregnancies, Rachel's death, and our break up all were cutting deep into your soul—I knew that."

"Did you ever think about contacting me?"

"Oh, yes, many times. But remember—I was married to Jim. He was extremely jealous of you after he knew about our relationship. Contacting you to talk would never have been an option as long as I was with him."

"Does little Bobby know who I am?"

"No. The only thing he knows about his real father is that he was someone I dated in college and that we were never married. He has never really asked. He wanted Jim to be his father, but Jim was very cruel to him, so Bobby has clammed up on this topic. My dad has stepped in and provided a role model for him over the years, and for that I am truly grateful."

"So am I. Your dad is a great guy. I hope he will accept me and forgive me."

Bobby then paused before continuing. He asked in earnest and sincerity, "Mandy, have you really forgiven me? Because if you haven't, we can't move on."

"Bobby, my love, I can say absolutely that I have, but I need to ask you a question as well."

"Go ahead. Get it all out."

"Have you forgiven me?" She asked.

"Forgiven you? For what? What did you do?"

"We know as dance partners that it takes two to tango. I was not innocent in all of this. I didn't have to see Dr. Barton. I could have let you know about Bobby these last few years. And I harbored hatred in my heart for you all this time, and you didn't even know it. Please, will you forgive me?"

Bobby looked again at his bride to be, and his eyes sparkled. "You are so amazing, Mandy Brooks. Look how I have wounded you deeply over the years, and you are asking me to forgive you. If it makes you feel bet-

ter then of course I forgive you. I love you too much to not forgive you."
They then embraced tightly and enjoyed another kiss.

As they continued to embrace in each other's arms Bobby relaxed
and laid his head on the back of the couch and sighed. Something was
obviously still on his mind, and it was clear to Mandy that he had more
to say.

"What is it my darling? You have to come clean with everything now.
No more secrets."

"It is not a secret, Mandy. It is a deep question."

"I am listening."

"Well, it is very funny that you and I are going to the same church.
Actually, you were right to laugh the other night when you found out that
I was going to church. That is hilarious, I know. Nobody would have ever
predicted such a thing a few years ago."

Mandy giggled. "I have to say, Bobby Childs, that you are full of
surprises."

"Well, forgiveness is a heavy topic. We talk about it every Sunday
when we say the Lord's Prayer. That prayer means a lot to me. I don't really know how to pray but that prayer really says it all. And it talks about
forgiveness."

"It really is a beautiful prayer isn't it? So simple but still it covers
everything."

"Yes, but the forgiveness part has me baffled. You can forgive me, and
I can forgive you. But I don't know how our kids can ever forgive us, and
most importantly, I don't see how God can ever forgive what I have done.
It is simply unforgivable."

Mandy was silent. She was not a trained theologian, and certainly her
own religious background was shallow, so she did not feel like she could
really answer Bobby's questions. But he was her husband to be, and he
was sharing hurts and doubts that needed answers. She knew she had to
try to help him make some sense of this whole matter.

"Bobby, I can only share how I have come to have peace in all of this.
But ultimately you have to make your own peace with God."

"So how did you come to peace about all of this? I think it would be a terrible burden for a mother to try to deal with the Dr. Barton situation and with Timmy and Tina."

Mandy took a deep breath and responded. "It hasn't been easy, and the scars will never go away. However, I began to pray a few years ago that God would show me a way to go on. At the time I wasn't sure that there was a God. In my mind I figured that if God existed, then he surely wouldn't be too concerned about me. How could the Creator of the vast universe ever think that Mandy Brooks was significant enough to care for?"

"I understand that thought totally. I know how insignificant I am. Catching touchdown passes and even winning the Super Bowl hardly qualifies for things of eternal value. One hundred years from now nobody will ever care what happened at this year's Super Bowl."

"But, Bobby, you are wrong. God does care. He cares about the little birds he made and when they die. He sees everything we do and wants to be a part of it. I had to come to realize that before I could understand forgiveness. When I hurt and cry he does too, and he wants me to heal. And when I blow it, he is ready to forgive because he knows how flawed we all really are. Until I understood this I was never able to understand his love and forgiveness for me no matter what I have done."

"So what makes you so sure of all of this?"

Mandy again grasped the cross around her neck as she responded. "Because he walked this earth too and experienced the same disappointments that we have. He was heartbroken and abandoned too. And because he experienced this as a man, he knows what I feel. And because he loves me more than I love myself, he forgives me. I have not earned it Bobby. He just offers it freely as his gift of grace. That is it. That is all I can understand. But because I believe it I know I am forgiven. And because I am forgiven I can be healed and move on."

Bobby looked again into the eyes of his beloved Mandy and responded, "I believe all of this. Being in church helps, but you have said it more clearly than I have heard before. And after hearing you, I now really understand. I believe, Mandy. I do believe.

They then both embraced each other tightly for a few moments.

Then Bobby began to pray out loud. Mandy joined him in reciting the prayer they had both known since their childhood:

Our Father, Who art in heaven,
Hallowed be Thy name.
Thy kingdom come, Thy will be done,
On earth as it is in heaven.
Give us this day our daily bread.
And forgive us our debts as we forgive our debtors,
And lead us not into temptation but deliver us from evil.
For Thine is the kingdom, and the power, and the glory forever. Amen..

When they ended the prayer, Mandy's face glowed. Bobby wiped tears from his eyes and smiled. They both knew something miraculous had occurred. Bobby Childs was reborn.

They continued to smile at each other for a few seconds and were lost in the majesty of the moment. Suddenly, they were taken back as the doorbell rang. They both realized that not all of the past had yet been discussed. Mandy sat nervously on the couch, as Bobby walked over and answered the door.

Jason O'Connor had arrived.

CHAPTER 12

Sammy Jensen left the Johnson home and headed immediately for his office at the *Seattle Post-Intelligencer*. He was ecstatic about the developing story he was uncovering. He sensed that he was on the verge of a extraordinarily big journalistic scoop that would be read nationwide. This was the kind of story that he had wanted to write his entire career, and now it appeared that he was sitting on some information that, if written properly, would uncover some scandalous activity and generate a large readership.

Sammy just had one major concern about his potential scoop. His source—Mandy's ex-husband, Jim Harrison—was not particularly credible. Jim Harrison was an admitted alcoholic, and, as Mandy's ex-husband, he obviously had a personal vendetta against her. Further, Sammy was certain that the Harrison divorce file, if reviewed carefully as a public file, would show a bitter dispute and paint Jim as an angry husband who would stop at nothing to hurt his former spouse. Because of all of this things, Sammy knew that he had to have written documentation of the details he was uncovering before he dared go public with the story.

As he entered his office he immediately went to his desk and called his editor. He let the editor know that he wanted to delay the publication of "The Brotherhood" series until Monday, the week of the Super Bowl. He explained that he was verifying some additional information that was needed before he could complete the series and just needed a few extra days to do so. Upon approval of the delay he then called Jim Harrison.

"Hey, Jim, it's me, Sammy Jensen, at the *Seattle P-I*."

"What's up, Sammy? How can I help you further?"

"Glad you are still interested in doing so. I need your help to verify some of the information you gave me."

"You name it, and then count it done, Sammy, boy."

"OK, it is a simple request, but this may be hard to accomplish in a timely fashion. And I know you are reluctant to do this, but I need for you to get me that letter you said was written by the Thomlinson girl to Jason O'Connor."

"Why? Don't you believe me?"

"Hey, man, you are a lawyer, and you know better than to ask such questions. This isn't a question of believing anybody. It is a question of proving what I am alleging. This story is just too big of a bombshell to go to print without written documentation."

There was a long moment of silence before Jim Harrison cleared his throat and then responded, "Mandy kept that letter in a safe at our home. When she moved out, she took that safe with her. She was very careful that the letter be safeguarded. I assume it is still there."

"Do you mean to tell me that over all the years that you were married to her you did not read that letter?"

"Listen, Sammy, I already told you that it was in a sealed envelope. Mandy never read the letter as far as I know. She said she knew its contents because apparently her friend Rachel told her about it before giving it to her."

"Well, since nobody—including your ex—actually has read the letter, it would be careless of me to assume what it says and go to press with this story unless I have read the letter first. I am not willing to risk my credibility with this story, unless I have that letter in hand, and it confirms all that you have told me."

Jim paused for a moment, thinking about a way to proceed. He no longer lived with Mandy and could not come into her home uninvited and remove the letter. As much as he wanted the story to go forward, he was not willing to risk a felony charge of breaking and entering to get the documentation that Sammy was requesting. However, he believed that his ex-wife might be convinced to cooperate if given a few incentives to do so. He approached that possibility with Sammy.

"Sammy, I have no way of getting into my ex's home and obtaining the letter, but I think there may be another way to skin this cat."

"I am anxiously awaiting your suggestions," Sammy said.

"OK, do you ever pay to get information for a story?"

Sammy laughed. "Not usually. A sports reporter like me never seems to be chasing a story where that would be necessary."

"Well, I think that Mandy would listen to a request of this nature if we offered her a couple of incentives to cooperate."

"Incentives? You mean something in addition to money?"

"Yes, you see if I am reading you correctly, I think that if you were forced to choose between writing a story that provided information on the college playboy activities of both Childs and O'Connor or a story that just talked about O'Connor and was silent on Childs that you would choose to go with the latter."

"That's a tough call, Jim. Both stories help provide the picture I am painting in my articles of Childs and O'Connor as prima donna athletes who got everything they ever wanted and ran over people to do so."

"OK, I understand that, but I am telling you I need incentives to get this letter for you. We can offer Mandy money, of course, but we need to offer her more."

"Like what?"

"We tell her that if she cooperates with us, then you will not mention in your article her sexual escapades with Childs, their son, or her termination of pregnancy with Dr. Barton. She will know that she is off the hook if she just gives us the letter."

Sammy paused. He wanted to write about the Childs situation and about his son. He liked the story line that was developing that showed Bobby Childs to be an irresponsible playboy who mistreated women and failed to pay support for a child of his for ten years. Yet, if he had to choose between one scenario and the other, he definitely wanted to reveal the secret life of Jason O'Connor. This was a bombshell that he wanted to get out to the public in the worst sort of way. In addition, he disliked Jason from the beginning of his career in Seattle, and now Sammy had an opportunity to expose him for what he believed him to be—an underachiever who did not deserve the public adulation he was receiving.

"OK, Jim. I am considering this. Tell how you would proceed if you were to give her these kind of incentives."

"I would go to Mandy and first just offer her money. I know she needs it even though I am stuck paying her alimony for a few more years. I think an offer of a couple thousand dollars would probably get her attention."

"I know for sure that my editor and boss will not go for that," Sammy responded.

"Sammy, my friend. Count it done. Don't sweat it. I will pay the money even though I would make it seem like it is coming from you."

"You want this story to go forward bad enough for you to pay that kind of money?"

Jim laughed. "I have more money then I ever will need. That is nothing to me. It is chump change. Don't sweat it. Count it already done."

"OK, and if she balks and refuses?"

"I don't think she will do that, but if she does then I would come back with the other incentive. I would tell her that I believe that you would not print any information about her and Childs and their son if she cooperates. But I wouldn't tell her that unless she balks at accepting the money."

"I see. So, we attempt just to pay for her cooperation. If she agrees the complete story is in tact. If not, then we provide her with the promise to lay off of her and Childs in the story."

"You got it! It's that simple. Now trust me on this one, Sammy. I know this woman. I am sure that the money angle will work, but I am positive that if she balks then the promise to keep her out of the story will definitely pay off."

"So, how do you plan on going about this anyway? We are pressed for time. The editors have agreed to delay the articles until next Monday, but you must have all the information to me by Saturday at the latest so I have enough time to go ahead with the story line."

"I will call Mandy tonight and tell her I want to see her and talk about the alimony situation. I will tell her that I would like to provide her with some extra funds and that I want to make amends for the tension between us. That should be enough to get a meeting."

"When can you meet her?"

"Well, when she finds out that money is involved, I am sure that she will clear her schedule to meet me. I will suggest perhaps Thursday or Friday night after work."

"OK, Jim. You go for it, and keep me posted. But I want to emphasize to you that I will not run the story without this documentation. I simply have to see and read the letter before I go to print."

"I understand. I will get the job done on this for you, Sammy. Trust me. I know how to handle this woman."

Jim Harrison ended the conversation and sat at his desk feeling smug. In his heart he did not want to let Mandy off the hook. He wanted the information about Bobby Childs and their son to be in the press. He wanted to humiliate his ex-wife in public with information about her private life and her secret medical appointment with Dr. Barton. He knew what he was going to do. He would promise to Mandy that if she cooperated with Sammy Jensen and provided the letter, that Sammy would not write about her and Bobby. But he would not promise that somebody else would not write about them.

He smiled to himself as he picked up the telephone and dialed for information for the *Seattle Times*—the competitor newspaper to the *Seattle Post-Intelligencer*. He dialed the number received and asked to speak with Edwin Greene, the sports columnist for the newspaper.

"Ed Greene, here. How can I help you?"

"Hello, Mr. Greene. My name is Jim Harrison. I am an attorney in town and a big fan of your work on the sports pages of the *Times*."

"Thanks, Mr. Harrison. You are too kind. Now, how can I help you?"

"I believe that I have some information about Bobby Childs that you may be interested in having."

"Is that so? And why do you think I might be interested in this information?"

"Well, let me tell you that it is tough information to have, but I think the public is entitled to know all that goes on in the lives of these sports figures that we pay millions of dollars to watch."

"Mr. Harrison, I don't have a lot of time to waste. I think you need to just tell me straight what it is that you have, and then let me decide if I want to pursue it."

Jim then took five minutes to give Ed Greene a brief summary of what he knew regarding Bobby Childs and Mandy Brooks. He was careful to not divulge too much information because he wanted to set up a personal meeting with Greene after he had spoken with Mandy. However, as he spoke he could tell that Greene was listening intently.

"Bobby Childs is a big sports hero and one of the most popular celebrities in Seattle these days. So why should I burst the bubble and slime him right before the Super Bowl?" Ed Greene retorted.

"Because if you do not then I believe that Sammy Jensen will."

"Sammy? He is on to this story too?"

"I can tell you for certain that Sammy intends to break this story sometime next week— the week of the Super Bowl. I think you could probably beat him to the punch and publish it first. It would be a great journalistic coup for you if you did."

Like Sammy Jensen, Ed Greene was a competitive journalist. He had learned over the years that being the first to report a story of major interest was the key to the success of a journalist. Nothing would please him more than to get one over on his professional rival Sammy Jensen.

"Listen, Harrison. You have given me some things to think about, but I have to know you are for real and can deliver credible information. How can I be sure of that?"

"I am planning to meet with my ex-wife this week to talk about the whole matter. You see she is very angry with Childs for dumping her and not supporting their son over the years. I think that she would probably be willing to talk to you if the price is right."

"If the price is right? Are you talking about some kind of payoff to her to give us some information?"

"Sure. It is done all the time in your profession to get the kind of information you need. Right?"

"Yeah, it is done on occasion, but I have never had to do that to write a sports story. This is highly unusual."

Jim Harrison paused before responding. He knew that he was dangling a carrot in front of a very hungry reporter who wanted to beat Sammy Jensen to this story. After a few seconds of silence, Jim spoke again.

"Well, Ed, I am sorry if I am wasting your time. I just thought that you might be interested in pursuing this story. With the Super Bowl coming up, it is rather timely don't you think?"

"OK, Harrison, you have my attention. You said that you were going to talk with your ex-wife sometime this week. So why don't you meet with me on Saturday with the information I should have. I won't write anything unless I personally confirm this story with your ex-wife, so you should arrange with her a time to talk to me. If she agrees then we can go for it."

"Well, for her to talk she needs some incentives you know."

"I can't promise anything on that right now. Just get me some good information on Saturday, and we will work out the details that are needed to have a great story."

"All right. I will call you at the end of the week and let you know how my communication with her has gone. Then we can talk further."

The ending of the call was not to Jim's satisfaction. He knew that Mandy would never talk to Ed Greene to enable him to write about her relationship with Childs. And, in fact, he wanted any story written to place Mandy in the worst possible light in the public eye. It was hardly plausible to believe that Mandy would cooperate at all in such an endeavor. Perhaps, he thought, that trying to get Ed Greene to do a story on Childs and Mandy was unrealistic. Yet, he did have this option to pursue if all failed in his attempts to get the letter from Mandy's grasp.

He began to scheme about how he would accomplish this. If he failed he would urge Greene to go ahead with the story on Childs anyway. Being an experienced and successful trial lawyer, however, Jim Harrison did not plan on failing in his mission.

CHAPTER 13

Jason O'Connor got out of his car slowly. He was not looking forward to the meeting that lay ahead. As he walked up the stairs to the door, his felt knots and pains in his stomach.

Bobby opened the door and greeted his friend. "Hey, Jason, buddy. Come on in. We have been waiting for you." Immediately upon entering, Jason saw Mandy sitting on the couch in the living room. She smiled at her old friend whom she had not seen in over ten years.

Mandy walked over to Jason who was obviously tense and guarded. She gave him a hug and spoke. "Hi, Jason. It has been a long time, but it is so good to see you again."

Jason responded with a grunt. "That remains to be seen now, doesn't it?" He took a seat on the chair adjacent to the living room couch.

Bobby poured his friend a drink and sat on the couch next to Mandy as he spoke. "So how did it go over at the Johnsons? I guess that Wagner hammed this up pretty good for the press. I hope that these poor people weren't too offended by the display."

"Wagner was his typical self. The cameras were all out in force, and it was the show he intended it to be. You can see it all on television tonight if you have the stomach to watch."

"How did you feel about it? asked Bobby.

"Listen, man, these people are really great people. Joe Johnson is a pastor in an inner city church, trying to help others. His wife, Helena, is a Vietnamese American citizen and seems to be very involved in their ministry. They have a handicapped child named Moses whom they adopted. They simply should not be exploited at all by Wagner for PR purposes. I am totally offended by this."

Mandy seemed interested when Jason mentioned Moses. "Did you meet Moses? How serious is his handicap anyway?"

"He has a condition known as Down's syndrome. He has some level of mental retardation, but to me that isn't the serious part. He has a rare degenerative blood disease that will eventually take his life. Joe and Helena have scheduled him for a blood transfusion soon, but the doctors are not hopeful that the procedure will significantly prolong his life."

"Why is that?"

"Apparently the disease is extremely rare, and only a blood donor who is genetically related to him will have much of an impact on his condition. Since he is adopted, they don't know who this might be because the records of his blood relatives don't exist."

"The adoption records don't show who the birth mother and father are?"

"No, Joe and Helena filled me in on this. The adoption was very strange. Apparently Moses's birth mother left him on the steps of the adoption agency when he was a newborn with no information about herself. Nobody has a clue as to how to track her down."

Mandy became exceptionally still and silent upon hearing this news. She noticed that Jason had been avoiding looking at her when he talked, and she realized that her presence was incredibly difficult for him.

Jason finally looked at Mandy. "I understand that Sammy Jensen has been prying into all of our private lives and apparently thinks he has some big scandal to break out in the news. How come you didn't tell Bobby about his son years ago? Why now, Mandy? Don't you understand what a distraction this is and what a mess it could be for us to deal with?"

Mandy paused for a few seconds before responding. She understood Jason's suspicions and wanted to deal with them calmly. She knew at the end of the discussion the information she had to give him would be devastating, and it was important for her to remain cool.

"Jason, first of all, if I wanted to do harm to either you or Bobby, do you think we would be talking now? I would have obviously just given Sammy all the information he wanted and let him print his story. Instead, I refused to talk to him and called Bobby to warn him. And I told him about some information I had to warn you as well. I don't want Sammy to print anything. He just wants to create a scandal that will slander all of us, and I want to try to work with you and Bobby to stop him."

"So why didn't you tell Bobby about his son years ago? Why now?"

Bobby Childs interjected, "Jason, please hear me out on this one. Mandy and I have gone over all of this. I am totally satisfied that she did what was reasonable. It is my fault for abandoning her. Her husband wouldn't have allowed her to talk to me, and I certainly didn't give her the room to come to me anyway. She did what she thought was best at the time."

"You didn't answer me fully. Why now?"

Mandy responded this time. "Because, Sammy Jensen has been given information by Jim, my ex-husband, about little Bobby, and Jensen wants to print a story painting Bobby as a wild playboy who sired a child years ago and hasn't paid support. He wants to talk about my previous pregnancy with Bobby and how it was terminated. He also wants to write about your relationship with Rachel."

Jason was silent. He did not want the conversation to go further, but he knew that it must. "Didn't Rachel see Doctor Barton as well? Bobby, wasn't that the doctor in Spokane that you referred us to?"

"Yeah, Jason, that is the guy," responded Bobby.

Mandy sat still and looked at both Bobby and Jason and realized that now was the time for her to provide the long hidden information that she had been harboring for years. She got up from the couch and walked over to the table in the dining room where her purse was sitting. She reached in and pulled out a sealed envelope that had yellowed with age. Both Jason and Bobby were intense as she came back to the couch and sat down. All sat in cold silence for several seconds before she spoke.

"I want you both to know that I care about you deeply. Bobby, you are the love of my life. You always have been and always will be. If what I am about to share changes what we have talked about earlier today, then I understand. I only want you in my life if you choose to be there for me."

She then looked at Jason. With a completely open and honest heart, she spoke to her long estranged friend.

"Jason, we had some great times together in school. My best friend in the world—Rachel Thomlinson—loved you. She cared about you more than you could ever understand or know. But I cared about you too. I was in love, and still am, with your best friend Bobby Childs. But you were my friend too. I was so proud of your accomplishments on the football field. And even after I left both of you that night long ago in the fraternity, I followed your careers. Jason, when you came to Seattle two years ago, my interest in football was renewed, and my dad, my son, and I all became Seahawks fans. You can imagine how intense our fan loyalty grew when Bobby joined you this season."

Bobby and Jason remained fixed upon Mandy as she continued to speak, and she found more strength as she shared her feelings and thoughts. Mandy continued more forcefully.

"I am just trying to tell both of you that I cherish the memories of what we all were together. I know that we can't repeat the past. I know that we can't undo the mistakes made. I know that we can't bring Rachel back. But I want the future to be different. I believe that it can be. I believe that we all can still mean something to each other. But before that can happen, Jason, you must have something that Rachel meant you to have. It was written for you, but I know that she wanted Bobby to know its contents as well."

Mandy handed Jason the envelope that was in her hand. "Jason, you must read this letter. It was written to you two weeks before Rachel died. She told me the contents; although, I have never read it. She sealed it in the envelope and gave it to me for safekeeping while she contemplated sending it. She was afraid that if she kept it, she might mail it in haste and then regret that decision. She died without telling me what to do with the letter. But I honestly believe that she wanted it to be eventually given to you. I have kept it all these years not knowing if you should have it, until now."

"But you know for certain that I should have it now?" Jason asked.

"I know for certain that now is the time," responded Mandy. "Please read it and once you are done I will answer any questions and fill you in on the detail."

Jason's hands trembled as he struggled with opening the envelope. He finally tore it open and took out the one sheet that was inside. The sheet contained a typed letter addressed to him. It read as follows:

Dearest Jason,

It is now the end of October, and much has happened since we departed last May. My last communication in August simply said, "Problem taken care of," but I am not sure that you quite understand what I meant. I need to fill you in on the details.

Before I do, however, I want you to know something. Jason O'Connor—I love you with all my heart. My heart was broken when we said goodbye. You seemed calloused and thoughtless in the manner that you addressed me. Perhaps I should have been more understanding as to what you were feeling at the time. I know that it couldn't have been easy for you to hear the words "I am pregnant." Maybe I should have given you more grace for not responding to me in the manner that I wanted, but the past is the past.

Jason, I terminated my pregnancy, but not in the manner that you have assumed. Instead of going home for the summer, I stayed in Moses Lake with Mandy's aunt. She is a nurse-midwife who provides care for pregnant women.

I did not terminate my pregnancy by seeing the doctor in Spokane. He had seen Mandy earlier this year and was cruel and brutal to her. Mandy talked me out of doing that. Instead, both she and I lived with her aunt who took care of me over the summer months.

At the very end of the summer, I went into labor prematurely and had a baby boy. Mandy's aunt delivered the baby at her home. There is no hospital record of this birth. My parents did not know it because, as you recall, they had taken a trip to Europe for the summer. I told them I could not go with them because I was doing an internship with a midwife to get some credit to get into the nursing program at school. They believed me and didn't ask further questions.

Jason, the baby was very sick and tiny. Since he was two months premature, I had not yet made a decision about adoption. I was very scared, and Mandy's aunt insisted that I turn the baby over to the state authorities so that he would be given a home with an adoptive family. Somehow I couldn't do that.

A couple of days after the baby was born, Mandy and I dressed him in very warm clothes and wrapped him in a blanket. We put him in a small cradle, and then drove to Seattle. Mandy's aunt did not know about this. We went to an adoption agency on an early Saturday morning and left the baby at the front door of the agency. We stayed in the parking lot of the agency until someone came to the door. Once we saw that the baby was seen, we drove off. Nobody followed us, so I believe that we went undetected.

I noticed that the Seattle papers printed some stories on this situation for a few days, but I also read that the baby was eventually adopted and that all would be well.

Jason, I know that this must be a shock to you, but I just couldn't have handled it any other way. We can now relax knowing that our son is alive and making a family very happy. I am sorry that I did not talk to you about this, but I felt that you didn't want to see me again.

I know that things can never be the same between us. But I want you to know that I love you and will always love you. Nothing can ever change that.

I am rooting for you to win the Heisman Trophy this year. Nobody else is as deserving as you.

I will always be your biggest fan.

Loving you forever,

Rachel

Jason stared at the letter for minutes after he had completed reading it. Finally, he crumpled it in into a ball and threw it at Bobby. He then sat still in the chair with his face buried in his hands, and Bobby uncrumpled the letter and read it. After reading it, Bobby remained in stunned silence awaiting word from either Jason or Mandy before he spoke.

"I am sorry, Jason, to be the bearer of this news," Mandy said. Jason remained silent with his head in his hands. "I can answer any questions you have," she continued.

"Do you understand what all of this means?" Jason said. "I have a son that I have not known about for ten years, and just like you did with Bobby, you have kept this information from me. I know you had your reasons, Mandy, and actually, I think I understand those reasons, but you should have come forward sooner. Words can't describe to you what I am feeling now." Jason then buried his face in his hands and began to cry, as both Bobby and Mandy looked on helplessly.

Mandy spoke again, "Jason, remember that Sammy Jensen has been talking to my ex about all of this. Sammy wants to do you harm with his article. Maybe the three of us together can talk about ways to thwart his plans."

Jason responded, "I saw Sammy today at the Johnsons. He was very interested in the circumstances surrounding their adoption of Moses."

He then sat up straight, as if startled by a noise. He looked at Mandy and Bobby and asked, "You can't possibly believe that Moses could be my son could you?"

Both Mandy and Bobby gasped and breathed huge, loud sighs. "I don't know what to think Jason," said Mandy. "It sounds like it could be plausible."

"Well, tell me more about the day you two dropped the baby off at the agency."

"Rachel was panicked. The baby was dreadfully sick, but Rachel did not want to call the state authorities nor go to the hospital. The day before we went to the agency, I went to the local library in Moses Lake and got out a Seattle phone book. I looked under the heading "Adoption Services" and found the number and address of Bethany Services in Seattle. I then called and got directions."

"Why didn't you just go to the hospital and drop the baby off there?

They would have called the state, and Rachel would have been off the hook."

"Rachel was really afraid, and I was concerned about my aunt. She helped that summer because she loved me, and I insisted that she help us. But she knew she was acting very unprofessionally and possibly could lose her professional license over this. She knew that medical records needed to be kept and that she should be reporting her activities to a supervising physician. But because Rachel was scared that her parents would find out, my aunt kept quiet about it all and watched over Rachel that summer. It was a shock when Rachel went into labor prematurely. The baby was born two months ahead of schedule in August."

"Were you there when he was born?"

"Oh yes, I helped my aunt deliver. The baby was so tiny and so weak. We were all very, very scared."

Jason again buried his face in his hands and began to weep. "This all seems so very strange. It is like a nightmare that won't end. I am not sure I can ever forgive you, Mandy. Tell me that this is just a joke, and I will get up and go away."

Mandy Brooks walked over to Jason and put her hand on his shoulder as he continued to cry. "Jason, my friend. I will understand if you hate me the rest of your life. All I can say is that I loved Rachel and wanted to help her. I am so sorry I have kept this secret from you for so long. I hope some day you will find it in your heart to forgive me."

"So give me more detail about the day you dropped him off at the agency. Believe me, I need to know more about this."

Mandy responded, "It was only two days after he was born. My aunt said she was going to have to take the baby in to the hospital and that scared us both. We got up very early that morning and Rachel dressed the baby warmly. She had been trying to nurse him, but it was clear that he was sick and dehydrated. She wrapped him in a warm blanket and put him in the small portable crib we had. My aunt was still asleep and didn't hear us leave."

"And you drove all the way to Seattle then?"

"Yes, we arrived at the agency around eight in the morning. Since

I had called earlier, I knew that nobody would be arriving until around nine. Rachel held the baby in her arms for a minute as we sat in the car in the parking lot. We both cried a lot. Finally, Rachel put him in the crib and made sure he was comfortable. She left a few things of hers in the crib with him but did not write a note. She took the baby out of the car and placed the crib at the front door of the agency. About five minutes later, someone came and saw the baby. We immediately drove off."

"What did Rachel leave in the crib?" Jason asked as he began to gain his composure.

"You know what Jason—I did not ask her, and to this day, I honestly don't know. She was so distraught. As we drove off she was crying uncontrollably, and I was just trying to console her telling her that she did the right thing. We drove back to Moses Lake that very same day."

Bobby had been listening to all of this quietly, not knowing how to respond. The details of the story were breathtaking to him, and he felt that his irresponsible actions had played some role in this drama that was unfolding before them all.

Jason continued to question Mandy. "So when you saw her last, how was she doing and what did she tell you about the letter I just read?"

"Well, it was late October—a couple of months after his birth—and she seemed to have recovered emotionally to a point that we could talk. Her mom and dad still had no clue about all of this. Rachel wanted to talk about you a lot. She loved you Jason and wanted you to know about your son. The newspapers apparently picked up on the story for a while, and Rachel followed it carefully and was satisfied that, at least according to the news accounts, the baby was going to be adopted to a loving family. I know that she hoped eventually that you and she would get back together and that she could share all of this with you."

Mandy's voice choked with emotion. "Rachel's death was such a shock to me. When she died, everything changed. Death has a way of changing things forever."

Jason suddenly stood up as if he had been startled by something and began to pace back and forth and reflected upon all that had been said. An incredulous thought came to him and he said: "Are you two thinking what I am thinking? This story sounds so close to what Joe and Helena have shared with me about Moses. Could it possibly be that Moses is my son? Sammy Jensen sure seemed interested in knowing more about the adoption of Moses. Is he on to something here?"

Mandy and Bobby were dumbfounded by the possibility of what Jason was saying. "I don't know what to think, Jason. My ex knows all of these details, and it appears that he has been talking with Sammy. Has Sammy been trying to get an interview with you?"

"Oh, yes. In fact, I am supposed to give him thirty minutes tomorrow after practice. That is all that I told him he can have, but I did promise it to him. I know that he is up to no good. And now it appears he is on the verge of uncovering the scoop of his life. Everything seems to be falling into place for him. Does your ex know about this letter?"

"Yes. Jim knows everything. I was married to him for seven years. He never asked to see the letter though, and now since we are divorced, he does not have access to it. If you want, we can destroy it right now."

"No, I want you to keep it. I don't want it, but it was written by someone special to all of us. Please hold on to it as a keepsake. I just need to be sure about Moses. I will go over to the Johnsons after practice tomorrow to ask some more questions."

Mandy took the crumpled letter, smoothed the wrinkles out, and then folded it neatly. She placed it in a pocket in her purse.

Bobby finally spoke. "Jason, what are you going to do if you find out that Moses is your son?"

Jason just stared at his friend without saying a word. Their eye contact said it all. The story that had unraveled before them was just too improbable to even contemplate a response.

Mandy broke the silence. "Jason, I can't tell you what to do. But we do need to be concerned about Sammy Jensen, don't you think?"

Jason responded, "I am supposed to talk to Sammy tomorrow. But I am going to put him off until I can talk again with Joe and Helena. I have to find some answers myself before I know what to do or say."

Jason then abruptly got out of his chair and walked toward the door. He turned and looked at his friends and spoke again.

"You probably think that I am mad at you, Mandy. I certainly was at the beginning of our conversation, but now, for some strange reason, I am not. Something is going on that I cannot explain. I need to tell both of you soon about a dream I had two nights ago. It must have something to do with all of this."

Mandy and Bobby struggled to respond. But no words came.

"I need to be by myself. Tomorrow after practice I will go and talk to Joe and Helena. That's all I can say now."

With that comment, Jason left Bobby's house, and Mandy immediately fell into Bobby's arms, struggling with her emotions. Bobby felt numb. He could do nothing but hold her tight and stroke her hair. His own body trembled from the stress and emotion of the moment.

"Oh, Bobby. What is going to happen to us all over this?"

"I don't know, Mandy. I just don't know."

CHAPTER 14

The shrill sound of the alarm clock at 6:00 AM on Wednesday morning brought an excruciating pain to the delicate and injured head of Jason O'Connor. He sat up in bed and rubbed his eyes, trying to wake up, but his eyes would not open. He immediately flopped back down and dozed off for another ten minutes until the alarm rang again, causing him to reach out and swat the clock off the nightstand. He had been through an enormous amount of stress the past few days and was totally exhausted. He just wanted a day off to be by himself and try to understand what was transpiring in his life. The previous day had been so exhausting, both physically and emotionally, that he was not able to think clearly when he got home from Bobby's place. In fact, he was so numb at that time that all he wanted to do was sleep. But this was a new day, and his mind began to race with the details of his life that were unfolding.

Events had come at him at supersonic speed since the play-off victory over St. Louis: his head injury on his winning touchdown run; the second blow to his head outside the stadium on his way to the hospital; the haunting dream of Rachel that very night; Bobby's reconnection with Mandy Brooks; his meeting with Joe, Helena, and Moses; and the discovery that Moses could be his son all were events of such magnitude that his body was ready to collapse from exhaustion, even after a long night's sleep.

Jason finally rolled out of bed knowing that he needed to be at the stadium by 8:00 AM to go over the day's practice plan and schedule with Wagner. He immediately opened his front door to retrieve the morning paper and on the front page of the *Seattle P-I* he saw his picture embracing Moses with Joe and Helena standing on the side smiling. The headlines read, "Seahawks Superstar Touches the Life of Handicapped Youngster."

Jason began to peruse through the article, which went into detail about the Johnson family, describing Joe and Helena and telling readers about their inner-city church. The article went on further to describe Moses and his handicapped condition. It mentioned the obvious fact that Moses was the adopted child of the Johnsons and how the three family members—an African-American male, a Vietnamese female, and a Down's syndrome white child—constituted a highly unusual make-up for a family. The article then talked about the presence of Jason and Wagner in the Johnson home and how the presentation of the Seahawks season tickets brought joy to this impoverished family.

"I am sure that Wagner is pleased with this portrayal of himself as a wonderful and compassionate philanthropist," Jason mumbled as he read on. When he completed the article he turned to the sports section and saw the Wednesday column of Sammy Jensen entitled, "Sentimentality Still Alive and Well in the NFL." Jason smiled as he read Sammy's comments.

Sammy started off his article by announcing that publication of his long awaited series on "The Brotherhood" was being postponed until the following Monday in order for him to have more time to "verify sources." Sammy then began to discuss the events at the Johnson home the previous day. He wrote in part:

> The world of the NFL can be brutal and violent. NFL football is not only known for its bone-crushing play on the field that can literally cripple an individual but also for its "dog eat dog" business practices where only the careers of the fittest athletes survive to play for more than a few seasons. Yet, the NFL does have a softer side. And this softer side was evident yesterday in the home of a former small college football lineman—the Rev. Josiah Johnson, affectionately known to his friends and family as "Joe."
>
> I was privileged to be at the home of Joe and his family along with Jason O'Connor and Paul Wagner who expressed their gratitude to Joe for his alert reaction to a falling concrete beam that

could have permanently ended Jason O'Connor's football career. Wagner expressed it best when he turned to Joe and told him that Seahawks fans everywhere were thankful for his preparedness and then presented to the Johnsons the coveted season tickets for next year. (Current popularity of the Seahawks makes this a very valuable commodity, worth several thousand dollars.)

Joe Johnson is a humble man who accepted the gift with meekness and appreciation—an uncommon trait for the likes of celebrities like Wagner and O'Connor. But the true joy of the moment came from the facial expression of Moses, the Johnson's adopted ten-year-old son who has Down's syndrome. Upon learning of the gift of season tickets, Moses, who has been raised in the ways of professional football by his adopted father (a die-hard Seahawks fan), jumped into the arms of O'Connor, giving the big Seahawks quarterback a hug that brought tears to the eyes of those of us fortunate to witness the event.

Yes, NFL football can be brutal. Yes, NFL football can be a violent sport where only the fittest of the fittest survive. But NFL football can also bring joy and happiness to those for whom the fortunes of life have been sparse. The joy shown yesterday on the face of Moses Johnson, a handicapped boy, is proof that the Seahawks magic performed by Jason O'Connor and company this season has touched many.

As Jason put down the paper to pour himself a cup of coffee, the phone rang. According to the caller ID, Jason saw that it was a call from none other than Sammy Jensen. He pondered for a moment as to whether he should answer the call but decided that he had to talk with Sammy eventually to cancel their appointment. He was glad to get this over with early.

"Good morning, Sammy. Nice comments in today's paper," Jason said as he answered the phone.

"Well, thank you, O'Connor. I am not used to such compliments from the likes of you."

"Don't mention it."

"Well, I am just calling to set up a time after practice today to meet for our interview. I will be hanging around the locker room all day, so you tell me what is convenient."

"Listen, Sammy, I am going to put you off for awhile on this one. I have a very important appointment to get to after practice, and I just don't have time for this today."

"Come on, O'Connor. I have been counting on you so I can get this project completed. You obviously don't have complaints about my article this morning, so you should trust me on this."

"Like I said, Sammy, it has to wait. Another important matter has come up, and I simply can't accommodate you today."

"So when can we talk? I have a deadline on this thing."

Jason wanted to hang up the phone and let Sammy fend for himself. Yet, he knew that Sammy was on to something that could result in a very hurtful and negative story to not only him but also to his friends Bobby and Mandy. He paused before he responded. "OK, Sammy…I hope I don't regret this, but we can talk on Saturday. The team flies out to Miami on Saturday afternoon. I will give you thirty minutes at the airport prior to leaving. Take it or leave it."

"Thirty minutes? Now listen I need at least an hour to go over some things with you."

"Like I said. Take it, or leave it, Sammy."

"Come on, Jason. The entire city is waiting for these articles because they want to know more about their exalted football heroes. You and Childs are hot commodities these days in the public eye, so these articles are important because they will give the public what they not only are demanding but what they deserve."

"What they deserve? What in the heck are you talking about Sammy? Why does the public deserve to hear gossip and innuendo that will destroy people's reputations and hurt them? You must be joking man. The public has no right to this kind of information."

Sammy began to get testy. "Why do you think I am going to print gossip and innuendo, O'Connor? Where is your head? Have those two blows to your skull rendered you incompetent to understand what this is about? Or, are you simply paranoid? These articles are going to provide the public with a bird's-eye view of the two most popular men in town, and I believe, on the whole, will be very complimentary. Why are you so mistrustful of me anyway?"

"I am not buying it, Sammy. You have exactly thirty minutes on Saturday, and that is it. Take it, or leave it."

Sammy let loose a long, frustrated sigh before responding. "OK. You don't give me much choice, and I can't force you to talk. I have to take what I can get. I will be there at the airport on Saturday. Saturday night is my deadline to finish these articles up, but they will be a lot more informative if you can give me more time."

"You will be fine, Sammy," Jason said as he abruptly hung up the phone. He next turned on *Morning Sports Talk* as he got ready for the day. Jake McGee and Robin Everson were taking calls on the Super Bowl, and Jake announced that he had Joe Johnson on the line for a brief interview. Jason immediately perked up and turned up the radio to listen while he shaved.

Jake McGee did a brief introduction of Joe Johnson, and then began his questioning. "I have on the line right now the Reverend Josiah Johnson who, as most of you sports fans know, made headlines on Sunday night by rescuing Jason O'Connor from serious and maybe permanent injury from a falling concrete beam. Good morning sir."

"Good morning, Jake. I am a big fan of your show."

"We appreciate it. It is listeners like you Joe who make this job of mine a wonderful experience. Now, let me ask you a few questions. Most sports fans in Seattle have been intrigued by what took place outside the stadium last Sunday as you tackled Jason O'Connor to push him out of the way of a falling concrete beam. Could you just briefly tell us what happened?"

Joe laughed and then responded. "You know, Jake, it happened so fast that I am not sure about all of the details. All I know is that for some reason I diverted my attention away from Jason O'Connor and Coach Wagner for just a brief second. My eyes directly connected with the beam that began to fall, and I instinctively reacted. I screamed out a warning, and then lunged toward Jason knocking him away from the beam as it crashed to the concrete. I sure feel bad that maybe his head was further injured from this."

"Well, the Seahawks front office tells us he will be ready for the game. I think Seahawks fans realize that if you hadn't reacted so quickly, the beam would have hit him, and who knows what damage that would have done."

"Yes, that beam weighs several hundred pounds."

"Joe, the papers all carried a story this morning about the meeting you had yesterday with Coach Wagner and Jason O'Connor. Could you give us a little bit of your perspective on this meeting?"

"Robin, I just want to publicly thank Coach Wagner and the Seahawks front office for their kind gift of season tickets for me and my family. I don't believe I did anything out of the ordinary. You or anybody else would have done the same thing. But I am very thankful to be able to be a season ticket holder for next season. Coach Wagner and Jason O'Connor were both very kind to stop by and give this gift to us."

"I understand that you have a handicapped son who is a big Seahawks fan. How did he respond to this gift?"

Joe chuckled. "Moses, our son, was thrilled. He is a big Jason O'Connor fan, and as the papers showed this morning, he hugged Jason when he was told the news. I can't tell you what that kind of happiness for our son means to my wife and me." Joe paused a moment and his voice cracked with emotion. He then continued. "Moses is handicapped and also suffers from a terminal blood disease. We are not sure how much longer he will be with us, so this gift is very special."

Jake McGee began to wrap up the interview but expressed his desire to continue the conversation at a later time. "We don't want to intrude into your family's private matters, but I would like to have you on again to talk about Moses a little bit more and see if, perhaps, the public can help out in some way. I understand he is going to undergo a blood transfusion in the very near future."

"Yes, Jake, that is true. On the Friday before the Super Bowl, Moses will be receiving a full blood transfusion in hopes of alleviating the problems he is now having. We would have loved to wait until after the Super Bowl for this procedure so that Moses wouldn't have to be in the hospital recovering during the game. However, his situation is very serious, and we just couldn't wait any longer given the rapid decline in his condition. We are all saying our prayers that it will be a success."

"Well, Joe, count both Robin and me in on those prayers. The story in the papers this morning about Moses was very touching, and I know I speak for Seahawks fans everywhere when I wish you and your family, and especially Moses, the very best."

Jason turned off his radio as the interview ended. His mind raced as he contemplated what he had just heard. If he, in fact, were Moses's father, his blood donation could save his son's life and extend it for years. Yet, giving blood, he was almost certain, meant that he would not be physically able to play in the Super Bowl.

Jason knew that he had to see Joe and Helena as soon as possible to find out the answer to the question that was most on his mind. Is he Moses father? He knew that as soon as practice ended he must drive to the Johnson home and talk to them about the matter.

The meeting that morning with Wagner to review the practice schedule for the day was mundane and routine. Wagner did not mention anything further about the Johnsons, nor did he comment on the stories in the morning papers. Wagner was totally focused on preparation for the Steelers and the Super Bowl. Jason, however, was not so inclined. His mind was on Moses and Rachel, and he continued to play back in his mind the way Moses had hugged him and the details of his dream on Sunday night.

Paul Wagner noticed that Jason seemed distant and distracted in the meeting. He abruptly commented, "O'Connor, what is with you today? Is the head all right?"

"It still aches, Coach, but it is feeling better."

"Well, glad to hear it. Now, if you don't mind, would you get that head of yours into the detail of our work today? We can't pull this thing off without your total concentration. Are you with us?'

"I am with you, Coach. Don't give it another thought," responded Jason. In reality, however, football and the Super Bowl were the very last things on his mind.

The Seahawks' practice was intense that day. Zach Morrison took all the snaps from center as the team prepared its arsenal of offensive weapons. However, Bobby Childs noticed that the passing game in practice was once again only short passes and ignored the deep threat that was his specialty. His frustration with this portion of game preparation was growing by the minute, and his patience with Wagner and his game plan was being severely challenged. As the team took a break, he once again confronted the coach with his bewilderment about the failure to work on the deep-passing routes.

"Coach, what is going on here," he said to Wagner at the break. "I haven't received one deep pass from Morrison all week. Don't you think it would be wise to work on that aspect of the game, just in case Jason doesn't make it back."

"Just cool it, Childs! Who are you to question me? Jason will be back, and we plan on starting him, so I don't think you have anything to worry about. Just knock off the questions. I know what I am doing."

Practice continued in a very uninspired manner. The spark necessary to charge the team and prepare them emotionally for victory was lacking. Nobody could quite understand why this was happening, but it was clear to all who observed that the Seahawks were just going through the motions. Little spirit seemed to be in the effort.

After practice most of the team headed immediately for the locker room to avoid the press. Wagner and Jason went straight to the pressroom to face the onslaught of questions from the Seattle sports media. The questions came immediately upon the entry of Wagner and Jason into the press room.

"Coach Wagner, could you give us an update on Jason's situation? Are you still confident that he will be your starter come Super Bowl Sunday?"

"Absolutely! Nothing has changed, fellas. Jason O'Connor is getting stronger by the minute and will be ready to take the snaps from center from the beginning to the end of the game."

Jason looked away, trying not to show by his facial expressions his feelings of contempt. Although he would never let his injuries get in he way of his opportunity to play in the Super Bowl, Jason sincerely questioned whether his physical condition would allow him to play at full strength. His head still hurt, and his vision was blurry at times. He strongly and correctly suspected that Wagner hadn't told him the truth, and because of this, he was disdainful of his coach.

"What do you say about that, Jason?" Are you going to be ready?"

"Well, let me say it one more time, and hopefully this will be the last time I have to say it. Nothing—and I mean absolutely nothing—is going to keep me out of that game, except maybe an act of God. I hope this finally settles the matter. Next question please."

"Coach, will Zach Morrison be able to carry the load in the event Jason is not able to do so or gets injured again?"

"Zach Morrison is a veteran and, of course, will be able to handle the job if called upon. However, let me tell you again—Jason O'Connor is going to be our quarterback and take the opening snap from center at the Super Bowl."

Another reporter asked, "Why hasn't Morrison been throwing the long ball more in practice? Is he physically able to throw the long ball these days? He certainly hasn't had much experience this season in doing so."

"Look, I have already told you. Jason O'Connor is going to be our starter for the game. In the very unlikely event that he is injured and has to be taken out, Zach Morrison will be ready to go. We have all the confidence in the world in both of our quarterbacks."

The press conference continued on for thirty more minutes with more questions being asked of Jason regarding his ability to play and his readiness for the challenge of the Steelers. Jason fended off each question by repeating his answer that by now had become a mantra. "Only an act of God is going to keep me out of this game. Only an act of God."

Paul Wagner finally announced that there was time for one more question and waiting for such a moment was none other than Sammy Jensen. Wagner acknowledged Sammy's request to be heard, and Sammy rose to make his inquiry.

"Jason, I want to change the topic here just a little. Yesterday, I and a few other reporters were able to witness an astonishing event at the home of Rev. Josiah Johnson. We were all moved by the sight of the Johnson's handicapped son, Moses, embracing you in joy at the news of his family receiving season tickets. Could you share with all of us what went through your mind when that happened?"

Jason was stunned. He stared directly at Sammy trying to compose himself before speaking. He was not sure how to answer without giving away his emotions and thoughts. After a few brief moments of reflection, Jason responded.

"Like anybody would be in that situation, I was touched. I have been blessed with athletic ability and a strong body to do things that very few people can do. Sometimes I really don't appreciate how blessed I really am."

Jason felt his emotions swell as he was talking. He continued.

"I certainly haven't appreciated the impact this Seahawks season has had on people—until now. When Moses hugged me, I finally understood. I realized at that moment that this team has brought a lot of happiness to people. I understood that people, like Moses, who can't throw a football, run, or tackle have been brought a lot of joy from our efforts this season. I don't want to let them down. They are the reason that I want to win this game. Our victory over the Steelers will be for them."

Jason paused again to fight back the tears that were beginning to fill his eyes. The reporters in attendance were frozen in amazed silence at this unexpected show of emotion, and all eyes were on him as his voice cracked. The cameras were flashing and rolling as he continued.

"Frankly, my experience with Moses was quite humbling. I am not sure I will be the same again. And I want to say right now that this game is dedicated to him."

This was an unexpected moment that had just been witnessed and put on tape. All present understood that these heartfelt comments about the handicapped youngster, who had embraced him, were also going to be the lead story in the headlines the next day.

After this show of emotion, Jason abruptly got up from the press table and exited to the locker room. Wagner followed him. When they were alone inside the locker room, Wagner exploded.

"What was that all about? You just dedicated this game to a kid you met yesterday and won't see again the rest of your life? Now, isn't that just lovely. The press is eating it up. What is the matter with you O'Connor? I guess your head injury is more serious than I thought. Because of your lame-brained comments just now, this team is going to have to play along. So do you now suggest that we put stickers on our helmets saying 'Win one for the little retard?'"

Wagner then raised his voice and moved right in front of Jason's face as he continued his tirade, shouting, "You listen to me, buster. I call the shots for this team, and that means that I, not you, will determine to whom we are dedicating this game. And I am not going to pander to the sentimentalities of little old ladies by dedicating this game to some retarded cripple! Do you hear me?"

It took all of Jason's will power to restrain himself from physically assaulting Wagner. As Jason angrily glared at his coach, Wagner realized that he had crossed the line. He saw the anger in Jason's eyes and stepped back. As he turned to go to his office, he quipped in a nonchalant manner, "Just remember who is boss here, O'Connor, and all will go well."

Jason quickly went to his locker to change into street clothes and leave. It had been a long day. He was exhausted, and this encounter with the Seahawks head coach had done nothing to ease his stress. He quietly packed his items and left the stadium, wanting to be alone with himself. His journey to Joe and Helena's home was a trip he was dreading but was necessary to answer the question that was lingering in his mind. If, in fact, Moses was his son, as he seriously now suspected, his life would be changed forever.

The Johnson home was located in the toughest part of the inner city and was a thirty minute drive from the stadium in rush hour traffic. On his previous trip to the Johnson resident, Jason was totally unobservant of the decaying nature of this part of the city. However, on this journey, for some reason, Jason began to notice the blight of the neighborhoods of the inner city and the depressed spirit that accompanied it.

It seemed to him that every intersection that he passed was accompanied by an abandoned, dilapidated building. And it seemed to him that every street corner was inhabited by at least one seedy character who was clearly interested in making trouble. At one intersection stood a young girl, in her early teens, who was dressed seductively and smiled at his car while motioning for him to stop. Jason shook his head sadly as he continued on his journey.

At another street corner he saw a circle of three young men who were obviously up to no good. If he ever saw a drug deal in the making, this was it. One of the men in this circle was a few years older than the other two and from the way he was dressed it looked like he was profiting nicely from his exploitation of his younger associates. Jason again shook his head realizing that he had just entered into a world with which he was unfamiliar.

Jason had grown up in a farming community and went to college in a small rural setting. His life in the NFL exposed him to big city life but only to the finer aspects of metropolitan living. He had not seen the seedier side of the big city that included crime, drugs, prostitution, and mayhem. On this drive, however, he began to take notice that another side to life existed outside of the privileged existence he had enjoyed as an NFL quarterback.

Jason finally pulled up in front of the Johnson home. As he parked his car, he contemplated what he was going to say and how he would say it. He was unsure of the exact words that would come, but he knew that he could not leave until he had an answer. His legs felt weak as he walked down the cement pathway to the residence. His hands shook as he knocked. After a few nervous moments the door opened, and he was pleasantly greeted by Helena Johnson.

"Oh, Jason, how nice to see you," Helena exclaimed. "What an honor for this visit. Please come in and sit down."

Jason walked slowly and deliberately into the home and sat down on the living room couch. His subdued demeanor indicated to Helena that something was on his mind.

"I am sorry I did not call before I came, but I need to see both you and Joe. Is Joe available?"

"He is next door at the church right now. There is a special prayer meeting going on for Moses. Many of the church members are there with him. You can go over if you want, but he won't be available to talk for a few hours. After the service he has patrol duty."

"Patrol duty?"

"Yes. The Seattle Police Department has deputized him to patrol the neighborhood during various nights of the week. This is his night. He will probably be gone until around nine tonight, but I am sure he will let you ride along if you like."

Jason smiled and replied, "I just might do that. Joe seems like the kind of deputy people wouldn't want to mess with."

Helen returned the smile and sat quietly waiting for Jason to share more of what was on his mind. After a few moments she softly spoke.

"Moses would be happy to see you, but he is sleeping right now. He sleeps a lot these days."

"Helena, be honest with me. How is he doing?"

Helena struggled with her response. "Not good, Jason. We have a blood transfusion scheduled a week from this Friday—right before the Super Bowl. He sleeps a lot these days—sometimes eighteen hours in a day. I am so afraid that one these times he just won't wake up."

Jason was choked up as he saw Helena struggle to find words. He responded, "Do the doctors give any prognosis for him? Is there some reasonable expectation given for improvement after this transfusion?"

"Nobody really knows, Jason. Moses has had two transfusions before, and after each one there seemed to be a little more life to him—for awhile. But gradually he has gotten weaker. After we discovered his condition (around the time we adopted him), we were told that the odds were not good for him to live past the age of twenty. We have always been aware that our time with him would be short, but he is only ten right now. We are praying for a miracle. We really would like to have another ten years with him."

"You really do love him, don't you?

Helena burst into tears. She covered her face in her hands as she struggled to gain her composure. Jason sat uncomfortably on the couch, not sure what to do. He waited patiently for her to respond.

"Most people don't understand this. They see him as a handicapped child and assume that he must be a burden to us. But really he is such a joy. We probably need him more than he needs us. Moses is the sparkle in our lives. Joe lives for the special times he can have with Moses. And the wonderful Sundays outside Qwest Stadium with Moses listening to the radio and hearing you play have been so special. We are just praying that Moses will live to be able to go to those games next year and watch you in person."

Jason was struggling inside. He wanted to ask Helena more about Moses and the conditions surrounding the adoption, but he knew that such questions needed to be asked while Joe was present. He stood up and went into the dining room to look at his portrait. Helena followed.

"That is some picture," Jason said with a chuckle. "Growing up on the farm back in Mansfield, I never would have guessed that one day I would be the inspiration of an artist."

"You are the inspiration to more than just an artist, Jason." Helena said. "You have brought joy to many—including my son."

Jason smiled at his host and then stated, "So Joe is over at the church? Why don't I go over for awhile and see if I can catch his eye. Maybe he will let me ride along with him on his patrol afterwards."

"Joe would be so thrilled to share that with you, Jason. Please go ahead. Just walk in, and find a seat in one of the pews; although, I think there may not be many seats left. I know a lot of people planned on attending."

"Thanks, Helena. I will come back here with Joe afterward. I need to talk with both of you for a bit."

Helena looked puzzled but responded, "I will be here. I don't think Moses will be awake, but I will look forward to the company."

Jason gave his host a brief hug, and then exited the home. He quickly walked next door to the small church building. As he approached, he could hear inside joyful singing and clapping. He walked in the back of the church. Joe had a microphone in his hand and was singing the lead as the choir joined in the background. It was an old time gospel hymn familiar to Jason from his childhood days at the Mansfield country church.

See the little baby.
Amen.
Lying in a manger.
Amen.
On Christmas morning.
Amen, Amen, Amen.
See him in the temple.
Amen.
Talking with the elders.
Amen.
How they marvel at his wisdom.
Amen, Amen, Amen.
See him on the seashore.
Amen.
Preachin' and a healing.
Amen.
All the blind and the feeble.
Amen, Amen, Amen.

Jason smiled as the song continued. It was accompanied by drums, guitar, bass, and keyboard, and the clapping of the congregation to the lively beat made it impossible not to stomp one's foot to the rhythm. As the music continued, Jason, noticed that this church was indeed unique. The pews were filled with black faces, white faces, brown faces, and yellow faces. Young and old were all in the church sanctuary, led by this big, charismatic, black pastor who was singing with the passion of a professional gospel singer.

He was amazed as he looked more closely at the people in the church who had gathered to sing and pray. It was obvious that nobody in this church, except for him, enjoyed any means of personal wealth. It was clear that these people all were struggling and that many of them were living in poverty. He noticed several people in wheel chairs clapping to the music. Not far from him sat a person who appeared to be blind, who was broadly smiling. And a complete row of hearing impaired church members sat in a pew, as a person stood in front of them signing the words of the songs.

Joy surrounded Jason, and he felt it deep inside of him. He wondered how people like this who had so little in their lives could actually believe that they had so much. He wanted to know the secret to their contentment. Jason had not been in church for years. As a child, his grandmother made him go to church every Sunday, and he had heard all of the Bible stories many times over. Yet, the loss of his parents at an early age caused him to tune out any deep thoughts of God and what life was all about. Football had become his god. Football was his religion and, until this very day, was all that mattered to him. Now, however, as he listened and observed the demonstrations of joy in the lives of the people around him, he was deeply moved and wondered if he had missed something all of these years.

The choir and instruments quickly moved on to song after song as the congregation joined in the singing and worship. After a few more tunes, Joe again grabbed the microphone and led them all in a peppy country style hymn.

> *Some glad morning when this life is over I'll fly away.*
> *To a home on God's celestial shore. I'll fly away.*
> *I'll fly away oh glory, I'll fly away.*
> *When I die, Hallelujah bye and bye,*
> *I'll fly away.*

The emotional level rose, as the congregation stood clapping, singing, and stomping to the rhythm of the music. Jason could not help but join in, as he remembered this hymn being sung at his church when he was a small child. Finally, the music ended. Joe motioned for the congregation to be seated, and then grabbed a microphone to speak.

"Thank you all for being here tonight for this very special service. Helena would love to be here, but Moses is not doing well, so she stayed home. She is, of course, here with us in spirit."

Joe finally noticed Jason sitting in the back of church. Upon seeing him, Joe smiled a big, hearty smile and said, "We are honored tonight with a special guest. He came in late, so most of you did not see him here, but ladies and gentlemen, let's give a big welcome to Seahawks quarterback, Jason O'Connor."

A gasp went through the audience as people realized who was in attendance. After a brief moment, the congregation burst into loud applause and stood to their feet in a standing ovation. Jason was moved but also embarrassed. He really did not want anybody to know he was present.

Joe continued to smile. When the ovation ended and the congregation sat down, he said, "I told you, Jason, that you were loved here. Thank you so much for being with us tonight."

Joe then became solemn as he continued to talk. "We are here on a very serious matter. This congregation has been blessed over the years by a young boy named Moses. To some in our society, Moses just takes up space and consumes resources; he is a useless eater who should have never been born. To some, he has nothing of value to offer. To some, he is considered a burden and a life not worthy to be lived."

"To Helena and me, however, Moses is a gift from God." A member in the back of the church shouted a loud "Amen," and then the entire congregation stood up and applauded. Joe was in a sermon mode now as he paced back and forth in front of the audience.

"To this congregation, Moses is a gift from God. He has taught all of us how to be compassionate and caring. He has taught us how to care for those less fortunate. And he has taught us to laugh. Yes, he has taught us to not take ourselves too seriously and to laugh at ourselves when we do the silly and stupid things we are prone to do."

"Preach it, brother," shouted another congregant as Joe continued on.

"Well, tonight we are gathering in honor of Moses and to ask the Lord for a miracle."

A woman in the front shouted out, "Yes, Lord, please give us a miracle tonight." The congregation again stood and applauded loudly, with many petitioning out loud for the Lord to hear and answer their prayers.

Joe waited for a moment to let the crowd settle back down, and then continued to speak. "I have to tell you that Moses is not doing well. He sleeps most of the day and night. He is very weak. You all know that a blood transfusion is scheduled a week from this Friday and we, of course, ask for your prayers. But the doctors are not optimistic. They say that only blood from one who is genetically related could possibly have a impact and improve Moses's condition. But we all know the circumstances of his birth and that finding such a donor would truly be a miracle.

"I want everyone to bow with me now as we ask for this miracle. For those of you who want to come forward and kneel in front of the church to pray, please feel free to do so. If you want to remain in your pew and silently pray that is fine too. You just pray in the way you know how. I will lead us."

Many people came forward and knelt, while others stayed in their pews and quietly waited for Joe to direct their actions. When all had settled in, Joe led the congregation in a prayer. His deep booming voice filled the church sanctuary with his petition.

"Our gracious and almighty, God," Joe prayed, "thank you for all your blessings."

Many "Amens" were heard throughout the congregation as Joe continued.

"And thank you, Lord, for the most precious gift of all—the gift of life." Again many "Amens" and "Thank you, Lords" were heard throughout the audience.

"Tonight, Lord, we are most thankful for your gift to us of Moses. This gift has taught us all how to love. He has taught us all how to care for others."

"Amens" were again heard throughout the congregation as they fervently joined in with the prayer.

"So, Lord, tonight we ask you for a miracle. You know the blood transfusion coming up has little chance of improving life for Moses—at least that is what we have been told by the experts. But we ask you tonight to confound those experts and to revive the life of this precious little boy who we all love."

Joe continued to pray, and the congregation continued to join in agreement with the vocal and sometimes very loud "Amens." Jason was silent and taken back by what he was witnessing. He had never before seen such purity, such innocence of spirit from people when they prayed. These people really believed that they were talking to a God who cared. Since the death of his parents, Jason saw God only as an angry, mean ogre in the sky who enjoyed making life miserable for mere mortals. These people saw God much differently. The prayers moved him, and, for the first time in many years, Jason prayed as well.

The service ended after about forty-five minutes of solid prayer from Joe and the congregation. Immediately after the congregation was adjourned, admirers and well-wishers surrounded Jason. Ladies of the church hugged him, wishing him God's speed in his recovery and in the upcoming Super Bowl. And many teenage boys sought his autograph while their female peers stood by, swooning over the handsome Seahawks bachelor. Finally, Joe interrupted the gathering and dismissed the crowd, saying that Jason needed his space and rest if he were going to lead the Seahawks to victory.

After the group of admirers disbursed Joe stated, "Well, Jason, my friend, it is such a pleasant surprise to see you tonight. How about coming along with me for a ride as I patrol the neighborhood for a few hours?"

"I am delighted that you would ask me, Joe. Let's get out of here."

CHAPTER 15

Mandy Brooks stirred the spaghetti on the stove as she prepared dinner for her dad and son. Details of the last few days filled her mind. She agonized over the situation that Jason faced in regard to Moses. Also, her revived relationship with Bobby Childs excited Mandy, and she desired with all her heart that this new love relationship would remain steady. Yet, she still could not shake feelings of insecurity. The lonely years of abandonment by him could not easily be forgotten. She knew that if they were now going to be together and raise their son in a family setting, there would be many issues to deal with, and this prospect frightened her.

As the water on the stove began to boil, the phone rang. Mandy went to answer the call. It was her ex-husband—Jim Harrison, who appeared to be quite sober and unusually friendly.

"Hey, Mandy, how are you doing, sweetheart? I wanted to call and just say hi."

"Yeah, right, Jim. Just get to the point, and make this brief. I am in the middle of fixing dinner."

"Aw, come on now. Don't be so irritable. I know things have not been civil between us for awhile, but at one time in our lives we were married. Don't you think you ought to bury the hatchet?"

"What do you want, Jim?" Mandy sharply responded.

"OK, listen, let me be brief for a minute, and I will let you go."

"Please be brief. I thought that was what lawyers were best at."

Jim chuckled. "Cute come back, Mandy. Nice one."

"I mean it, Jim. If you don't tell me what you want, I will hang up on you," Mandy replied as she raised her voice a decibel.

"Well, I don't think you would want to do that since it would cost you some money that is coming your way." Jim smiled to himself as he knew he had Mandy's attention by that comment.

"I am listening, Jim, so tell me what is on your mind."

"That a girl. I knew I could get your attention someway. Now listen, I am serious when I say this. I am sending you your alimony check tomorrow as I always do, but I would like to give you a little bit more this month."

"Oh, really? And why is that?"

"Could you use an additional five thousand dollars?" Jim asked her in a tantalizing fashion.

"Well, not if it means that you are expecting something from me in return."

"No, Mandy, I am not really expecting anything except for you to listen to me and seriously consider one request. That is all I am asking. I would like to meet with you in person this Friday to talk about this. I will bring you the check if you agree to my request. You know that my checks are always good, and this check will just be a little extra above and beyond what I owe you in alimony."

Mandy smelled a rat. She knew that Jim had been providing information to Sammy Jensen to help with the upcoming articles that would smear Bobby, Jason, and herself. She suspected that Jim's request was related to this. Her immediate instinct was to hang up the phone, but she also wondered if it would be smart to play along for awhile to see what Jim and Sammy were up to.

"You are not going to tell me what it is that you want now?"

"No, sweetie, I want to talk to you in person about it. So how about meeting me Friday evening after work? I will bring the check to give to you at that time."

"What if I don't agree to do what you want?"

"Well, I guess I won't be able to give you your bonus then, will I? But I think if you hear me out you will probably agree that this is the best thing to do. And I know the extra money will come in handy for you and little Bobby."

Mandy thought for a moment before responding. She was not going to betray her friends, but she thought that perhaps if she met Jim she might be able to find out some important information. Maybe she could persuade him to stop working with Sammy to defame Jason and Bobby. Maybe she could even convince him to get Sammy to cancel his articles.

"OK, Jim. I am not making any promises, but I will meet you on Friday."

"Wonderful. How about 6:30 Friday night at the coffee shop around the corner from your place? This won't take long, and it could result in a nice windfall profit to you."

"I will see you then, Jim. And remember, I am not promising anything other than to hear you out. Is that clear?"

"Very clear, Mandy. You won't be sorry you have agreed to meet me. I will see you on Friday."

After hanging up the phone Mandy felt sick to her stomach. She felt as if she needed to take a bath and clean herself off. As she began to rethink her decision to meet Jim, she suddenly looked over to see the boiling pasta spilling over, making a gigantic mess. Her conversation with Jim was so intense that she had forgotten to turn down the heat on the stove.

Her dad walked into the kitchen just as she ran over to clean up the sticky noodles and the water that had boiled over and was now on the floor. She looked at him in frustration and said, "Sorry, dad. I have a lot on my mind. Do you mind taking Bobby out for dinner and giving me some time to myself? I need to think about some things."

"Of course, sweetheart. No problem. We will go get some pizza. You do what you need to do."

"Thanks, dad. I love you," Mandy said as she walked upstairs to her room to meditate.

"I love you too, sweetie. We won't be gone long."

Mandy sat on her bed for a moment to try and understand what had just taken place. She questioned whether she had done the right thing in agreeing to meet Jim. She also knew that now was the time to test her newly revived relationship with Bobby Childs. She picked up the phone and dialed his number. Bobby answered after just one ring.

"Hi, sweetheart, it is me, and I just need to talk. I may have just done something very reckless," Mandy said.

"Well, baby, I am sure that whatever you did is fixable. Let's talk about it."

"I just don't know what is going on with Jim—my ex. He just called me and was very nice. He offered me more support money this month if I would do him a favor."

"And what was this favor?"

"He didn't say. But he promised me an additional $5,000 if I grant his request and said he wanted to meet with me to discuss it further."

"What did you tell him?"

"I hope that I have done the right thing, Bobby. I told him I would meet him and hear him out this Friday after work. I have no intention of doing anything to harm you or Jason, but maybe if I talk with Jim I can find out more about what is going on and persuade him to lay off."

"Do you have any idea of what he is after?"

"Yes. I believe that he wants the letter from Rachel. He didn't say that exactly, but that could be the only thing that he would want from me."

Bobby was silent for a few moments. If ever there were a situation conducive for Mandy to betray him, this meeting would certainly present such an opportunity. However, the thought did occur to him that if she betrayed him, he would deserve it.

"You know you can't trust this man, Mandy. He is really sick and wants to destroy us."

"I know that, Bobby. Should I call him back and tell him I have changed my mind and won't meet."

Bobby thought again for a few moments before responding. He was not sure what would be accomplished by Mandy meeting with, Jim. On the other hand, perhaps there was an outside shot that such a meeting might bring an end to the effort to defame him.

"You know something, Mandy. What do you have to lose? You just might get some additional information from him that would be helpful. Who knows? Maybe he will even listen to reason. But if he doesn't, then we will be in exactly the same position we are right now. So, there is nothing to lose by doing this. I think you should meet with him."

"I am scared, Bobby. Jim can be abusive when he doesn't get what he wants."

"But you will be meeting in a public place, right?"

"Yes, we are to meet at the coffee shop around the corner from me."

"Tell you what, you meet with him, but I will plan to be at the mall just down the street from you. If there are any problems at all, you can call me on my cell phone, and I will be there in less than five minutes."

"You will be there for me if I need you?"

"Absolutely, Mandy! Trust me."

Upon hearing this Mandy had a flashback to that day ten years earlier when Bobby had said the very same thing. Her stomach knotted. Could she really trust him this time?

Mandy was relieved for the support and protection from Bobby. Yet, she felt some apprehension in this new relationship. The past cannot be buried easily, and she knew that time would be the ultimate indicator of whether or not Bobby Childs could now be trusted. Perhaps this situation was a test of his sincerity and new commitment to her. In the current circumstances, however, she had no choice. She had to once again place her trust in the integrity of Bobby Childs.

"Thank you so much, Bobby, for being available. I can't tell you what that means to me. I will call you right before I leave for the meeting—around 6:00 o'clock, and if there are problems at all, you will get a call on your cell. If you do get that call please hurry. It will mean I am in trouble."

"I will have a lead foot on the accelerator to get there. Count on it." Bobby paused briefly before he continued. "Mandy, there is one more thing I want to say."

"What is that, my love?"

"Thanks for the second chance."

Mandy smiled a big smile that could be felt over the phone. She responded.

"Thanks for being available and supportive. I know you probably need to go now, but there is one more thing to ask."

"I am listening."

"This request isn't so serious. How about coming over for dinner tomorrow night after you get out of practice? Does six o'clock sound good?"

"Of course. What are we having?"

Mandy laughed and said, "I think I will be fixing spaghetti."

"My favorite dish. You remembered! I will bring a little wine, some garlic bread, and some dessert."

"Perfect. Dad and Bobby will be pleased to see you. We can tell them about the Super Bowl trip then and maybe figure out a way to tell them about us."

"It's a date. Good night, precious. I love you."

Mandy's hands shook as she heard those words of endearment. "I love you too, Bobby. Good night."

CHAPTER 16

Jason sat in silent contemplation as Joe drove out of the church parking lot. Joe could tell that something was on his mind.

"So tell me, Jason, what's up? I don't think you made this trip to see me just to talk about football."

Jason smiled. He did not know where to begin. Their eyes met, and Joe knew that some serious discussion was about to take place. Joe took the lead in the conversation.

"Two nights a week I patrol about ten square blocks in this part of the city. The Seattle police department has deputized me to do this. It is a special program that the mayor and city council implemented a few years ago. It helps keep the streets safer at night here."

"I remember reading about this when I came to Seattle. Apparently, it is having some success."

"Yeah, I think so. I am well known in this part of the city, and frankly, people don't want to mess with me. If there are some problems that I see, I just call them in on my cell phone to the police dispatcher and help arrives within a matter of minutes."

"I bet you have some exciting stories to tell."

"Not really. Many of the kids growing up in this part of the city have known nothing but crime and drugs their whole lives. I have tried to help give them an alternative at our church, but sometimes I see a few of them on the streets at night up to trouble. It bothers me, but I do what I can."

Joe looked across the street and noticed a young girl who was dressed seductively trying to flag down cars. He motioned to Jason to look, and Jason immediately recognized her as the girl who had tried to flag him down earlier on his way to see Joe and Helena. Joe turned his car around and headed toward her. He rolled down his window, as he intended to address her once he got close enough.

She initially thought that she had tracked down a customer, but when Joe pulled up she knew that she had attracted the wrong guy. Joe spoke to her as he pulled up alongside.

"Ebony Mason, what in the heck are you doing out here at this hour? Does your momma know what you are up to?"

"My momma doesn't care, Joe, and, frankly, neither should you. It is none of your business. You aren't my daddy, so just beat it, and leave me alone."

"You are wrong on both counts girl. It is my business, and I do care. Now get in this car, so I can drive you home."

"Stick it, Joe. I ain't going with you."

"You get in this car now, or I will get out and put you in."

Ebony immediately gave Joe an obscene hand gesture, darted across the street, and began running down an alleyway. Joe was unable to position his car in a manner to follow and cancelled any attempt to go after her. He looked at Jason and said, "This part of the city is full of kids like that. They grow up on the street and that is all they know. Young Ebony is headed for an early grave, just like my momma, unless someone can get to her and turn her life around. The Lord knows that I am trying."

"You seem to know her mother and family."

"Oh yes. Her momma comes to church on a regular basis. She was addicted to crack for years but got her life straightened out. Unfortunately, her daughter seems to be following her earlier lifestyle, not the latest one."

"And her daddy?"

Joe smiled at Jason and responded, "Who knows where he is? Ebony has been raised her entire life by her momma. She has never met her father."

Joe continued to drive up and down the neighborhood streets hoping to spot the young girl, but it appeared that she had successfully ditched him. Changing the subject he then began to inquire about Jason's background.

"So, Jason, tell me about your upbringing. From what I have read it appears that you are a farm boy from Eastern Washington."

Jason laughed and replied, "Oh yes, a regular hick from the sticks. It is funny that a guy with my background would be where I am today."

"Tell me about your parents."

Jason became melancholy as he pondered a response. "My dad died when I was very young. I hardly remember him. It was a farming accident. And my mom died a few years later from a very strange blood disease. I was raised by my grandmother in a small farming town named Mansfield. It is almost in the direct center of the state."

"I was raised by my grandmother too," said Joe. "The street life took my mother at an early age, and I never knew my daddy. Gramma Grace raised me. I was hell on earth for her until age sixteen."

"What turned your life around?"

"The Lord got a hold of me real good, and then I discovered football," Joe said with a laugh. "Nothing like that game to let a young buck get his aggressions out."

"So God and football changed you, huh? I never had thought that God was very interested in the game."

"So you don't pray before games?"

"Well, yeah. It is a ritual for every NFL team I have been on, but I don't think the guys take it too seriously. I think they do it more out of superstition."

"How do you feel about it?"

"Me? Well, frankly, I think God probably has a whole lot of other things he is concerned about. He is busy running the universe and football is probably pretty near the bottom of his agenda."

"I wouldn't bet on it," said Joe.

Jason was now fascinated with this African-American preacher who seemed to live and breathe football. "Come on, Joe, are you trying to tell me that in the eternal scheme of things, it matters to God who is going to win the Super Bowl?"

Joe chuckled a little, but then responded, "Listen, the God I believe in cares about every aspect of our lives. He knows the number of hairs on your head, Jason. So of course he cares about football and your upcoming game."

"Does he care who wins?"

Joe laughed again. "I am not sure of that, but I know he cares that you do your best. He is the one who gifted you with athletic ability. It gives him great pleasure to see you run and throw and use those physical gifts to the best of your ability. If you lose the game, God will cry and hurt with you, and he will probably rejoice with the Steelers, but winning and losing aren't as important to him as you doing your best and showing off the gifts he has given you. When you do that, he is pleased at his creation. It makes him happy. And I know that no matter what the outcome of the game is, God wants you to enjoy yourself because he is the one who made you."

"Wow," said Jason. "I have never really thought much about those things. I guess I have pretty much shut God out of my life since my mom died years ago."

"Yeah, I know that feeling. I had a friend of mine when I served in Vietnam who was very special. We called him Sparky."

"What happened to Sparky?"

"We were out on a mission, and he took a bullet in his head." Joe's voice began to crack as he related the story. "He died in my arms. I cried to God to save his life, but he didn't."

Jason remained silent, as he knew that his new friend was recalling some painful memories. Joe continued.

"Sparky and I used to pray together and read the Bible at night. That was the one thing that kept me sane over there. Sparky assured me that God was protecting me and that there was a purpose in my life. I believed him, and his counsel gave me great comfort."

"But God didn't spare his life. Were you bitter?"

"Oh yes. For awhile I wondered if there was a God who cared. I missed my friend so much."

"But you aren't bitter now?"

"No, sir. I have worked this through and, in fact, I believe that I am stronger in my faith because of Sparky and what happened."

"How did you eventually come out of that trauma still believing in a loving God who cares."

Joe looked at Jason intently before answering the question. "Jason, we all die. Some sooner than others, but we all die. Some of us will live a good long life and experience many things. Others, like my friend Sparky, will die young. In the end, however, we all die and pass over to the next life. That is a fact. It doesn't matter how long we live down here. What matters is what we do with this gift of life while we are here. Sparky died when he did because it was his time. My time will come later. But Sparky made a difference in my life while he was here, and for that I am grateful to God. If it hadn't been for Sparky, I wouldn't be doing what I am doing now. I am not bitter at God for taking Sparky—it was Sparky's time. I am grateful to God for giving me the chance to know Sparky and grow from that relationship."

This speech impressed Jason. He saw that Joe was a man of deep convictions who was not bitter about the setbacks he had known in his life.

Jason wanted to dig deeper into the conversation so he inquired, "Joe, do you believe in heaven?"

A big smile came to Joe's face as he emphatically responded. "Oh yes, brother. Absolutely! I believe in heaven. I know in my heart that it exists, and I hope to see you there someday."

Jason again smiled and said, "And what do you think we will do up in heaven, Joe? I mean, forever is a long time."

"Well, first it is not what we will be doing up there that will take up our time; it will be who we will be with and will finally see that will totally engulf us."

"I don't follow you."

"Listen, we are all lonely people down here. We try to fill our lives with things we think matter. 'Stuff' is what I call it. We just fill our lives with 'stuff' so that the pain of loneliness won't be so strong. But in the end we are still lonely. And that is because we were created not to be alone but to be at one with the Lord. In heaven we will be at one with the Lord, and there will be no loneliness. And when we are at one with him we won't worry about doing things— doing stuff—to fill our lives. We will just enjoy being with the one who created us for his purpose."

"So there is no football in heaven?" Jason said laughingly.

"Well I think we will play as much football as we want. And you know something, Jason O'Connor? When you get there, the Lord is going to run out for a pass and see if you can hit him right on the numbers with a deep one. And all the residents of heaven are going to be watching and cheering the biggest touchdown pass you ever made." Joe's face beamed as he spoke.

Jason was deeply moved. He was describing a devoted and loving friend, a father who cares, and one who understands everything that Jason feels. He thought to himself: "Could this possibly be true?".

"Joe, I need to ask you something very serious."

"I am listening, buddy."

"Does God show you heaven in dreams?"

"I am not sure what you mean, Jason."

Jason then began to share with Joe about his girfriend, Rachel, and about her death. He was careful not to talk about the baby and the adoption—that would come later in the evening. For now, Jason just poured his heart out and shared about his dream of Rachel and the great divide that prevented him from coming to her.

"Was that a dream of heaven, Joe? And if so, how come I could not come to her? Why was there that abyss that prevented us from being together?"

Joe pondered a response for a few seconds.

"I can't tell you if that was a dream from God or not and whether that was heaven. But I do understand why the divide was there, and why you couldn't cross it. There is only one way to cross that divide—only one way to get to heaven and you, my friend, in the dream weren't ready to do so."

"So how does one get to heaven? Is there a bridge across the great divide to get there?"

Joe smiled another big toothy smile and looked at his friend. "I am glad you asked. I have committed my entire life to answering that question for people."

Joe began to speak further but suddenly stopped as both he and Jason heard a loud, dramatic scream and cry for help. Joe immediately pulled his car over to the side of the road and got out to listen again. Jason joined him on the side of the car. They heard the voice again screaming, "Please stop. Please somebody help me. Help me." Joe recognized it as the voice of Ebony.

"The voice came from that alleyway over there. Let's go."

Jason and Joe sprinted toward the alley as they heard the voice call again. Joe carried his cell phone on him and while on the run he dialed the emergency number to the police department and requested help. A dispatcher promised that assistance would be on the scene within minutes.

As they entered the alley they saw about fifty yards ahead of them Ebony and two men. One was holding her arms tightly behind her back while the other was fondling her body, laughing, and beginning to undress her. The two appeared to be either intoxicated with alcohol or high on drugs.

Joe shouted as he pressed forward. "OK, you two punks, let her go and give it up, before I make you sorry you came out tonight."

The man who had been fondling Ebony immediately pulled out of his jacket a knife and brandished it at Joe and Jason. He recognized Joe as they came closer and addressed him directly.

"OK, preacher man. You think that you can handle me, huh? Well, come closer, and we will find out now won't we."

Joe and Jason halted abrubtly as Joe addressed his antagonist. "James Mathewson—what do you think you are doing? Now I have called the police, and they will be here in a few minutes. You have nowhere to run. Your back is to the wall, son, and you have nowhere to go. So I suggest you just put that knife down and let Ebony go."

The young man who was holding Ebony immediately released and took off running, only to be tackled by Jason, who pinned him to the ground. Ebony ran and hid in back of Joe as he continued to address the assailant. Joe's steely eyes met those of the young man holding the knife. As the drugs burned up his body, he become more disoriented. He continued to point the knife at Joe, but his hands shook, and his resolve weakened.

Joe continued his verbal assault. "You know, James, I knew your daddy well. He was a fine man. What do you think he would think of you now? Is this anyway for his son to act? What happened man? How did you get so messed up?"

"Don't come near me, Joe. Come any further and I'll…"

"You'll what? You gonna knife me, James? Is that what you have turned into? You drop out of school and hang around with the slime of the neighborhood. You let drugs ruin your body and now this? Now, you are gonna knife me because I am here stopping you from doing something stupid?"

A police car pulled up in front of the alleyway with its lights flashing, and two officers immediately jumped out. Upon seeing the situation they pulled their revolvers and shouted. "Get out of the way, Joe. We will handle this from here."

Joe and Jason drew back, taking Ebony with them, and the police officers took over. James and his friend both looked at two guns pointed their way. Finally, James dropped the knife, and he and his compatriot were immediately apprehended and handcuffed. They were led to the police car, and the officers talked to Joe, Jason, and Ebony to find out what had transpired. After about thirty minutes of fact finding, the officers drove off with the two young assailants in the back of the car. Joe and Jason drove Ebony home, just a few blocks down the street. As she got out of the car, Joe said to her, "I hope this is a lesson, young lady. I am going to talk with your momma tomorrow and let her know what you are up to. I think you would be wise if you got back in school."

Ebony, still shaken by her experience, responded. "OK, Joe, whatever you say. Thanks for being there tonight. I know I don't deserve it."

Joe and Jason drove on, and Jason took a deep breath. "Wow, Joe. Who said your life isn't exciting? My heart is still beating hard. That was quite an aerobic workout we just had."

"This is my battlefield, Jason. This is my mission field. And if I can influence just one life for the good, then I have accomplished a lot."

"You have touched more than one life, Joe. You have touched many lives—you have touched my life."

They drove back to the Johnson residence in silence and collected their thoughts. Helena opened the door for them as they approached and immediately noticed that they had had some excitement. She commented, "Well, goodness, look at you two. You both look like you have had a race with the devil. I hope you won."

Joe responded, "You are close, Helena. It was one of those nights that got your heart pounding hard, that's for sure."

He then proceeded to tell his wife about the incident with Ebony Mason. Jason sat on the couch pretending to listen, but in reality was lost deep in thought preparing questions in his mind. Joe wound down his story of the evening, he looked over at Jason and realized that the subject was about to change.

"Sweetheart, why don't you get us something good to eat like ice cream as we relax and talk with Jason?"

Helena went to the kitchen to prepare the treat, and Joe and Jason moved into the dining room to eat. As they sat down Jason looked up on the wall at his picture again, admiring the painting. Helena returned with two chocolate sundaes and some hot cocoa. These were Joe's favorite treats that allowed him to relax before going to bed at night.

"Moses is still asleep," Helena said. "He has slept over sixteen hours today." She looked at Joe with a grim and sad expression. Jason clearly saw her pain and decided it was time for him to make his inquiry.

"Can you tell me more about the blood transfusion? Why is it that the doctors don't believe it will be successful?"

Joe responded, "Well, they are not totally negative about it. We all hope and pray for the best. But I think that this will be the last transfusion for him."

Helena looked at Jason and added, "There is no guarantee that this one will be any different, but it is clear that unless we have it done, Moses will probably be comatose before long. He is just getting weaker and weaker all the time. Because of his rapid decline, every day is precious."

"Couldn't you wait a little longer for the transfusion to take place?"

Jason asked. "Perhaps more time is needed to find the right donor. Certainly there are records that would indicate who might be genetically related to Moses."

"We have scheduled the procedure for the earliest day available for the doctors and, at the same time, that would allow for a reasonable effort to try to locate a donor. We have balanced the two concerns here. If a blood-related donor is not found, we will simply go with whatever blood is available at the blood bank. But this simply can't be put off any longer. I even worry that he may not make it until the scheduled day of the procedure."

Jason continued his line of questioning. Doesn't the adoption agency have the records that show who his birth parents are? Didn't Moses' parents leave anything that would identify them? Anything left from which finger prints could have been taken? Anything like that?"

"Well," said Joe, "there was a little chain necklace left in the basket where the baby was lying. The adoption agency said that it undoubtedly belonged to his mother, but there was really nothing on it to identify her. There was no name, no initials—nothing to determine who she might be."

Helena added further. "We have kept that little necklace as a keepsake. We know that somewhere there is a young woman who obviously loved Moses and wanted to do the right thing. Maybe someday she will come forward and let us know her. Until then we have this necklace that allows us to think of her. She gave life to our son and for that we are truly grateful."

Jason froze. He knew that if he proceeded to ask questions, the mystery might be solved. The thought occurred to him, however, that if he ended the discussion at this point, he could walk away and not be confronted by a sense of right and wrong. If he didn't really know the truth, then he had no duty to act one way or another. Continued ignorance in this matter would be a blessing.

On the other hand, Jason knew deep inside that he would never have peace until he had an answer. He knew that his dream of Rachel meant something and was sent to alert him to something dramatic about to take place in his life. He knew that he had to continue. He had to know the truth.

"Is it possible that I could see that necklace?" he asked.

Joe and Helena both looked puzzled at the request, but had no objections. "Sure," said Helena. "Hold on, and let me go get it." Helena returned with the necklace in her hand. She placed it in Jason's palm, and he squeezed it tightly in a clenched fist. He was deathly afraid to open his hand and take a look.

When he finally looked at the necklace he knew the truth. He was holding a chain necklace, and on the chain was the English ha'penny that Rachel had given him so long ago. He closed his eyes as his mind flashed back to the moment when sweet and innocent Rachel Thomlinson gave him the coin as an act of love, hoping that one day she and he would be like two English ha'pennies—coming together becoming one whole penny.

Jason placed his head in his hands and began to weep. He cried loudly and unashamedly, as Joe and Grace looked on in amazement. They had no idea of the truth and were puzzled. Joe reached over and gently touched the shoulder of his friend.. Helena wiped tears from her eyes. She didn't totally understand all that was transpiring, but she sensed that something major regarding Moses was occurring. Both Joe and Helena felt totally helpless as they watched the sobbing professional athlete. Finally, Jason got control over himself and sat up. He cleared his throat and began to speak very deliberately.

"I am sure that you two don't have any idea as to why I have behaved this way. I am embarrassed. I know that you don't fully understand."

"Don't mention it, Jason." Joe said. "It is obvious that you have something on your mind. Would you like to talk about it?"

"I need to be by myself right now, Joe. I have a lot to think about. I am sorry if this leaves you in the dark, but I have to go and be by myself."

Jason got up from the table quickly and headed for the door. "Thank you both so much for your hospitality. I will call tomorrow and explain some things, but for now I have to go."

"Whatever it is, my brother, I want you to know that we will be praying for you," said Joe as he put his arm around the shoulders of the big Seahawks quarterback.

"Yes, Jason," said Helena. "We will be praying tonight for you."

Jason fought back the tears. "Thank you so much. I will be in touch tomorrow night." Jason quickly exited out the front door and hastily walked to his car. He did not know exactly where he was going or where he would end up.

Jason drove away from the Johnson home at a high speed.

CHAPTER 17

Jason drove his car through the streets of inner-city Seattle, heading nowhere in particular, and not noticing anything as he passed by. While he was driving, his cell phone rang. He looked at the number calling him and knew that he had to answer. It was his friend Bobby Childs.

"Jason, buddy, Mandy and I have been worried about you tonight. Are you OK?"

"I don't know, Bobby. I just don't know," said Jason in a manner that indicated he was under great stress.

"What did you find out from Joe and Helena?"

Jason paused for quite awhile before answering. "It is all true, Bobby. Moses is my son. Rachel left a necklace with him when he was a baby. It was a necklace that she had also given me. I recognized it immediately. He is my son, Bobby." Jason's voice began to quiver with emotion.

"Wow. This situation is something out of the twilight zone. So what are you going to do?"

"I don't know yet, Bobby. Moses is in serious condition and needs a blood transfusion. I am the only one who can supply the blood that has a chance of helping him."

"What happens if he doesn't get the transfusion?"

"He will die and probably soon. Even if he gets the transfusion, there is little hope unless the donor is related and close to his genetic make-up. Apparently, that is the only hope that exists."

"Do Joe and Helena know that you are his father?"

"Not yet. I am going to talk to them tomorrow after I figure out what I should do."

"What are you going to do, Jason?"

"I hope an answer comes to me quickly because I am not sleeping until I decide."

"Where are you now? Let me come and be with you for awhile. I think you could use some company."

"Thanks, buddy, but I need to be alone right now. I will stay in touch. We will talk more tomorrow about this after practice."

"OK, but you feel free to call me at anytime tonight if you need me. You have the number."

"I will, Bobby. Thanks for your friendship."

"I need to ask you a favor, Jason. It is all related to this mess we created."

"Go for it man."

"Mandy received a call from her ex-husband Jim Harrison. He wants to meet with her on Friday night and give her some extra money."

"Well, good. I am sure Mandy could use that."

"No, it is not good. Apparently Harrison wants something from Mandy and will pay her only if she gives it to him."

"And what do you think he wants?"

"Mandy is pretty certain that he wants Rachel's letter to give to Sammy Jensen."

"It figures. So, is Mandy going to cooperate?"

"No, Jason. Trust me on this. She would not betray you or me. I know that in my heart. But she is going to meet with him."

"So why is she meeting with him? Why doesn't she just tell him to stick it?"

"Mandy believes that she might be able to talk Jim out of going ahead with this whole thing. He is probably the only person who can stop Jensen from writing his piece because he is the only source Jensen has. At the very minimum Mandy believes that she will be able to get some more information out of him that will be helpful to us or at least prepare us for what is coming down."

"OK. I have no control over any of this, so what is this favor you want from me?"

"Mandy is afraid of her ex. He has been violent in the past. She has agreed to meet him at a coffee shop near her home. It is a public place that should be safe enough. But she wants me close by in case he gets out of line. She will call me on my cell immediately if she needs help. I will be at the mall near her house—about five minutes away—and can immediately be there if needed. I would like you to be with me."

"When are they meeting?"

"Six o'clock on Friday night. We can go to the mall after practice and just hang together. If I don't get the call, then we are not needed. What do you say?"

"All right. Why not? I think by Friday night I will need the company."

"Thanks friend. Take care of yourself tonight and remember that I am only a phone call away."

"Don't mention it."

Jason hung up the phone and found himself heading toward a small beach off of Puget Sound known as Alki Point. He got out of his car and walked toward a bench on the boardwalk. The bench overlooked the water and faced the spectacular nighttime skyline of the city.

Jason sat pondering what he was supposed to do with the knowledge that he had a son who was seriously ill. He knew that only he could supply what was needed to save the life of Moses. Yet, Jason knew that if he were the blood donor for the operation, he would undoubtedly be significantly weakened and unable to play in the big game. His head continued to hurt from his concussion, and he knew that anything that further weakened him physically would eliminate him from playing.

Jason now seriously prayed. Even though he had been raised by his grandmother in a religious environment, he had never really learned how to pray. Now, however, he was confronted with a situation in which nobody could help him except God. His inner spirit cried out to the Supreme Being that he believed existed but who seemed very distant from him at this time.

Jason looked up at the clear, starlit sky as he prayed and noticed a dazzling shooting star across the heavens. He immediately thought of his dream where the ocean view skies lit up like a fireworks display with numerous shooting stars, and then his mind flashed back to his child-hood.

He recalled walking as a young child with his mother along a sandy beach in Eastern Washington at Lake Chelan—a large lake in the central part of the state. The walk occurred at night, and the sky was clear and full of visible stars—much the same as it looked to him now. He remembered his mother pointing and exclaiming, "Oh look son, a shooting star. Every time that happens God is sending to earth a guardian angel to protect one of his children." Jason smiled to himself as his thoughts stirred up fond memories of his mother.

He then began to feel anger and resentment toward God as he asked himself: Do guardian angels really exist? If so, where were these guardian angels when Rachel needed them? And where are they now when Moses needs divine intervention?

As he asked these penetrating questions, an answer came that con-victed his soul. He perceived no audible voice; yet, he heard the answer as clearly as if someone had spoken directly to him. The voice was loud and shook him to the core as it answered back forcefully, "Where were you?"

Jason sat on the bench stunned. He knew he had failed Rachel. He had abandoned her at her most vulnerable time in pursuit of his own selfish interests. He wanted to make things right with her, but her death ended any ability to do so. Even though ten years had passed since she died, he was now grieving and mourning her loss as if her death had just occurred.

He could not go back into the past and correct his mistake, but he was now confronted with another crisis, partly of his own doing, and he could respond differently this time. Moses was the most vulnerable human being he had ever met. Yet, this young boy was full of energy and loved life. He brought joy to all who knew him, and he needed a miracle. Only Jason could provide that miracle for him. Perhaps, Jason thought, he himself was the guardian angel that Moses needed.

Jason sat staring out at the water, watching the ferry boats cruise across Puget Sound, lighting up the night sky. He again looked up to the heavens and saw yet another shooting star. "The angels must be busy tonight," he softly mumbled to himself.

Time seemed to stop for him as he sat contemplating the newly discovered details about his life. As a professional athlete, he had arrived at the pinnacle of success. He was only one step away from achieving the ultimate in professional football. Quarterbacking a victory in the Super Bowl would undoubtedly place him on a track to end up in the NFL Hall of Fame and guarantee sports immortality. Yet, strangely, he was empty inside. It seemed that all of his successes and all of the fame and notoriety he had achieved could not take away the deep guilt, insecurity, and loneliness he felt within. At this moment in time, he felt that nothing—not even NFL football fame and fortune—could fill the deep hole in his heart.

Jason continued to pray. He had faint memories of his father and happy memories of his mother. He thought of his grandmother who had raised him and passed on several years before he achieved his football success. His grandmother had cared for him the best she could after his parents died. She raised him in church and laid the foundational values for his life. He was grateful to her and what she had done to care for him.

Jason wondered if these people from his past were together this very moment observing his struggle. Maybe, he thought, they didn't care. Maybe, he thought, God doesn't care, and his emotional turmoil was his just reward for living a life of selfishness. Maybe, he thought, this was his punishment for the way he had treated Rachel.

His mind flashed back again to a scene from his childhood. In this memory he was sitting with his grandmother at the old Mansfield country church listening to a guest preacher. He did not remember much about the sermon except for the strange lisp in the voice of the preacher. Despite the obvious speech impediment the preacher was somehow connecting with the congregation as he spoke. And Jason, a young boy of around ten, was listening.

"There is a a a heart-shaped vacuum in the lives of every human being," the preacher said. "And this vacuum tries to suck up everything it can in order to be filled. But no matter what goes into the vacuum, it is never permanently filled because what goes in lasts only for a season and then it is gone. The only thing that will permanently fill that vacuum is God. He is the only one who can satisfy the longings of the human heart. He is the only one who can fill the void and give you peace."

The words "give you peace" were the words Jason needed to hear most on this night. Peace had never been in his life. Nothing he had achieved in football had given him peace. In fact, quite the opposite seemed to be happening to him as a pro quarterback. The more success he achieved, the more turmoil he experienced. But it was peace that he wanted.

Jason bowed his head on the bench and breathed the cool air of the water front. He prayed for peace. His heart cried out in sorrow for what he had done to Rachel, and he asked for one more chance to do the right thing.

Suddenly Jason heard a voice speak to him, and he was momentarily startled. He looked immediately behind him to see a man who said, "Hey, you are Jason O'Connor aren't you? Wow, I am so happy to meet you tonight."

Jason stood up to face this intruder who offered a handshake and said, "My name is Josh. And let me tell you that I am your biggest fan."

Jason began to relax and smiled. He was frankly glad for a reprieve from his troubled thoughts. He put out his hand in friendship and responded, "Nice to meet you, Josh. You startled me."

"Oh, sorry about that," Josh chuckled. "I have a tendency to do that at times. Do you mind if I sit here and talk a little? I am just such a big football fan that I am honored to meet you."

"Sure, why not? I could use a little company tonight."

Josh sat on the bench and was quiet for a few moments. Jason remained deep in thought. The moment was awkward.

Finally, Jason spoke. He was glad for the company and thought that a little idle conversation would help to calm him down.

"Well, obviously you know what I do for a living, but tell me about yourself, Josh. What do you do?"

"I build bridges."

"Bridges? OK, you are an engineer then. You are one of those smart guys who were given all the brains when it came to math and science."

Josh laughed and said, "Perhaps, but you are one of those guys who received all the physical talent and athletic ability." He paused and then added, "And all the pretty girls too."

That last comment stung Jason as he remembered again the one pretty girl he had abandoned. He responded sadly. "I know that is the image of pro athletes—that they have their pick of the available ladies. But you would be surprised to know that there has been only one lady in my life, and she left long ago."

Jason immediately changed the subject. "So you are a big Seahawks fan, I take it?"

"Oh yes, I have been to all of your games. I have followed your career from the beginning. I know all of your moves. You have wound up this city like no one before you."

Jason again smiled and responded, "So what brings you out so late tonight Josh?"

"Well, I don't sleep much. And I love to come to the beach and be alone at night sometimes. It is very peaceful here," he said as he looked out at a large ferry boat traveling on the waters headed toward port at the city of Seattle. "Yes, there is nothing like the Seattle skyline view from here. It is simply gorgeous."

Josh then began to probe Jason. "So what is the latest news about your condition? Are you going to play against the Steelers? You know the fans of this city have been waiting a long time to revenge that Super Bowl loss to the Steelers a few years back. You have to play to make sure that happens."

Jason responded, "You know, Josh, I am glad you asked that question. Because frankly I really am not sure I will be playing in the big game."

Josh sat expressionless as Jason continued. "My head still hurts bad. I am not sure I have been told the complete truth about the extent of my injuries, but something has come up that may take me out of the game regardless of whether or not my injured head does."

For some reason Jason was feeling very comfortable talking with this stranger. He felt like they must have met sometime in the past and inquired. "You know, Josh, I feel like we have met before. Have we?"

"Like I said, I have been to all of your games. I am sure that maybe you have spotted me in the crowd on occasion."

"Well, that is highly unlikely considering those games have over 70,000 people in attendance every Sunday."

Another brief moment of silence occurred before Jason continued to speak. Jason needed a friend on this night. He needed someone to just listen to him. Josh made him feel very relaxed, and he began to open up to him.

"Do you believe in guardian angels, Josh?"

Josh smiled and replied. "Absolutely. How else can you explain all the close calls you have survived in your life?"

Jason nodded but then said, "Well, if they exist they seem to be rather selective in providing protection don't you think?"

"Interesting comment, Jason. Tell me more of what you are thinking."

To his great surprise Jason opened up completely to this stranger. He did not care anymore if his hidden past was made public. He figured that Sammy Jensen was going to do that within a short time anyway, and, thus, he had nothing to lose by sharing with Josh. So he talked.

He told Josh about his relationship with Rachel Thomlinson and what had transpired during their college years. He told him about her death and how for years he had buried the wounds. Living with such buried wounds had made him more driven in his professional life as he mistakenly thought that success and fame on the football field would compensate and bring about healing. He then told him about the dream he had earlier in the week and how it had been haunting him. He then opened up and told him about Joe, Helena, and Moses and the dilemma he was facing.

Josh just sat and listened intently. When Jason finished, he felt like a huge burden had been released. Just talking about these things to this stranger seemed to bring some kind of inner peace, and for that he was very grateful.

Silence ensued between the two for quite sometime after Jason stopped talking. He finally looked at his new friend and asked, "So what advice can an engineer give to a professional jock on these matters? Any comments, Josh?"

Josh stood up and walked toward the water. He looked up at the stars as if talking silently to somebody else. He then turned to Jason and said, "I know you will do the right thing. But you have to understand that the power and ability to do the right thing does not come from within you. You have no more ability to do what is right than a dog has the ability to fly."

Jason was taken aback at these comments. He had not been prepared for this stranger to suddenly wax philosophical. Jason walked over to Josh and responded.

"Really, now? Do you think I would be here tonight if I knew exactly what I should do or how I should do it?"

"Jason, my friend. You know what to do. You know what is right. You just are lacking the strength and ability to do it. That's all."

"And where does that strength come from, Josh? Where do I find the wherewithal to do what is right, here?"

"For years you have had a heart of stone. Rachel's death hardened you. You were unable emotionally to confront what had happened, so you hid your wounds deep within and hardened your spirit to things of eternal significance. Now your heart of stone is softening, and you are beginning to receive a heart of flesh. Your new heart is one that will empower you to understand and do the right thing."

Jason responded again more forcefully to this stranger, who seemed to know more about him and his inner workings than anyone Jason had ever known. "So tell me, Josh, please tell me. What is the right thing to do?"

Josh began to walk away as Jason watched with eyes that pleaded for an answer. Josh responded. "You were in the process of finding that strength before I interrupted you tonight. If you continue on, you will find your answer."

Josh continued to walk away as Jason stood speechless. He then turned to look at Jason and said, "Don't worry though. I know you will play in the Super Bowl, and you will have the greatest game of your life." With that comment the stranger walked around a corner into the night and out of sight.

Jason O'Connor remained at the beach for several more hours, reviewing in his mind the different scenarios that possibly could occur regarding Moses. But he knew that only one of these scenarios was the right one to pursue.

As he sat on the bench contemplating these matters, he felt loneliness as he had never before experienced. He was sure that nobody could understand these overwhelming feelings of isolation. They were intense. They were haunting. They were physically painful, and he felt them throughout the foundation of his being. The intensity of these feelings was so powerful that Jason fell to his knees, holding his face in his hands, and sobbed, crying out for help.

Once again, Jason's mind flashed backed to scenes from his childhood. Once again, he was in the country church with his grandmother, listening to the visiting preacher implore the congregation to make their lives right with God. He replayed over in his mind a picture of the congregation singing a hymn while the preacher urged people to come forward and turn their lives around.

Tears came to his eyes as his memories crystallized. He knew that something had happened to him as a child at this church meeting so long ago. Something had happened that he had hidden for years. Now, however, that experience had returned. He remembered his grandmother with her hand on his head praying for him. And he remembered how he, a young boy, had earnestly prayed to ask God to fill the hole in his heart. He remembered the peace of God coming into his soul. It was a peace that had been woefully absent during his teen and adult years. But now, at this moment of truth, this peace returned, and it bounded into his heart.

Jason got up and walked over to the edge of the boardwalk on the shore of the Puget Sound. He looked up at the stars once more, and to his amazement, he saw another shooting star. He smiled and wiped the tears from his eyes.

He now knew what he had to do regarding Moses. There was no question in his mind. He had no fears or doubts about the course that now must be pursued.

CHAPTER 18

Thursday morning came too early for Jason, as he had gotten to bed well after midnight. Yet, he was feeling refreshed from his encounter and was experiencing unusual vitality and strength. His injured head no longer ached, and his body exhibited uncanny energy as he bounced out of bed upon hearing the alarm.

He went about his usual morning ritual of shaving, showering, and eating breakfast when the phone rang. It was Paul Wagner.

"Listen, O'Connor, I need you to come in a little early today. We have a number of matters to discuss, so don't dilly dally around. Get here as soon as you can."

"I am just finishing up breakfast, Coach, and will leave right after that."

"Don't be late," Wagner gruffly replied before hanging up the phone.

Jason quickly finished his breakfast, and then picked up the phone to call Joe Johnson before he left. He knew the course that he must pursue. There was no answer to the call, so Jason left a message on the recorder.

"Hey, Joe and Helena, its me, Jason. I am sorry for leaving so abruptly last night. But I need to talk to you today as soon as possible. I will call you after practice. Also, I need to know the name of the doctor who will be administering the blood transfusion for Moses."

Jason arrived at the stadium about forty-five minutes before he was expected. He went directly to Wagner's office. The door was open, and Wagner was talking on the phone. Wagner motioned to Jason to sit down. He then quickly ended his conversation and directed his attention to his star quarterback.

"So how are ya feeling today, O'Connor? How is the old noggin doing?"

"Well, Coach, I can honestly say that today it really feels fine. No pain. No aches. Feels almost like new."

"Glad to hear it," replied Wagner as he got up out of his chair and began to pace. "Listen, I apologize for what I said yesterday regarding that Johnson kid. It was out of line, and I know it teed you off." He was obviously uncomfortable in making apologies and admitting that he was wrong, but as he paced in his office, it became clear to Jason that he had something else on his mind.

After a few uncomfortable moments Wagner spoke, "Listen, Jason, I have not been totally candid with you about your head injuries."

Jason looked at his coach with a blank stare and no response. Wagner continued.

"The doctors are telling me that you shouldn't play. They believe that the blows you took to the head were just too serious to risk another hit."

"I am not surprised," said Jason. "But I don't think it changes things."

"Well, listen, O'Connor. I did a lot of soul searching last night. I didn't sleep well. All I could think about was you and your ability, or in-ability, to be ready for the game. In the process, I faced some pretty ugly things about myself.

"Nothing means more to me than winning this game. Nothing! But I have to tell you, it won't be worth it if you suffer another serious blow. We probably can't win without you. Everybody knows that. But I honestly could not live with myself if I played you knowing what I know and you were injured again. It would not be pretty."

While Jason was astonished at hearing, what appeared to be, a softer side to his coach, he was also calm as he listened. He had made his decision regarding Moses, so he was not expecting to play anyway, but now he was being given a way out of his dilemma. He wouldn't have to tell Wagner about being the donor for the blood transfusion and, thus, would most likely be too weak to play. Rather, now he could just obey doctor's orders and sit out of the game because of the head injury. Nobody had to know about his decision to help Moses.

"So do you think Morrison will be ready to step in?" asked Jason.

"Absolutely, Jason." Wagner replied in an unconvincing manner.

Jason stood up and chuckled. He then shook his head and looked directly at Paul Wagner. He knew he had to control his response because he was feeling a surge of anger. He knew that his hot-blooded Irish temper might get the best of him if he let it, so he took a deep breath and then responded.

"OK, Wagner, listen, I know all about Zach Morrison. I know he is seriously injured and has been all year. I know he can't throw the ball more than thirty yards down field and that will not work to beat the Steelers. This puts you in a pretty tough spot now doesn't it?"

Wagner normally would respond to such a challenge with a belligerent retort. However, the stress of the situation overcame him. He now knew that the secret about Morrison was known by Jason. With this realization, he quietly walked back to his big leather office chair and sat down.

"You know, O'Connor, I am glad somebody else knows about this. It has been an incredible strain to keep in. And because of it, I was on the verge of putting your permanent health in danger. I won't do that. I am a big boy, and I am responsible for my actions. The press will want to know why I didn't put Morrison on the injured reserve list at the start of the season and get another backup quarterback. I am going to be the story from here on out. I can take it because I deserve it. But boy I tell you, this has to be the most frustrating time of my career. We have gone almost a week since beating St. Louis, and we still have not been able to focus on beating the Steelers."

Jason's anger slowly began to subside, and he truly felt sorry for his coach. Wagner had believed in him enough to give him a chance in the NFL. Before coming to Seattle his career was mediocre at best, but it was Wagner who gave him a second chance. Now, this big tough NFL coach was demoralized and defeated after coming so close to achieving the utmost in professional football. On the eve of the greatest sports spectacular in the world, Paul Wagner was ready to quit.

"Coach, I want to tell you something, but the details have to wait a couple of days."

"Don't play games with me, O'Connor. I am telling the press after today that you are not playing. I am letting them know that your injuries are just too severe to risk it. So if you have anything to say, you must speak up now."

"No, listen to me. You have to wait. I frankly am very grateful to you for my opportunity to play in Seattle, and I do not want you to be the fall guy for this at all. Let me take the blame."

"Now how do I do that, O'Connor?"

Jason sighed. He was not sure how to respond because he was not sure yet of the details. He had made up his mind that he would be the blood donor for Moses, but he had to talk with Moses's physician to know more detail as to how that would affect his ability to play. He was pretty sure that giving the amount of blood needed would weaken him to such an extent that he would not be able to play, but he needed more information.

Jason responded slowly, "Listen, Coach, I am going to tell the reporters today that I am playing. I am going to tell them that my head is fine, and you must go along with this. By Saturday I will have a different story and will voluntarily take myself out of the game. It will be totally my decision, and I will be the fall guy—not you."

Wagner twisted his face in confusion and said, "That brain of yours really has taken a hit. What you just said makes absolutely no sense. Why would you take yourself out of the game?"

"Since you are going to pull me anyway, does it matter?"

"Stop the bull, O'Connor. I want to know what you are up to."

"Just don't announce anything right now. I will give you more details in a day or so. When the time comes, I will announce I am not playing, and the press will come down on me, not you."

"Now why would you want to do that?"

"Maybe because I have come to realize that there are some things more important than football. There are some things more important than the Super Bowl."

Still bewildered Wagner responded. "And what, may I ask, is more important to you than winning the Super Bowl? Why after all these years when you are at the top of the game would you take yourself out of this opportunity?"

Jason got up from his chair to leave. As he walked toward the door he said, "You will understand shortly, Coach. Just don't say anything now."

Wagner, feeling more perplexed than ever, responded, "I thought you said that it would take an act of God to keep you from playing?"

Jason smiled at his coach and replied, "That is exactly what has happened, Coach—an act of God." He then walked out of the office and into the locker room to get ready for the day's practice.

The day's practice was routine. Jason watched on the sidelines as Zach Morrison called most of the plays during the scrimmage. He and Wagner did not talk much, as the tension between them was mounting. Reporters in the stands noticed that Jason was not on the field working with the team, and serious questions began to surface.

The questions at the press conference after practice again focused on the physical condition of Jason O'Connor. Sammy Jensen led the way with the first question of the day.

"Coach, we couldn't help but notice that Jason O'Connor did not take one snap from center today during the practice. Can you give us an update as to his physical condition and if he is going to be playing against the Steerlers?"

Jason, sitting at the table with Wagner, jumped in to answer before the coach could respond. "I feel great today—just like new. I am ready to take it to the Steelers and can't wait to be there."

"If that is so, Jason, then why were you not out there throwing the football?"

"Just precautionary measures." Jason pointed his finger at Wagner and continued. "The coach here is a conservative, as we all know, and he simply wants to make sure that I am 100% ready to go before I have any contact."

Ignoring Jason O'Connor and looking directly at Coach Wagner Sammy Jensen continued the interrogation. "Coach, it is highly unusual for a starting quarterback to be so absent from activity during a week of practice leading up to the Super Bowl. Can you simply play it straight with us about this? Are you guaranteeing that Jason will be ready to go as the starter come Super Bowl Sunday?"

Wagner's temper began to flare up, as he did not like being questioned in this manner. He stood up and gruffly retorted, "I am tired of saying the same thing over and over to you guys. Nothing has changed. Absolutely nothing. So don't question my decision on how to run practice. I know what I am doing."

The press conference continued for twenty more minutes with reporters not letting up on the issue and questioning why Jason's medical reports had not been released to the public. Wagner and O'Connor artfully dodged the questions and stayed together on their insistence that Jason would be playing. The event was tortuous to both of them, and they were relieved to end the conference and return to the locker room.

"OK, O'Connor. I gave you what you wanted. Now I expect to get some more specifics from you before long. When do I know exactly what you are up to?"

"Coach I will be ready to talk detail by Saturday. I will meet you early at the airport and go over everything. We can talk about handling the press then."

"Till Saturday? I don't know why I have agreed to this, but we can't back off now. I have a feeling that I am going to be crucified by the press no matter what happens here, but I know one thing. You are not physically ready to play football, and I won't allow it."

Nothing more was said between the two as Jason walked back to the locker room to get ready to leave. Bobby Childs was waiting for him as he approached the locker and sat down on the bench. Both were silent for a few moments before Bobby spoke.

"So, buddy, are you OK? Mandy and I were really worried about you last night. Where did you go, and what did you decide?"

Jason smiled at his friend. "You know what, Bobby? For the first time in my life I feel peace. It is a great feeling. I know that no matter what happens that all will be well in the end. And I know that it really doesn't matter if I play in the Super Bowl. It really doesn't matter."

Bobby Childs sat stunned for a moment and then spoke. "So you are going to give blood for Moses? I assume that will make you too weak to be able to play."

"I am calling Joe and Helena in order to set up a chance to meet with the doctors. I know that I will have to give a lot of blood, and that will make me pretty weak."

"And you are sure this is what you want?"

Jason chuckled a little and then responded. "You know, Bobby, I met an interesting guy last night in whom I confided about all of this. His name is Josh. I don't know where he came from, but he was there at the beach when I needed someone to talk with. He gave me some pretty good advice. More importantly, though, he gave me some perspective on life, and I now have great peace about all of this."

Bobby sat in silence for quite awhile and simply breathed deep sighs. He looked at his friend with new respect. He just wanted to be supportive.

"You know, Jason, buddy, this has been an incredible week. The news about my son, Bobby, and your son, Moses, is simply breathtaking. I feel strangely that a burden has been lifted."

"How so?"

"The night Rachel died was the most tortuous night of my life. She was my friend as well as yours. When Mandy walked out on me that night my life went down hill. I deserved it when she walked away, but it was still painful. I was not the same from that point. You remember how bad we played in the Rose Bowl that year, and our careers in the NFL, until recently, were nothing to be proud of."

Jason replied, "Yes, when Rachel died my heart died too. I was so cruel to her, and I never had the chance to tell her I was sorry." Jason's voice began to crack. "I never got the chance to tell her that I really did love her. I was so selfish."

"I know what you mean. I died on the inside that night as well. But my life has been resurrected by meeting Mandy this week and seeing my son. I have been given a second chance. I am a lucky guy. Few people get the chance to correct a serious wrong he or she has done. But I have been given such a chance."

Jason smiled. "And I have been given a second chance too. I failed Rachel, but I won't fail our son. He means everything to me now. I will not walk away from him."

Bobby got up to leave and put his hand on Jason's shoulder. "You need some company tonight? Mandy and I would love to have you join us. We are having dinner at her place and telling her dad and Bobby all about our plans."

"That's OK. Not tonight, Bobby. We will spend tomorrow night together after practice at the mall. You go and enjoy your night with your new family."

Bobby smiled and then walked out of the locker room, leaving Jason with his thoughts. Jason picked up his cell phone to call Joe and Helena Johnson and fill them in on the details. Again, he received the greeting on the answering machine and left another message.

"Hey, Joe and Helena, it's me Jason. Look, I really need to talk with both of you tonight, so please call me when you get in. This is important and urgent. I won't go to sleep until we talk."

As Jason ended his call and walked out of the locker room. As he exited the stadium, he smiled to himself. He knew that he had made the right decision, and nothing he could ever achieve on the football field could compare to what he was now feeling inside.

It was peace. Wonderful peace. And from this peace, he felt joy within himself. He knew that all was well.

CHAPTER 19

As soon as Jason entered his front door, his phone rang. When he saw that it was Joe Johnson, he immediately picked up the receiver.

"Hey, Joe, glad to hear from you."

"It sounded very urgent, Jason. I am sorry we were not available. We were at the hospital talking with Moses's doctors. Helena and I have been worried about you since last night. Are you OK?"

"Actually, Joe, I couldn't be better. I have had a huge weight lifted off of my shoulders, and I owe it all to you."

"Well," responded Joe, "I am glad to hear it, but can I ask for a little more detail?"

"Sure, Joe. Get Helena on the line, will ya?"

Upon Joe's request Helena got on another phone in the house. After greeting Jason and telling him her concern for him she said, "Jason, I have prayed for you so much last night and today. I know that something is on your mind. How can we help you?"

"Helena, as I told Joe, you two have helped me more than you ever can imagine. And now I want to help you and help Moses as well."

Jason then began to share about his romance with Rachel Thomlinson and about her death. He told them about his dream and then about the emergence of Mandy Brooks into his life. Finally, he told them about Rachel's letter and what it meant. He told them that he was the birth father of Moses. He then became silent hoping for some response.

Helena began to weep as she understood what Jason had said. Joe was speechless for a moment but then spoke up. "Are you certain that all of this is true?"

"Yes, Joe, the ha'penny necklace was the one that Rachel gave to me.

And the story that Mandy has told about how Rachel's baby was placed for adoption matches perfectly with what you know about the adoption. I am without a doubt his father."

Joe struggled to find words as Helena continued to weep. "So it really is a very small world, isn't it?" Joe finally said.

"Joe and Helena, listen to me now. There is a reason I have told you all of this. I plan on being the donor for Moses's blood transfusion. I will give whatever amount of blood is needed to save his life."

Helena responded as the tears continued to flow. "Jason, the blood transfusion is set for Friday, and the doctors tell us that they can't wait any longer if we are to have any hope of a recovery."

"I know that, Helena."

"But you can't give the blood. You have to play in the Super Bowl. I am sure that if you do this, you won't have the strength to play."

"That is probably true, but I need to find out for certain from the doctors. Although, today Coach Wagner told me that he is not going to let me play because of my head injuries, so it most likely won't matter anyway. But regardless of what giving blood will do to me physically, I have made my decision. I failed Rachel badly. If I had acted like a real man, she would be alive today. I am not going to fail our son. I have been given a second chance, and this time I am answering the call."

Joe, fighting back tears, responded. "Helena, we prayed for a miracle. And God has answered our prayers big time."

Jason was struggling as well with his emotions but continued the conversation. "I need to speak with Moses's doctors about this as soon as possible. I want to know how much blood I can give. I am going to give as much as I possibly can."

"We will call the doctor immediately and arrange for you to speak with him," said Joe. "Are you available later tonight? Perhaps we can have a conference call together."

"You set it up, Joe, and I will be here waiting. Just get a hold of the doc, and then we will all talk."

"We will be back in touch as soon as we know anything. Don't go anywhere, and stay by the phone."

"Hey, Joe and Helena, there is one more thing I need to share with you."

"Go ahead, my friend," responded Joe.

On Saturday I am giving an interview to Sammy Jensen for the series of articles he is writing about Bobby and me. I plan to tell him about Rachel and Moses and my decision to give blood. He wants some dirt on me for his story, and I am going to have to give it to him.

"Now why would you do that?" Helena asked.

"Sammy wants to smear my friend Bobby Childs in his story, but he wants to hammer me more. I will let him hammer me as long as he lays off of Bobby."

Joe and Helena were silent. They were puzzled by this new information and not sure how to respond.

Jason continued, "I just wanted you both to know this so you are not surprised by the articles that will be coming out next week. Joe, you are a hero to this city, and it will make you look really good. You are the guy who stepped into Moses's life when he had been deserted by his parents."

Joe responded, "Jason, so much information has come to me that I am not assessing everything properly right now. Let's talk more about this after we hear from the doctor regarding the transfusion."

"Sure thing. I will be waiting for the call."

Jason had a wonderful feeling of satisfaction about what had just transpired. For Joe and Helena, the long prayed for miracle was coming true. They hugged each other tightly, and then Joe called Moses's primary physician to tell him the news and arrange a conference call.

Two hours later, Jason's phone rang. It was the anticipated conference call with Joe, Helena, and Dr. George Wesley.

Dr. Wesley immediately spoke. "I find the information given me by Mr. and Mrs. Johnson to be truly remarkable, Mr. O'Connor. I am assuming that you want information on the procedure and how much blood you will be giving."

"That's correct, Doc Just get straight to the point, and tell me how giving blood is going to affect my physical strength."

"Well, Mr. O'Connor, you cannot give more than three pints at a time, and then it will take a while for you to recover your strength."

"How much is needed?"

"We are doing a complete blood transfusion, which means that the entire blood in Moses's system will be replaced."

"So my three pints won't be enough for him, I assume?"

"That is correct. We will have to have additional blood from another source to do the entire transfusion."

"So how long would I have to wait before giving another three pints?"

"Oh, Mr. O'Connor, your blood system would need at least a week—maybe ten days—to build up before you could do that. You will be very weak from this and will need time to recover. And I dare say you will not be in any condition to play football."

"I figured as much, Doc But let me ask you this. Could I give three pints this weekend and then another three pints on the next Friday just before the operation?"

"That is highly unusual, Mr. O'Connor. You will be severely weakened if you do and will need time to recover."

"I will do it. I can recover fine over time. Doc, can I give on Saturday in the morning?"

"Of course, anytime will do. We will keep the blood preserved until needed for the operation."

"And then I can give another three pints on Friday right before the operation?"

"As I told you before, that would be highly unusual, but yes. Just understand that you will be severely weakened and will need several weeks to recuperate."

"That's all I need to know. Let's plan for the first sample to be given on Saturday morning around ten o'clock. Would that work?"

"Mr. O'Connor, I want you to know that what you are going to do is very serious. It will have immediate affect on you physically, and there will be no way you would be able to play in the Super Bowl. I just want to make sure that you know what you are doing."

"I fully understand, Doc. Unless Coach Wagner changes his mind about the seriousness of my head injuries, I won't be playing in the game anyway. But the Super Bowl is not what is most important to me now. Please just work out the details, and I will be in touch with Joe and Helena later."

Joe Johnson was so moved by the conversation that he could hardly speak. With a quivering voice, he said, "Jason, you are truly a guardian angel right now sent to us at just the right moment."

Jason responded, "A guardian angel? Perhaps. If so, I have been a little late in reporting for duty, but I am here now, and that is what counts."

Jason paused a brief moment before continuing. "Joe, as I mentioned in our previous conversation, I need to let you know that I am going to be divulging all the information about me and Moses to Sammy Jensen for the story he is writing. I hate to invade your privacy, but trust me about this. I have to strike a deal with him, so he will lay off saying some very hurtful things about Bobby Childs and his college girlfriend Mandy Brooks."

Joe responded, "It appears that you are always thinking of others these days, Jason. Listen, I have no problem with the press reporting on all of this. They are bound to know sooner or later, and it is probably a good idea that you are in control of the story at the beginning."

"Thanks, Joe, I appreciate your support."

"I am the one who should be giving the thanks, Jason."

CHAPTER 20

F riday's practice went quickly for Jason. He and Wagner spoke very little, but the coach made it clear that he wanted to talk further after practice. Wagner was obviously edgy and nervous about what was going to happen and what would be revealed by Jason.

In the locker room after practice Bobby Childs approached Jason to remind him of their time later the evening at the mall.

"Jason, are you going to be OK? I look forward to our time tonight, and we can talk about more of the detail that is going on."

Jason smiled and said, "I honestly couldn't be feeling better. I am concerned about Mandy meeting with her ex tonight. I think that guy is trouble. But don't worry, I am going to make sure that Sammy is not going to slam you two in his articles. Count on it."

"Well, how are you going to manage that one?"

"I have an interview with Sammy tomorrow at the airport about a half hour before the team boards the plane. I will tell him everything about Rachel, Moses, and me, but I will do so on one condition—that he lay off of you and Mandy and keep the information he has on you two out of the paper."

"Jason, we are all in this together, man. You can't do that."

Jason O'Connor smiled again at his friend. He stood up walked over to Bobby and put his hand on his shoulder. "Oh yes I can. And I will."

"Well, then, do you think Mandy still needs to meet with her ex about this? If Sammy agrees, then there is no need that she subject herself to more of his abuse."

"I think she should go ahead and meet him because we do not know how Sammy is going to respond. If he turns my request down, we will hopefully have some additional information from Mandy's ex to counter what he wants to do."

"So you are willing to sacrifice your reputation and let Sammy smear you in order to protect us?"

"I wouldn't put it quite that way. First, I hardly see how Sammy is going to smear me. Facts are facts. I did a very bad thing with Rachel and am paying for it. But I am also doing a good thing about Moses. I think the public will be forgiving to me."

"You are taking yourself out of the Super Bowl voluntarily. Do you really think the crazy Seattle sports fans will think kindly of you for doing that?"

"Whether they do or do not is out of my control. I can only control what I do, and I have to live with myself for all the decisions I make. I could not live with myself if I abandoned Moses right now, and he dies."

Jason walked toward the press room for the press conference as Bobby followed. When Jason came to the door he said to Bobby, "One more thing. Tell Mandy to please bring Rachel's letter with her tonight, and I will pick it up from her. I am going to give a copy of it to Sammy tomorrow."

"Are you sure you want to do this?"

"I am more sure of this than anything I have ever done." With that comment Jason stepped into the press room and mounted the platform to sit by his coach, Paul Wagner.

This press conference was particularly trying for Wagner. Questions continued about Jason's availability to play. Many questions related to the clear observation that Jason was not taking part in any of the play running or calling on the field. And on this particular day Jason was in his street clothes, standing on the sidelines merely watching with no interaction with his coach. The press was beginning to sense that Wagner was not telling the complete story, but the Seahawks head coach held his ground during the interrogation.

Wagner tried to finesse his answers as best he could, but it was clear that the reporters were not satisfied with his continued insistence that Jason would be playing. Jason remained mute throughout the questioning until the very end, when he finally spoke up.

"I don't know why you guys continue to beat a dead horse. Coach Wagner has repeated it over and over again. Can't we move on to other topics, such as how the team is looking overall in our Super Bowl preparations?"

Sammy Jensen then spoke. "So, Jason, why were you not participating in the practice today? We haven't really heard the latest update from you yet."

Jason replied in a teasing and joking manner, "Now, Sammy, you know that you and I are going to have an exclusive talk tomorrow, so are you sure you want me to tip these other guys off on the big scoop I am going to be giving you?" The reporters laughed.

Finally, the torturous press conference ended, with the reporters unsatisfied with the responses given. Wagner and Jason walked out of the press room relieved to be free of their interrogators.

Wagner spoke to Jason as they entered the locker room. "OK, O'Connor. I honored your request. Now you better tell me what is going on and what I can expect. I am not going to face the press again until I know what you are planning."

Jason walked into Wagner's office and sat down. He waited for his coach to stop pacing back and forth before he spoke. Finally, as Wagner sat in his chair, Jason opened up to what was going on. He told the coach all about his past with Rachel and the birth and adoption of Moses. He told him of his decision to be the blood donor for the transfusion and how that would render him unable to play in the Super Bowl. Wagner was stunned.

"Words cannot express what I am feeling right now," Wagner said. "This is eerie. Just plain eerie."

"Well, Coach, it also gets you off the hook regarding me not playing."

"How do you figure that?

"It is simple. I am voluntarily taking myself out of the game to give blood for Moses. It is my decision—not yours. Nobody has to know that my head injuries prohibit me from playing. That is our secret. I become the bad guy in this scenario, and you are off the hook."

Wagner looked at Jason skeptically and replied, "You don't think the press will give me hell for not replacing Morrison with an adequate backup for you?"

"Maybe they will and maybe they won't, but the main story is going to be me voluntarily stepping down to give blood for Moses. To some I will be a hero, but I think to most I will be a sentimental jerk who let the team down, but at any rate I will be the story—not you."

Wagner took a deep sigh and said, "Jason, I can't let you play with the injuries you have received, and that is the bottom-line. So you go ahead, and do what you need to do. I am sure that things will work out for Moses, and who knows, maybe we can pull off an upset of the Steelers with Morrison at the helm. That would be a great way for him to go out."

"Yes, it would. I am meeting Sammy Jensen at the airport. He doesn't know anything yet, but I suspect that he has strong suspicions. I will give him a copy of the letter from Rachel, and he will have quite a story to write. It will be the news story he has been waiting for his whole career to write. It will be the entire story for the rest of the week leading up to the Super Bowl."

"And how about you, Jason? This has to be a tremendous burden and pressure for you to handle."

"Strangely enough, Coach, I am at peace. For some reason I believe that meeting Moses and doing what I am doing was supposed to happen in the grand scheme of things. However this thing turns out, I know that all of this was meant to happen for some greater purpose."

"Greater purpose?" Wagner asked sarcastically. "If a greater purpose exists in this situation, it will be at the expense of us losing the Super Bowl. Now please tell me why anybody should be happy about that?"

Jason thought for a moment before responding. He was not quite sure what to say. His whole life in professional football had been pursued with one ultimate goal in mind—winning the Super Bowl. Now, however, he was telling his coach that a greater purpose existed that transcended winning the ultimate prize in his profession. His response was short.

"Coach, I know you don't understand. To be frank, I don't understand it all either. But I know what is right. And what I am doing is the right thing. That is all I can say now. Maybe it will be clearer to both of us later on."

Wagner was clearly unnerved by all of the detail his mind was processing. He was a man of enormous pride. What Jason was planning to do would possibly preserve his reputation by focusing the press on Jason's decision to give blood and not on his own errant judgment in failing to secure an adequate backup quarterback.

Wagner got up from his chair, walked over to his star quarterback, put his hand on his shoulder, and said, "Jason, my friend, go ahead and do this. You have to face yourself in the mirror every morning. And nothing is worth being in a position where you despise yourself and everything you have done. We are going to be OK. I will fill Zach Morrison in on everything tonight, and we will face the press tomorrow."

"Just so you know, Coach, I am not flying out with the team tomorrow. I am going to the hospital to give some blood right after my interview with Sammy Jensen."

"I hadn't planned on you coming along, but I want you with the team though next week for moral support and to help me on the sidelines."

"I won't be flying out until a week from tomorrow, if I am strong enough to come at all."

"What are you talking about?"

"I am drawing some more blood a week from today. I want to give as much as I can for the transfusion next Friday. I am told that I will be very weak, and it will take awhile to recover."

"Well, Jason, I want you there if possible. Your presence is important as a morale booster, if nothing else."

"I hope I can make it, Coach. I hope so."

CHAPTER 21

Upon arriving home after practice, Bobby immediately picked up his phone and called Mandy to touch base on the upcoming events of the evening. He was concerned about her meeting with her ex-husband, and wanted to make sure that all of the details were covered before she met him. When Mandy answered the phone it was clear that she was under a great deal of stress.

"Oh, Bobby, I am so glad you called me. I have been out of my mind all day today. I need you more than ever now."

"You know you don't have to meet with him tonight. You can just call the whole thing off."

"No, I really feel strongly that I have to do this. We have to find out what he and Sammy Jensen are up to, and then come up with a plan to thwart it. Maybe we can't do anything to stop this, but at the very least, I will find out some detail before we have to read about it in the papers."

"I will be with Jason tonight at the mall. I want you to have your cell phone on you. If at anytime he threatens you or gets out of line, call me. We will be there in less than five minutes."

"Thank you, Bobby. I trust you."

Those three words—"I trust you"—tore at Bobby. He vowed that he would make himself worthy of Mandy's trust this time. He had lost her trust long ago but had now regained it. He was not going to lose it a second time.

"Mandy, everything will be all right. I am here for you and will never abandon you again." Bobby could hear Mandy cry over the phone as he continued his assurances.

"Rest assured that if this guy gets out of line, he will not only have to deal directly with me, but he will also have to face the wrath of Jason O'Connor."

"Thank you, Bobby."

"There is one thing. Jason asked me to request something of you."

"And what is that?"

"He wants you to bring Rachel's letter, so he can pick it up later on."

"Why does he want the letter?"

"I was afraid you would ask. He is going to talk to Sammy Jensen tomorrow morning and tell him all about Rachel and Moses. He is going to give Sammy a copy of the letter to use in the story."

"Oh no, Bobby, you have to talk him out of that. He can't do that. It will be playing into Sammy and Jim's hands."

"Well, first, we shouldn't worry because Jason assures me that he will not release the letter until Sammy agrees not to write about you and me. He wants to keep private all of our dirty laundry."

"So Jason is willing to take the entire hit on this and protect us? Why?"

"He is quite a guy. Something happened to him last night when he was by himself. He is a changed man. He is at peace with himself. He plans to be the blood donor for Moses's transfusion and take himself out of the Super Bowl."

"Oh my! He is going to do that? He is going to sacrifice his career to give blood for Moses?"

"Yes, he has made the decision and won't be deterred. I am numb from all of this. Especially in his decision to try to protect our privacy."

"Oh, Bobby, we can't let him be the fall guy in this. We are not innocent, and if Sammy wants to slime Jason, we are part of the story and should be mentioned as well. We just can't let him sacrifice his reputation like that."

"I tried to talk him out of it, but he is Irish you know. That's as hardheaded as they comes. I know Jason O'Connor better than anybody. When he sets his mind to doing something, you can't stop him. That is why he is such a great quarterback. He is too stubborn to lose. But he has made up his mind that he is going to intervene in order to save the life of his son Moses. I think that Rachel would want that."

"So do I," Mandy said quietly.

"There will be other Super Bowls, but there will never be another Moses."

"Yes, you are right. I will bring the letter with me."

"Mandy, I am concerned about this meeting tonight with your ex. If Sammy agrees to Jason's terms, then there is no need for you to meet with Jim. I am not sure you have to go through with this."

"Well, first, we don't know if Sammy is going to agree with Jason's demands. And if he doesn't, then perhaps my meeting with Jim will provide us with enough information to at least defend ourselves when Sammy tries to slaughter us in the press."

"That is what Jason said as well. Two great minds think alike."

"So I think I should go to the meeting tonight. You will be close by, and it is in public. I will be fine.

"OK, we will be at the mall waiting for you. If everything goes well, then call me around eight o'clock, and we will come over to defuse. If you have problems then call me immediately. If I get a call from you before eight, then I know we need to come."

"I understand the plan, Bobby. We can do this thing."

"There is one more thing I need to say before we hang up."

"Yes, what is it, Bobby?"

"I love you. You are my precious angel. Thanks for the second chance."

Mandy choked up as she responded. "I have always loved you, Bobby, and I always will."

Bobby Childs hung up the phone with mixed emotions. He was legitimately concerned for Mandy's safety and felt the stress she was feeling, but he was also very happy that he had reconnected with her. For the first time in his life, he was experiencing love. He was excited about his new life with Mandy Brooks and their son, and he knew that now, more than ever, was his time to be the protector for these two.

Bobby met Jason at the designated place in the parking lot outside the mall. They both knew that they would not be able to go into the mall because if they did they would be overrun with Seahawks fans and admirers. Such was the burden of celebrity status.

When Jason drove up, Bobby got into Jason's car, and the two long time friends began to talk. "What a week we have had," said Bobby. "How are you doing tonight?"

"I am feeling better and stronger than I have for days. It is funny, but football just doesn't seem so important now. Moses is who I care about."

"I am not sure that the Seahawks fans and front office will see it the same way. Are you ready for the firestorm your announcement is going to make?"

"Indeed I am. Indeed I am."

Jason put his seat into a reclining position and closed his eyes while sighing deeply. Bobby remained quiet for a few moments before speaking.

"You know, Jason, I am feeling the same way. It is funny. On the one hand, I want to beat the Steelers more than anything. The Super Bowl is everything we have dreamed about in our careers. On the other hand, I am beginning to understand that there are much more important things in life than a game. Mandy and my son are far more important to me than winning the big game."

"What a difference one week makes," responded Jason. "In a way, we both have been given a second chance to correct some big mistakes. I only wish that Rachel were alive for me to tell her how sorry I am. At least you have been given a second chance to work this out with Mandy."

Bobby replied, "I didn't realize it until I saw her this week at the restaurant, but my heart died the night she walked out of the fraternity house. I ached all of these years. When I reconnected with her, I became alive again."

Jason looked at his friend and smiled. "Mandy is a good woman, buddy. You better treat her well this time around, or I will have to rough you up some."

Bobby laughed. "Now that is one thing I don't want to happen. A guy your size carries a pretty good wallup, and I don't care to mess with you."

The two men both laughed as they began to reminisce about their friendship. They talked about life in college and how together they had torched the football field at old Wazzu. They talked about the times the four of them had together on campus, and, of course, they talked about Rachel and Moses.

"So what are your plans as far as being with Moses after the transfusion? I assume even if all goes well, he doesn't have a lot of time left."

"If Joe and Helena let me, then I will be as much involved in his life as a father can be. It will be up to them."

"I guess I am lucky on this point," replied Bobby. "Mandy wants me to be involved with our son. And I plan to make up for lost time."

Suddenly, Bobby's cell phone rang. He noticed on the caller ID that it was Mandy. He immediately answered but could only hear a loud male voice screaming obscenities.

"We gotta go now man! Mandy is in trouble!"

Jason put his car into high gear and sped out of the parking lot, squealing the tires as he accelerated the vehicle. They sped toward the coffee shop where Mandy was with Jim Harrison.

CHAPTER 22

Earlier that evening Mandy had driven to the coffee shop to await the entrance of Jim Harrison. She was nervous and questioned if meeting him were wise. As requested by Bobby, she brought with her Rachel's letter to give to Jason later in the evening.

Jim Harrison staggered into the coffee shop ten minutes late and intoxicated. He slowly walked over to Mandy's table to sit down, smelling of booze. She felt total disgust upon seeing him but struggled to avoid showing her revulsion.

"Hey there, babe. You are looking good tonight. How about some play time afterward, unless, of course, you are planning to meet loser boy Childs someplace."

"Jim, just get to the point. I don't want this to go on too long. Just say what you have to say, and then let's end this matter."

"Well, OK, little miss iceberg. I was just trying to be friendly. It's OK though because I think what I have to say will interest you."

Jim then pulled out of his coat pocket a check and handed it to Mandy. The check was made out to her in the amount of five thousand dollars but was unsigned. Jim smiled broadly as he watched her facial expression when seeing the check.

"Now, I know you and little Bobby could use some extra cash, and I am willing to provide it for you. But, of course, there is one thing you have to do for me before I will sign this thing."

Mandy stared at the check for a moment. She had no intention of doing what he wanted and was not seriously contemplating taking this bribe. She did, however, want to know what was going on between Jim and Sammy Jensen, so she played along.

"OK, Jim, tell me what you have in mind. I know that you and

Sammy Jensen are planning something big in the papers to trash Jason and Bobby. I suspect you are wanting me to cooperate with you."

"You are a smart girl, Mandy. All I want from you is the letter Rachel sent to Jason. Just give me the letter, and I will sign your check. That is pretty simple now isn't it?"

"And what are you and Sammy going to do with this letter? Honestly, Jim, I don't know why you have such a hatred for me that you want to destroy me in this process. What did little Bobby and I ever do to you to deserve this?"

"Mandy, dearest," Jim said sarcastically. "You just don't get it, do you. I don't intend to destroy you at all. Just give me the letter, I will sign the check, and Sammy will not mention you at all in his news articles."

"He has told you that?"

"He has given me his word. He is intrigued with the story about Jason and Rachel and wants it verified before he prints it. That is it. His interest in you and Childs is merely secondary."

"Why does he want to destroy Jason? Jason is the biggest sports hero Seattle has ever seen. I just don't understand this."

"Don't you think that the public has a right to know about the celebrities whom their hard earned dollars support? Jason O'Connor has made millions from sports fans in this area. I think they are entitled to know a little bit more about their investment. And that includes the bad news as well as the good news."

Mandy looked straight into the eyes of her ex-husband before she responded. She surprised herself in feeling some compassion for this man who was totally enslaved by his desire to destroy others.

"Rachel Thomlinson was my best friend," she said. "I have never had a friend like her and probably never will in this life. I cherish the memories of her. You are asking me to destroy her reputation ten years after she died. Why can't you just let it go, Jim?"

Jim began to become hostile and raised his voice. "Don't get so self-righteous with me, Mandy Brooks. I know you well enough to not let you be so sanctimonious. Money means more to you than anything—that's why you probably are trying to hook up with loser boy Childs. But what has he given you the last ten years? Nothing. Absolutely nothing. He abandoned you and turned his back on you. As for me, I took you in as my wife and gave you a lifestyle you relished. I continue to support you monthly, and now I am giving you a chance to improve your life. Where should your loyalties be?"

"Improve my life? You want to improve my life? Just tell me Jim how betraying my friends and the memory of my best friend will improve my life. I have to look at myself every morning in the mirror, and I like what I see these days. I won't like the reflection if I do what you ask."

Jim Harrison responded angrily, "My, oh my, aren't we the self-righteous one. And all this moralizing coming from someone who gives birth to a little bastard out of wedlock."

"That's enough, Jim. If you think continuing to assassinate me with your tongue will get you what you want, you are wrong."

Jim Harrison reached across the table to grab Mandy's wrists and pull her face toward him. Mandy pulled back from his physical advances realizing that agreeing to this meeting was a big mistake. She jumped up from the table and put the strap from her purse around her shoulder. Jim noticed Rachel's letter sticking out of the purse and smiled to himself.

"I have had enough, Jim. You are not getting the letter. Tell Sammy to write what he wants, but I am not betraying my friends. You can keep your stinking money."

Jim followed Mandy out of the door into the parking lot of the restaurant. When she got to her car he became aggressive and agitated and stepped in front of her, blocking her ability to open the car door.

"Get out of my way, Jim, and leave me alone. If you don't move now, I will call the police."

"Don't you walk away from me, Mandy Brooks. Don't you ever walk away from me. Nobody does that." Jim began to curse and shout obscenities in her face, and then swung his hand across her cheek with a violent slap knocking her to the ground.

"Now, give me the letter, or I will take it from you forcefully."

"I am calling the police," said Mandy as she struggled to get her cell phone out of her purse. When she reached for the phone, Rachel's letter fell out of her purse and onto the ground. Jim immediately grabbed it, pushing Mandy away as she struggled to keep it from him.

Jim shoved Mandy to the ground again while placing the envelope inside his coat pocket. He shouted more obscenities at her while she dialed Bobby Childs on her cell phone.

"Go ahead and call the police you little slut! See what I care. I have connections with the police department and the city prosecutor. They won't touch me."

He lifted his new found trophy—Rachel's letter—high above his head in triumph and shouted, "So you brought it after all. I knew you would see it my way. The problem now though is that my offer expired back in the restaurant." He then took the unsigned check and tore it up into little pieces, laughing hysterical as he did so.

Mandy began to sob and pleaded with him to give the letter back. In a cruel and taunting demeanor, Jim mocked her voice and then said, "OK, maybe I will give it back if you beg for it."

He then cruelly laughed at her as she struggled to get back on her feet. "Come on now. Go ahead beg for it. I want to hear you beg for it," he shouted in her face.

While Jim was shouting further obscenities at her Jason O'Connor's car pulled into the parking lot at top speed. Upon seeing Mandy's distress, Bobby immediately jumped out of the car and ran toward Jim Harrison. Jason followed closely behind.

"Back off now mister, or you will be one sorry cowboy," Bobby shouted.

Jim Harrison turned around to see the two Seahawks players and burst into a hysterical and cynical laugh. "My, oh, my. If it isn't the dynamic duo coming to the rescue of a damsel in distress. What are you going to do to me, Childs? Punch me out? Go ahead, and try if you dare. If you touch me, I will enjoy suing your sorry behind into bankruptcy."

Bobby and Jason slowed up and began to walk slowly toward Harrison as Mandy immediately ran into Bobby's arms, sobbing. Childs looked at Harrison as he held her and demanded to know what was going on.

"I have never met you before, and I don't care to do so again. But let me make something clear to you buster. Don't you ever come close to this woman again."

Harrison again laughed and responded, "OK, loser boy. It is a deal. I have what I want anyway, and you cannot stop the things that are about to happen." He then pulled out the letter, and looking at Jason, he continued his taunts.

"You know something, O'Connor. I knew you were a phony from the start. You try to portray this all-American boy image to the public, but wait until they get a load of what is in this letter. That will tarnish your squeaky clean image a little now, won't it?"

Mandy screamed at her ex. "Give me back the letter Jim. Give it back now, and I won't call the police to have you arrested for assault."

Jason also responded, "I have nothing against you, sir. I don't even know who you are. Just give back the letter, and we will forget that this whole sorry incident happened."

Jim again laughed his wicked laugh as he tucked the letter into his coat pocket. He then responded, "I love it. I love it. You two guys are petrified of what I have and what it will do to your big shot reputations. Well, listen, fellas, and listen good. The gig is up. You two phonies are going to be exposed for who you are, and there is nothing that you can do or say to stop it."

Bobby let go of Mandy and began to move toward Jim Harrison in an aggressive manner. Upon seeing the move, Jim taunted him even louder. "Come on, tough guy. Try it now. Just try to take this from me." As he continued his tirade, he walked backward toward the highway laughing and taunting as he went.

Jim Harrison did not see what was headed his way as he continued to walk backward, away from Bobby's moves. Coming down the road at a frightening speed was a van, whose driver was not prepared for what was about to happen.

Mandy noticed the van first and saw that Jim was about to step onto the road in front of the oncoming vehicle. She became alarmed and shouted a warning to her ex-husband just before he stepped into the street. She screamed, "Jim, look out! Get back! Get back!"

It was too late. His body was immediately hit and mangled. He was thrown through the air and landed directly on his head. He was killed upon impact.

Jason immediately ran over the body to see if he could help while Mandy fell into Bobby's arms, crying hysterically. Bobby reached for his cell phone to call for assistance as a crowd began to gather.

Traumatized, Jason stood over the body in disbelief. Bobby dialed for emergency help on his cell phone, but it was clear that Jim was gone. At the sight of the mangled body, Mandy buried her head in Bobby's chest and sobbed.

The siren of the emergency vehicle could be heard in the distance, and Jason continued to stare at Jim's body. As he did, he noticed that Rachel's letter was still in tact in Jim's coat pocket. He reached down and pulled the letter out, placing it in his own pocket.

CHAPTER 23

Saturday was a complete whirlwind for Jason, Bobby, and Mandy. They got home well after midnight on Friday after giving statements to the police about the accident. Plus, the shocking events of the evening required that the three of them remain together for a while to defuse.

Jim Harrison was a despised little man in their eyes, but, despite his depravity, none of them wished upon him such an untimely end. This catastrophe particularly distressed Mandy, as she struggled with an intense sadness over the incident. Bobby provided great comfort to her and assured her that everything would work out for everyone's overall good. Such was the new found faith of Bobby Childs.

Jason and Bobby were up early on Saturday as they went to the airport to join the team. Jason was introspective watching the team board the plane as he waited to speak to Coach Wagner for a final briefing. Standing silently off to the side while the team boarded was Sammy Jensen, patiently bidding his time to interview the Seahawks quarterback.

Wagner approached Jason to quickly converse before boarding the plane. His eye contact with Jason indicated that he also was deep in thought and experiencing inner turmoil.

"OK, O'Connor, so you aren't going on this flight with the team, but I am expecting you next week after the blood transfusion. I have made arrangements for you to fly out next Saturday morning to join us in Miami. There is going to be a lot of hoopla in the media this week over what you are about to do. I suggest that you lay low as far as the media, but I know you well enough to understand that you will make your own decision on that one."

"I don't know what I am going to do after talking with Sammy today.

I will take it day-by-day. I know that the media will be demanding interviews and updates." Jason looked over to the other side of the gate and
saw Sammy Jensen looking at him intensely as he waited his time to connect. Wagner saw him as well and simply sighed.

"Well, Jason, we need you for moral support in the locker room. The
team doesn't yet know what is going on—except I did fill Zach Morrison
in on the details, like I said I would. We will debrief them once we land
in Miami. Just be on that plane next Saturday and help raise our spirits.
Promise you will do that."

"I can only promise that I will try, Coach. I have a feeling that I am
not going to be real strong by next Saturday."

Zach Morrison came alongside the two. He was ready to board but
was anxious to say something to Jason before doing so. His eyes met
Jason's for a moment, and then he spoke while Wagner listened quietly.

"Wagner filled me in on what is going on, and I have just talked to
Bobby Childs about it. I am in shock."

"You will do fine, Zach," Jason said. "It is a great way for a guy like
you to end his career.

"Listen, Morrison," said Coach Wagner. "You are to keep your lip
zipped on the plane. Do you hear me? I will be debriefing the entire team
when we land in Miami. Then, and only then, will they be getting the full
story. It will come from me—not you. The team will be able to read all
the details in the papers the next few days anyway, so keep it to yourself
for now."

Zach nodded and walked over to the gate to board the plane. He
looked depressed, as if he were headed to a funeral—not the Super Bowl.

Wagner quietly walked to the gate with Jason by his side. Both men
contemplated the upcoming events of the next week. Before boarding,
Wagner commented, "I want to win this game more than anything,
O'Connor. Most pundits say that we can't win it without you. I tend to
agree. But for some strange reason, I agree with you, O'Connor. I think
all that is about to happen was meant to happen. As far as I am concerned,
we are going to play with everything in us to win this thing. And deep
down inside I really believe we will."

"I have confidence in you and the team, Coach. The Seahawks are destiny's team. Remember that."

Wagner turned and walked through the gate toward the plane. Jason smiled to himself as he watched. He felt that something unbelievable was in store for everyone. Inside he sensed an upcoming adventure that had not been anticipated just one week before. He knew that whatever events unfolded in the next week were meant to happen. He sensed that some unseen, guiding hand was in charge of these things, just like a conductor in front of a symphony orchestra. It was Jason's role to simply play his assigned part in the drama that was about to take place.

Jason turned and slowly walked toward Sammy Jensen for the scheduled interview. Sammy was puzzled as to why Jason was not boarding the plane with his teammates. He assumed that perhaps he would be leaving on a later flight but was not sure why. However, as Jason got closer, Sammy noticed in Jason's hand what looked like could be the letter from Rachel Thomlinson. He congratulated himself and sensed that what he was seeking would be given to.

Jason commented after they sat down to talk, "I assume you are aware of what happened last night to Jim Harrison."

"Yes, it is very sad. And I want you to know that I was not behind whatever happened to precipitate that horrible accident. Jim Harrison merely told me that he had a meeting with Mandy Brooks to request that she verify some information for me."

"Jim Harrison was an abusive monster to Mandy, and he threatened her last night. You really ought to be ashamed of yourself for working with such a guy."

Sammy was quiet. He looked away from Jason before finally responding. "Listen, Jason, I did not want this thing to go the way it did. I am a reporter and just have a nose for a good story—that's all. It was never my intent that Jim or anybody get hurt. I just wanted to write a good story and have it backed up by the facts."

"Well, you may be on the verge of your story. I have something that might help, but I am not talking at all about it unless I get assurances from you."

"What do you need from me, Jason?"

"I will give you everything you want, including the letter from Rachel Thomlinson, but only if you agree not to write anything about Bobby and Mandy. Leave them out of this."

"You are asking a lot, Jason. They both play a critical role in this story. How can I do that?"

"You have no choice. If you want the letter, you must agree to this. You must be silent about their romance and the fact that they had a son out of wedlock. You must be silent on her previous pregnancy and how it was terminated. You must just focus on me and my relationship to Rachel Thomlinson. Believe me—what I can share with you will be enough for you to have the scoop of your life. But you will only have it if you agree to my terms."

Sammy sat still as he contemplated Jason's demands. He knew that without Jason's cooperation, he had nothing to write. Jim Harrison was dead, and Mandy Brooks was not talking. Jason apparently had the letter secure, and without it, Sammy had nothing to verify the storyline. Jason had him over a barrel, and he knew it.

"OK, Jason, you have my word. A deal is a deal. Bobby and Mandy's relationship and their son are off limits. Nobody will know about that."

Jason smiled and said, "You know, Sammy, I think we might even like each other by the time this is over. Why don't we just go somewhere else for a long conversation, and let me fill you in on some things."

The two men left the airport together and arrived at a local restaurant. They sat down in an isolated booth that allowed them to talk in complete privacy. After briefly ordering drinks, Jason began to talk about Rachel Thomlinson.

Jason shared everything about his relationship with Rachel and her pregnancy. He let Sammy read the letter and filled him in on the big bombshell in the story—the indisputable fact that Moses Johnson, the son of Joe and Helena, was his biological son. Jason then shared about the upcoming blood transfusion and the need for the blood donor to be genetically related. He next talked about his decision to be the needed blood donor.

Sammy listened in amazement, as he now understood that Jason O'Connor, by his decision to be the blood donor for Moses, was voluntarily taking himself out of the Super Bowl. He knew that he was sitting on the sports story of the year—perhaps of the decade.

The two men talked for over an hour, and Sammy took meticulous notes as they spoke. Finally, Jason looked at his watch and said, "Sorry, Sammy, but I have an appointment to draw blood at Providence Hospital in twenty minutes. We have to end this. You can call me later for more detail if you need it, but I have a feeling that I have given you plenty of material to use."

Sammy was beginning to feel some guilt over how he had so harshly judged Jason O'Connor's character. He now saw Jason in a different light. "Jason, I know I have been hard on you. But I no longer don't want to hurt your reputation. I know you don't believe me, but I promise you it is true. Before today I was feeling pretty antagonistic toward you, but I won't destroy you now with this information. You are doing an incredibly noble thing. My story will reflect that."

Jason again smiled. "I can't tell you how to write the story or what to say. You are a professional. Just do what you think is best. I am at peace with all of this."

With that comment Jason O'Connor walked out of the restaurant. Sammy Jensen remained in his seat in awe of the story that had been revealed to him. He jotted down a few more notes before leaving to go to his office and work on the scoop of his life.

Jason traveled to Providence Hospital for his appointment to draw blood. He checked in with Moses's physician, who explained the procedure and how much blood was to be taken. The doctor once again made it clear to him that by giving as much blood as he was—three pints—he would be significantly weakened and unable to undertake much physical activity. He also told Jason that he should just go home and rest for the next few days to build up his strength before the second blood draw in seven days.

Jason sat in the waiting room as the medical staff prepared for the draw. He closed his eyes for a moment to relax when he felt a tap on his shoulder. He opened his eyes and saw before him Josh—the stranger he had met and talked with earlier that week at Alki Beach.

"Josh, what are you doing here?"

"Well, I come to this hospital often as a volunteer. There are a lot of needy people here who just need a kind hand and smile from somebody."

"Well, my friend, sit down for a few moments while I wait. I think you know what I am here for."

"Yes, you told me all about this possibility when we met. However, you had not made up your mind as to what you were going to do when I left you."

"Yeah, I had to do a lot of soul searching, but once I did, it was an easy choice to make. I have no doubts or regrets."

Josh smiled at Jason and said, "You have made the right choice my friend. Well done." He then asked, "Are you going to be able to play in the big game?"

"Hardly. I will be very weak after the draw today, and I will barely have recovered before they take the second draw a week from today. It is OK, though. There will be another day for football. There will never be another Moses."

Josh stood up to leave, continuing to smile. His eyes pierced Jason's as he reached out and placed his hand on Jason's shoulder. "I said this to you the other night. I am not sure you heard it, so I will say it again. You will play in the Super Bowl, and it will be your greatest game ever."

"Thanks, Josh. I appreciate your confidence and support, but it will take a real miracle from God for that to happen."

"I think that is what God is in the business of doing—miracles." The eyes of these two compatriots met again, and Jason was strangely warmed.

"Thanks, Josh. I appreciate the encouragement."

"You are more than welcome. I will see you next Friday. I will be here at the hospital again to volunteer. And yes, I will also see you in Miami."

"You are coming to the Super Bowl?"

Josh laughed. "I already told you that I am your biggest fan. I wouldn't miss it." With that comment, Josh turned and walked away. Jason closed his eyes once again and leaned his head back.

As expected, Jason was very weak after the draw. Joe Johnson showed up just before the procedure and volunteered to drive him home. Jason gladly accepted the offer. He was feeling lonely and needed the company. The two men said little to each other in the car on the way home, but Joe again expressed his deep gratitude to Jason for his sacrifice.

"Words can't express how thankful we are for you Jason. You are a true hero."

"Joe, when all this is behind us, I want to spend as much time as possible with Moses. I don't want to intrude on your relationship with him, but I really want to get to know my son. There is a lot of lost time to make up for."

Joe Johnson exhibited his big toothy grin and said, "I was hoping you would want to do just that. The three of us will do a lot together. It will be wonderful."

"Thanks for accepting me into your lives, Joe."

"Thank you for coming into our lives. What a difference one week can make."

As they drove up to the front of Jason's residence, Joe asked, "Need some company tonight? I would be glad to come in for awhile and just chill with you."

"Thanks, Joe, but I am OK. I really just want to get to bed early. I am totally exhausted."

As soon as Jason opened the door, he was greeted by the phone ringing. He looked on the caller ID and saw that it was Sammy. He hesitated slightly before finally answering.

"OK, Sammy, make it quick because I want to lie down and get some sleep."

"I don't want anything Jason. I was just calling to see how you are doing and if you need anything."

"Well, that is mighty nice coming from you, Sammy. But I am fine. I feel really weak—weaker than after I first injured my head, but I will be fine. Thanks for asking."

"Jason, I just want to let you know that I am breaking the story in tomorrow's Sunday morning paper, ahead of schedule. This is going to be the news story for the rest of the week, so I hope you are prepared for the onslaught of requests for press interviews."

"I am ready, Sammy. I am not sure I will take any more interviews, but I am ready for all the questions that are going to come my way." After the conversation ended Jason went into his bedroom and he immediately fell into a deep slumber.

CHAPTER 24

On Sunday morning the story of Jason O'Connor, Rachel Thomlinson, and their son Moses finally broke in the sports section of the *Seattle Post-Intelligencer*. Sammy Jensen's work was the lead story and covered two full pages of text. The national media immediately picked up the story on the newswires, and sports pundits across the country were abuzz with discussion and analysis of the drama.

Jason slept hard the night before and was groggy when he awoke midmorning to the annoying sound of his telephone ringing. The story had been out for a few hours at that time, and it didn't take long for the phone calls to start. This call was from Paul Wagner.

"So, O'Connor, how are you feeling? You better be prepared for the onslaught that is about to take place."

"Thanks, Coach. I am real tired. I just want to go back to bed and sleep. I think I will turn my phone off and ignore it the rest of the morning."

"Yeah, maybe that is a good idea. I gathered the team around last night and told them what was up. Needless to say, some of the guys are really angry. Others are just bewildered. Your pal Childs is running interference for you and trying to talk sense to the team."

Jason smiled and responded, "Bobby is a loyal friend."

Wagner continued, "The team will be issuing a statement shortly for the media. I thought I would run it past you before we do."

"Go ahead and read it to me."

Wagner cleared his throat and began to read the carefully scripted statement. "The Seahawks regret that Jason O'Connor will be unable to play in the upcoming Super Bowl. Jason has made the decision to undertake efforts to preserve the life of his son. We cannot criticize such actions and wish his son a speedy recovery."

"That sounds fine, Coach. You are going to have to fight off the reporters down there all week. I know that this is all they are going to want to ask about."

"I am ready to handle it. Right now the team has to get their focus back, so I am closing all practices to the press. We will have a very short press conference after each practice session, and I will say as little as possible about your situation."

"Good luck, Coach. It won't be easy."

"Listen, O'Connor, I want you on that plane next Saturday to come down to Miami and join the team. In fact, I am expecting you to be there."

"How well do you think I will be received?"

"The team loves you, O'Connor. You are their leader. Some of the guys are angry and don't understand, but that is all the more reason why you need to be in the locker room with them."

"I can handle it. I am just not sure that I will be strong enough to travel."

"Suck it up, O'Connor. Just be there. You are a strong athlete. You can handle this."

Jason turned off his phone after talking with the coach and attempted to rest. He wanted to be free from what he anticipated would be a heavy onslaught of calls and press inquiries. His instincts were correct. The press—both national and local—saturated the air waves and news wires with commentary and detail of the story. Many media sources were trying frantically to contact Jason for comment.

Jake McGee and Robin Iverson highlighted the story on their Sunday edition of *Morning Sports Talk*. Jason listened as he lay on his bed with his eyes closed.

"Good morning sports fans. This is Jake McGee along with my sidekick Robin Everson bringing you the latest in sports news this Monday morning. And boy do we have a sports story to talk about today, don't we, Robin."

"Yes, Jake, I am in shock over the revelations in this morning's *Post-Intelligencer* from Sammy Jensen regarding Seahawks Quarterback Jason O'Connor. Sammy will be with us in a few minutes to talk about this drama, and we are trying desperately to contact Jason O'Connor for comment."

Jason smiled as he lay on his bed listening. He was now extremely happy that he had turned off his telephone.

Robin Everson continued. "In case you sports fans are not yet aware of the story, it has been reported that Jason O'Connor has voluntarily taken himself out of the Super Bowl in order to be the blood donor for a handicapped youngster who is undergoing a blood transfusion on the Friday before the game. The story gets a little bizarre and reveals that the youngster is, in fact, Jason's son from a relationship he had in college. The child's mother was killed in an automobile accident shortly after giving birth, and the child was adopted by a Seattle area couple."

Jake McGee picked up the story line. "And sports fans this story really gets interesting. The boy, age ten, is the adopted child of Rev. Josiah and Helena Johnson. In case those names do not ring a bell, Joe Johnson is the person who saved Jason's life a week ago by pushing him out of the way of a falling concrete beam in the Qwest stadium parking lot."

"It doesn't get any stranger than this sports fans," said Robin. "The Seahawks front office has now confirmed the story with a brief comment, but we haven't heard yet from Jason O'Connor. We are trying to get him on the line, so stay tuned."

Jake McGee continued, "We now have Sammy Jensen on the line with us. After we talk with him we will be taking your calls and comments. Good morning, Sammy."

"Good morning, guys. Again, as always, it is a pleasure to talk to you two."

Robin started in with the interview. "Sammy, these revelations are astounding. How did you confirm these facts? Did you talk with Jason O'Connor about them?"

"Oh, yes, Robin. Jason and I had a long conversation this last weekend, and I can verify everything in the story. Jason provided me with a copy of the letter that his girlfriend, Rachel Thomlinson, had written to him shortly before her death. All the facts are clearly documented."

Jake McGee asked the next question. "What would motivate a guy like Jason O'Connor, who has worked his whole professional life to get to the Super Bowl, to now refuse to play because he wants to be a blood donor for this transfusion? It just doesn't make sense to me."

"Jake, I think you are underestimating the impact that Jason's relationship with Rachel Thomlinson had on his life. They were in love, and her death devastated him. He did not know that their son had been born and adopted. He thought that she had terminated the pregnancy earlier in the summer, before his senior year at Washington State. When she died, he buried the tragedy in his mind and tried to move on with his life. The events of this last week have brought back to him the memories of Rachel. I think the opportunity to play in the Super Bowl pales to him in comparison with what he perceives as his opportunity to redeem himself from his failed relationship with Rachel."

"Thank you, Sammy," responded Robin. "We are going to the phone lines to take your calls for Sammy Jensen. Good morning, you are on *Morning Sports Talk.*"

"I am one Seahawks fan that is totally disgusted with this hot shot quarterback of ours. Listen, he can give blood in two weeks. Nobody would think anything of that. In fact, I think he would be applauded for being so noble. But his actions now are guaranteeing certain defeat for the Seahawks, and we fans have a right to question his judgment and be angry."

Calls continued to come into the program, with most expressing the same sentiments. A few, however, were sympathetic and even complimentary to Jason. One such caller said, "Hey, listen guys, there is more to life than football and the Super Bowl. What Jason O'Connor has chosen to do is to attempt to save the life of his son. That is a very noble gesture, and he should be commended for it. Lay off him, will ya."

Jake, Robin, and Sammy continued to talk back and forth and field questions from the listening audience. Most of the comments were negative, and eventually Jason grew tired of hearing himself being publicly bashed and turned off his radio. He closed his eyes to get some much needed rest.

The rest of the week saw more of the same kinds of reactions. Reporters tried in vain to contact Jason, but he made himself unavailable for comment by not answering his phone or even going out. To the public, Jason O'Connor had gone AWOL, and he was being highly criticized for not explaining himself and being absent from the public discussion.

Coach Paul Wagner was not as lucky. Everyday after the Seahawks' workout, he had to ward off questions about the matter. His attempts to change the topic of discussion from Jason O'Connor to the Seahawks' strategy of beating the Steelers were largely unsuccessful. At every press conference, he had to repeat over and over the standard front office sound bite that "Jason O'Connor has made the decision to attempt to save the life of his son and not play in the Super Bowl. We cannot criticize him for that."

As the week slowly passed, Jason's strength gradually returned. However, he was keenly aware that another three pints of blood would be drawn on Friday morning, and such a procedure would significantly weaken him. The blood draw was to happen at 11:30 in the morning, and the blood transfusion for Moses was to take place at 1:00 in the afternoon. He assumed that the time of the blood draw and transfusion had not been leaked to the press by the hospital staff, but he also suspected that the press would get wind of the time and be present to hound him with questions.

Jason slept hard on Thursday night. Before he dozed off, he knelt down in front of his bed to pray. On this night, nothing seemed more natural to him than to humbly bow and petition the Almighty for strength to continue on.

Jason's prayer was humble and concise. "Lord," he prayed, "thank you for Moses. Thank you for Rachel. Please use my sacrifice to give Moses life. And give me strength to carry on. If there is any chance I can play in the Super Bowl, please make it happen. If not, I understand and won't complain."

Jason awoke early on Friday morning. The sun had not yet risen, and the city streets were quiet. He sat in his living room to meditate and be by himself. He was at total peace. Nothing he had done in his life seemed more right than what he was about to do.

Jason arrived at the hospital one hour before his scheduled blood draw. He was anticipating the media to be present, so he had arranged to be received by security guards through a back entrance. After entering he was ushered to a secure area on the second floor of the hospital to await further instructions. As he sat alone with his thoughts, his new friend Josh approached him.

"Hey, there! How are you feeling today?" Josh asked as he sat down by Jason.

"I expected to see you here today," said Jason. "They must trust you an awful lot to let a volunteer up in this secured area."

Josh smiled and then chuckled. "I have connections here so I pretty much can come and go as I please. I wanted to make sure that I was here for you today. I expect that things have been tough for you this week."

"I have been able to handle them. I have just avoided the press and haven't shown my face in public, but I know what people are saying. I can't say that I blame them much. They simply don't understand."

"You'd be surprised at the support for you out there," said Josh. "More people than you realize are rooting for you today."

The two men were interrupted by a nurse who approached Jason and said, "Mr. O'Connor, the doctor will be with you shortly to explain the procedure in detail. Since you went through this procedure just last week, he will be brief, but we do want to hear any questions that you may have."

"I really don't have any questions, nurse. I understand what will transpire."

"You will be extraordinarily weak from this blood draw, and the doctor wants you to stay overnight. I know that he will not want you driving home."

"Thanks, nurse. That is probably a good idea."

At that moment, Joe and Helena Johnson walked into the room. Jason got up and gave them both a big hug. Helena's eyes filled with tears as she embraced him for a long time. Finally, as they separated Jason said,

"I want you to meet my new friend Josh." He turned to point to Josh but found that he was no longer in the room. He had quietly exited.

Joe and Helena looked bewildered, as they saw nobody else present with them. Embarrassed, Jason chuckled as he said, "Well, he was here a minute ago."

Joe responded, "Jason, my friend. We are here for you today. Moses will receive the transfusion later this afternoon, and we will keep you posted on his progress. I will be glad to come pick you up tomorrow and take you home. I know you will not be in any shape to drive."

"Thanks, Joe." Jason gave Helena another big hug as they prepared to exit the room and be with Moses. A short time later he was summoned to his room for the blood draw.

The procedure did not take long. He hated needles, and having them poked into his veins for the draw was not a pleasant experience. He felt his already diminished strength zapped from his body as the blood was drawn into the container by the side of the bed. After the procedure ended, the blood-filled container was quickly carted away to be used for the blood transfusion for Moses. Jason was then wheeled into a private room set aside for him to recover. He immediately fell into a deep sleep.

Jason did not know how long he had been sleeping, but his next conscious moment came as he felt a hand touching his arm gently. He opened his eyes and recognized Josh standing beside the bed.

"How are you feeling now?" Josh asked.

"Hey, man, nice to see you. I am feeling really groggy. I just want to sleep. That is all. I just want to go to sleep."

Josh looked at Jason compassionately. "I know that this has been a very grueling procedure for you—both physically and emotionally, but you are going to recover rapidly."

"Is that what the doctors say? Well, that is good news, but what about Moses? Do we have any word on him yet?"

Josh smiled. "I can emphatically tell you that Moses will be fine. Your blood is exactly what was needed to strengthen him. Of course, because of his disease, he will not live into his elderly years, but your gift of life has given him many more years than expected."

Jason closed his eyes and smiled. He thought of Rachel and wished that she were present. His heart ached to see her again, and he longed for her to know the good news.

"You are thinking of Rachel right now, aren't you? I can also tell you that she knows about all of this and is very happy and proud of you."

"Hey, you never told me you could read minds. How did you know that?"

Josh laughed and said, "You are an easy man to read."

"Well then, Josh, tell me this. Are the Seahawks going to win the Super Bowl?"

Josh again laughed. "Most definitely, and you are going to play a major role in the outcome. I have told you that twice before. Now it is about time that you believe me."

Jason opened his eyes. He was feeling extremely weak and could hardly talk. He struggled to catch his breath and respond. Finally, he commented with a hardly audible voice.

"Josh," he said, "you are the eternal optimist, but look at me. I am so weak I can hardly talk. How in the world do you think I can get up out of this bed, fly to Miami, and play in the Super Bowl? I am afraid that unless you can work some miracle here, I am going to be in bed for a few days. Are you some kind of miracle worker, Josh?"

Jason began to doze off. His mind floated back and forth between a deep slumber and a semiconscious state of cognizance. His eye lids were half shut, and Josh looked upon him intently.

Josh gently placed his hands on Jason's forehead, looking deeply into his half-closed eyes. He then gazed upward as if looking beyond the structural barriers of the ceiling and the four walls that confined him. His look pierced through the hospital building, sending energy into the great beyond. He closed his eyes in deep meditation as he communed and interceded with the Providential Being who controls all things in conformity with his sovereign will.

As Josh continued to look through the confines of the hospital room, he quietly spoke in an audible voice. "Thank for hearing this request," he said to an unseen being whose presence filled the room with a divine serenity that had the power to calm raging storms and raise the dead. The room was electrified by this presence, and the great cloud of witnesses in the spiritual realm was silent and in awe of what was happening.

Josh intensified his touch on Jason's forehead, and, looking deeply into Jason's eyes, his own eyes burned. Josh's innermost being was ablaze with the essence of the divine, and healing power rushed through his veins as he continued to press his hands against Jason's forehead.

Josh once again said to Jason, "You will play in the Super Bowl, and it will be your greatest game ever."

A few more moments of meditative silence followed with Josh gazing into the eyes of the Seahawks quarterback, who was drifting in and out of consciousness and was unaware of what was transpiring. Finally, Josh smiled and looked one more time into the heavens in gratitude. He then quietly walked out of the hospital room.

Less than five minutes after Josh left, Jason's eyes opened, and he bolted up from his semiconscious state with the energy of one who realizes that he is late for work and needs to move quickly. Just as he sat up a nurse walked into the room to check on him.

"How are you doing, Mr. O'Connor?" She asked. "You need to lay back down and get some rest. It is the doctor's orders."

Jason responded aggressively and with all his faculties in place. "Doctor's orders? Oh yeah, well I need to get out of here and catch a plane. I have a football game to play in."

The nurse laughed. "You are too weak to do that, Mr. O'Connor. Please don't be difficult now. Just lay down and relax."

Jason looked at the young woman for a moment, gave her his patented smile of charm, and then laughed. His laughter was hearty and loud. It was so loud that he could be heard outside the room and down the corridors of the hospital wing. The nearby attending doctor rushed into the room to see what the commotion was all about.

"Hey, doc, I need to get up and get out of here. I have to go to Miami and join the team. We have the Steelers to beat you know."

The young doctor looked dumbfounded as he witnessed the energy level of Jason O'Connor. Just as he began to comment, Joe and Helena

Johnson walked into the room. Jason immediately and vibrantly acknowledged the presence of his friends.

"Joe, it is great news about Moses, isn't it? I am thrilled that all is
going well and that he is going to recover."

"We don't know that yet. The doctors say that it will take at least
twenty-four hours before they can assess any progress."

"Oh yes we do know it! I know it for sure. You can bank on it! Now
listen, Joe, I need to get out of here and get down to Miami."

Joe and Helena looked perplexed and glanced at the doctor. Jason's
energy level was highly unusual for someone who had just given a large
amount of blood.

"Mr. O'Connor, we are hopeful for the best for Moses, but it is just
too early to give a prognosis."

"No, it is not too early. I know for sure that Moses is going to be fine.
Josh told me."

"Who is Josh? There is no doctor in this hospital with that first
name."

"Josh is not a doctor. He is one of the volunteers who help out here
with patients. He was just in the room giving me the good news."

The doctor and Joe glanced at each other with puzzled looks. The doctor, being completely perplexed, did not know how to respond to Jason's
insistence. Joe, however, was beginning to understand and smiled.

"I am sorry, Mr. O'Connor, but unlike some hospitals, we do not
use volunteers here at all. Even if we did, we would not allow them to
be in this area of the hospital where serious medical actions are being
undertaken."

Jason was becoming agitated. "Well, then explain to me how Josh got
in here, and how he has all this information on both Moses and me?"

"There is no Josh, Mr. O'Connor. You have been hallucinating and
need to lay back down and get some rest."

Jason tossed his body back on the bed with a frustrated sigh. Perhaps,
he thought, this was just all a dream. He pondered for a moment if he
were losing his mind. After a few moments of silence, however, he realized that he was not crazy. It didn't really matter whether a person named

Josh had talked to him because he knew in his heart that Moses would be OK and that he had the strength to play in the Super Bowl. He could not explain all of this rationally, but he believed it to be true.

Jason sat back up in his bed and forcefully said, "I don't care if you believe me or not." He then jumped out of his bed and began to get dressed. All in the room stood speechless as they witnessed the energy level in which he went about dressing himself and preparing to exit.

After getting fully dressed, Jason looked and winked at Joe and Helena Johnson. Both Joe and Helena now understood that something supernatural was in play, and they smiled at their friend. Joe said, "Jason, I will take you to the airport tomorrow. You have a plane to catch."

The doctor responded forcefully, "I will not allow this man to leave. He needs to rest and recover. He cannot go anywhere!"

Jason laughed. "Are you gonna stop me, Doc? I am getting out of here."

Joe and Helena hugged each, and then Joe said, "Let's go, Jason O'Connor! We have a Super Bowl to win!" Joe Johnson then let loose with a loud shout that reverberated and shook the hospital wing. "Go Seahawks!"

Despite protests from the doctor, Jason bolted out of the room with Joe and Helena following closely behind. Nothing could stop him. The Super Bowl awaited. The war within him had been successfully fought and won. Jason had to now take care of the less serious challenge of beating the Steelers.

CHAPTER 25

Immediately after arriving home, Jason called Coach Paul Wagner. He wanted to let him know that not only would he be on the plane the next day but that he would also be ready to play. He was astounded at how good he felt. Even his injured head seemed to be completely healed.

Wagner was surprised to hear from Jason so soon after the blood draw. "How are you doing, O'Connor? I expected you to be sleeping most of the day to get your strength back."

"Listen, Coach, I am doing fabulous. I can't explain it, but somehow my strength has been completely restored. I am coming down on the company charter and will be ready for action on Sunday."

"Now hold on, Jason. I told you that I wasn't going to risk further injury to your head, and I meant that. The doctors have emphatically said you are not to play. It is just too risky. I am going to follow their advice on this one."

Jason tried in vain to successfully convince the coach otherwise. However, he realized that at least for the moment he was not going to persuade Wagner to change his mind. Finally, in frustration he said, "OK, Coach, I think you just need to see me for yourself tomorrow night after I get in. I know you will realize that I can play and lead this team."

"I will be glad to see you, O'Connor, but unless the docs tell me something else, I just won't allow you to play. You took a couple of lethal shots to the head, and we want you playing for us in the future. I don't intend on going to your funeral anytime soon."

Jason hung up the phone feeling discouraged. He intended to use all of his persuasive powers to convince the coach to play him when he got down to Miami. For the moment, however, he went about packing and getting ready for the trip.

About two hours had passed when the phone rang. It was Paul Wagner, who now seemed very concerned about the mental wellness of his quarterback.

"Listen, Jason, I just got off the phone with your doctors, and they told me what happened at the hospital. They say you have been hallucinating and seeing people who don't exist. They are also very concerned that you checked out of the hospital and ignored their orders to keep resting. What in the world is going on with you?"

"Coach, I have never felt better. I can't explain exactly what has happened, but I can tell you that I think a miracle is taking place. I know I can play."

"So tell me about the imaginary hospital volunteers that you like to talk to."

"Is that what they are saying? That I talk with imaginary people?"

"Listen, Jason, you have suffered a lot of physical trauma lately. You have received two blows to the head and gave away a significant amount of blood. You are obviously not completely together in all your faculties. You need to rest"

Jason was becoming more and more frustrated. He felt annoyed and responded in an agitated manner. "All I can say, Coach, is that I am feeling great, and you will see that tomorrow when I arrive."

Paul Wagner was silent. He wanted to believe Jason, but he knew the doctors' concerns, and he was very afraid of the consequences of another serious blow to Jason's head.

"OK, listen, O'Connor. We will talk tomorrow night. You are going to be flown down in the Seahawks private jet. The media has been hounding me all week about your whereabouts, and I intend to keep them guessing. When you get here, you are going to be carted off to the hotel where we are staying and ushered in the back entrance. You are not to talk to the press at all. Do you understand?"

"I understand. And I agree."

"You will room with Childs tomorrow night, and I want you to spend some time with Zach Morrison to prep him for the game. He is not feeling confident about starting, but I know that you can help him with that."

"So you are telling me that I won't be playing?"

"Yes, sorry, Jason. It is just too big of a risk. Unless the doctors tell me otherwise, you are going to have to sit this one out. If you remain healthy, there will be other Super Bowls."

Jason again hung up the phone in frustration, but he was not going to give up. He believed that it was his destiny to play in the big game, and he was more confident than ever that, if allowed to play, he would bring victory to the Seahawks.

Jason did not sleep well that night. His mind was on all of the events that had transpired over the week, and he was confused on the significance of his encounter with Josh, if indeed Josh existed. Perhaps, he thought, his mind had been playing tricks on him. Perhaps, Josh was, as the doctor in the hospital said, just an imaginary person conjured up in his mind—just a hallucination.

On the other hand, thought Jason, if Josh were not real, how could anybody explain his sudden physical recovery? Jason never felt better in his life. As a professional athlete, he knew his body and how to read it. To him there was simply no rational explanation for his renewed energy level and complete mental focus on the Super Bowl. Jason believed in his heart that Josh was real, but he couldn't comprehend exactly who Josh was and why he had suddenly popped into his life at this time.

After hours of tossing and turning, Jason finally dozed off. He awakened after only four hours of sleep but again felt a surge of energy as he prepared to leave for his flight. Joe Johnson was expected anytime to drive him to Boeing Field in Seattle to catch the Seahawks company plane to Miami.

As he waited for Joe's arrival, he glanced at the sports section of the morning paper. The main article was commentary from Sammy Jensen. The editorial entitled, "Where Is Jason O'Connor?" read in part:

For a full week now Jason O'Connor has been nowhere to be seen. The sports world has been shocked by the revelations concerning O'Connor's son and Jason's decision to sit out the Super Bowl. Perhaps the Seahawks quarterback would receive more support and sympathy from Seahawks fans and the media if he would simply come forward and explain himself. Alas, Jason O'Connor has been absent. He has not shown his face in public, and the Seahawks front office has been woefully quiet on the details of this bizarre tale.

JASON O'CONNOR—WHERE ARE YOU? EXPLAIN ALL OF THIS TO US. WE DON'T UNDERSTAND. YOU OWE YOUR LOYAL FANS THAT MUCH.

Jason knew that his avoidance of the press the past week was going to generate this kind of commentary. He still remained satisfied that he had made the right decision to avoid public discussion and lay low. The last thing he wanted was to have the press hounding him as he mentally prepared to undertake the blood draw for Moses.

Joe Johnson finally arrived to take Jason to the airport. On the drive over Joe was very talkative and excited about the Super Bowl, but Jason remained quiet and for most of the drive listened with amusement to Joe's enthusiasm. Finally, Jason spoke.

"You know that Wagner told me I am not going to play in the game?"

"What? You have got to be kidding. Why would Wagner pull such a bone-headed stunt like that?" responded Joe.

"He just doesn't believe that I will survive another pop to the head. The doctors are telling him to keep me out, so he is doing just that."

Joe shook his head in disbelief. "I know something miraculous has occurred here, Jason. That is all I know. In fact, miraculous things have been happening every since we met."

Jason looked at Joe and smiled. "You are right about that. It will be interesting to see how this story all turns out. Maybe someday I will write a book about it."

"Oh yeah? And tell me, Jason, what would be the title of the book?"

Jason thought for a few moments before answering. "I think I will call it *Destiny's Team*. That is what we are. I just hope I can play a role in that destiny tomorrow."

"You know, I have this strong feeling that somehow that is going to happen."

"Funny that you say that because that is what Josh told me as well," said Jason. He paused for a moment and then continued expressing his thoughts.

"Joe, do you think this Josh guy is real, or am I going crazy?"

Joe thought for a moment before speaking. "All I know is what I have seen over the last two weeks. Everything that has happened—beginning with your appearance into our lives, to you becoming the blood donor for Moses—has been an answer to our prayers. So, I think that Josh is real and is another piece of the puzzle that is being divinely put together."

Joe and Jason looked into each other's eyes and both smiled. They both strongly believed that they were main characters in an unfolding drama.

The coast-to-coast flight from Seattle to Miami was mentally exhausting for Jason as he continued to play over in his mind the different scenarios of what would transpire in the next twenty-four hours. He desperately wanted to play in the game on Sunday but was totally baffled as to what he could say or do to change Wagner's mind.

Jason was met by Paul Wagner at a secluded private airport in Miami. They got in the limousine and headed for the hotel where the team was staying. Wagner was subdued and distant as they drove along, and Jason had to take the initiative to break the ice.

"So, Coach, would you not agree that I look fit enough to play tomorrow?"

"Looks are deceiving, O'Connor. I am concerned about the condition of your brain. It is what is inside the package that matters, and the doctors have confirmed with me today that what is inside your skull is not in good shape."

"Coach, all I can say is that I know I am fine and can play. You have to give me a shot."

"I suppose that imaginary character you talked with has confirmed this? What did they say his name was? Was it Josh?"

Jason was silent. He simply was not sure what more he could say. It was clear that Wagner was not budging, and, barring some unforeseen miracle, he would be watching the game in his street clothes.

Wagner continued, "Listen, Jason, I need you to spend some quality time with Zach Morrison tonight and go over the game plan with him. He has the jitters and needs a confidence booster."

"So, how is his back these days? I don't expect that he will be throwing the ball much unless his condition has improved."

"Yeah, you are right. We have worked out a game plan where there will be a lot of short passes—nothing deep."

"How in the world will that win this game? If the Steelers realize that the long ball to Bobby is not a threat, then they will immediately adjust and take away even the short passing game. You can't win that way, Coach."

"Well, it is all we have to go with."

"No, it is not. I can play. I am telling you now that I can play. I don't understand all that has happened, but I know I am OK. It is a miracle."

Paul Wagner looked at Jason longingly. He desperately wanted to believe him, but Wagner was a practical man. In his worldview there was no room for miracles.

"Jason, I want to believe you. I really do, but I just can't. I will not risk more serious injury to you. When these injuries first happened, I was hoping for the best and refused to accept the truth. But I could not live with myself if something more serious happened to you. You have a future with us. There will be other years and other Super Bowls. I want to coach you five years from now. I am sorry, but it is just too risky to play you."

The limousine was silent for the rest of the trip. Jason was feeling intense disappointment and emotions were building inside him. Paul Wagner, not normally an emotional man, was also struggling. As they finally pulled into the back entry of the hotel, Wagner spoke one more time.

"We will have your bags taken to your room on the second floor. Here is the key. Childs and Morrison are in there now waiting for you. Please just get up there, and don't say anything to anybody. I do not want the press to know that you are here."

"Are you telling me that they don't know that I am in Miami?"

Wagner laughed. "Yes. It is being called in the media the 'great disappearance of Jason O'Connor.' The press simply does not know where you are at right now. They have no idea that you are going to be here. In fact, except for Childs and Morrison, the team doesn't know you are in town either. The team will see you tomorrow in the locker room, but I want to keep you away from the press for now."

Jason quickly headed for his hotel room, and, in order to not be recognized, he made every effort to avoid eye contact with people in the hotel. Upon entering his room, he immediately noticed Bobby Childs and Zach Morrison in deep conversation. They had been in a serious discussion, and Bobby had shared with Zach the details of his past with Mandy.

"Hey, guys," said Jason. "Why the somber looks on your faces? You both look as if you have lost your best friend."

Bobby immediately got up and gave his friend a hug. "Man if you aren't a sight for sore eyes. I can't tell you how hard it has been all week without you here."

Zach Morrison chimed in. "It is so good to see you, Jason. I know this sounds strange for me to say, but I sure wish you were going to be in the lineup tomorrow instead of me."

"Thanks, Zach. I know you will do fine."

"And how are you doing?" Zach asked.

"You know what? Strangely, I am feeling better than I have in ages. My head doesn't hurt, and I am not feeling weak at all from the blood draws. I have tried to get through to Wagner that I am fine, but he is refusing to listen. He says that he doesn't want to take the risk of further injury to my head."

"So, you are definitely not going to play tomorrow? Bobby asked.

"I am afraid so. At least that is what Wagner is saying now."

Bobby and Zach both sat silent in response. All three of the men in the room understood that the odds of the seriously injured Zach Morrison being able to move the Seahawks offense effectively was questionable. Because of the reality of the situation, all three felt a sense of impending defeat.

Zach Morrison finally spoke. "Well, I guess we are just going to have to try harder tomorrow to convince Wagner. But Jason, if you don't get in the game, I want you to know that I am going to give everything I have to win this game. You have become an inspiration to me in more ways than one, and I don't want to let you down."

"That is kind of you to say, Zach, but I am not sure why I am such an inspiration. Most of the people in Seattle hate me now. At least that is what the papers seem to indicate."

Zach cleared his throat and nervously looked down at the floor. It was obvious that he had something more to say but was lost for words. He struggled to speak what was on his mind. Finally, the words came.

"I want both of you to know something about me. I know that I have this reputation of a do-gooder. I am someone who always seems to be getting involved in some cause and lending my celebrity status to advance the particular issue."

"Yeah, well you had egg all over your face when you tried to fight for and protect the closing of that art gallery awhile ago," laughed Bobby. "But, yes, Zach, we all know you have a social conscience."

"I want you two to know that there is a reason I have been such a social crusader over the years. Nobody knows what I am about to tell you. I want to explain why I have the current reputation that I do."

Jason, intrigued with the direction the conversation had headed, said, "Go for it, Zach. We are all ears."

Zach Morrison began to pace up and down in the hotel room as he nervously talked about himself. "In my early years in the NFL, I had quite the reputation of a swinging bachelor—a lot like your reputation now, Childs."

Bobby smiled and thought to himself, "If Zach only knew the real truth, he would be amused."

"I had women all over me. I could have had a different woman every night of the week and, in fact, there were some weeks that I did do exactly that. I used woman for my own desires and pleasure and then discarded them. I wounded several very deeply."

Jason and Bobby looked at each other. They both definitely could relate to what Zach was saying. Zach continued sharing.

"But there was one woman who got into my heart. Her name was Wendy. She was sassy and sexy and knew how to connect with me. She loved me, and, although I didn't want to acknowledge it, I loved her. We lived together for a couple of years."

"Didn't the tabloids publish your picture with her a few times followed by some steamy, gossipy tale?" asked Bobby.

"Yeah, they did and that's Wendy that those stories refer to. All of those stories were truly garbage, of course, but I loved the press coverage," responded Zach. "But Wendy and I had a dark side. One day she shared with me that she was pregnant and wanted to get married. I was enraged and flew off of the handle."

Jason closed his eyes fighting back the tears. All he could think of was Rachel.

"I set her up to go see that Dr. Barton in Spokane—you guys know all about him. I thought that Barton would take care of the problem quickly. That would have been a convenient solution to my predicament. However, Wendy argued with me. She begged me to marry her and help raise our child. But I was very insistent and even cruel to her as I pressured her to see Barton."

Zach struggled to find words. His eyes filled with tears. "She finally made the appointment. She was told it would be a simple procedure and over in an hour. But there were complications because she was further along in her pregnancy then we had thought." His voice became soft, and he could hardly be heard in the room as he said, "She was butchered on the operating table."

Bobby and Jason remained still as they listened. Bobby was thinking of Mandy and how he forced her to see Barton. And he was thinking of their twins, Timmy and Tina, whose lives were snuffed out by the so-called safe and legal procedure of pregnancy termination.

Zach's voice was quivering now as he spoke. "She came home after the surgery but was very sick. She was bleeding profusely the next morning, and I rushed her to the hospital. It was too late. She died from a loss of blood. Her uterus had been perforated and damaged severely."

Zach paused one more time in an attempt to stop the tears. He was unsuccessful. He finally blurted out between sobs, "I never got a chance to say goodbye. I never got a chance to say goodbye."

Bobby and Jason both began to weep in response to the heart-wrenching story. In America men are told that they shouldn't cry. It is seen by some as a sign of weakness. It is seen by others as a silly feminine reaction to stress. But in this hotel room, on this night, three very masculine professional athletes sat together in a room where the sense of loss felt by all was real, and they all unashamedly let the tears flow.

After a few minutes, the onslaught of emotions subsided, and Jason spoke up. "So that is why you have been the social crusader all these years? Somehow you think that by doing so you can redeem yourself from this horrible mistake you made years ago?"

"Exactly. You got that right my friend," replied Zach.

Bobby spoke up in response. "Zach, I have a similar story of pain, as I told you before Jason arrived tonight. But what I didn't tell you is that there is hope and redemption for anything we do. We can't earn forgiveness, but we can accept it. It is a free gift from God if we only believe."

"I wish I could believe that, Bobby, but the guilt and the pain are too great for me to do so. I don't see how I could ever be forgiven for what I have done."

Jason responded. "Forgiveness comes not from within ourselves but is a gift that comes from beyond. Of course you can't forgive yourself, Zach. You don't have the ability to do so, but God easily forgives. All you need to do is ask and believe. We all make mistakes, Zach, but if we don't let go and allow God to give us a clean heart, we will only end up destroying ourselves."

Zach listened intently. He wanted to have what his two teammates had recently discovered—peace. Nothing he had done in his life—good deeds, contributing to worthy causes, standing up for justice—had bought him the peace his life so desperately needed. And nothing he attempted wiped away the guilt, stained permanently on his conscience, for what he had allowed to transpire with Wendy.

Jason concluded his comments with a simple request. "Zach, I only know of one thing that we all can do to help you. There is only one thing to do."

"What is that?"

"We need to pray. Can we do that now?"

"Sure," said Zach. "What have I got to lose?"

Jason and Bobby knelt by the side of the bed, and Zach followed. They all poured out their hearts, seeking cleansing for their souls and tranquility to their spirits. In the sacredness of the moment, the one who makes all things new responded to this act of contrition and humility.

CHAPTER 26

Super Bowl Sunday had finally arrived. Other such games in the past had received intensive public relations build ups the week before kickoff. This particular game, however, was second to none in its elaborate celebration of that American cultural event known as the Super Bowl. The pregame entertainment set the stage. It was billed as a "Blast from the Past" and focused nostalgically on sixties rock and roll, highlighting music from the Beach Boys, the Beatles, and the Rolling Stones.

The week long media build centered primarily on the absence of Jason O'Connor from the Seattle lineup. The news stories concentrated on the conventional wisdom that the Seahawks would be unable to move the football rushing against the Steelers defense. Sports pundits agreed that the passing game was the key to beating the Steelers, but without Jason in the lineup, it was questionable whether the Seahawks would be successful.

Jake McGee and Robin Everson started the day off early in the morning with their radio call-in show. Their discussion continued to highlight the bizarre events of the week that had preceded the game. Jake began the broadcast with a pessimistic assessment of the Seahawks likelihood of winning.

"Robin, we have to be realistic about the Seahawks chances without O'Connor at the helm. Zach Morrison has had his moments of greatness in the past, but he has not played one down all season. The reports of the Seahawks week indicate that he was doing very little passing in practice. Is he going to be able to connect with Childs today with the long ball? That is the question to ask, and it is the key to the game."

"Jake, if I can change the subject just a little, I would like to comment on the total absence of Jason O'Connor from the public arena this last week. Nobody in the media has been able to talk with him, and the Seahawks front office has been very quiet about his whereabouts. We don't even know if he is with the team today."

Jake McGee commented, "We have picked up rumors that Jason O'Connor is with the team in the locker room, but we haven't been able to verify this. The inside reports from the hospital after his blood draw indicate that he left the hospital on Friday, the same day of the procedure, but nobody has seen him or talked with him since."

"I think it is safe to say the we won't be seeing Jason O'Connor in the game today," said Robin. "But frankly, Jake, the Seahawks organization could have been a little more forthcoming in providing us with some details regarding his whereabouts and his physical condition. I think Coach Wagner and the front office have a lot of explaining to do after this game."

Jake McGee responded, "I have just gotten word of some more information on this, and we want to go down to the field with Sara Gleason, our sideline reporter for the game. Good morning Sara. What news can you give us about the whereabouts and condition of Jason O'Connor?"

"Hi, Jake and Robin. We have unconfirmed reports that Jason O'Connor is with the team right now but will not be suiting up for the game. He apparently is very weak from the drawing of his blood this last Friday, and sources tell me that because of his weakened condition, he is unable to contribute anything to the Seahawks' effort today. There is also the question of whether he has sufficiently recovered from his severe head injuries two weeks ago to be able to play, but, as has been their pattern of communication this last week, the Seahawks front office has avoided providing more detail on this."

"Thank you, Sara. OK, Seahawks fans," replied Jake, "this is the best information we can give you right now. But stay tuned, as we hope that more information will be forthcoming."

The atmosphere inside the Seahawks locker room was quiet. Jason sat in his street clothes talking to select teammates as they dressed and mentally prepared for the game. Some of the players were too angry with Jason to talk to him. Others were just bewildered at the events of the week and said very little. Bobby and Zach stayed close by their friend for support, and tried to project a positive atmosphere in the pregame setting.

Zach Morrison knew that he would not be physically able to do the job needed to defeat the Steelers. His back injury had worsened over the previous months of the season, and he was fighting excruciating pain in his shoulders whenever he attempted to throw the football for any distance. He, of course, kept such information to himself. Only Jason, Bobby, and Wagner knew the extent of the physical disability from which he was suffering.

As the team was preparing for the game, Jason received a call on his cell phone from Joe Johnson. Joe was in the hospital room with Moses and Helena, and they had the television set turned on to view the game.

"Jason, brother, I just wanted to call and see how things are going. Will Wagner allow you to play today?"

"I am afraid not, Joe. He is pretty adamant that he doesn't want to risk further injury to my head. So I am not even suiting up."

Joe was silent for a few moments. He sighed and then finally responded. "Listen, Jason, I can't quite explain why I feel this way, but I just know that somehow you are going to make a difference in this game today. We are continuing to pray that Wagner will change his mind."

"Thanks, Joe, and by the way, how is Moses doing?"

Joe Johnson laughed a hearty laugh. "Moses is sitting up and acting normal. He is watching the television set very intensely with us, and by all signs it appears that he is going to be doing fine when he gets out."

"That's great, Joe. Thanks for the good news. Please give Helena my love, and tell Moses that I love him."

"We all love you big guy. You mean the world to us. We will see you in a few days and celebrate the great Seahawks victory in person."

"Thanks, Joe. I love you too. See you in a few days."

Before addressing the entire team, Paul Wagner asked Jason and Zach to meet with him briefly in the coach's office. The mood was somber as they walked in and shut the door behind them. Wagner got up from his desk and paced a bit. He looked at both Jason and Zach as he struggled with the exact words he wanted to say.

"Jason," he blurted out. "Unlike other many voices in the media and public this week, I am not one that is critical of you at all. I hope and pray that your son will respond to what you have done and improve. You have given to him the gift of life and in doing so have sacrificed a great deal. In the eternal scheme of things, I think that what you have done is far more significant than playing in the Super Bowl."

Wagner continued, "There will be other Super Bowls, but there will not be another Moses. I want you to lead us in those future Super Bowls, so I am not going to risk serious injury by playing you today."

The coach then looked at Zach Morrison and said, "Zach, you have been put in a very difficult situation, but you are a pro. You have had a wonderful career. I can't think of any better way to finish it than by playing in this game today. I need to apologize to you for my negligence in not allowing your back to heal properly after your surgery. It was inexcusable. But I know you will rise to the occasion today."

The locker room atmosphere continued to be subdued, as each Seahawks player quietly concentrated on the job he needed to perform to be successful. Wagner did not give much of a pregame speech or pep talk. His demeanor indicated that he was lacking the passion that he usually exhibited for big games.

Just before the Seahawks prepared to enter the stadium tunnel that led to the playing field, Bobby Childs stood up and briefly spoke.

"I for one intend to give everything I have to this game today. I know all of you will do the same." He then looked over at Jason and said, "Some in this locker room right now have given more than any of us ever could contemplate giving. My friend Jason O'Connor has sacrificed his ability to play with us today so his son could live. Our sacrifices this week pale in comparison to this kind of giving."

The team quietly took in the words of Bobby Childs as he continued. "Things have happened to me this week that have changed my life forever. I want to win this game more than anything, but I want to win for reasons that are much different than they were one week ago. There are now people in my life who I care about more than life itself, and I want to win this game for them. There are people out there who live without hope and need to see us defy the oddsmakers and win this game to prove that nothing is ever hopeless. There are people out there who need to understand that miracles do happen if you believe. I, for one, believe in miracles, and I believe in this team."

Bobby dramatically paused for a moment and looked again at his friend Jason O'Connor. He then screamed at the top of his lungs, "So, I say let's go out there, kick some butt, and win this one for Moses!"

The Seahawks entered the playing field to the deafening sound of screaming football fans. The Seattle fans were in full force and rocked the stadium with their cheers as the Seattle theme song "Hold on Tight to Your Dream" blasted through the stadium.

Jason O'Connor stayed behind in the locker room on orders from the coach. Paul Wagner had decided that his presence on the sidelines would be too great of a distraction for the team. He knew that if Jason were seen, he would be mobbed by the sideline reporters, and the team would undoubtedly lose its focus. Jason reluctantly and sadly sat in the coach's office watching the game on television.

The first half of the game started out as an unmitigated disaster. Seattle failed to move the football after receiving the opening kickoff. The Steelers then drove seventy-five yards in ten plays to score and led 7-0. On their very next possession, the Seahawks fumbled and lost the football, and the Steelers drove to the twenty yard line of the Seahawks, kicking a field goal and making the score 10-0 at the end of the first quarter.

The Seahawks offense continued to sputter and accomplish very little. It was clear that Zach Morrison was not going to be able to run the offense effectively unless he threw the ball downfield to his receivers, but, because of his back injury, he was unable to do so. The Steelers defense picked up on this obvious flaw in the Seattle offense and began to bury the Seahawks' running attack with linebacker blitzes and a stone wall defensive line.

In the second quarter, the Seattle defense stiffened and the game settled in to what appeared to be a defensive battle. The Seahawks offense continued to struggle and failed to move the football, but the Steelers did not do much better.

With less than one minute left in the half the Seahawks got the ball again and attempted to tighten the score. Wagner signaled to Morrison for a bootleg run around the right side of the offensive line. Zach did not have the speed of Jason O'Connor who ran this play to perfection, but with sufficient blocking, he had the ability to pick up some decent yardage. What happened next, however, was disastrous.

Upon getting the snap from center, Zach received some excellent blocking as he turned up field. For a moment it appeared that he was going to get ten or fifteen yards on the run. However, just as he began to intensify his speed he was met with a bone-crunching tackle from a Steelers linebacker whose helmet landed violently into Zach's back. The pain of the hit was excruciating, and upon being knocked down, Zach fumbled the football. The ball bounced up and was caught by a Steelers defensive back who ran for a touchdown. The score now read 17-0 in favor of the Steelers as the first half ended.

Zach Morrison remained stretched out on the field, writhing in pain and unable to get up and walk. Seahawks trainers immediately attended to him and called for a stretcher. Eventually an ambulance was summoned to take Zach to the hospital for x-rays and observation. He was clearly out for the rest of the game.

Sara Gleason cornered Paul Wagner on his way to the locker room for a comment. "Coach, it doesn't look good for Zach Morrison. What are you going to do? Will we be seeing Jason O'Connor in the second half?"

As he continued his quick pace to the locker room, Wagner responded tersely, "We have to get final word on Morrison before we decide anything. It is time to regroup. We will be ready for the second half."

Jake McGee and Robin Everson gloomily assessed the Seahawks' fortunes during their halftime commentary, in light of Morrison's injury. Jake started out, "With Morrison out now, the Seahawks simply do not have anybody to run the offense. The only quarterback left on the team is rookie Dennis Martin, who has not played one down in his whole pro career."

"To be honest, Jake," responded Robin, "the young rookie can't do any worse than what Morrison did in the first half. Sadly, we watched a pathetic performance by a veteran who has blown his chance to end his career in glory."

The Seahawks locker room was silent as the players received word of Zach's condition. Jason was sitting at the end of a bench gazing intently at Paul Wagner, who was pacing back and forth attempting to decide how to respond to the injury of Morrison. He knew that playing the rookie Martin would virtually guarantee defeat, but he was also resisting the compulsion to allow Jason to play.

After slowly pacing back and forth, Wagner looked at Jason and their eyes met. Jason's look was intense. Wagner could not turn his head away from the piercing gaze in Jason's eyes.

Paul Wagner suddenly stopped pacing and cleared his throat. The eyes of all the Seahawks players were on him as he walked into the center of the locker room to address the team. The drama of the moment cannot be understated. The dropping of a pin could have been heard in the intense stillness that engulfed the locker room atmosphere.

Wagner picked up a football and placed it under his arm. He then looked over at Jason and calmly stated, "Get suited up, O'Connor. You are going in the game." The entire Seahawks team roared its approval with cheers. Their spirits were ignited and the mood changed from one of despair to one of hope. There was a feeling in the air that history was in the making. Every Seahawks player now believed what Jason O'Connor had been saying to the media for the last two weeks—they were destiny's team.

Wagner and the assistant coaches went over some defensive sets to implement in the second half as Jason was having his ankles taped by the trainers. The Seahawks would start the second half on defense, and the coaches wanted to shake up the Steelers offense with some additional linebacker blitzes and defensive sets.

No speech was given by Wagner or anybody as the team prepared to depart for the football field. The inspiration felt by the knowledge that Jason O'Connor would play was enough motivation for the team, and they left the locker room emotionally charged. Jason stayed behind to continue suiting up and getting taped by the trainer. He would enter the stadium and the playing field shortly after the opening kick off to start the second half.

After receiving the kickoff to start the second half, the Steelers offense worked its way for two first downs, and it appeared that they were in total control of the game. However, as they lined up to run the next play, they all were shaken by the roar of the crowd. For some unknown reason to the players on the field, the entire stadium erupted in thunderous cheers and chants. The noise from the crowd was so loud that the Steelers offensive line could not hear the cadence from the Steelers quarterback, and the referees had to stop play to give the crowd time to quiet down.

The crowd, however, continued to scream and cheer, as they were responding to something the players on the field could not see. Jason O'Connor had entered the playing field from the tunnel that comes from the locker rooms. His entry onto the field was perhaps the most dramatic moment in Super Bowl history.

When Jason walked onto the playing field and toward the Seahawks sidelines, he was overcome with emotion as he heard the roar of the fans and felt the excitement that his presence had generated. He looked over into the crowd and saw a face he recognized. It was his friend Josh, and Josh was whooping it up with the rest of the fans yelling encouragement. Jason's and Josh's eyes met briefly as Josh raised his fist in the air and shouted, "Go for it my friend, you can do it. Go for it!"

Jake McGee was going wild in the press booth. "This is incredible! This is unbelievable, Seahawks fans! All week we have been asking the whereabouts of Jason O'Connor, and we have wondered if he was going to play. Now before our very eyes he is on the sidelines with the Seahawks team in uniform, and it looks like he will be leading the team in the second half. Let's go down to our sideline reporter for more information. Sara, can you tell us anything?"

Sara Gleason responded excitedly, "Jake, it is simply pandemonium down here around the Seahawks bench. The team is emotionally ignited by the presence of their leader. Jason O'Connor is here with the team and appears to be ready for battle. He is now huddled up with Coach Paul Wagner, apparently talking strategy."

"Sara, have you been able to talk with Jason at all? What has he told you?"

"Well, Jake, I briefly asked him if he was going to play and what the second half strategy would be. And Jake, I gotta tell you that the look in his eyes was one of steely determination. Wow, you should have seen those eyes. This is a man on a mission."

"What did he say?"

Sara laughed. "All he said was that he was going to quote 'take care of business' end of quote. He is now with Coach Wagner plotting offensive strategy."

Jake McGee continued his commentary to the listening radio audience. "Well, the presence of Jason O'Connor is, of course, very exciting, but remember sports fans, the Seahawks are behind 17-0 right now, and the Steelers are driving for another score. It is going to take a monumental team effort to bring them back from the brink. Jason O'Connor can't do it alone."

The presence of Jason on the sidelines sparked the Seattle defensive unit. Suddenly the Steelers ran up against a brick defensive wall. Three plays later they had lost yardage and had to punt. A very long kick put the Seahawks back on their own eight yard line—ninety-two yards away from a score. Now Jason O'Connor and company had to go to work.

Wanting to show that he was in charge and physically up to the task Jason called a bootleg run on the very first play. It was the same play that Zach Morrison was injured on before the end of the first half. This time, however, everything worked to perfection.

Jason turned the corner around the right end of the offensive line and darted up field with the football. He stiff armed a Steelers linebacker and ran over a defensive back before picking up seventeen yards and a first down. The crowd was electrified.

As the drive continued, Jason completed a few short passes to bring the Seahawks to midfield. In the huddle he looked at Bobby Childs and said, "OK, let's do it. Let's thread the needle and get on the scoreboard."

"Right on brother," said Bobby smiling broadly and sensing the emotional energy of the moment.

The next play was executed perfectly. Jason dropped back with the football and released the ball in precise timing with the pass route Bobby was running. The ball hit Childs on his numbers just as he began to accelerate between the two Steelers defensive backs. He easily outran his pursuers and sprinted down the field for a touchdown. After the successful extra point conversion the score now stood at 17-7.

The remainder of the third quarter saw the teams trade possessions of the ball for several series. The Seahawks defense stubbornly held its own and denied the Steelers any meaningful scoring opportunities. Jason was sharp in his passing moving the team up the field on several occasions only to have the efforts thwarted by penalties.

At the beginning of the fourth quarter, Jason moved the team effectively again into Steelers territory. It was third down and seven from the Steelers twenty-five when Jason launched a pass over the middle to Bobby Childs who was wide open. Bobby caught the ball on the run and appeared headed for the end zone when for some inexplicable reason he lost control of the ball and fumbled. The ensuing scramble ended with the Seahawks recovering the ball but not scoring the needed touchdown. Three plays later they settled for a field goal and the score stood at 17-10 with less than eight minutes to play in the game.

The Seattle fans were growing restless as they anxiously waited for the Seahawks defense to hold and get the ball back into Jason's hands. The Steelers, however, had other thoughts. They took the kick off and methodically drove down the field into Seahawks territory, mixing short passes with runs up the middle. With two minutes to go in the game, the Steelers were threatening to score from the fifteen yard line. A quick trap up the middle took the ball down to the one yard line and it looked like the Steelers were ready to pound the final nail in the coffin of the Seahawks.

The crowd was on its feet screaming at high decibel levels. Seattle fans were urging their defense to hold tight and give Jason one last chance to perform his magic. On the next play the ball was given to the Steelers fullback who lunged over the top of the offensive linemen in front of him. At the height of his leap, he was met with a ferocious hit from a Seahawks linebacker and the ball flew out of the running back's arms rolling away from the goal line. An alert Seattle defensive lineman picked the ball up and began to run as the delirious Seattle fans screamed. He was brought down on thirty yard line by a flying tackle from the Steelers quarterback that saved a touchdown.

Seattle had one last chance. There was one minute and thirty seconds left in the game. The Seahawks were seventy yards away from a touchdown with no time outs remaining.

Jake McGee summed up the situation in a drama-packed, emotional voice. "Seahawks fans this is what this game of football is all about. This is what makes the NFL so great. Seventy yards now stand between Jason O'Connor and new life for the Seahawks. We have never had a Super Bowl go into sudden death overtime before. If the Seahawks score it will be a first. And I just want to say to all of you fans out there that no matter what criticisms one can muster against Jason O'Connor, and there are many, no one can deny that he has given this nation today a thrill that will not be duplicated in a very long time. If the Seahawks win today, it will be because of their superstar quarterback, Jason O'Connor."

Jason went to work running the Seattle offense with precision. He immediately completed three short passes—two to Childs— to put the ball at midfield with fifty-five seconds left on the clock. The next play was an incomplete pass, which stopped the clock and gave Jason a chance to go to the sidelines and speak with Coach Wagner.

"OK, Jason, I want you to bootleg it again around the right end. They will be expecting a pass so pump fake one to Childs before you take off. I think you can pick up some yardage this way, but make sure that you get out of bounds to stop the clock."

Jason responded, "After that we should just throw to the end zone. If I can get a first down here, we should have time for about four passes. I know that Bobby is good for at least one of them."

"You make the call, Jason. Just get a first down here, and we will worry about the rest of the game after that."

Jason made the call in the huddle and urged his line to block for him like never before. He took the snap from center and immediately pumped faked a pass in the direction of Bobby Childs. He then took off running at full steam for the corner. The offensive line was superb in executing the blocking scheme. Jason turned down field and was finally tackled out of bounds on the thirty yard line—a twenty yard pick up. The crowd was going berserk. Thirty-seven seconds remained on the clock.

Jason next made the call for a pass to Bobby in the corner of the end zone. He knew that Childs was going to be double teamed so he let Bobby know that the throw would be very high to avoid an interception. It could only be caught if Bobby were able to leap high enough and pull it in.

The pass was incomplete, going over Bobby's head. There was time for three more attempts but this most recent play had serious consequences. Immediately after his release, Jason was hit ferociously by a three-hundred-pound Steelers lineman. Jason's head hit the turf hard as he went down. He was stunned and upon impact and realized that his previous skull injury and concussion had not sufficiently healed for him to escape this kind of blow without further injury.

Jason was out for a few seconds. When he opened his eyes he saw the Seahawks trainer and Wagner standing over him and helping him to his feet. His vision was blurry, and his head was throbbing in pain. Wagner's worst fears were becoming reality.

Jason immediately looked at his coach and said, "I'm OK, Coach. It is nothing. We have time for three more plays, and we can do this thing. Don't even think about taking me out now."

Wagner responded. "I don't have anybody to replace you if I did. But are you sure you can go on?"

If this were a regular season game Jason, knew that he would have to go to the sidelines and sit out the remainder of the game. But this was the Super Bowl, and everything was riding on his ability to perform in the next half minute.

Jason briefly looked down the sidelines and saw a familiar figure standing with his teammates looking at him and urging him on. It was Josh. Jason was completely puzzled as to how Josh had been allowed to come down to the sidelines, but he was glad to see him and felt his encouragement. Jason smiled at his friend and then responded to Wagner.

"No matter what I say, you won't believe me, Coach. So just keep me in, and let's take care of business. Trust me. We are going to win this game."

Wagner patted Jason on the back and simply said, "You are the man, Jason. We couldn't have gotten here without you, and we can't win without you. Go for it. Just don't let them hit you in the head again."

The Seahawks fans roared their approval as they saw that Jason was going to stay in the game. The look of his teammates in the huddle also expressed relief. What they didn't know was that Jason's vision was so blurry that he could not even read the numbers on their jerseys.

The next two passes to the end zone were well off the mark, as Jason's vision was becoming more blurred by the moment. The Seahawks were now facing fourth down with eight seconds left on the clock. Everybody in the stadium knew that the next play would be a pass to Childs. The Steelers set up their pass prevent defense to make sure that Childs was doubly covered and would not catch the ball.

In the huddle Bobby looked at Jason and asked how he was feeling. Jason replied, "All I know is that I am seeing three of you."

Bobby smiled and replied, "Oh yeah? Hey, I think that was a line in the *Rocky* movies. So do what the trainer told Rocky to do."

"And what is that?"

"Throw to the guy in the middle. I guarantee that he will catch it this time, but make sure it goes to the guy in the middle."

Jason smiled back at his friend. He then looked around at the rest of his teammates and said, "OK, guys, this is what we have been working for all season. Let's not fail."

Jason then said to Bobby, "This one is for Mandy and little Bobby."

Bobby replied, "It is also for Rachel and Moses."

Jason took the snap from center and dropped back in the pocket to pass. Bobby broke for the corner of the end zone facing two defenders who were with him every step of the way. The pass rush was intense as the huge Steelers defensive line, acting like ruthless assassins, barreled in on Jason.

Jason was hit by two defensive lineman just as he released the ball. The pass was a perfectly thrown projectile and headed directly toward its intended target in the corner of the end zone. Jason landed again hard on the turf hitting the back of his head. He did not see the results of the play but could hear the roar of the crowd as Bobby jumped high between the two defenders and miraculously pulled in the pass keeping his feet in bounds and scoring the touchdown.

Jake McGee screamed into his broadcast microphone, "TOUCH-DOWN! TOUCHDOWN! TOUCHDOWN! O'CONNOR HAS DONE IT AGAIN. HE FOUND BOBBY CHILDS IN THE CORNER OF THE END ZONE AND THREW A PERFECT PASS FOR THE SCORE. THE MIRACLE MAN COMES THROUGH ONCE MORE!"

Jason once again had a difficult time getting up. His head hurt worse than ever, but he was not going to let anybody know about it. The all important extra point was coming up and needed to be made to send the game into overtime.

Jason looked to the sidelines as the Seahawks place kicker came on the field. He again saw his friend Josh standing next to Paul Wagner smiling at him and giving him the thumbs up. Jason shook his head wondering how in the world that guy was allowed to be next to Wagner on the sidelines.

The team lined up for the extra point attempt, and Jason knelt behind the line to hold the ball for the kicker. His head was throbbing, and his vision was more blurred than ever. He called the signals and awaited the snap from center for the extra point that everybody assumed would send the game into overtime.

The center snapped the ball to Jason, but because of his blurred vision, he mishandled the football, as it bounced off his hands and bounded behind the kicker. Jason immediately ran to pick it up as several three-hundred pound Steelers defensive linemen were on his tail.

Jake McGee called the action for the radio Seahawks fans. "The ball is snapped and…oh no…Jason O'Connor has fumbled the snap, and the ball is bouncing away. O'Connor has picked it up back at the twenty yard line and he is…HE IS GOING TO RUN IT. HE GETS A BLOCK AND IS FREE. HE HAS ROOM. HE IS AT THE FIVE AND DIVES FOR THE GOAL LINE. HE SCORES! HE SCORES! JASON O'CONNOR HAS JUST SCORED A TWO POINT CONVERSION AND THE SEAHAWKS WIN 18-17. THIS IS TOTALLY UNBELIEVABLE!!!!!"

The stunned crowd was now going crazy in a manner never seen before at a Super Bowl game. Jason O'Connor had engineered an incredible comeback for the Seahawks, and his superhuman run for a two-point conversion sealed the victory.

His Seahawks teammates mobbed him in the end zone as he attempted to get up. Coach Paul Wagner was also mobbed and received the ritual water soaking given to winning coaches of the Super Bowl.

The stadium crowd was beside itself, as were fans from all around the country who watched the game on television. The joy expressed by Seattle fans was indescribably sweet, as their beloved Seahawks were now the Super Bowl champions.

In the stadium Mandy Brooks, little Bobby, and her dad jumped for joy and hugged each other, and in an isolated hospital room, Joe and Helena Johnson hugged and wept. In that hospital room a young boy named Moses was jumping up and down on the bed in excited celebration of what he had just witnessed.

Moses's strength had returned.

CHAPTER 27

As soon as the hoopla and commotion on the field quieted down, the postgame award ceremony began in front of all the fans in the stadium. In the middle of the field, on a quickly assembled stage, the commissioner of the NFL announced the winner of the coveted Most Valuable Player Award. The award went, of course, to the Seahawks quarterback, Jason O'Connor. Jason was immediately interviewed by the television network announcer.

"Jason, tell us what was going on in your mind after you fumbled that snap from center on the extra point?"

Jason smiled and quipped, "I guess I just wanted to make this game a little more exciting." The stadium crowd laughed as he continued. "Seriously, I dedicated this game to my son Moses. I made a promise to him that I would bring back the game ball to him. I don't break my promises."

The crowd roared its appreciation in response to Jason's humble demeanor. They were unaware, however, of the fragile condition of Jason's skull due to the violent hits he had taken during the game.

Jason continued to speak and express his appreciation to the Seahawks organization, but his vision was becoming more and more blurred as he talked. His speech was also becoming slurred, and he felt very weak. His knees suddenly began to buckle, and he vainly grabbed the microphone stand in an attempt to keep from collapsing. Finally, Jason fell unconscious in front of the stadium crowd and the national television audience. Immediate attention was given to him, but Jason remained unconscious as emergency help was summoned. Jason was quickly transported to the closest hospital by an ambulance. Coach Paul Wagner jumped into the back of the ambulance to ride with Jason to the hospital.

The national audience and the stadium crowd were stunned at this dramatic turn of events. The happy, celebratory atmosphere in the stadium immediately changed to one of quiet and somber anguish. The tears of joy that had pervaded the eyes of many Seahawks fans just moments before now became tears of sadness and concern.

During the ride to the hospital, Paul Wagner talked to Jason, attempting to get a response, but Jason remained unconscious and seemed barely alive. The big, tough Seahawks coach fought back tears as he pleaded with Jason to open his eyes and talk to him.

At the hospital Jason was immediately transported to the intensive care unit and placed upon life support systems to stabilize his vital signs and keep him breathing. The attending physician ordered a CAT scan to determine the extent of the cerebral damage The results of the scan showed severe and significant hemorrhaging in Jason's brain. The prognosis was not good. The doctors held out little hope for recovery.

Coach Wagner and Bobby Childs were the first to receive the news about Jason's condition. Bobby immediately called Joe and Helena and told them that the situation was serious and that Jason had slipped into a coma. Upon hearing the news, Joe and Helena obtained tickets to Miami on the first flight available the next day, so they could be by Jason's side.

Mandy stayed over in Miami that night to be with Bobby and to keep watch with him at the hospital where Jason remained in a comatose state. The next morning Coach Paul Wagner, who had also stayed over in Miami to monitor Jason's progress, joined them. When Joe and Helena finally arrived, they too were allowed to visit the hospital room where Jason remained unconscious. The mood was solemn as the group stood around Jason, talking to him in hopes that he would wake up.

As the day continued on, Jason seemed to respond somewhat to the voices. He opened his eyes a couple of times, smiling at Mandy and Bobby before closing them again. Such a gesture gave everyone hope that he would eventually recover.

Finally, Joe Johnson asked to lead the group in a prayer for Jason. They all gathered in a circle around Jason's bed and bowed their heads as Joe prayed.

"Lord, we are asking you now for another miracle. Our brother Jason is in pretty bad shape, Lord. I know we are being selfish asking for this, but we really want to have him around for awhile longer. Please Lord, if it be your will, bring him out of this coma, heal his body, and bring him back to us. Amen."

Mandy wiped the tears from her eyes as she and Bobby repeated, "Amen." Paul Wagner struggled with his emotions, trying with all his strength to keep the tears from coming. Helena hugged her husband and buried her tear-stained face into his big, burly chest. Joe Johnson stood upright, holding his wife, and continued to pray silently.

After a few moments, Jason opened his eyes and looked at each of his friends. He was happy to see them, but he couldn't figure out what had happened. Everyone in the room took heart that he was making eye contact, as it was clear that he could see them and was aware of their presence. Mandy leaned and kissed him on the cheek. He did not verbally respond, but he did smile.

Paul Wagner looked at Jason and said, "Come on, O'Connor. You can do this. Just one more comeback is all that I need. I know you have it in you, Jason. Just one more comeback."

Jason then noticed that, in addition to his friends, Josh was in the room. Josh smiled broadly upon making eye contact with Jason, and it was clear that he wanted to say something. Josh's lips did not move, but his facial expressions and a nod of his head indicated that he wanted Jason to come with him. Josh, in fact, pointed to a closed door at the end of the room. Josh walked over and placed his hand on the knob, ready to open and reveal what was on the other side. Josh again motioned with his hand for Jason to get up and walk to the door.

Jason sat up in bed in response to Josh's urging. Strangely, it appeared to him that his friends around the bed did not notice that he was sitting up. He then pulled his body over the side of the bed and stood up. The life support tubes that were connected to him slid off and fell onto the floor. Again, none of his friends seemed to notice that he was out of bed, standing on his own, and unconnected to the tubes that had kept him breathing.

Jason opened his mouth to speak to Bobby and Mandy, but before he said anything, he looked at Josh who compelled him to walk over to the door. Jason complied. He walked past Bobby and Mandy who appeared not to notice that he was walking away from the bed.

As he approached the door, Josh reached out and squeezed Jason's hand tightly, and then gave him a warm and affectionate embrace. "Well done, my friend," said Josh. "Well done."

Josh then opened the door, and blinding light came rushing into the room, like a sudden bolt of lightning in the pitch black of the night. Jason was awe struck by the brightness that engulfed him. He fell to his knees and closed his eyes.

Josh helped Jason to his feet saying, "It is OK. It will take just a few moments for your eyes to adjust, but you just have to see what is in front of you."

Jason opened his eyes to look, but the brightness was still blinding. However, the longer he looked the clearer the picture became. Finally, his eyes adjusted, and he saw what Josh was talking about.

Through the door and directly in front of him stood a beautiful, green meadow. The brightness of the picturesque landscape was indescribable, yet, there was no apparent sun in the sky. The sky was cloudless and was the deepest blue color Jason had ever seen.

Josh looked at his friend and simply said, "Do you want to come in?"

Jason replied, "What is in there anyway?"

"In there lies your destiny, Jason, and the fulfillment of all your desires and dreams. It is the place you were meant to be from before the beginning of time. There is a mansion waiting for you, and there are a lot of people anxious to see you again."

Jason turned his head and looked at his friends who were standing around his bed. His heart ached to see the most important people in his life so sad. They were all huddled around the bed and tears were freely flowing from all of them.

Jason looked at Josh and asked, "Can I say good bye before we go?"

Josh responded, "Of course you can my friend. Of course you can."

Jason walked back over to the bed and looked into the faces of his beloved friends. Mandy was uncontrollably weeping with her head place on Bobby's chest. Bobby had tears streaming down his face. Joe and Helena were in a deep embrace, and Helena was sobbing while her husband held her tightly in his arms. Joe Johnson's eyes were closed, tears were running down his cheeks, and his head was lifted up to the heavens as he continued to silently pray. Paul Wagner was on his knees crying with his head face down on top of the bed as he unashamedly wept.

Jason looked down at the bed and saw himself lying peacefully with his eyes closed. A nurse came into the room and sadly pulled a sheet over his face.

Jason desperately wanted to comfort his precious friends. He felt helpless and unable to do anything to soothe them. He then saw Josh walk into this circle of his friends. His unseen presence provided the needed consolation. Josh put his arms around Mandy. He embraced Bobby and held Helena tight. He hugged both Joe and Paul Wagner, and as he did, tears streamed down his face as well.

Josh finally walked over to Jason, gently put his hand on his shoulder, and said, "They will all be fine. They are being taken care of. In fact, one day all of them will walk through this very same door."

"Even Coach Wagner?" asked Jason.

Josh laughed a big, hearty laugh. "Yes, even Paul Wagner. All of the events over the last two weeks have caused him to seriously question his values and who he is in relation to God. He is a man on a journey right now, and what he is experiencing is necessary to bring him to the place in his life that will ensure that his journey ultimately leads him to this door."

"So everyone will eventually come here?"

"Everyone is invited here, but not all will come," Josh said sadly. He then grabbed Jason's hand and asked, "Are you ready for an everlasting adventure?"

Jason smiled and said, "Absolutely. Let's go. I can't wait."

The two walked through the door. Josh shut it behind them, and immediately upon its closure, the door and its frame disappeared. All Jason now saw in front of him and behind him was the plush, green meadow and bright blue sky above. He also heard in the distance familiar angelic voices in melodic harmonies beckoning him to come.

Josh then tossed to Jason a football that suddenly appeared in his hands. He laughed and pointed straight ahead saying, "OK, Mr. Quarterback, there is a lot of real estate ahead of us. How about you throwing me a long ball. Let's see if I can run a pass route as good as Bobby Childs."

Josh then ran straight ahead with blazing speed as Jason faded back with the ball in his hands. He planted his feet like the NFL quarterback that he is and launched the ball toward the streaking Josh who was exhibiting incredible speed down the meadow. Josh was almost out of sight when Jason let loose with the football that soared into the air and seemed to fly for miles before it landed right on Josh's chest. Josh caught the ball on the dead run. He then turned around and spiked the ball as if celebrating a winning touchdown catch.

Looking at Jason he exclaimed, "You are going to be better than ever with those passes as time goes on. But I promise to catch everyone thrown to me."

Running to catch up, Jason asked his friend, "Man, where did you ever get that speed? Bobby Childs could not have run that route better."

Josh continued to laugh and urged Jason to follow him as he now was running toward the angelic music. The two continued striding straight ahead looking like two children playing tag in a school play yard without a care in the world.

Jason suddenly experienced the strange feeling of déjá vu. He was sure he had been in this place once before. Then he remembered his dream about Rachel. He realized that he was now standing on the same meadow that was in this dream. Since he had been here before, he knew that someplace up ahead they would have to slow their pace and eventually stop. The great uncrossable abyss awaited them.

Josh continued to run and urged his compatriot to follow suit. They tossed the football back and forth as they laughed and ran toward their ultimate destination. Finally, Josh slowed his pace to a standstill. He began to walk very deliberately as Jason followed. Josh and Jason walked to the very edge of the great abyss that separated them from the glorious land ahead. They heard the angelic voices calling them forward and the brightness of the land across the divide was still somewhat blinding to Jason's eyes.

Josh looked across the abyss to the land beyond and turned to Jason and asked, "Shall we cross over?"

"Well, Josh, I have been here before, and there is no way to get to the other side. I know I tried. It just isn't possible."

"You are wrong my friend. There is a way to cross. I know because I built a bridge to get to the other side."

Jason looked intently into the eyes of his friend. "You built a bridge?"

Josh laughed. "Remember when we first met. I told you that I build bridges." He pointed to his right and said, "And here it is. The bridge to get to the other side. It is the only way to get there."

"I was here before in a dream and could not find any way to cross. I did not see the bridge then. How come?"

"It was not your time to cross," answered Josh.

"But it is my time now?"

"Yes, my friend. It is your time now."

"There is no other way," continued Josh. "Many try to get to the other side by avoiding the bridge, but they always fail." Josh then pointed to his left at a person who was familiar to Jason.

Jason looked and saw Jim Harrison, Mandy Brooks's ex-husband. Jim stood at the edge of the abyss, looking down into it and then across to the other side. He was assessing his chances to get over by jumping.

Jason called out to him. "Jim, you can't do it. We have a bridge over here. It is the only way. Please don't try it. The divide is too wide for you to jump. Nobody can do it on their own."

Jim Harrison looked up and recognized Jason immediately. He laughed and screamed curses at Jason, and then stepped back several paces preparing to leap.

Jason became more insistent in his efforts to divert Jim from this suicidal act. He urgently screamed, "Jim, I am telling you—you can't make it. Don't do it! You just need to come with us and cross over on the bridge."

Jim Harrison totally ignored the warnings and the pleas. He was about twenty yards away from the edge of the abyss when he began to run as fast as he could. Jason took off trying to intercept him with a tackle before he reached the edge. His efforts failed.

Jim got to the edge just ahead of Jason and jumped with the strength of an Olympic champion long jumper. The effort was very impressive for any human being to make, but it was not enough to carry him to the other side. Jim's superhuman attempt got him less than halfway across the divide before he began to lose momentum and fall. He realized that he would not be successful and began to scream at the horror of what he was facing. There was no way to save him. He fell screaming in terror until he could be seen no more by Jason who stood helplessly watching at the edge of the abyss.

Jason looked over at Josh who witnessed the incident. Josh had tears in his eyes. Jason desperately wanted to hear an explanation. Josh again sadly shook his head and said, "There is only one way. It is the bridge I built. It is the only way."

Jason slowly walked back to Josh, and together they began to walk toward the bridge. Jason was contemplative of what he had just witnessed. He did not yet fully understand the gift he had been given. He asked Josh the question heaviest on his heart. "So why do some people choose to cross over on the bridge and others refuse and attempt to do it on their own?"

"All are invited to cross by way of the bridge, but not all choose to do so. Most people are too proud to admit that they need help. Their pride tells them they can do it on their own. To think otherwise would be to admit weakness and human beings are loathe to do that."

"So instead they just ignore the obvious, live life dangerously, and figure that all will be well in the end because they tried their best. Is that it?" Jason asked.

"That sums it up pretty well," said Josh.

Josh and Jason finally came to the beginning of the bridge. Josh said as they briefly paused, "I built this bridge for all to use. It cost me everything I had. But I also built it especially for you, Jason O'Connor. It is my gift to you. I built this bridge for you before the foundations of the earth were laid."

"I know that the land on the other side is indescribably beautiful, and it will be, as you said, an everlasting adventure, but I am curious about a few things, Josh."

"Don't be afraid to ask me anything you want," Josh replied.

"Well, will I know people on the other side?" Jason was, of course, thinking about Rachel, his parents, and his grandmother.

Josh smiled broadly and replied, "Oh yes my friend. All of those you are thinking about right now are eagerly waiting for you to cross the bridge and hug you again. In fact, there are some people you haven't met yet who are enthusiastically waiting to see you when you get there."

"Really? And who are these people?"

Josh responded, "There is a guy named Sparky who has been watching and enjoying your story. He can't wait to shake your hand."

"Sparky? You mean Joe's friend from Vietnam? Wow! But how does he know me?"

"On the other side is a great cloud of witnesses who are aware of what goes on in the land where you previously lived. Many were watching you and rooting you on. And they are all so very proud of what you did and what you accomplished."

Josh continued, "There are a couple kids wanting to meet you as well. They are big fans of yours. Their names are Timmy and Tina."

Jason was overwhelmed to hear this news. "You mean Bobby's and Mandy's twins? They are here? And they want to meet me?"

Josh laughed. "Timmy can hardly wait for you to throw him a football. He claims that he can catch as good as his Dad. And they are excited that someday both of their parents will be joining them and you in the land across the bridge."

More questions filled his mind so Jason continued to inquire. "I am concerned about the special friends I left behind—Bobby, Mandy, Joe, and Helena. You said they will all join us here one day, but in the meantime what will become of them?"

"You need not worry, my friend. Your life story has brought them all together. They are well taken care of. The four of them will become a very tight-knit family, and they will bless many while they reside in their temporary abode. Little Bobby and Moses will be as close as blood brothers, and, as I said before, all of them will eventually join us in the land across the bridge."

Jason stood silent, attempting to comprehend all that had been said. He had so many more questions to ask, but he also understood that he was not under any time constraints. He now had forever to ask such things. He was overwhelmed and placed his head in his hands as if to cry for joy, but no tears came. Instead, his face glowed from happiness.

Josh said, "Tears don't exist here. They are wiped away from everybody's eyes and are no more. Neither is there anymore sorrow, pain, and death. All of these things are gone now. This is a new order and an everlasting adventure for all who come."

Both Josh and Jason now stood at the beginning of the bridge and looked across to the land ahead. Jason knew that his life had just begun.

Josh then reached out his hand and said, "Let's go join the celebration."